"You really should leave," she said,
her voice sounding husky.

"Perhaps I should."

She nodded.

"Otherwise, I might do something inexcusable."

What was wrong with her? Her pulse shouldn't be racing. Her breath shouldn't be tight. She should move away, away now, before he came closer, bending his head and pressing his lips against her temple.

She closed her eyes, feeling his breath on her ear.

"Such as toss you onto that settee," he whispered, "to see how much of your book is real and how much imagination."

KAREN RANNEY

The Virgin of Clan Sinclair

AVON

An Imprint of HarperCollinsPublishers

AVON BOOKS
An Imprint of HarperCollins*Publishers*
195 Broadway
New York, New York 10007

Copyright © 2014 by Karen Ranney LLC
Excerpt from *The Witch of Clan Sinclair* copyright © 2014 by Karen Ranney LLC
Excerpt from *The Devil of Clan Sinclair* copyright © 2013 by Karen Ranney LLC
ISBN 978-0-06-224249-5
www.avonromance.com

First Avon Books mass market printing: June 2014

Avon Trademark Reg. U.S. Pat. Off. and in Other Countries, Marca Registrada, Hecho en U.S.A.
HarperCollins® is a registered trademark of HarperCollins Publishers.

Printed in the U.S.A.

10 9 8 7 6 5 4 3 2 1

*To Flash the Wonder Pooch, aka Sir Barksalot
and Mr. Mouth*

Chapter 1

Drumvagen, Scotland
May, 1875

His lips skimmed down her throat and hovered at her shoulder.

"I knew you would taste like a sweetmeat."

Lady Pamela shivered.

A teasing smile curved his lips.

Pressing one hand against his chest, she moved back.

He countered by grabbing her hand, turning it, and pressing a tender kiss to her palm.

"You have to leave," she said.

"I am not leaving you until dawn comes, my dearest. Even then, I will have to be pulled from your arms by a host of your servants."

"I've my reputation to consider," she murmured.

He laughed, easing her closer until her cheek was pressed against his shoulder. She held back her sigh with some difficulty, closing her eyes and reveling in the feel of him.

"Banish me, then, lovely. Send me away with a ges-

*ture. Give me the word and I'll leave your chamber,
your house, and even your life if you wish it."*

*How could she possibly send him away? If he left,
he'd take her heart with him, not to mention the glorious pleasure she felt in his arms.*

"That woman is the most annoying creature it's ever been
my misfortune to know!"

Ellice turned and stared at her mother.

Enid was advancing on her, determination in every line
of her face.

Quickly, she flipped over a page in her manuscript so that
none of the writing showed. Putting her pen down, she addressed her mother.

"What has Brianag done now, Mother?"

Enid stopped, narrowed her eyes and pointed at the door.

"That creature!" she said, singling out Brianag with that
one imperial finger. "That abomination! That—That—That
housekeeper!"

Her mother's face was becoming a mottled red, her mouth
pursed up until it resembled a furled rose.

Oh, dear.

Her mother dropped her arm, resuming the march toward her.

Any moment now she was going to notice the stack of
pages on the surface of the desk and demand to know what
they were.

That would be a disaster of the highest magnitude, worse
than when they were living in London and pretending not to
be poor.

Ellice stood, turned and faced her mother, blocking her
view of the manuscript.

"She's done something to upset you. What is it?"

Her mother stopped, frowned at her, and took a deep
breath.

"That vile and despicable creature has insulted you!"

"Me?" That was a surprise.

Her mother nodded. "She bragged about her granddaughter getting married."

"How is that insulting me?" Ellice asked, genuinely curious.

"She intimated that you would never marry. That you would remain on the shelf. That no man would ever want you. That I could not arrange a marriage for you as swiftly as she had acted the matchmaker for her granddaughter."

The first three points weren't troubling, especially since they were probably true. The last comment, however, had her staring wide-eyed at her mother.

Oh, dear.

Her mother was looking at her with such intensity that Ellice wished she would blink. Finally, Enid nodded just once, a sign that she'd made up her mind about something.

Once determined on an action, her mother never changed course.

Calm. She needed to remain calm, that was all. She wouldn't fidget, which was as her mother had often told her—a nervous habit, one her sister, Eudora, never had. Nor would it do any good to let her mother know she was terrified. Eudora had always been poised and in command of a situation.

"You're of an age to be married," her mother said, moving through the sitting room, touching objects Ellice had brought from London to give her a bit of comfort in the Scottish countryside. A book Eudora had given to her on her fifteenth birthday. A sketch of her brother, Lawrence, framed in silver. A small porcelain statue, called a Foo dog, that resembled a wrinkly lion more than any dog she'd ever seen.

"You're not a child anymore, Ellice. You need to give some thoughts to a home and family of your own."

She was aware of her own age and circumstances, perhaps a bit more than her mother, who occupied herself with quarreling most of the day.

Because of Macrath's generosity, she and her mother had been given a home at Drumvagen, almost as if they were family in truth, instead of claiming only a tenuous relationship.

Virginia, Macrath's wife, had once been married to Ellice's brother. After Lawrence's death, Virginia had fallen in love with Macrath Sinclair, a Scot who made even Ellice's heart pound occasionally, especially when he looked at Virginia across the room with that certain look in his eyes.

Perhaps it was that look that had sparked her imagination. What would she feel if a man looked at her in that way, or treated her as if there was nothing more important in the world than her?

The problem was—she didn't want just any man for a husband. Where did she go to find another Macrath?

Her mother was still walking through the sitting room, her substantial skirt and train grazing the tables and brushing against the wall.

"Why should I marry?" Ellice asked. "I'm perfectly happy." A bit of a lie but was it necessary to be honest all the time, especially about something so personal?

Her mother drew herself up, shoulders level, hands clasped tightly in front of her. Enid was a short woman, one whose bulk made her appear squared. A small yet disquieting enemy if she wished to be.

"Marriage is a woman's natural state, Ellice."

"You're not married."

"I have mourned your father all these years, child. I do not wish to replace him in my affections."

Not once had she ever heard her mother speak fondly about the late earl. Whenever Enid referred to her long dead husband it was in an irritated tone, as if his demise had been solely to annoy her. Now she was claiming to feel affection for him? Ellice didn't believe it. She was not, however, unwise enough to make that comment.

Enid, Dowager Countess of Barrett, never forgot a slight, even one from her own daughter.

"Is it truly necessary that I marry?" Ellice asked. "Could we not find a small cottage somewhere? Not every woman marries."

"Only if they are desperately poor and without family. Or," she said, eyeing Ellice, "they are of a temperament unsuited to be a wife." She abruptly sank into a chair. "Tell me you haven't done anything to shame the family."

She eyed her mother. Was she supposed to be a child, ignorant of how, exactly, they came to be living at Drumvagen?

If Virginia hadn't bent the rules of society, with her mother's encouragement and collusion, they wouldn't be living in this grand house, each given a lovely suite, and treated like family members.

Perhaps it was best not to pursue that topic of conversation at the moment.

"No," she said. "I haven't done anything to shame the family."

She wanted to—did that count?

"Thank the good Lord and all the saints for that, at least." Enid fanned the air in front of her flushed face.

Should she tell her mother she was still a virgin? Not because she was all that virtuous and proper. The groom she'd met last year had been remarkably handsome, with soft green eyes, a quirk to his lips, and a Scottish accent that made her toes curl.

He'd been new to Drumvagen and hadn't known who she was. He'd kissed her soundly, leaving her to wonder at what she hadn't experienced. He'd gone on to work in Edinburgh, but she remembered him sometimes, and wondered what he might have done if he hadn't heard someone coming.

Society, however, would have skewered her had she done anything shameful. So she was left to view the smoldering looks between all the couples in her life, catch the sight of swollen lips and flushed cheeks and pretend she had no interest in such things.

What a silly notion.

Mairi had been the one to educate her, if only by accident. Macrath's sister was knowledgeable about a whole world of things, one of which was passion. Ellice could tell that from the way she looked at her husband, at the laughter they shared, not to mention Mairi's love of lurid novels.

On one of her visits to Edinburgh, she'd discovered two of Mairi's favorite books, devouring them on quiet afternoons when she was alone in the house, accompanied only by the servants. She learned a great deal from *Memoirs of a Woman of Pleasure* and *Tom Jones*. Coupled with her observations of life in Scotland, she'd gotten a very good education, enough to realize that Drumvagen was teeming with passion.

"Is there any reason I should rush to be married?" she asked. Other than her mother's wish to best Brianag?

"You are not getting any younger. Do you wish to be dependent on Macrath's charity for the rest of your life? A poor sad female reading in the corner of the room, hoping no one notices her?

Well, she did that now. She'd learned to keep silent, retreating into herself. At least she could write her feelings. Every word she'd never spoken, every thought she wasn't supposed to have, went into her manuscript.

Lately she'd had a great many adventures in her imagination, all of them centered around Lady Pamela.

Lady Pamela wouldn't meekly sit back and let someone else plan out her life. She wouldn't acquiesce to a marriage simply to have a place to live. She'd create her own world, with a smile and a promise in her eyes.

Men would drop at her feet.

Her mother stood, brushing down her skirts.

"Eudora would have been married at your age, child. No doubt I would have been a grandmother by now."

"Do you want to be a grandmother?"

To her surprise, her mother seemed to consider the question.

"Once I was in my own establishment, surely. What would truly be preferable is if your husband could defray my expenses so I wouldn't have to use my own money."

Now she was not only supposed to be married, but to be married well? What else did her mother want, a title? She didn't bother to ask. As the Dowager Countess of Barrett, of course she wanted a title for her last remaining child.

Where was she supposed to find a titled bachelor in Scotland? No, if she were going to get married, let him be handsome, gifted with a sense of humor, and that indescribable deliciousness that some men had. She wanted to feel the air charged around him. She needed him to look at her with eyes that smoldered with passion.

"We can afford to stay in Edinburgh for a few months," her mother said. "Long enough to find a husband for you, even if he is a Scot."

The glint of determination in her eyes warned Ellice.

For the next months she would be paraded in front of every available man, given endless lectures on decorum, especially peppered with comments about how her dear, departed sister had been so much better at everything.

Nor would she have a moment to herself. She'd be in her mother's company every hour of every day until she was married.

Why had the housekeeper challenged Enid?

Ellice didn't say a word as her mother sailed out of the room with the same disregard she'd shown entering it.

Suddenly, the suite was too close and confining.

She threw open the window to breathe in the spring air, heavy with the sweet perfume of roses and heather. To her right was the rolling glen beckoning her to come and walk. *Sit here awhile and dream your thoughts on this flat rock.* How often had she done that?

The day was enchanted, like most days at Drumvagen, promising its inhabitants tranquility and joy. Wagons would rumble down the road from the village bringing provisions. People would walk from the house to Macrath's laboratory. The staff would be intent on their tasks, as they were even now. Someone was whistling, and before the day was out she would probably hear someone singing.

If she belonged here, she'd feel blessed. Because she didn't, all this happiness was simply too much.

She felt like she had in London after Eudora's death. Her mother had retreated to her rooms, leaving Ellice to find her way through grief. She couldn't chastise the servants for the occasional laugh or jest. Their joy never touched her, however, and that's what she felt at Drumvagen as if she were in a bubble that prevented her from experiencing the happiness of others.

She wasn't unhappy. She just couldn't borrow someone else's emotions. She couldn't live off Virginia's joy. Even her mother's constant harping at Brianag was to be envied because it was heartfelt and real.

What did she feel?

Anxious and impatient for her life to begin. Not what her mother wanted for her, but what she wanted for herself.

Perhaps that's why her book meant so much to her. She felt every page of it, every paragraph, every word. The love Lady Pamela experienced for Donald was the love stored away in Ellice's heart, just waiting for the right person. The passion Donald and Lady Pamela knew was hers. The yearning each felt was what sat, impatient and heavy, in her own heart.

She wanted to be away, leaving her suite, Drumvagen, and all of its inhabitants behind.

Mostly, she wanted to be away from who she was. She

wanted to be someone more courageous, like Mairi. Mairi didn't chafe under the role circumstance had given her. Instead, she molded life to fit her, like Lady Pamela.

Nor was Mairi the only courageous person she knew. Everyone at Drumvagen was strong-willed and memorable: from Virginia, who had challenged society's rules, to Macrath, who created an empire from an idea, to her mother and Brianag.

She was the only one people ignored. *Oh, yes, Ellice,* people probably said, wrinkling their brows to summon an image of her.

Poor dear girl, she's Enid's daughter, correct? Pity the other one didn't survive. Heard she was a beauty, but this girl?

Brown hair and brown eyes and a completely malleable nature, they would say, describing her. Once, she'd been endlessly chastised for speaking out of turn, for saying what she thought. Years of being castigated had taught her to keep silent.

Taking the manuscript, she tied a string around it to keep all the pages together. It wouldn't do to lose one here or there, not when she'd worked so hard on the book.

Holding it against her chest, she opened the sitting room door, looking both ways. Once she was certain no one was there, she made her way down the corridor to the servants' stairs. She would go and work in the cottage. Virginia had made the place available to her and ever since it had been a sanctuary.

Through her words she'd become someone else, someone memorable and unforgettable, a woman of courage and daring, someone who captivated others, especially a man her equal. She'd have auburn hair and startling green eyes. She'd laugh with abandon and keep every man who looked at her in thrall.

She'd be Lady Pamela.

In the pages of her manuscript, she released every thought

that trembled unspoken on her lips, every secret wish, and every torrid desire.

Lady Pamela wouldn't accept marriage to anyone simply because her mother wished it. No, she would be fiercely opposed to such a bloodless union. She would demand a say in her own life.

Virginia had altered her future herself. So had Mairi. Her mother had done the same, which was why they were living in Scotland.

Was she the only weak woman at Drumvagen? She was very much afraid she was.

The distant rumble of thunder warned her. She didn't care. She'd go to the cottage even in the pouring rain and remain there while the windowsills wept and the floor grew muddy.

She skittered to a halt at Macrath's voice, ducking around the corner just as he and a stranger appeared.

"I'm grateful you decided to call," Macrath said. "I've had questions about your father and the original architect for years."

"I've often thought of Drumvagen," the stranger said. "It's featured prominently in my childhood memories, especially the grotto."

She peered around the corner.

A man stood there, his back to her. As tall as Macrath, with black hair to match, he was attired in a dark blue suit. She wished he'd turn so she could see his face. His voice alone was intriguing.

Scottish English varied even within Drumvagen. Brianag's manner of speaking was vastly different from that of the maids. Nor did the maids sound like Jack, Hannah's husband.

This stranger's accent was Scottish in certain words and very English in others.

"Had your father planned to incorporate the entrance into the house?"

"I was hoping he would," the man said. "It's a wondrous place for a boy with an imagination."

"My own son considers the grotto his."

The man laughed. Ellice's toes curled, the first time they'd ever done that at a simple sound. Oh, if he would only turn.

Perhaps he had a misshapen nose. She'd consider a scar to be dashing, but crooked, black teeth would be very off-putting.

"I'm surprised we haven't met before now," Macrath said. "With you being Logan's friend and the distance not that far from Edinburgh."

The stranger lived in Edinburgh?

An hour earlier she wouldn't have given the thought an iota of life. An hour earlier, before her mother announced her new plans, Ellice would have pushed aside the notion and laughed at herself.

She might write of a daring, shocking woman, but it was quite another thing to be that person. But was she simply to wait until circumstances happened to her? Was she never to act on her own?

Ellice looked down at herself. This morning she'd worn a blue dress with bone buttons, white cuffs, and collar. She and her mother had instituted so many economies over the years that it was difficult to relinquish the habit now. The dress was like most of those in her wardrobe, constructed for long wear and serviceability, able to withstand the laundry and fade only a little over time.

Because of the bustle her mother insisted on—after all, just because they lived in Scotland was no reason to be fashion heathens—the dress was a little shorter than it should have been, revealing a glimpse of her ankles. At any other time, she would have been embarrassed to be seen in such old clothing. Right now, however, it was perfect for the plan that was bubbling up in her mind.

The stranger might be persuaded to think her a maid at Drumvagen.

If she waylaid him, would he take her to Edinburgh? She wasn't above begging. Would she need to tell a story? Would he believe she needed to visit a sick mother in the city? Or that she was pining for an errant lover?

If she must, she'd tell a tale, something that wouldn't cast Drumvagen or Macrath into disfavor but would appeal to the stranger's better impulses.

If he had any better impulses.

Perhaps he was a slaver, or a smuggler wishing to purchase Drumvagen for his evil uses. Had he come to scope out the land before leading his flotilla of ships to fire on the great house?

No, Macrath seemed to like him, and Macrath was a good judge of character. Besides, the stranger knew Logan. Any friend of Mairi's husband had to be a decent man.

Clutching the manuscript to her chest, she crept to the front of the house—the better to avoid Brianag—and slipped out the massive double doors.

The minute Ellice saw the carriage, she changed her plans.

The visitor to Drumvagen didn't travel in a normal equipage. Instead, his team of four horses pulled a brougham, a massive carriage similar to a mail coach.

She would not have to flag down his driver after all. She wouldn't have to throw herself on the visitor's mercy. She would not have to grovel.

Instead, she was simply going to hide in the carriage.

To her relief, the driver was nowhere in sight. She neared the carriage with a nonchalant walk, glancing over her shoulder to see if anyone was watching her from Drumvagen.

Virginia was in the Rose Parlor. Brianag was no doubt giving orders to the maids. Macrath was escorting his visitor around the house, which only left her mother and the children, both of whom she adored. Whenever Alistair saw her, he ran toward her, arms spread wide as he screamed, "Leese!" His sister, Fiona, was only a year old, but she was already beginning to emulate her brother in not only her affection, but her shouts of glee.

But she didn't see any childish face pressed against a windowpane. Nor was her mother standing there admonishing her with a look.

She couldn't hide in the rear of the carriage. Two trunks were stored behind the brougham and secured with a leather flap from the top of the vehicle to the fender.

She could only wonder about Macrath's visitor. Was he a world traveler? Where had the visitor gone before coming here? Was he truly returning to Edinburgh? What if he wasn't? What if he was going to Kinloch Village and from there to America or an even more exotic location? What if he was traveling on to Inverness instead?

She didn't want to get trapped in a city with no funds or friends, but if she returned to her room to get some money from her stronghox, there was every possibility the stranger would leave before she got back.

Worse, she might be seen by Brianag or her mother before she could return to the carriage.

No, she was simply going to assume that what she'd heard was correct. The visitor was returning to Edinburgh. Once in the city, she'd find a conveyance to take her to Mairi's house, where the driver would be paid.

She glanced back at Drumvagen.

The darkness on the horizon, as well as the swelling wind, gave evidence of a fierce storm to come. Drumvagen stood up to the elements well, a house buttressed against all types of weather. The snows of winter melted from the edifice as if in apology for marring the perfect beauty of the twin staircases or four towers. The winds that came off the ocean pressed against the brick and the rows of windows without effect.

Every time Macrath returned to the house, he had the

driver stop just before the curved approach and simply stared at his home. Anyone could tell how much he loved Drumvagen and how proud he was of the house he'd finished building.

By leaving, Virginia and Macrath would probably think she'd rejected their kindness. They'd both effortlessly enfolded her into their family. She didn't want to hurt either of them, but her mother wouldn't be stopped.

Either she took this opportunity or she ended up being married to someone her mother chose.

In one of Macrath's carriages, the seat lifted up, revealing a storage area. This carriage was easily the size of Macrath's. Would it also boast a secret compartment?

Entering the carriage, she ducked down beneath the window. The carriage smelled of leather, which was understandable because of the leather seats. But why should it smell of lemons?

To her wholehearted relief there was a compartment beneath the seat. Only she was very sure she wasn't going to fit, not with the bustle her mother insisted she wear. Every morning Ellice tied on the garment that looked like a fishtail hanging over her backside.

No one at Drumvagen, except her mother, cared if her dresses hung correctly, plumped from the rear.

In order to fit into the compartment she was going to have to remove the hated thing.

She put the manuscript into the compartment, then hurriedly reached beneath her skirts, finding the ties to the bustle and slipping it off. Folding it into as compact a size as she could, she pushed it, too, into the compartment.

In a normal carriage the journey to Edinburgh would take four hours. It was altogether possible they might reach the city in less time in such a vehicle as this.

Ellice entered the compartment, kneeling before wedging herself in sideways. The space smelled of wet boots and horse.

She was more than willing to be a little uncomfortable in the short run. After all, her freedom was at stake.

Telling herself to be as brave as Lady Pamela, she closed the seat on top of her.

In minutes she'd be on her way to Edinburgh. She'd take her own life in her hands and determine her own future.

Along the way, perhaps she'd get to see the stranger's face.

Chapter 2

Ross Forster wished he'd not made this sudden stop at Drumvagen. Being here was the result of a foolish impulse, one that had appealed to him at the time.

The house Macrath Sinclair had rescued was only an hour or so out of his way on a fine spring morning.

Seeing the magnificence Sinclair had created didn't ease his life in one whit. Nor had the sight of Drumvagen made him feel better about what was a series of poor memories. He had satisfied his curiosity, that was all.

His father had sold the place to Sinclair without a qualm.

"What do I care?" he said. "I'll never return to that monstrosity."

He wondered what his father would have said to see the finished house, the four towers each topped with a cupola, the twin staircases curving out toward the drive as if to welcome each visitor to Drumvagen.

During one of his dozen or so attempts to get in good graces with his wife, Thomas Forster had determined that what his family needed was a change of scene. A house near the ocean, perhaps, where they could retire when needing to escape the vastness of Huntly. He'd selected the land, acquired an architect, and played gentleman builder long enough to instill a dream in his son.

They would all move to Drumvagen and live a life of familial warmth and affection. His parents would never argue about his father's behavior. His mother would never scowl or weep at night. He would be their darling child, not ignored but celebrated. He was adept at rowing? Great job, son. He was brilliant in his studies? Congratulations, boy, you've worked hard.

Such a bucolic existence was never to be, but the dream had died hard.

Eventually, he'd gone away from school, creating his own life as far away from his parents as he could manage. He'd been clever at mathematics, which amused him. What skill he'd acquired had gone into doubling the fortune he'd eventually inherited.

"Would you like to see the grotto?" Sinclair asked.

He hesitated only a minute, the eight-year-old boy within him nearly quivering with excitement.

He followed Sinclair to his library, startled to discover that the entrance to the grotto was cleverly concealed behind a bookcase in the man's library.

The last time he'd been here he'd trailed behind his father like an appendage or fashionable accessory, an heir Thomas had created to satisfy the dictates of his rank and family but little more.

As a child Ross had been terrified to speak up or do anything to call attention to himself. The grotto, however, with its echoing sounds and sheer beauty had brought him out of himself.

"Is it a miracle, Father?" he remembered asking

The round stone room with its window view of the ocean and the hole in the ceiling, almost like a chimney, had seemed a special place to the boy he'd been.

"Perhaps it's that, Ross," his father had said, looking around. "A magnificent place for a party."

His father had never seen the beauty of the place, only that it was a location to drink himself into a stupor.

"It's not changed," he said now, the air heavy and salty. Frothy swells danced on top of the ocean as if waving to him. The seabirds' cries echoed through the grotto, called his attention to where the sea and sky met like long-lost friends.

"I doubt it would," Sinclair said, striding to the door on the other side of the grotto. "Not after thousands of years."

He followed Sinclair, curious because he'd not been allowed to come this far on his previous expeditions. Nor had he been permitted in the grotto by himself. Not because he was too precious to lose or that people worried about his welfare. He was simply a commodity, a fait accompli, the heir, and it would be a chore to make another one of him.

He walked out on the beach, the wind buffeting him. Why had he come here today? His father had been dead for years. Why was he suddenly compelled to face his ghost?

His anniversary was tomorrow.

The blow was strong enough that he nearly reeled. Was that why he was here?

He wanted to run until the sudden constriction in his chest was eased and the feathery memories in his mind blew away.

"Beg pardon?" he asked, realizing Sinclair had asked him a question.

"I asked at what stage you'd last seen the house."

"The foundations had been done," he said. "And some of the interior planned out. Not the library, of course, or the entrance to the grotto. If you like, I'll send you the plans for the house."

Sinclair's smile was one of boyish eagerness. "I'd be very happy to see them. I've often wondered about the original details of Drumvagen."

He was glad the man had kept the name.

His father had sworn that he was going to change it as soon as he could get the locals to understand. It didn't matter that a castle had once sat on this very ground, or that history had bled into the very earth here. He'd wanted, Ross remembered, to call the structure Forster House.

Perhaps it was a good thing his plan never came to fruition.

Two years into the project Thomas proved to be as bored with Drumvagen as anything decent he attempted. He and the architect had argued over money and more. The architect hadn't liked his father's vision for the house, or perhaps he'd simply seen Drumvagen as more, something along the lines of what Macrath Sinclair had envisioned.

"I always wondered what happened to Drumvagen. I like what you've done with it."

Sinclair smiled. "At first, it was a showplace," he said. "A way of proclaiming that I was successful. Now it's my home."

His father would never have transformed the house in such a way. Drumvagen—or Forster House—would have been a hedonist's paradise, not a place where running feet and childish laughter punctuated the conversation of adults.

"Thank you for this," he said, turning to Sinclair. "I've come unannounced and uninvited, but you've been very kind."

His host scanned the skies. Despite the early afternoon hour, it was becoming as dark as night.

"Stay," Sinclair said. "A storm is coming, and a storm off the ocean is no small thing."

Dark clouds were merging with an equally inky sea. Lightning speared from the boiling clouds, accentuating Sinclair's words.

"I couldn't put you out."

"I've seen ships almost come to ground when their captains thought to outrun one of these beasts," he said. "I can't send you away in this."

As swiftly as the storm was moving, he might not make it to an inn.

"If you're certain," Ross said, unwilling to expose his coachman to the danger of a lightning filled storm.

"My only regret is that you won't get a chance to meet my wife." Sinclair turned and led the way back through the grotto. "She isn't very visible nowadays." Here the other man seemed to fumble. "She's near to term with our third child," he finally said.

Ross nodded, understanding.

Slowly, he followed his host back through the grotto and up the passage to the library.

Here at Drumvagen he'd been young, naive, and filled with hope. Perhaps his willingness to stay overnight was because today, of all days, he needed some memory of happiness.

Ellice wasn't afraid of the dark. A good thing, since the compartment was as black as a winter night at Drumvagen.

She never knew, until this exact minute, how much she disliked being confined in a small area. Closing her eyes didn't seem to help, either.

Had Eudora, in her coffin, felt the same? *Oh, don't be nonsensical, Ellice. Eudora was dead. She couldn't have felt confined.*

The space, however, was most definitely coffinlike.

A scream slid up her throat. She bit it back and took several deep breaths, admonishing herself to be calm. When she felt the carriage rock, as if someone had entered, she sighed in relief.

They would be on their way shortly and Edinburgh was just a few hours away. She could bear anything for four hours.

She lay there with her arms crossed over her chest, wondering if her hands would begin to tingle because of the constriction. The pose reminded her of how Eudora had been buried.

Even in death Eudora had been beautiful and poised.

Tall and statuesque, with a regal looking face and demeanor, Eudora was everything she was not, elegant, graceful, and attuned to people. Eudora knew, immediately, if someone was out of sorts, sad, or happy. She exerted herself to please others and they rewarded her with praise and admiration.

Ellice knew she was only granted confused glances.

When she was younger and living in London, she was guilty of a great many societal faux pas. She spoke without thinking and she fidgeted endlessly. Now, after years of training herself, she remained silent for the most part and tried very hard to remain outwardly calm.

However, she wasn't feeling excessively calm at the moment.

Her poor sister had been relegated to a hurried funeral and burial surrounded only by her immediate family because of the way she died. Everyone had been afraid of smallpox. Fear of the contagion seemed to cling even to the dead.

She'd stood there at Eudora's grave, knowing that nothing would ever be the same. Nor had it been.

At the moment, she could almost imagine herself dead as well.

What if someone locked the compartment? Would this carriage prove to be her last resting place? Would she lie here forever, the spiders casting their webs around her decaying body?

Mairi wouldn't have been afraid. But then, Mairi probably wouldn't have hidden in a compartment. She would have demanded that the owner of the carriage give her passage to Edinburgh. For that matter, she would have demanded the same of Macrath, her brother.

Mairi was her idol.

Mairi demanded the world give way. She didn't remain silent in the face of opposition. She didn't worry about how to silence Brianag and her mother. She simply accomplished it.

Everything Mairi wanted, she achieved. She'd married a man who made Ellice's heart flutter almost as much as Macrath. Logan was the epitome of all things manly and brave. As the Lord Provost of Edinburgh, he had cut a formidable figure. For Mairi, he'd resigned his position and become a private citizen again.

Love could do that to a man.

Of course, neither Mairi nor Logan would admit that's why he'd done as he had. But it had been obvious at their wedding that the two were deeply in love, enough for each to sacrifice for the other.

She sighed, wondering if she would ever feel that emotion. At least she'd been able to channel her feelings into her manuscript. If the hero looked a little too much like a compilation of Logan and Macrath, tall, broad-shouldered, with strong features and black hair, that was to be understood. She was surrounded by handsome Scottish men.

The heroine didn't look anything like her. No, that would have been too odd. The heroine was a brave and courageous woman of great beauty, who used her appearance to bend men to her will. She was an earthy seductress with auburn hair and penetrating green eyes that could see deeply into a man's soul.

When she smiled, men wanted to fall at her feet. When she kissed them, they sighed in delight. When a man touched her, Lady Pamela breathed words into his ear, taunting him to continue.

She never worried about her virtue, her unmarried state, or her future. She lived life to the fullest, plucking from each day a memory to mark it as different from the others.

A thump above her head brought Ellice back to her surroundings. The sound made her think someone had placed something on the seat above the compartment. Was it something heavy? Would it prevent her from opening the lid once they'd arrived in Edinburgh? Would she be trapped here forever?

She squeezed her eyes shut and forced herself to take several deep, calming breaths. The musty air made her want to cough, but that was the last thing she could do. She had to remain undetected.

She closed her eyes and tried to relax. Lying half on her side, she wasn't at all comfortable. The compartment might be deep but it wasn't wide. She had to draw her knees up until they were pressed against the front.

Was this what it felt like to be in a coffin?

She could almost hear the earth pressing down on the top, hear the wails of the mourners. Had Eudora felt the same?

Don't be foolish. When you're dead, you're dead. No one feels or hears anything. Or at least no one had come back from the dead with reports on what it was like.

Would they place roses on her bier? She truly loved roses, especially Drumvagen roses. The rose garden Macrath had created for Virginia was only a few years old, but it was filled with old plants he'd acquired from as far away as France. Every spring they bloomed and scented the air for weeks and weeks.

All she could smell now was dust.

She wrinkled her nose when a sneeze threatened. That would never do. A sneeze would announce her presence as loudly as a shout. Here I am—trespasser!

No, she would be better off sleeping. But if she did, she might miss when they arrived in Edinburgh and be trapped in a locked stable, only released when someone opened the bay doors days later. How would she ever survive without water and food?

She couldn't breathe.

She had to calm down. None of what she imagined could come to pass. Very well, perhaps it could, but it wouldn't.

They would arrive in Edinburgh, the owner of the carriage would disembark. The coachman would be concerned about his horses, leading them away to their stalls. She would emerge from her hiding place, obtain a conveyance to Mairi's house, and then her plan would begin in earnest.

Mairi would read her manuscript, want to publish her book, and her future would be assured.

Her mother wouldn't be able to plan her marriage to a stranger. She wouldn't be required to live a life she didn't want. Instead, she would be just like Mairi, choosing her own destiny. She would write more stories about adventuresome women in the throes of lust. She might even experiment a little on her own to ensure she got all the details just right.

She would become a lady of letters, someone to whom women would point in admiration. *There she goes, Ellice Traylor. She wrote that scandalous book, you know. Have you read it?*

She could almost hear the guilty giggles now.

Women would read her book in secret, their cheeks reddening. They would marvel at *The Lusty Adventures of Lady Pamela* and wonder if they, too, had the courage the heroine had demonstrated.

Would her book incite others to explore the world with more adventure?

For that matter, would the book inspire her?

Why else would she be hiding in a stranger's carriage? Lady Pamela would have done exactly this. In addition, her heroine would have discarded her bustle in the same manner.

Or perhaps she would have simply seduced the owner of the carriage and he would have gladly given her passage to Edinburgh in exchange for a little tumble on the leather seat.

Her face warmed as she thought of such an adventure taking place only inches from her. The stranger would be overcome by her beauty, of course. He would undress her slowly, each garment removed with a reverent air. He would kiss each area he unveiled, the curve of her neck into her shoulder, the skin above her shift.

He would touch her breasts, bend to kiss each nipple while excitement raced through her.

She was brought back to herself by voices.

Lifting her head, she tried to make out their conversation but couldn't. To her surprise, however, they were moving, the carriage lurching as it started.

She lifted the seat up to discover that the carriage was empty.

They turned, the sharp curve throwing her shoulder against the compartment. She bit her lip hard, tasting blood, and felt the carriage turn again.

The road to Edinburgh didn't wind around like this.

Abruptly, they stopped, the rocking of the carriage a sign the driver had dismounted.

To her horror, she heard Brianag's voice, the words echoing.

"When you've settled your horses, ask one of the lads to bring you to the kitchen. We've a fish stew and bread baked this morning."

They weren't going to Edinburgh. Instead, all she'd done was hide in the carriage while the driver took it around to the stables.

She couldn't leave the carriage for fear one of the lads would see her. Worse, they'd report her behavior to Macrath, who would feel duty bound to talk to her mother. That conversation would doom her to weeks of lectures, and might well escalate her mother's plans.

In an attempt to gain her freedom, she'd only made matters much, much worse.

Chapter 3

The library door opened to admit Drumvagen's housekeeper. Ross had the thought that regardless of how many times he met her, he would probably always be startled by her appearance.

Tall, with broad shoulders, she appeared almost like an Amazon. Her square face was matched with square lips and a jaw that jut pugnaciously out at the world. Her graying hair indicated that she was an older woman but her face was curiously unlined, making him wonder at her age.

Attired in a red and black tartan skirt and white blouse, she had a feathered brooch pinned at the base of her throat and a glare in her eyes.

She nodded just once in his direction, then evidently dismissed him.

"The Earl of Gadsden has agreed to be our guest, Brianag," Sinclair told her. "Would you please show him to the guest chamber?"

By the time they made it up the stairs, the rain was pelting the windows like pebbles. He was even more appreciative of Sinclair's hospitality; he wasn't a fool to travel in weather like this.

Even in the midst of an increasingly fierce storm, Drumvagen was an oasis of safety, an example of man's thumbing his nose at nature. When the lightning flashed from cloud to cloud, followed by deafening peals of thunder, the house stood impervious. None of the walls vibrated. The floors didn't shake. The structure was as solid as a mountain and as defiant.

The housekeeper led him to a broad oak door with a brass handle and stepped aside.

"You'll be settling in, then," she said, nodding at him again. "The boiler works, but I imagine you'll discover that on your own. I'll send a maid to take you to the dining room promptly at six. In the meantime I'll see that your coachman is settled."

When he thanked her, she didn't respond, merely left him standing in the hall, staring after her.

He entered the room, unsurprised to find that the comforts of Drumvagen extended to its guest chambers as well. He'd been given a bedroom with an adjoining bathing chamber, one that opened into a second bedroom.

Deep blue curtains were open, revealing a view of a turbulent sea, lightning flashes illuminating boiling clouds for just a second before plunging the world in darkness again.

He doubted his mother would miss him at home, not as long as there was a new arrival of purchases. Nor was there anyone else who would miss him at Huntly. Strange, that the realization should pinch now when it never had.

Perhaps it was the noise of Sinclair's household. He could hear children laughing and someone singing not far away.

How long had it been since Huntly was filled with the sounds of children? Or had it ever been? Or was the house too large to be tamed in such a way?

He pushed the thought aside, along with the strange discomfort of the comparison.

Drumvagen wasn't the first disappointment he'd ever experienced at his father's hands, but it was a first lesson learned. Thomas was easily bored and not equipped to handle any problems. Over the years, he'd begun to understand that his father's way of handling any crisis was to go off and get drunk in the company of willing hangers-on, people who realized that his father was as devoid of morals as he was flush with cash.

At last count, Ross had four illegitimate half brothers. Each was left a small fortune at his father's death. Thomas had been less concerned about the three girls. One of Ross's first decisions was to give each a matching amount of money.

His second task, and one that had occupied him since ascending to the earldom, was recouping what was left of the Gadsden honor.

As profligate as Thomas had been in sowing his seed in other places, he had only one legitimate child. As his heir, and the fifth Earl of Gadsden, it had fallen on Ross to attempt to undo decades of scandal.

A task that wasn't as easy as simply announcing that he wasn't his father.

Everywhere Ross went, his surname alone conjured up memories of glorious debauchery. Just last week a companion had regaled him with tales of how Thomas hired a performing troupe to entertain his guests. Various exotic animals were paraded through the man's house, defecating at will and terrifying the staff.

Ross had heard similar tales over the years.

People remembered a reprobate. From the distance of years, Thomas had become less menacing and more hail-fellow-well-met. People saw him as less of a bastard and more of a boy in a man's body.

Too bad Ross couldn't say the same.

At least Sinclair had no stories to tell, no episodes of violent temper to recount, no profligate spending or wenching the length and breadth of Scotland and England.

He himself was not his father's son. If anything, he was a creature that scandal had made.

Where his father had defied society, Ross embraced it. He was deferential to matrons, polite to young girls, and respectful to white whiskered men who would advise him on everything from his appearance to his investments.

Let the gossips go and talk about the Earl of Dumfries with his penchant for horse racing, or the Duke of Barnett who was rumored to have sired a bevy of children from the girls on his staff.

The fifth Earl of Gadsden was as proper as John Calvin.

He didn't covet Drumvagen but he came close to envy when remembering the expression on Sinclair's face when he spoke of his wife and children.

Drumvagen had become a home, one that Ross didn't have even at his beloved Huntly. The sound of laughter was rarely heard in his house, unless it was an errant maid before being severely lectured. A man didn't speak of his wife heavy with child or bear a look on his face half of desperation and half exuberant joy.

He'd created order at Huntly, a regimen worked out since he took over the earldom. He knew the exact number of maids and footmen he employed, the costs of their salaries, uniforms, days off, and the cleaning supplies required to keep Huntly spotless. He knew how many horses were stabled and the exact amount of feed they received each day, along with their exercise regimen. He was kept aware of the number of barn cats and hounds on the estate. Each repair to the house or the outbuildings was carefully calculated and planned in advance.

He made meticulous notes and had a daily schedule he consulted often.

Yet he hadn't remembered his anniversary. The date had blindsided him.

Cassandra had been a beautiful woman. Her laughter still echoed in his mind. She was the perfect wife and would have been a glorious countess.

She never got the chance, dying two years after they'd wed. He'd been a widower more than twice as long as he was a husband.

His widowed state had made him a romantic figure. Girls sighed at him. Women fluttered their eyelashes. The widows of his acquaintance were predatory, and the mamas of every eligible female in the whole of Edinburgh bore down on him with fire in their eyes.

He avoided social engagements when he could or, when he was forced to attend, remained in the males-only bastion when the host was clever enough to create one, and begged off when it was possible.

Frankly, he was surprised that he hadn't gotten a reputation for being sickly. He'd invented so many coughs, possible contagions, and stomach ailments, he was bound to be thought of as a hypochondriac.

He knew why he remained on the top of the Edinburgh marriage mart. He was alive, an earl, and single—all three qualified him to be a husband. The only problem was that the idea of marriage was abhorrent to him.

Unfortunately, most of the females of his acquaintance insisted on making him out to be a Scottish Heathcliff.

To them he was a creature from a fevered novel, a brooding hero plucked from the pages. He was as far from a romantic figure as that fool Heathcliff, wandering the moors when he should have applied himself to some sensible pursuit like repairing his home or purchasing cattle.

Baying at the moon never got a man anything but a hoarse voice.

The darkness was so complete, no matter how wide she opened her eyes, Ellice couldn't see anything.

The carriage maker was to be commended. No cracks existed in the floor, and the compartment beneath the seat was perfectly joined, permitting not one thread of light.

She heard people moving around the carriage, felt the wheels roll a little as the brake was applied and the horses taken from their leads.

Someone laughed not far away and she smelled the pungent odor of wet hay, horses, and leather.

She was going to be late for dinner. Her mother would check her room and, finding her absent, would complain to the others at the table about what an ill-mannered chit she was.

I can't imagine where the girl has gotten to now. Eudora was never such, disappearing at all hours with no concern for others. When Ellice is here, she's almost a shadow. Never speaks. Never has an opinion. Dearest Eudora was such a conversationalist.

Only Virginia would know where she'd gone, but she wouldn't tell. Nor did she ever contradict Enid, but her glance always carried a measure of compassion. As if to say, *She is a trial, isn't she, Ellice?*

She waited until she didn't hear any more sounds, but just as she raised the carriage seat, she thought she heard one of the stable doors opening.

How was she to ever get out of here? The stables were always occupied, by either the stable master or one of the grooms. People were always walking in or out. Would they even notice her? If someone did, could she stop them from carrying the tale?

She forced herself to relax. She would have to miss dinner, that's all, including meeting the stranger who'd been convinced to remain at Drumvagen.

Her plan would have worked, too, if only he hadn't decided to stay.

She wasn't good at telling time without a watch. The minutes seemed to stretch on into eternity when she was waiting for something to happen. Fifteen minutes might have passed or it might have been longer. When finally it seemed as if the sounds in the stable were muted, other than the stomp and snorts of the horses, she opened the seat, grateful that the hinges didn't squeak.

Getting out of the compartment was a great deal easier than going in, and she took a moment to fluff her skirts and debate over putting on her bustle for the short scamper to the house. Would anyone see?

Yes, they undoubtedly would, and they'd go to her mother. Or, heaven forbid, Virginia.

No, Virginia wouldn't listen to tales about her. As for her mother, she couldn't even bear considering that conversation.

Your ladyship, did you know your daughter was cavorting about in the stable? Hiding in a carriage, she was, and acting as if she hadn't a care in the world.

No, that would never do.

She blew out a breath, wished she never had the idea of escaping Drumvagen, and opened the carriage door.

The nursery, on the same floor as the family rooms, was in chaos, the door firmly closed. That wasn't to prevent anyone from entering as much as it was to keep Fiona from leaving. She'd been walking for months now and was insistent on exploring. Everyone was afraid she'd tumble down the sweeping stairs in front of the house or the servants' stairs in the rear. Therefore, she was kept closely guarded, at least until she was capable of understanding and obeying instructions.

"No," to Fiona was merely a sound, one to ignore.

Today she was taking great pains in being even more obstinate, as she sat on the floor playing with a profusion of colored wood blocks and occasionally kicking one into submission.

Bedtime was rapidly approaching and tonight Virginia couldn't wait. She'd sent Alistair on ahead since he'd been quarrelsome all day. When Mary finished tucking him into his bed, she'd return for Fiona. Only twelve when she'd come to Scotland, the young maid had blossomed in the intervening years. At last count she had three suitors from Kinloch Village.

Virginia sat back, placed her hands on her stomach and wondered at the pain sweeping through her. This labor felt nothing like the two before.

Hannah sat beside her, intent on her needlework and eyeing her every few minutes. The maid had settled into Drumvagen and become a dear friend, their bond having grown since London. Hannah was happily married herself now and well on her way to becoming a Scot.

"You need to go lie down," Hannah said now.

"I'm having my child," Virginia said, forcing herself to smile.

Hannah's eyes widened but she didn't try to dissuade Virginia.

After all, she'd already proved everyone wrong when she gave birth the first time. She was in labor with Alistair only a few hours. Fiona's birth had been even faster. It seemed as if Providence had granted her the ability to have her children in a remarkably quick manner, a fact that had her darling Macrath in knots.

He watched her sometimes like he was afraid she was going to simply stop in the middle of the hall and deliver their child there.

"Have you told Macrath?" Hannah asked.

"Good heavens, no. He'd be circling me. Can you imagine?" She crossed her hands over the mound of her stomach and tried to smile again. The effort was too much, however, as another cramping pain stretched from her back to hug her in the depths of her womb.

Something was wrong.

"You're lips are nearly blue, Virginia," the maid said. "And I'm not liking your color. You should get to your bed."

She nodded, nausea sweeping through her. Her heart was beating much too fast. That had never happened before, either.

"It might be a good idea to let Macrath know."

Hannah grabbed the bellpull before reaching for Fiona.

A year and a half old, her daughter had the promise of beauty along with the Sinclair eyes. Her hair was black and curled around her shoulders. Her mouth was pursed in a pre-tantrum yowl as she reached for her blocks.

"Come with me," Hannah said. "We'll play a game."

Fiona smiled and thrust both hands at her, a signal that she was more than willing to be picked up.

Macrath must have given instructions that any request from her be answered at a racing pace because a maid was at the door in less than a minute.

"Would you send for Macrath, please?" Virginia asked, pain making her breathless. The maid disappeared as fast as she arrived.

Hannah put Fiona on her hip and held her arm out. Virginia gripped it tight and slowly rose from the chair. Her face felt cold and wet. Suddenly, she felt like she was going to faint.

Please, let Macrath get here first.

Her pace was agonizingly slow, the pressure building in her womb so that each step was torture. Before they were halfway to the suite, Macrath was pounding up the stairs.

After one look at her, he swept her up in his arms.

"You should have let me know," he said, bending to press a kiss to her forehead.

"I just have," she said, a spasm causing her to close her eyes.

Hannah opened the double doors and moved out of the way.

Fiona reached for her father but Hannah stepped back as Macrath entered the room.

She looked up just then, one hand gripping his shirt.

"Get Brianag, Macrath, please. I think something's wrong."

"Do it," Macrath said, his voice holding an edge.

Hannah nodded, descending the steps with Fiona in her arms.

Virginia palmed her husband's cheek, wishing his look wasn't so filled with fear. The pain suddenly cut her in two, washing away any thoughts.

Chapter 4

Ross found his way to the kitchen, grateful that Sinclair had offered his hospitality. In the hour since he'd agreed to stay, the storm had increased. Thunder muted every other noise but the rain drumming on the roof.

He followed the sound of laughter, entering the cavernous kitchen to find it filled with people.

His driver was separate from the others. Harvey would have been easy to find regardless, clad as he was in his mother's new livery of red and black.

His brown hair was askew and even in this fragrant room the man smelled of horse, not a strange fact since most of his days were spent with the horses and he lived above the stables.

"Is there anything I can do, sir?" Harvey asked.

"No, you go about your dinner," he said. "I'm just going to get some clothes for the morning." There was no need for the man, or any of Drumvagen's servants, to perform a task he could easily do himself.

"If you're sure, your lordship?"

At Huntly he had a staff that hovered night and day. These past two weeks had been marked by a curious freedom.

"I'm sure," he said, nodding.

With Harvey assuaged, although the man frowned as if in doubt of his competence, Ross left Drumvagen and headed for his carriage, dashing through the rain and getting soaked before he reached the stables.

The structure had been built of gray brick to match the exterior of the house. Long and rectangular, containing at least twenty stalls, it was draped in shadows and faintly illuminated by the last faint light of the gray day.

No one was about. No doubt all of Drumvagen's staff was arrayed in the kitchen. Only the horses were present, restless from the sound of the storm.

The smell of hay and leather surrounded him, bringing back memories of his childhood when he'd returned home from school. He'd visited all the servants at Huntly, finding in them the ease of simply being himself.

For years he'd been Master Ross, his hair ruffled by fond, work-weathered, hands. His teeth were inspected to praise the new ones that had come in since he'd been home last. He was measured against a beam in a stable not appreciably different from this one, his rapid height praised. Everyone noticed him. Everyone saw him. The feeling of belonging he'd experienced among the staff counteracted his father's disregard.

At Drumvagen, his carriage had been pulled into a large space in front of a double door. A rolling clap of thunder accompanied him as he went to the rear of the vehicle, untying the leather flap over the baggage area. He grabbed his valise and was turning to leave when the carriage door opened.

He watched as a female foot emerged, then a hint of petticoat and skirt.

"Who the blazes are you?"

The female in his carriage didn't say a word, merely turned and stared at him with doelike brown eyes.

Was she too afraid to speak?

He walked around to the side of the carriage. "Answer me now. Who are you?"

A small head shake was her only response.

"What are you doing in my carriage?"

She just stared at him.

He stretched out his free hand while smiling reassuringly.

"It's all right. You can't stay in there, you know. You must come out. Were you tricked by someone? Did you think it a fine game to hide in there?"

"I wasn't tricked," she said, grabbing the handle above the window.

"You're English," he said.

"And you're a Scot," she answered. "Is it so strange to find an Englishwoman in Scotland?"

"In my carriage, yes."

She still hadn't explained why she was there. After her quick look at him, he dismissed the idea that she was deficient. Her eyes sparkled with intelligence and perhaps something else.

Why did he warrant defiance?

"It's not that large a carriage," she said, giving it a dismissive glance. "One thinks it's a bit larger than it is, but it isn't, not really. It's quite confining, even for someone who isn't all that tall. I can't imagine what it would be like for someone like you, for example."

He stared at her. "Do you want me to apologize for the close confines of my carriage?"

She shook her head.

"No, I'm just explaining."

"Who are you?"

"You would want to know, wouldn't you? Or, more importantly, why I'm in your carriage."

"Yes," he said, when it was obvious she wasn't going to provide that information.

Her blue dress was smudged with dust, the white cuffs more than a little gray. Her shoes were scuffed as well but looked as if they'd been polished at one time.

He reached out and plucked a cobweb from her dark brown hair. She shivered in response, then focused her gaze on his hand.

"Were you and the spider acquainted?" he asked.

"I don't like spiders," she said. "But they're better than snakes. I haven't the slightest idea why God made snakes. He forgot their legs. Although a snake with legs would be even more terrifying, don't you think?"

He brushed off his fingers with his handkerchief. "If you think that bombarding me with speech will make me forget the question, you're mistaken. I'm known to have an excellent memory."

"Why?"

He stared at her again. "Why what?"

"Why do you have an excellent memory? Is it an occupational requirement? Was it something you were born with? I'm interested in a great deal, you see."

"Who are you? And why are you in my carriage? I warn you, I will not tolerate any deflecting maneuvers." When she didn't speak, he added, "If you're involved in something illegal, it's best to tell me now."

She smiled at him, such a blazingly happy expression that he almost reared back. "You think I'm doing something illegal," she said.

He slowly nodded.

"No one has ever thought I was doing anything illegal. I have conformed to the letter of every rule and regulation for the extent of my life."

"You really shouldn't look so pleased to be thought of as a law breaker. There are rules and regulations to limit human behavior for a reason."

"What reason? So that someone can say, 'Oh, you broke a rule, miss. Back to the schoolroom you go. Or, sir, you are in violation of that regulation. How very vulgar of you.'"

Her smile abruptly vanished. "Do not tell me that's why you have an excellent memory. Are you a magistrate?"

"I'm not, but why does the thought of a magistrate make you frown?"

"I think being a magistrate would be the most horrid job you could have, being judge over people, all pompous and proud."

"Who are you? And don't go off on another tangent."

"You're very tenacious."

"No," he said. "We aren't going to discuss my tenacity. Who are you?"

She took another step away from the carriage. "If you could only have one question answered, which would it be? Who I am or why was I in your carriage?"

"I think I deserve the answer to both, don't you? After all, it's my carriage."

She turned her head. His breath halted as he stared at her. Why hadn't he seen it before? The woman in his carriage, the one who'd emerged from his carriage like a Botticelli Venus, was beautiful.

Not in the way Cassandra had been beautiful, with glittering eyes and full, red lips. Cassandra's blond beauty might have faded in time, become handsomeness instead.

This woman's beauty was simple: well-defined cheekbones, a high forehead, slender nose, and stubborn chin. As the years passed she might grow even more attractive.

He suspected that her laugh would captivate, just as her tears would act like a razor to whomever brought them forth. Her smile had already charmed him, and now her silence incited his curiosity. Not about who she was and why she was here, but about more.

Who was the woman behind the smile?

"I hoped that you were going to Edinburgh," she said, just when he thought she wasn't going to answer.

"Are you escaping from an angry husband?" he asked. None of his concern, if she were. "Or escaping to a lover?" That was certainly none of his business, either.

Her cheeks bloomed with color. "I was going to tell you that," she said. "Oh, not about the husband, but the lover."

"Is it the truth?"

She shook her head. "I hadn't decided, however, whether to use that excuse if I was found. Or to tell you that I had a sick relative. It all depended on how kind you seemed to be."

He folded his arms and regarded her.

"Or you could simply be a servant wishing to escape to Edinburgh. Is that it? You're employed here and the isolation has finally gotten to you?"

"Drumvagen isn't all that isolated. There's Kinloch Village."

"Hardly exciting enough for someone as daring as you."

She laughed. He was right. Her laughter was enchanting. So, too, the sparkle in her eyes as she glanced at him. He'd never seen eyes as darkly brown as hers. With her dark hair she should have been a study in monochrome, but she wasn't. Her cheeks matched her pink lips.

"Who are you?"

"I don't think my identity is as important as yours. Your name isn't Donald, is it?"

God had a marvelously mischievous sense of humor. Not only had He taken her from London and deposited her in the wilds of Scotland, but He gave her a need to write down all the forbidden, odd, and wicked thoughts she had.

Then, in the most glaring demonstration of His power, God put this man in her path.

Or maybe it wasn't God at all but the Devil.

The carriage owner's features were so familiar to her that she could have sculpted him blindfolded.

His was a perfectly carved face graced with a Roman nose and high cheekbones. The hollows below them were shadowed, accentuating his leanness. His bold brow led to black mobile eyebrows. One was arched at her even now. Full lips looked as if they smiled often—only not at the moment.

His gray eyes were the color of a stormy sky, revealing no hint of his thoughts. She had the feeling she could gaze into his eyes for hours and never learn more about the man than he wished her to know.

But what kept her silent, every thought jelled in wonder, was his physique. He'd come to the stable attired only in dark trousers and a white shirt. Now the shirt was plastered to his chest, the rain having dampened the linen so it conformed to every contour and muscle.

What would he do if she placed her palms on him like she wanted? Just to touch, to see if his chest was as broad as it appeared or a mirage. Were those muscles truly as defined as they seemed through the fabric?

"Are you a farmer?" she asked.

"Pardon?"

"No, you live in Edinburgh, don't you?"

"How do you know where I live?"

"I overheard you talking earlier," she said.

Truly, her hands were itching to touch him. She curled her fingers into fists and deliberately looked away.

"You must box, then," she said. "Or be an equestrian." Something must account for his fitness.

"I'll ask the questions," he said. "None of which you've answered. Who are you and what were you doing in my carriage?"

His hair was slicked back, the ends curling at his neck. She wanted to touch him there, too.

What an utter temptation he was.

The man she'd imagined had been brought to life.

"What is your name?" she asked, feeling breathless.

He didn't answer.

"I'll tell you my name, shall I?" she said. "Then, you tell me yours."

If anything, his face grew stonier. "I see no reason for us to exchange pleasantries."

Even his voice made her shiver.

"Are you married?"

Had she shocked him? His lips thinned and those glorious eyes narrowed. He did not, however, answer the question.

"You wanted to know my name and why I was hiding in your carriage. All I'm asking is for a little reciprocation."

His teeth were clenched so tight that a muscle flexed in his cheek as he bent down, retrieved his valise, and strode away.

She scrambled to catch up with him.

Her hero was a great deal more personable. He inspired a woman's adoration. When he touched Lady Pamela, she trembled.

Donald even smelled good.

He stopped and turned, nearly knocking her over. She regained her balance, stepping backward.

"Were you sniffing me?"

She'd been lectured never to discuss a man's appearance in public or his failings. She knew better than to discuss personal subjects, like a man's income. One never flaunted one's wealth—or lack of it. Politics was a subject better left to others. Nor was she to ever talk about her health. In the smallpox epidemic that had killed her sister and thousands of other Londoners, she'd been unaffected. She wasn't to say so, since that would sound too much like boasting.

Sniffing, however? She didn't know the proper etiquette.

"Yes," she said, deciding to be honest. "I was. Do you use scent? Or fancy soap?"

How often did he need to shave during the day? Even

now a hint of beard shadowed his face, giving him an almost swarthy appearance. He looked the picture of a gentleman, but one with a touch of menace.

"I imagine Sinclair has his hands full with you on staff. Unless you were fired. Is that why you want to go to Edinburgh?"

"If I had, would you put in a good word for me?"

Her hero would have. Her hero championed the downtrodden, saved abused cart horses, and was a man to emulate and admire.

This man didn't look as if he'd go out of his way to help anyone.

"When I speak to Sinclair, I'll inform him of the circumstances, nothing more," he said, his eyes conveying frozen disdain.

Perhaps most people would have been put off by such a glare, but she'd been face-to-face with angry people for years. First, her brother Lawrence, who seemed to be in a foul temper most of the time. Then her mother, who didn't allow her title of Dowager Countess of Barrett to restrain her anger when she was annoyed. Brianag was an intimidating individual even on days when she was happy with the world. Nor would it do to forget Macrath. She'd seen him angry at one of his inventions once. He'd almost kicked it in frustration.

This man's words, however, made her stomach cramp.

"There's no reason to tell anyone I was in your carriage."

He frowned at her, resuming his stalking march to the door.

"Truly, there isn't. I'll simply go now, and you can return to the house."

"You expect me to ignore the incident?"

"Well, not ignore it exactly, but is there a reason to tell anyone?" she asked, following him.

Donald had a small dimple on his right cheek. This

stranger showed no sign of smiling. He brushed his fingers through his thick black hair, a habit Donald had as well.

"Were you fired? Did Sinclair give you an ultimatum to leave Drumvagen?" he asked, glancing at her.

"Do you always treat people's questions like bits of fluff in the air? You bat them out of the way when you don't want to answer."

"If you think that I'm going to continue this conversation with you, miss, you're mistaken," he said, almost to the door.

"My name is Ellice," she said. "My mother's name is Enid and my sister's name was Eudora. My mother has a penchant for names that begin with E. It could have been worse, I imagine. I could have been named Ephine or Eustacia."

He ignored her and opened one of the double doors. The rain was making a lake of the path to the house.

How could she possibly dissuade him from telling Macrath? By his carriage, he was a man of means. She doubted there was enough money in her strongbox to change his mind.

What was she going to do?

She could hear her mother now. *Why can't you be more like your sister? Eudora would never have countenanced such a foolish idea, Ellice. She would never have hidden in a gentleman's carriage. I despair of you, I truly do. You were not reared with such flibbertigibbet notions.*

"You can't tell him," she said. "Really. You can't. Please."

He glanced at her. "Sinclair doesn't appear to be a cruel man," he said. "I doubt you'll be punished."

"He won't understand."

She hadn't left a note and she should have. She hadn't considered that she would have to explain her actions to Macrath face-to-face. All she'd thought about was leaving.

The man didn't look the least affected by her plea. She'd often wished to possess that kind of sang froid but had never been able to master it.

"I'm certain he'll understand if you explain it to him, something you haven't bothered to do with me."

She blew out a breath. He was going to tell Macrath regardless of what she said.

"To better yourself is always a fine goal. You shouldn't be afraid of him."

"I'm not afraid," she said. She didn't want to explain about her book.

The book she'd left in the carriage compartment.

She turned and stared back at the carriage. Oh, no, what had she done?

"Go on ahead," she said, stepping back from the open door.

"No," he said, eyeing her with a narrowed gaze. "I don't think so. I suspect that the minute my back is turned, you'll disappear."

"You are a magistrate, aren't you? Why are you so determined to tell?"

"Why did he dismiss you? Were you guilty of theft?"

"Of course not!"

"Did he find you where you weren't supposed to be?" His eyes took on the frost of a Scottish January. "Like in the beds of his guests?"

She blinked at him. He truly did think she was an adventuress.

"You consider the matter amusing?" he said.

Her smile melted.

"Very well," she said, gathering up her skirts, too long since her bustle was in the compartment of his carriage. She would have to retrieve her undergarment and her book as soon as possible, but for now she had to face the situation she'd created.

At least, that's what Lady Pamela would have done. She put her chin up and walked through the rain, praying for a little more courage.

Chapter 5

Without caring if the stranger followed her, Ellice headed for Macrath's library. If Sinclair wasn't there he'd be with Virginia or even in his laboratory with his associates.

Macrath Sinclair had become wealthy by inventing a way to make ice. As a boy he'd had an idea, and made it happen through sheer perseverance and hard work.

She'd always admired him. Plus she liked him, which was a good thing since Virginia had always been like a sister to her.

He had not hesitated to include her and her mother in his family, had made them welcome at Drumvagen and ensured their every wish was granted.

Except, of course, the most important one—to have some control over her own life.

Mairi would have understood how she felt. Mairi had devoted herself to the cause of women's suffrage and women's rights for years now. She had founded the *Edinburgh Women's Gazette,* a paper devoted to women. She published anything of interest to a woman, from political leanings of various politicians—who were determined not to allow women to be treated fairly in society—to recipes and tips on how to manage a home. In fact, it was Mairi's publishing company that had published her mother's and Brianag's book.

Mairi would have understood.

Unfortunately, Mairi wasn't here right now, and as Ellice stood before Macrath's library door, she wished he wasn't, either. Why hadn't she waited until Macrath and Virginia visited Australia again to be rebellious?

If only her mother hadn't been adamant that she find a husband now.

Virginia was about to give birth to her third child, which meant Macrath wasn't going to budge from Drumvagen for months, if not years. He would do anything to keep Virginia safe, an attitude he had for all the women in his family, even her, which meant he wasn't going to understand.

But as much as she admired Macrath and Mairi's husband, Logan, she didn't want to be smothered by them.

Macrath would have wrapped his wife in bunting, but Virginia had a way of looking at him, the message in her gaze all too evident. *Back off, my darling husband. I am no schoolgirl unable to make decisions.*

Ellice's problem was that she was still a schoolgirl in Macrath's eyes.

"Are you afraid?" the stranger asked from behind her.

He was standing much too close. She could almost feel his breath on her neck.

Lemons. He smelled of lemons and leather.

What would he have done if she'd leaned back against him? Would he have supported her in his arms or would he have stepped away? Would he question her or lecture her?

She might turn and wrap her arms around his neck, lean in for a kiss in a way she'd imagined so many times before. His mouth would envelop hers, his tongue brushing against hers, his lips soft yet hard.

The taste of his mouth would fascinate her. His tongue would brush against hers, stroking that fire building inside. Her head would swim, but she'd pull back, look at him coolly just as Lady Pamela would.

Her palm would rest against his heated cheek and she'd say, so calmly that it surprised even her, *That was wonderful. I've dreamed of your kiss.*

Then, as he moved toward her, she would shake her head. *I've no time now,* she'd say, and move away in a gliding motion, leaving him to stare, desolate, after her.

"Ellice?"

She blinked her eyes to see the library door open and Macrath standing before her.

"What's wrong?"

When the stranger gently propelled her into the room by pushing on her shoulders, Macrath's eyebrows drew together in a most forbidding frown. She'd seen that expression before but it had been directed at something inanimate, Macrath's plans or a bolt that would not line up where it was supposed to go.

Behind her, she heard the stranger say, "She hid in my carriage. She wanted to go to Edinburgh but my staying here defeated her purpose."

Macrath stepped back.

"Ellice, is that true? Were you hiding in his lordship's carriage?"

"His lordship?" she asked, glancing over her shoulder at the stranger.

"Ross Forster, the Earl of Gadsden," Macrath said.

Gadsden should have told her, but no, he'd remained silent.

She frowned at the earl, but her irritation didn't change his expression one whit.

Both men looked at her until she realized she was supposed to sit. She didn't want to sit. She wanted to run upstairs to her room, close the door, and put a chair in front of it so no one could disturb her. If she wanted, she'd fume. Or perhaps she'd even weep. Or she might do both. She felt too close to tears at the moment and that angered her.

Instead, she pretended that she wasn't the least disturbed—

much in the way Lady Pamela would behave—and moved to one of the comfortable chairs in front of the fireplace.

Virginia often sat here reading. She wasn't here today and hadn't been for the last week. Her time was near and no one was taking any chances with her health. Her first child had been born after only four hours of labor. Her second had been half that.

"I'll have the baby before anyone realizes," she'd told Enid last week, and although she laughed at the time, she didn't realize that's exactly what everyone feared.

Macrath was well on his way to having the clan he said he wanted. The fact that his wife endured childbirth so well was a blessing. However, that didn't take the worry from his eyes or make him any easier to be around.

Like now, when his blue eyes were as intent as the belly of a flame.

"Do you want to explain your actions, Ellice?" He waved his hand in the air as if to erase his words. "No, let me re-phrase that. I want you to explain your actions."

Macrath indicated the nearby chair, but Gadsden shook his head, evidently preferring to stand. When Macrath seated himself behind his desk, the other man leaned against a book-shelf, folded his arms and looked supremely unconcerned.

Why should he worry? He'd done the proper thing. A das-tardly man would have compromised Lady Pamela in the stables. No, Gadsden had been suffocatingly proper, disap-pointingly so.

She'd been prepared to be even more of an adventuress, but he didn't give her the opportunity. He hadn't even tried to kiss her.

All she'd done was make the situation even worse, since her manuscript and her bustle now rested in the compartment of his carriage. However was she going to retrieve it?

"Ellice?"

She blinked up at Macrath, realizing he was waiting for an answer.

"I felt the need to go to Edinburgh," she said. Would Macrath take that as enough of an explanation?

Evidently not because he leveled that stare at her and asked, "Why?"

"To see Mairi."

He didn't respond, merely turned and looked at Gadsden. "Mairi is my sister," he said.

"And who is she?" Gadsden asked, glancing at her.

"She's a sister as well," he said.

The words bloomed in her chest, choking off her breath. She'd never expected Macrath to claim her like that, especially in front of a stranger.

She was not going to cry now.

"Then I should consider myself fortunate to be an only child," Gadsden said.

Annoyed, she looked at him. What a horrid thing to say. But then, Donald had been as cruel when he was hurting.

Had she wounded him somehow? Was his heart more tender than it appeared?

"Why did you need to see Mairi?" Macrath asked. "Couldn't you have sent her a letter?"

She stared down at her clasped hands. He would never understand the truth.

Drumvagen was a magnificent house but it was a prison, inhabited by jailers who dictated her every move. She couldn't leave her room without being assailed by people who wanted her to talk more or less, walk faster or slower, tell them what was on her mind or hold her thoughts. Between Brianag and her mother and even dear Virginia, she could not simply *be*, and that lack of freedom had made her do something rash and impulsive.

She was never rash and impulsive. She was docile and

agreeable. She was invisible. People could probably see through her, she was such a nondescript person.

Ellice stared at the front of Macrath's carved desk.

What could she say about Drumvagen that wouldn't offend him?

The door suddenly flew open and a wide-eyed maid stood there, breathing fast.

"Oh sir, Brianag says to come quick. Something's wrong. There's blood."

If the weather had been better, Ross would have left Drumvagen, rather than be an intrusion into what was a private matter.

He removed his sodden clothes and dried himself, dressing in the clothing he'd retrieved from the carriage. Tomorrow he'd be home, and grateful for it. As it was, he'd been gone for two weeks, time enough to be about his duties.

Because of the condition of Drumvagen's mistress, and the subsequent involvement of the housekeeper, a woman with a reputed skill at nursing, dinner was a tray in his room brought by a trembling housemaid.

He thanked her and ate, unconcerned that the fare wasn't the equal of that found at Huntly. Few great houses employed a cook the equal of his, or had such massive farms from which to obtain its food.

For a time, he contemplated the storm, grateful that he'd changed his plans as it raged across the sky like a child having a tantrum. Perhaps it was a testament to how soundly Drumvagen had been built that the house didn't even tremble beneath the worst of the thunder, only sat impervious adjacent to the sea.

Because of the cliff, there was no danger of ever being swamped by the ocean. Even so, the waves were the highest he'd ever seen, brought into stunning clarity by the streaks of lightning.

At the knock, he stood and walked to the door, thinking it was the maid come to get his tray. Instead it was Harvey, holding something in his hands.

"I'm sorry to bother you, sir, but I thought I should bring this to you."

Harvey stepped forward, proffering a stack of pages wrapped in twine.

"What is this?" he asked.

"It was in the carriage, your lordship." Then, to his surprise, the man's florid face deepened in color. "And this, too, sir." He reached into his coat and pulled out a garment, draping it over the pages.

Both men stared at it like it was poisonous. From the lace, he could tell it belonged to a female.

"It's a lady's undergarment," Harvey said, his voice barely above a whisper. "It wasn't in the carriage before, sir. I inspect the carriage every day, to make sure it's proper and all."

He was torn between assuring his driver that he hadn't accosted a female in his carriage and explaining the stowaway. He did neither, finding himself curiously without words.

Harvey nodded and backed out of the room, closing the door behind him.

He removed the offensive undergarment with two fingers and draped it over a chair next to the bureau.

What had the oddly named Ellice penned? A series of love letters? No, the pile of paper was too thick for that, unless she had an insatiable yearning for a young man. Even so, that depth of written devotion would be excessive.

Love poems? He could see the young woman doing exactly that. She'd be passionate in any encounter, overly romantic, and no doubt demanding.

Why had she been intent on traveling to Edinburgh?

Curiosity was not a valid enough reason to have any interest in her thoughts, movements, or future. Certainly not a justification for wanting to read her poetry. No doubt it was very bad poetry as well.

His hand stretched out and fingered the twine. He untied the bow, turned over the first page and read: *The Lustful Adventures of Lady Pamela, a novel by Ellice Traylor.*

So her name wasn't Sinclair after all and she'd written a novel. No doubt one of those bits of literature where the heroine is trapped in a castle and her virtue is threatened by a ghost.

He found himself smiling.

He thumbed through the stack, beginning to read somewhere in the first third of the book.

His skin was hot, his cheek nearly blistering her palm. She stroked her fingers over his jaw, feeling her own heat escalate. Inside, she clenched, anticipating when he claimed her, thrust into her, bringing her to pleasure.

He stared at the page, his smile disappearing. He read farther.

His eyes were no longer cool but were the color of smoke, as if he felt the same fire.

His hands grasped her shift and effortlessly tore it in two. Her breasts swung free as she draped herself over him, her nipples stroking his lips, daring him to mouth her.

What the hell had she written?

He sat on the end of the bed, skimming a few more passages, then skipped forward.

His face was narrow, his eyes gray. Tall, with broad shoulders, he was a commanding man but it was his mouth she noticed first.

His lips were full but not too full. His lower lip ached to be teased. She'd nibble on him there, then sweep her tongue over his lips to acquaint him with her taste.

He'd know the rest of her by the time the night was done.

Still farther:

His hand teased her breast, cupping it, squeezing the nipple, making it swell for his lips. His mouth was hot, his tongue flicking back and forth.

"Yes," she said. "Yes. More."

Instead, he released her nipple, painted her with his tongue between her breasts, then down to her abdomen.

Her flesh shivered at his touch and she clenched her fingers on his arms.

His tongue darted into her navel.

He raised his head. Their eyes met.

"More? Do you want more?"

"Oh yes."

Every stroke of his tongue weakened her. Every glance and knowing smile made her want to surrender completely.

She widened her legs.

"More," she said softly.

His hands slid around her thighs to cup her buttocks and lift her for his mouth.

Ross stood and walked to the other side of the room, turning to stare at the pages spread across the end of the bed.

What the hell had she written?

His face was warm, his trousers too tight, and he couldn't

reconcile the voluble girl in the stables with the author of that book.

Worse, he wanted to go back and read the rest and finish every damn page.

The hero looked like him.

Gray eyes weren't all that common. Only his father had possessed them in his family. The man's good looks no doubt played a small role in his lechery, in addition to his fortune and title.

Ross was tall and his face narrow.

What other similarities were there?

He told himself it was for research alone that he grabbed the pages, sat at the desk, and began to read from page one.

How could she possibly sleep?

Ellice lay on her bed, staring up at the tester over her head. Her mother had spent the last few hours with her, Enid's fondness for Virginia keeping her pacing. Ellice knew she would have liked to be with Virginia, but Brianag was queen in the sickroom and had refused admittance to anyone other than Macrath.

More than one maid walked the corridor, moving past Ellice's room with halting feet. A cloud hung over Drumvagen, and it was centered on the master's suite.

Galelike winds punched the windows, as if nature were insane with fury over the fate of such a good woman. Thunder shouted in the clouds above, the sound reverberating repeatedly until it was in her brain.

God was as miserable as the rest of the inhabitants of Drumvagen.

She got out of bed and knelt beside it, pressing her forehead against the mattress.

If she had anything at all, it was because of Virginia. When she and her mother needed a home, Virginia had provided one. When she needed a private place, Virginia had let her use the cottage. When she was at the end of her tolerance with her mother, Virginia had listened, sharing her humor and compassion. When she was sad, sometimes talking about London with Virginia eased the worst of the ache.

Now, Virginia lay abed, ten hours into a difficult labor, one rendering Brianag uncharacteristically silent.

Please, God, spare her. Is it always women's lot to die in childbirth? I don't understand how such a good person as Virginia could be taken from us. Who would mother her children?

God was probably going to extend a celestial finger through the clouds, His nail lit by an unearthly light.

You would challenge me, child? Would you tell me how to create the animals in the forest, the fish in the sea? Have you no respect for your God?

How odd that the god of her imagination sounded like her mother.

Sleep was not going to come tonight.

She stood, went to the armoire and selected another blue dress, this one with a plain blue collar and cuffs. She didn't care about her appearance. Who would see her, the very annoying Earl of Gadsden?

She'd seen the look on his face when the maid appeared at Macrath's door. The man had looked startled, then abruptly distant, as if giving birth to a child was an abhorrent act, one that offended him.

He was probably deeply asleep. Her eyes widened. He was probably deeply asleep, just the time for her to retrieve her book.

As a careful man, Ross limited his acquaintances to those who were reputable. He was never seen in circumstances that would give voice to speculation as to his intentions or his motives.

But as he put down the last page of Ellice's manuscript, he realized he'd been caught. Over the years, he'd learned to conquer the personal shame of his circumstances. Embarrassment, however, was a close cousin, and now it sat heavily on his shoulders.

He shouldn't have read the book. If he hadn't, he wouldn't now be perched on the edge of a precipice.

What the hell did he do?

Sinclair was occupied with his wife or he'd deliver the pages to him, along with a friendly warning to watch Ellice. She was evidently involved in a great many lurid activities. How else would she be able to write about such things?

Nor did he want to deliver the pages to Ellice herself. She'd ask him if he'd read the book and he'd be forced to admit that his curiosity had been greater than his common sense.

Or Harvey could deliver the manuscript to Ellice, explaining that he'd found it in the compartment below the seat. That would be the best solution, one that would eliminate his involvement completely. She needn't know he'd read the book.

She really must be encouraged to destroy what she'd written. Perhaps he could ask Harvey to suggest such a thing, along with a financial encouragement to do so. But how to do that without letting her know he'd read it?

Since he'd been so ensnared by her imagination that he hadn't yet undressed for bed, he donned his shoes, threaded his hands through his hair, and set out for the stables and his coachman.

Chapter 6

Ellice finished dressing hurriedly. She would never get a better chance to retrieve her manuscript and bustle than now.

Outside her door she saw two maids, both silently leaning against the wall. She walked up to them, whispering the question.

"How is she?"

The older of the two girls shook her head, biting her lips against words she didn't say.

Ellice's stomach twisted as she nodded in response. She deliberately blocked her imagination, unable to perceive of a world without Virginia. Life at Drumvagen wouldn't be bearable without the woman she considered a sister.

She left them, heading toward the servants' stairs and the back of the house. Three of the maids were sitting around the table, sipping at cups of tea. She sent them a commiserating smile and grabbed a shawl from a peg by the door, wrapping it around her head and over her shoulders.

A minute out the door she realized how foolish she'd been. By the time she made it to the stables, she was soaked through to her shift. She'd never experienced a storm like this at Drumvagen, hours and hours of intense rain, so heavy it felt like standing beneath a waterfall.

She opened one of the doors, grateful that the hinges were oiled often. Inside, it smelled of rain, damp hay, warm horses, and sodden wood.

Overhead, the storm was giving no signs of subsiding. Thunder rolled and roared and the rain continued. Did nature itself mourn for Virginia?

She said another quick prayer, wishing she could do more, just as she had in London when Virginia was sick with smallpox. All she'd been able to do then was keep reassuring the staff that Virginia would get well, that things would get back to normal and everything would eventually be fine.

Nothing ever did go back to normal, though, did it?

A faint yellow light illuminated the large space just inside the door. A stablehand sat on a chair, a watchman against fire and any other danger. Evidently he was exhausted from his day because he was asleep, his chin on his chest.

She tiptoed past him and down the center aisle. Only a few hours ago she'd been racing down this same corridor. This time she paused in front of one of her favorite mares, Lady Mary, and rubbed her face, the mare's hooves pawing the ground in greeting.

She returned to Gadsden's carriage, glad to see that there was no lantern or guard.

Those working at the stables slept above the stalls, on a second floor Macrath had expanded to include larger rooms for staff and visitors. No doubt the earl's coachman was sleeping there.

She sluiced as much of the rain from her face and hair as she could, hoping she didn't drip all over Gadsden's carriage. She didn't want anyone to know she was here.

After opening the door, she unfurled the steps, stood on the bottom one and reached over into the compartment, trying to forget the spiderweb the earl had brushed from her hair. There was no gigantic spider lurking in the darkness. It was not going to come dashing out at her, latch onto her hand, fix her with bulbous black eyes and fanglike teeth.

All she had to do was wrap the manuscript in her bustle to protect it from the rain and get back to her room, no one the wiser.

"Looking for this?"

She screamed and fell off the step.

Ross had been on the point of returning the manuscript and the garment to the compartment when he saw her enter the stables. At first he thought she had an assignation with a servant, but then realized she was heading for his carriage.

He'd only been a few feet away, but not fast enough to get there before her. Like it or not, he would have to return the manuscript directly to her.

When she screamed, he had no choice but to come out of the shadows, grabbing her as she fell, just before she reached the ground.

Now, she lay in his arms, staring up at him. He wished, almost fervently, for a lantern, some light to see her.

"I've brought your book back to you," he said, helping her stand. Releasing her, he went back to where he'd dropped the manuscript and her clothing. "And your undergarment."

She glanced away, the ceiling of the stable suddenly capturing her interest.

When he handed her the manuscript, she glanced down at it then up at him.

"It's not tied the way I had it," she said. "Did you read it?"

He should have told her that he'd simply retied the string because it was loose. Instead, he nodded.

He'd read the whole thing from first page to last. At first he'd told himself it was to ensure that he was correct in his assumption: *The Lustful Adventures of Lady Pamela* was a book of erotic literature. By the second chapter, however, he'd become intrigued in the story, enough to keep reading.

He'd read for hours, finding himself increasingly aroused, enough that remembering certain passages now would be unwise.

"You were on your way to Edinburgh with your book," he said. "Why?"

"Mairi and Logan own a publishing company. I want them to publish my book."

Stunned, he stared at her. "You can't publish it," he said.

She stood draped by shadows, her arms filled, her expression hidden by the darkness.

"Why can't I?"

"It's salacious. A proper woman wouldn't write such a thing."

"Then perhaps I'm not proper."

Oh, she was most definitely not proper, not after writing the scene in the tub. Or the one in front of the fire. Or the one using the chair in Donald's parlor.

He felt his face warm.

"You'll be ruined. Have you given no thought of how it would affect the rest of your family?"

"What do you mean?"

"I doubt Sinclair would care for the notoriety."

She shook her head. "You don't know Macrath. He doesn't care a whit about what people think."

"Then what about Virginia? Would she not be offended?"

At the woman's name, Ellice turned and walked away. He cursed himself for a fool and followed her.

"You can't publish it."

"Why does the book bother you that much?" she asked. "Is it because it's the story of a woman? If it was about a man, would you object? Like *Tom Jones*?"

"I shouldn't be surprised you've read that. What about

Justine or *Juliette*? Do you count the Marquis de Sade as one of your favorites as well?"

She didn't answer.

"Are you always this stubborn?" he asked.

He had the idea she was, but in a subterranean manner. She sucked you in with those big brown eyes and that tremulous smile. Then, just when you were feeling protective of her, she stood her ground like one of his Highland ancestors, feet planted, hands on hips, daring anyone to try to move her.

Only the truth would do.

"The hero looks too much like me."

She stopped and turned. The light wasn't any brighter here, but one of the horses eyed him with interest.

"People might infer a relationship between us."

"That's ridiculous," she said, turning and walking toward the door again. "Why should they? I'd never set eyes on you while working on it."

"Nevertheless, the hero looks like me. You live in Macrath's home. I'm asking for Logan's support in my election. Logan is Macrath's brother-in-law. Of course the relationship will be considered, especially if you publish the book."

"I've never heard of anything sillier," she said.

"The book could damage my career."

"No, I was wrong," she said. "*That* is the silliest thing I've ever heard."

She was talking loud enough to wake the groom, who started, eyes opening wide, then straightened on his chair, pretending he'd been wide-awake the whole time.

"I'm standing for election for representative peer in a few weeks," Ross said, lowering his voice. "There are four men in contention for two slots. Your book could cost me the election. The scandal could destroy any future chances I might have."

"There's no scandal involved," she said airily. "I have no

connection with you whatsoever. I have nothing to do with you. You are a thimble filled with water next to my ocean. You are a grain of sand to my beach. You are a tiny star in the sky. You're nothing to me."

She opened the door then and stood there staring at the sheet of rain. Without another word, she left him, disappearing into the torrent like a watery sprite.

Chapter 7

Ellice fell into an uneasy doze around dawn, only to wake in a few hours.

When she opened her door, she was greeted by silence. The maids had disappeared.

Please, God, no. Don't let anything have happened to Virginia.

She descended the stairs, finding most of the staff in the kitchen.

"Is there any news?" she asked.

The cook answered her. "Brianag says no progress."

How much longer could this go on? She left the kitchen without responding, wanting to be alone. The problem was that this was Drumvagen. There was no place to be alone.

The rain still fell, making the front lawn of Drumvagen look an extension of the ocean to their left. She heard her mother come down the stairs and into the family parlor, and deliberately walked in the other direction.

Even though she was desperate for a place to escape, she was chained by worry to the house. Because she was unmarried, she wasn't allowed at Virginia's side. Evidently, being a virgin meant she was supposed to be ignorant of all things, including how babies are brought into the world.

She walked into the Great Hall, a room even larger for it being empty. How strange, that of all the rooms at Drumvagen, the Great Hall was the one least used. They all crowded into other rooms, smaller but more cozy.

She walked a path around the room, wishing the day weren't so dark and the thunder so ominous.

A storm in Scotland was like nothing she'd ever experienced in London. Here, the elements felt alive, sentient. This storm was a raging monster that had grown in fury since yesterday.

Sometimes, she thought Scotland was more than a country, more than a rough and magnificent land with a border created by men, written on a map, and defended for hundreds of years. Scotland was almost a living creature that could turn and bite your hand if you didn't speak about it in fond and loving tones.

When she walked the hills and glens surrounding Drumvagen, she sometimes felt like she was being watched. Not by living inhabitants, but those who'd gone before, proud men and women who hated the English and now hovered over their land to protest her appearance.

For all her imagination, she didn't believe in the hundreds of folktales Brianag told the children. The trees weren't alive; they were simply trees. Brownies didn't do chores for obedient children. Sea creatures in the shape of horses didn't bedevil the coast.

Yet something about this storm was otherworldly, as if God were punishing them.

In the sunlight, the Great Hall was a pleasant place. The walls were painted the color of cream. Furniture was arranged in groups so that several different conversations could be held. Large fireplaces, each capable of burning a tree trunk, sat on either side of the room.

Now, rain dripped down the chimneys, seeming to bring a

chill with it. Wind from the sea buffeted the house, shivering against the windows.

She hugged herself and kept walking, the movement the only way to ease her fear. Turning the corner, she looked up to find the Earl of Gadsden standing there.

For an instant she recognized him. Not in the sense of knowing who he was as much as seeing the man he hid from the world. As if for that unguarded second she was some-how prescient and could feel his uncertainty and remnants of pain.

The sensation faded as quickly as it had come. He nodded to her, entering the Great Hall.

She whirled away from him. If her skirts flew about her ankles, she didn't care. If her face was flushed and her hair askew, she didn't mind, because it was only him. She turned back, looked at him and asked, "Are you still here?"

"The roads are impassable," he said. "Otherwise, I would have to decline your gracious hospitality and leave." His gray eyes were steady on her.

In London they never turned away a visitor. In fact, they were such a solitary group that any visitor, announced or not, was welcome.

Here in Scotland she'd never known Macrath to banish anyone, from a would-be investor, to a tinker, to a carriage filled with Lowlanders who'd gotten lost. Instead of sending them on to Kinloch Village and one of the inns there, he wel-comed them to Drumvagen and no doubt left them with an enduring memory of their visit.

He wouldn't be happy to know that she was practically pushing the Earl of Gadsden out the door. But he was with Virginia and had better things to think about than an annoy-ing Scot.

Very well, she hadn't thought him annoying before he'd demanded that she not publish her book. He'd been very attractive to her. He was still handsome, but she was dutifully ignoring that fact.

What she really wished was that she'd never been impulsive and hidden in his carriage. But then, if she'd remained in her room, she would never have met her hero in person. She would never have watched his eyes chill or that marvelous mouth firm in annoyance.

He wasn't quite smiling, but his face had changed.

"You do have a dimple," she said. "I've been waiting to see."

"Have you? What will it cost me?" he asked.

She blinked at him, confused.

"If it's money you want, I'll pay you not to publish the book."

She could only stare at him.

"Come, name an amount. I'll pay it if you promise to destroy it."

"Are you insane?"

Evidently, the Earl of Gadsden didn't like his sanity questioned, because his eyes grew even colder. He walked to the other side of the room, staring at the picture above the mantel.

Was he trying to guard against his baser urges? If he mastered them, perhaps he could tell her how. Despite being annoyed with him, she couldn't help but notice how well fitting his buff trousers were. Lady Pamela had never noticed a man's derriere. Perhaps she should. The midnight blue jacket fit his broad shoulders magnificently.

"Do you pick out your clothing or do you have a manservant do it for you?"

He turned his head, looking at her as if he'd just happened onto an interesting specimen of bug.

"I beg your pardon?"

"Why do people say that? Is it to stall for time? You know as well as I do that you heard me perfectly well. Why wouldn't you want to admit to a valet?"

"I have a valet. He's not on this journey, however."

"There, was that so difficult?" she asked. "I suspect you have a great many servants."

"Why do my personal arrangements interest you?"

She didn't know how to answer that. Everything about him interested her.

"Is there any news about Mrs. Sinclair?"

She was not going to talk about Virginia. Instead, she started walking again, pacing, trying to ignore him.

He made the shadowed room seem full somehow, as if he'd come with ghosts and they'd drifted off his shoulders to settle in the corners.

"Why does Sinclair insist on hanging this here?"

The question caught her off guard. She glanced at the painting he was studying, then smiled. The work had been done by an artist Macrath commissioned during the building of Drumvagen. The painter had captured the scaffolding, the wagons carrying the stone and wood to finish the interior of the house. The ocean was serene, the sky a brilliant blue, and the workmen and craftsmen looked like ants as they toiled in the bright afternoon sun.

"Drumvagen is his dream," she said. "Anyone who talks to him for more than a minute or two understands that."

She walked closer to the fireplace.

"You were going to live here, though, weren't you?"

He glanced at her. "I doubt it would have ever come to pass," he said.

"Why did your father never finish the house?"

Macrath had told them all about the earl who'd begun Drumvagen but walked away after a dispute with the architect.

He smiled. "My father was a stubborn man in some respects and showed remarkable lassitude in others. Drumvagen was an impulse."

"Well, I shouldn't say this, perhaps, but I'm glad. Otherwise, Macrath would never have found Drumvagen in ruins and made it what it was."

"A case of something good coming from folly. Could you not see your way clear to doing the same?"

"Are you saying my book is folly?" She didn't know whether to be insulted or pleased. He turned, faced her and folded his arms.

"I warn you, Miss Traylor, that I wield a significant amount of influence."

"Am I supposed to be afraid of you?"

"Change the hero's appearance, then. Agree to publish the book anonymously."

Slowly, she shook her head.

"Why the devil are you being so obstinate?" he asked.

No one had ever called her obstinate before. She'd been considered conformable, easy to sway, a malleable personality.

He took a step toward her. She didn't move away. How very tall he was, and in this light almost dangerous looking. His eyes were such a glorious shade, merging with the encroaching shadows.

"I can buy up every single copy and have them burned," he said, his voice low. "Or I can simply give you the money not to publish it. Wouldn't you prefer to have the funds?"

She really must step back. He had the strangest effect on her. She wanted to throw herself into his arms, wrap her legs around his waist, entwine her arms around his neck and demand he kiss her.

The scent of heather perfumed the air because Brianag insisted on filling vases with heather cut fresh every morning. Yet she still smelled him, a combination of leather and lemons.

She took a step back and he matched her movements, stalking her.

"I can give you a substantial sum," he said, naming an amount that made her gape. "In exchange, you would give me the book. A fair trade, don't you think?"

Once, their family had been on the threshold of poverty. She wasn't supposed to know it because her mother had made such an effort to hide the knowledge.

The idea of having that much money at her disposal now was heady.

She could live the rest of her life on the amount he'd mentioned. She could have her own establishment and live as she pleased. She could pen a dozen books featuring Lady Pamela and a man who looked nothing like the Earl of Gadsden, but her hero would speak like him, have that inflection in his voice when he was being sarcastic, that upturn of his lips that didn't mean amusement as much as disdain. But he wouldn't have gray eyes as hard and as brittle as shale.

She looked away, toward a shadowed sideboard and the murky mirror above it. The gilt frame looked dull, their figures barely visible, dark gray against a backdrop of nearly black.

He touched her face, so suddenly that she jerked, startled. He didn't withdraw his hand, though. Nor did he stop looking at her in just that way, as if he would steal her soul if he gazed hard enough.

What was her soul worth?

Not the amount he'd offered. Not ten times that amount.

"No," she said, the answer coming without conscious thought. Perhaps she was being obstinate. Or maybe she simply couldn't be purchased that easily.

"No?"

His eyebrows lowered as he stared at her. His gaze seemed to light on each feature as if he were comparing her to the beauties he knew and finding her lacking in so many ways.

"It's my book. My effort. My hours of thinking and worrying. Did I tell that right? Did I say it correctly? Will a reader understand?"

"Oh, I think you wrote it perfectly," he said, dropping his hand.

"You do?" Should she be so pleased at his comment?

"That's just the problem, you see. It doesn't read like a book. It reads like a journal. As if you've experienced all those things in reality."

She couldn't breathe.

"As if you and I had done all those things together."

A spear of heat traveled to the core of her.

"As if that episode on the desk happened in my library at Huntly. Or when Lady Pamela unveiled herself. That could have occurred in my bedchamber."

Her face was going to catch fire. Her lips felt singed.

"And the part about the attic? We have an attic just like that at Huntly. It's like you visited it, saw the small windows, pulled out that table from storage and dusted it with the back of your dress."

Donald had mounted Lady Pamela on that table in defiance of all propriety and reason. They might have been interrupted by a maid at any time.

She cleared her throat. "It's a work of fiction," she said. She could barely speak.

Was this part of his offensive? Torment her until she agreed?

"You really should leave," she said, her voice sounding husky.

"Perhaps I should."

She nodded.

"Otherwise, I might do something inexcusable."

What was wrong with her? Her pulse shouldn't be racing. Her breath shouldn't be tight. She should move away, away now, before he came closer, bending his head, and then she felt his lips pressing against her temple.

She closed her eyes, feeling his breath on her ear.

"Such as toss you onto that settee," he whispered, "to see how much of your book is real and how much imagination."

She shivered.

"Are you Lady Pamela?"

In her heart of hearts she was, but only partially. She dreamed, she envisioned, she imagined, but only as far as her knowledge could take her.

Was she to be punished for her curiosity? For wanting to know, for being impatient to know if the coupling between a man and woman was as wondrous as it seemed to be? The books she'd read had informed her about the physical act, but what about the emotions?

Virginia looked at Macrath and her eyes sparkled. Hannah smiled at her husband and her cheeks bloomed with color. Logan and Mairi were nearly combustible in the same room. Even she, a virgin, could feel the heat between them.

Was it so terrible to want to know?

His lips left her skin and she immediately felt cold.

Would he say something cutting now? He'd tried everything else, bribery and cajoling.

Then his lips were on hers. They were full, pillowy soft, urging her to forget her resistance and her will. She hadn't expected that softness. He wrapped his arms around her and she had no recourse but to allow him to do so.

She raised her head even farther, her mouth dropping open to welcome him. Fire raced through her at the touch of his tongue.

Take me. Take me on the settee, on the floor, standing up next to the fireplace, in front of the mirror.

Unbutton my dress and worship me with your hands, your lips, your mouth. Praise my breasts, trail your fingers through the hair guarding my womanhood. Enjoy me and let me do the same.

She wanted to be naked, or at least less clothed. She almost unbuttoned the first button of her dress, but his lips were on her throat now, making her forget everything.

Oh, she hadn't known about that spot. How delicious that was. And there, just behind her ear. She'd never imagined such a thing.

Her lips were lonely.

She reached up and wrapped her arms around his neck, standing on tiptoe to press herself closer to him. Even if threatened with all the fires of damnation, she wouldn't have released her hold. She should have stepped away, remembering who she was, their argument, and that the man who was kissing her so divinely was autocratic and annoying.

He lowered his head slowly as if to further torture her, and again softly lay his lips on hers. Just that and nothing more. No pressure or cajoling, just the soft acquaintance of the shape of his mouth, the texture of his lips, the taste of his breath. Gently, as if she might have otherwise been frightened, he threaded his fingers through the hair at her nape.

"Pamela," he murmured against her lips. "I think you are Pamela. A sorceress."

She would be anyone he wanted.

He tilted his head, slowly deepening the kiss, giving her a chance to refuse. One hand rested against her nape; the other was at her waist.

She didn't remember the room they were in, the time of day, or that Drumvagen was filled with people. Darkness shimmered beneath her eyelids, befuddlement clouded her mind. All she truly knew was him, the heat of his body, the furious beating of his heart, the soft, stroking excitement of his tongue.

Her fingers slid up to the back of his neck, danced in his hair, cupped the back of his head and pulled him even closer. They shared their breaths, excited each other, daring in a way that was ancient and ordained by their bodies, independent of their minds.

She wanted him. She had wanted him from the first

moment she heard him talking to Macrath, the first time she'd seen him, the living, breathing embodiment of her hero. She'd imagined him, created him, and God had taken pity and delivered him to her.

From somewhere far away she heard the crack of thunder. The windows shivered in their panes, breaking the spell, almost as if God called her back to herself.

Stepping back, she realized her hair had fallen from its bun. She pushed it out of the way, over her shoulders, and took one more step away from him.

He was the most dangerous creature in the world.

If she had the wit of Lady Pamela, she wouldn't have been embarrassed. Her heroine would have simply sailed from the room, her lips red from his kisses, uncaring when he stared after her longingly.

"Should I offer my apologies?" he asked.

Was she that much a hypocrite? She should have flounced from the room. Or screamed that he was accosting her. Instead, she wanted to throw herself into his arms.

"Oh, miss!" She turned to find Annie, one of the housemaids, standing in the doorway. Her face was florid, her eyes wide.

"What is it, Annie?"

Had the girl witnessed their kiss?

"Is it true, miss? Is the village flooded? One of the grooms said so and we've no one else to ask."

Her concerns faded beneath the girl's obvious fear.

"I don't know, Annie," she said, conscious that it was the first time anyone had come to her for help since she'd moved to Drumvagen. "But I'll find out."

With a last glance toward the earl, she left the Great Hall.

Chapter 8

Without stopping to grab a shawl, Ellice pulled open one of Drumvagen's massive doors, racing out into the slashing rain and down the right staircase. Twice she slipped on the slick stone steps and managed to right herself.

Once at the bottom, she picked up her sodden skirts and began to run across the glen, past the cairn stones where she often sat and read. She crossed a path that lead to the cottage in a roundabout way, heading for a growth of pines perched on the hill overlooking Kinloch Village.

The slope had become almost impassable, the grass gone, replaced by rivers of mud. Her feet sank to her ankles and each step weighed more than the one before. Her clothing was dragging at her, including the hated bustle. She finally resorted to bending over and clawing at the mud, determined to make it to the top.

The rain was blinding, the thunder so close it felt as if it were grumbling in her ear.

A hand on her elbow startled her. She glanced to her left to find the earl there, his hair slicked back by the rain and his clothes as sodden as hers. He gripped her arm and helped her get her balance. Together, they made it the rest of the way.

On a pleasant day she could have seen Kinloch Village, but this downpour was unlike anything she'd ever known. Now she could barely see past the bridge, if the stone footbridge had been there. The Water of Kinloch, normally a narrow, undulating river, was so wide and deep that it looked like the ocean.

Just beyond was Kinloch Village. Half of the houses clung to the cliff, their foundations carved into the stone. The rest would flood.

Hannah and Jack's house would be in danger, as well as those of most of the maids who didn't choose to live at Drumvagen. Every morning a contingent of them could be found walking toward the house, their laughter marking the start of the day, their smiles and quick conversation something she'd come to expect.

Ellice moved forward, the earl's hand dropping from her arm. Wiping her muddy hands on her dress, she stared toward the village, stunned by so much potential destruction.

She turned to face him. "The village will flood," she said. "What are we going to do?"

His features arranged themselves into a mask. Was he going to simply turn and walk away? Or worse, say something cutting and cold?

"We need to get back to Drumvagen," he said.

"We need to do something. I'm not a Scot," she said, raising her voice to be heard over the rain. "Nor am I altogether certain I like Scotland. But I can't sit by and let people lose their homes. You go back to Drumvagen. I'm staying here."

"What do you propose to do by standing there?"

"Something. I don't know. Something."

She folded her arms and stared straight ahead, trying to figure out something to do. Had Macrath any machines that might be moved into place to block the flow of the river?

Her face was sheened with rain, droplets falling from

her nose. She hadn't thought to grab a coat or a shawl, but it would have been soaked in only minutes anyway.

"Can you sew?" he shouted at her.

Surprised, she turned to look at him.

"Can you sew? We need to get back to Drumvagen and see if your housekeeper has any extra muslin. We need bags filled with sand to serve as a dam against the river."

She blinked at him. Bags of sand? Would they work? At least he'd come up with an idea. She didn't have one.

Turning, she descended the hill with Gadsden at her side.

The next hours proved her initial thought of him correct. The Earl of Gadsden was very much like her hero, Donald.

She'd never seen anyone work as tirelessly. He was ahead of all of them in filling the wagon with sand, shouting orders, commanding the men who'd come in the dozens from Kinloch.

Drumvagen wasn't in danger because the house was on a much higher elevation than the village. Even if the water did come this far, only the basement would be affected.

They set up operations in the gazebo. The white painted structure, nestled in a clearing in the woods, was equidistant between Drumvagen and the village. There, they finished sewing and loading the sandbags before carting them down to the river. The gazebo also served as headquarters for information. The maids who weren't involved with the sewing came to bring them news from the house, along with tea and food. In turn, they learned the status of the flooding, to take back to the house.

Ellice had no patience for needlework, but this was nothing like the intricate footstool patterns or samplers she'd done as a girl. Instead, this was production stitching. Ten of them worked side by side in the gazebo. Two of the maids cut muslin into large squares while the rest of them sewed. Once the bottoms and sides were done, each bag was passed to one of the men, who filled it with sand so the top could be stitched.

Thanks to Brianag's militaristic planning, there were seven bolts of muslin in the attic, and Ellice prayed it would be enough to help protect the village.

Virginia's condition had not changed. She was in and out of consciousness—that information gleaned from a pale and drawn Hannah, who'd helped her carry the bolts to the wagon.

"I can't leave her," Hannah said.

"Of course you can't," Ellice said, hugging her. They'd each given the other strength when Virginia was so ill with smallpox in London a few years earlier. Now they needed to remain hopeful, just as they had then.

"Go and tend to her," Ellice said. "She's in my prayers, and the prayers of every person at Drumvagen."

Would that be enough?

Thunder roared overhead as if God Himself had heard her. *Strike me, God, and not Virginia. I, no doubt, deserve it. She does not.*

They worked for hours, darkness no clue to the time. The skies were boiling black, the thunder constant, the rain unremitting. Someone lit lanterns and hung them on the eaves of the gazebo. Two of them were immediately doused by the sideways rain. They were relit and placed inside the structure, at a careful distance from the pile of muslin ready to be stitched into bags.

She pricked her finger so many times her blood christened each finished bag, but it hardly mattered. No one was going to point to it and say, "Look at what a despicable job Ellice did. How terribly gauche."

They worked silently, the thunder and rain too loud for normal conversation. The only time anyone spoke was when the same young man who ran the bags to the river returned with news.

"The water's at the outskirts now," he said. "The earl doesn't think it'll rise higher, but we need more bags."

"We're working as fast as we can," Ellice said, glancing at the other women.

Each of them looked tired, pale, and worried. Either their thoughts were filled with Virginia's suffering or with their own homes and those of relatives in Kinloch.

"He knows that," the boy said. "But the earl said that we still need more. He said to tell you he's bracing the fortifications on the south side of the river, hoping that will keep most of the flooding from the village."

"What about my house? Do you know anything?"

Ellice glanced over at the girl who'd asked, one of the maids new to Drumvagen. She'd found the girl crying in the parlor one day, afraid of Brianag and miserable in her new job. She reassured her at the time that everyone felt the same about the housekeeper. Had the girl settled in? Or was she wishing she'd found work anywhere else?

"The earl said that none of the houses are affected yet," the boy said, "only the church, but we should be able to repair any damage once the water goes down."

"Go to Drumvagen," Ellice said, giving him orders, when she never gave orders to anyone. "Tell them we need any bolts of cloth still in the attic. I don't care if it's silk or satin. If there's no more cloth, tell them we need extra sheets and pillowcases."

"Yes, miss," he said, and began running through the rain to Drumvagen.

An hour later they had two more bolts of cloth and all the extra sheets Drumvagen possessed.

Toward evening, Cook sent food to the gazebo with food for all of them. Ellice made the decision to send four of the maids to Drumvagen to get warm and dry and sleep for a few hours. When they returned, she and the other women would rest.

After being wet for so long, she felt like a duck. A very

waterlogged duck who never wanted to see a lake or pond or body of water again for a long time. Or rain—dear God, please let them be spared rain for a while, although drought was not something for which to pray.

She thought it was probably early morning when the rain eased. All she was certain of was her fatigue. Her lips were numb with cold and her entire body seemed to shiver all at once. She couldn't feel her fingers but kept stitching.

At first she thought she was mistaken, but then realized that the pounding on the gazebo roof wasn't as strong as earlier. Several of the other women glanced up, and more than once she met a pair of eyes, the hopeful look making her wonder if they were finally being spared.

She bit off a thread, placed the bag to the stack at her right and stood, her legs feeling strange after having been sitting for so long.

Slowly, she walked to the gazebo steps, standing there to watch as the rain subsided. When she tilted her head back, she could see a section of midnight blue sky and stars. Clouds scudded across the sky, revealing a bright moon, white and full.

One by one the other women joined her.

"It's a miracle," one of them said, tears bathing her face.

"Hardly a miracle," another answered. "The rain's stopped, it has. Finally."

"What about the flooding?"

"I'll go and see, then," one of the women said, and she was soon joined by the others.

"Go," Ellice said when they hesitated at the steps. If she lived in Kinloch, she'd be as anxious to see if her house had been spared.

Returning to the bench where she'd sat for so many hours, she began to stack up the bags. The rain might start again and they might need more sandbags.

She closed her eyes for a moment. She couldn't sleep yet. Nor was it safe to return to Drumvagen until she knew if the danger was over. The river might continue to rise.

No one had come in the last hour with news. How was Virginia faring? A tear fell from beneath her closed lids and she brushed it away.

Weeping never accomplished anything, did it?

Chapter 9

Ross found Ellice sitting in the gazebo, leaning against one of the support posts. At first he thought she was asleep, but she opened her eyes and looked at him as he climbed the steps.

"You're tired," he said, sitting down beside her.

"I could sleep sitting up, a needle in my hand," she said with a small smile.

Her brown eyes were red-rimmed, as if she'd been weeping. He wanted to ask, but concentrated, instead, on the news he had.

"We saved the village, I think. Four houses were damaged as well as the church, but everything else was spared."

She closed her eyes. "Good. Good."

Reaching out, he grabbed her left hand.

"I'm not a very good seamstress," she said, trying to pull away.

He wasn't letting her. Instead he examined the tips of her fingers.

"How many times did you stick yourself?" he asked.

"A dozen. Two. I don't know."

For a moment they sat in perfect accord, the only sound the rain droplets pattering from the trees.

She took a deep breath and released a sigh.

Two tears traced a path down her cheeks.

"What is it?" he asked, concern overwhelming any caution. "Has something happened?"

"It's Virginia. It's the flood. It's my mother. It's Scotland. It's everything."

"You've no news of Mrs. Sinclair?"

She shook her head.

He handed her his handkerchief. She nodded in acceptance, even as her weeping started in earnest.

"I'm just so tired," she said, blotting at her face. "That's all."

He wasn't given to impulsive gestures but couldn't sit here and witness her pain. Extending his arm around her, he pulled her close. She grabbed his shirt with a death grip, turned and burrowed against him.

He shouldn't have moved to comfort her. He should have expressed his regret about Macrath's wife, explained the duties he'd given the men of Kinloch, and retreated. Hopefully, the end of the rain meant that the roads were passable. If so, he would leave Drumvagen as fast as the horses could carry him.

Instead, he held her as she cried, wishing he could reassure her that everything would work out for the best. The regrettable fact was that women died in childbirth. A man could have a succession of wives, and in many cases did.

Still, because she was so fully engulfed in her pain, he had to say something.

"You love her very much."

She nodded against his chest.

"I never met her."

She began to weep more, clutching the handkerchief to her mouth to muffle her sobs.

He decided that the best avenue was to simply remain silent, so he did, holding her against him and listening to her cry.

Finally, it seemed she was done. She pulled back, blinking up at him with reddened eyes. Her face was pale, her lips swollen outside their borders.

He wanted to kiss her, brush his tongue against those pillowy lips and inhale her breath. Because he almost never allowed his impulses mastery over him, except with her, he didn't. The need to do so was a warning, however, one he noted and wouldn't forget.

"It shouldn't be happening," she said. "She's never had any trouble giving birth. But it's been going on for so long now."

Since he had little knowledge of childbirth, he was left without anything comforting to say. The fact that they shouldn't be having this conversation was a moot point. He shouldn't be holding her in his arms, either.

"Why is an Englishwoman living at Drumvagen?" he asked, hoping to distract her.

To his horror, she began to weep again, again soundlessly, large tears falling down her face in militaristic precision, one after the other.

Her eyes would swell shut if she didn't stop crying.

He found himself rocking her, a discordant movement he'd never before performed, the sole purpose of which was to comfort the woman in his arms.

"Virginia was married to my brother," she said, her voice choked by tears. "But he died."

"I'm sorry."

"He was very sickly. No one expected him to marry, but he did. I used to tell myself it was a love match, but it wasn't, not really. I think Lawrence hated Virginia. And poor Virginia did her best to be a wife but Lawrence didn't care anything about her."

He wasn't in the position to pass judgment on anyone's marriage since his own had been so lamentable.

"After my brother died, there was no money, nothing that wasn't entailed along with the title."

"Title?"

"He was the Earl of Barrett," she said.

He pulled back a little, staring down into her face. He really should be leaving now. He shouldn't be captivated by the sight of a tear caught on her lashes, or her perfect nose, slightly pink. Those lips were even more intriguing, so he made himself look away, staring out at the forest beyond the gazebo.

He glanced down to find Ellice still looking up at him, her eyes liquid pools of chocolate.

Their gaze caught and held, the seconds ticking by in solemn regularity. He felt drawn to her like a magnet. Pulling away would be a difficult task.

He must for his own safety. This woman with her guileless eyes, soft heart, and lurid imagination was a danger.

"Ellice," he said, her name a warning.

"I'm not normally so unrestrained," she said. "I don't normally tell anyone what I'm thinking or feeling. I am sorry. You didn't deserve all my confessions."

Was the rosiness of her complexion due to her tears? Or was she blushing? If so, it was hard to believe that this woman with her air of innocence was the author of *The Lustful Adventures of Lady Pamela*.

Her mouth was slightly open, the bottom lip so plump and succulent it begged for a kiss. He looked away, hoping that would be enough to curb his response to her and summon his common sense.

"If you wouldn't tell anyone about my behavior, I'd be very grateful. I'm tired, that's all it is. I'm worried, too. Virginia is like my sister."

He silenced her by grabbing her face between his hands and placing his mouth on hers. For a moment she was still speaking, the sensation of her lips moving beneath his intriguing before her mouth fell open in surprise.

She tasted of tears and honey, a combination that had him reeling.

This sweet girl was the same one who'd imagined the

bathing scene in her book, who'd described several sexual positions he'd never considered. He found himself wanting to try them. Even more, he wanted to know if Lady Pamela was her double while Donald was his.

Her hands gripped his shoulders, but not to push him away. He wanted to pull her onto his lap, cuddle her closer, slowly unfasten her blue dress with its bone buttons to see if her shift was lace trimmed like Lady Pamela's.

Her tongue darted out to touch his, slide against his bottom lip and retreat again.

He tilted his head, deepening the kiss, needing this in a way he'd never before needed a kiss. He inhaled her breath, gave her his in exchange, and felt his heartbeat jump when she moaned.

Fire traveled through his body when she wrapped her arms around his shoulders, her hands traveling to stroke the back of his neck.

She was trembling, and he caught her closer until he could feel the press of her breasts against his chest.

He hadn't felt this surge of lust for months or perhaps even longer. Had he ever been lost in a kiss?

"Is this entirely appropriate?" a voice asked.

She flew out of Gadsden's arms and stared, horrified, at Macrath.

In the lantern light he looked terrible. His eyes were sunken and surrounded by dark shadows. His beard looked as if he hadn't shaved for days. His hair was unkempt, falling down on his brow.

"Virginia?" she asked, pushing back her dread.

"She's out of danger, Brianag says." His voice carried the weariness of the world.

She closed her eyes and said a swift and fervent prayer.

When she opened them, Macrath was staring at her, a look

in his eyes she'd rarely seen and never directed at her. Gadsden was not the only man who could affect a cold stare. This one chilled her down to her bones.

How did she explain being in Gadsden's arms? Or kissing him?

"And the baby?" she asked.

Macrath nodded, as if just remembering his child. "A healthy baby boy. A large child, Brianag says."

He looked past her to the earl.

"In my library. Fifteen minutes."

He turned without another word and left. She'd never seen Macrath be so rude, but she couldn't blame him for his words or the look he'd leveled at her.

She was so thoroughly in the wrong that there was nothing she could do or say.

"Apologies are in order," the earl said in that proper voice of his, the one she was beginning to think of as his Pontificating Tone.

"From me to you? From you to me? From you to Macrath? From both of us to everyone?"

She wished she were a better person. If so, she'd want to undo these last few minutes. The truth was, she'd wanted his kiss, wanted another even now.

She couldn't even look at him. If she did, she knew she'd be trapped by those startling gray eyes. She'd stare at him until she lost her senses again. She'd let him kiss her and perhaps ravage her in full view of Drumvagen and the chaos within.

When she stood, he made no move to stop her. She sincerely hoped he wouldn't play the gentleman now and insist on escorting her back to Drumvagen.

She needed to get as far away from him as she could, as quickly as possible.

"I wondered if you'd imagined everything you wrote. Or had you researched your book."

She stood still. "And your decision?"

"It's not imagination, is it? You're very practiced, aren't you?"

His accusation stripped the words from her.

Once, she might have been overjoyed at his thinking she was experienced. Now she was strangely hurt.

She left the gazebo, refusing to look back.

Why the hell had he said that? Why had he tossed words at her that made her face pale and her eyes widen? He'd been a pompous prig. He didn't want scandal in his life, true, and everything about Ellice hinted at danger in that regard, but he'd no right to hurt her.

He wanted to go after her, apologize, perhaps even explain that it was better if they weren't in the same room together, especially now after they'd kissed not once, but twice. He paired the memory of her kisses with the scenes she'd written, knowing that the two would forever be entwined in his mind.

Ellice Traylor was no virgin or demure miss right out of the schoolroom, despite how innocent she seemed.

He returned to Drumvagen feeling justifiably chagrined. He'd abused Sinclair's hospitality and took full responsibility for the scene the man had interrupted. He had better sense than that, given his family history.

From now on he would do his damnedest to limit being in her company, since he couldn't control himself around her. He wouldn't forget himself again. He would never again allow his emotions full rein, and if he couldn't do that, he'd simply avoid her at all costs.

Conscious of his appearance, he entered the back of Drumvagen, a little embarrassed when the maids and cook exclaimed over him.

"You're a miracle, you are, sir, and thanks we are that you were here in our time of need," one of the maids said.

Another offered him a towel. "I've warmed it in the stove. I'll get another for your hair, shall I?"

Cook had a fragrant stew waiting, and he would have gladly sat at the kitchen table and eaten his fill had Macrath not been expecting him.

"I'll send a tray to your room," she said when he explained that he was on his way to visit with his host.

Sinclair answered at the first knock, and he pushed in the door to find the other man standing in front of a fire.

Sinclair glanced over his shoulder at Ross. "Come in. If you're as wet as me, the fire will be welcome."

"It's been a long time since I was dry," he said, joining Sinclair.

For a few moments neither spoke, the silence surprisingly companionable. He'd expected to be lectured as to proper behavior, but after glancing at the man, he realized Sinclair was as exhausted as he was.

They'd fought their own battles in the past day and a half and he had the inkling that Sinclair's was the more difficult of the two.

"I'm very happy to hear about your wife."

Sinclair nodded.

When he didn't speak, Ross subsided into silence. Should he broach the reason why he was here? Or simply excuse himself and allow the man to rest?

"I hear I owe you a great debt," Sinclair said.

"No debt is owed."

Sinclair turned to face him. "You saved Kinloch. Some say single-handedly, and the Scots here are not given to awarding praise where it isn't due."

"You would have done the same," Ross said. "But you were occupied."

"Why did you? It's not your land."

That comment surprised him.

"Because the situation demanded it. People were going to lose their homes."

"Yet there was nothing in it for you, other than my thanks."

"Must there be some gratification in every deed?"

"I would have thought so, especially of you," Sinclair said.

"You're saying I act only to better my own circumstances," Ross said carefully.

"I'm saying that's the impression I got of you. Why shouldn't I? I'm aware of your wealth, Gadsden. I've seen Huntly. I know you've political aspirations. Was that why you helped the people of Kinloch?"

"I came to apologize for my behavior with Miss Traylor, not to defend my actions to you, Sinclair."

"Nor do you need to do the latter, Gadsden." Surprisingly, the other man smiled. "I don't think your efforts were politically motivated. And I am grateful, more than you know."

Before he could speak, Sinclair held up his hand. "As far as the former, it's to Ellice you owe your apology. Have you?"

Ross speared his hands through his hair.

He wanted to ask about Ellice and her history. Who was she, really? Evidently she wasn't the charming ingenue she pretended to be. No woman could kiss that well without some practice.

Had she a reputation in London? Was that the reason Sinclair had made a home for her and her mother in Scotland?

"No," he said, "I haven't apologized to her."

"Then I would appreciate if you did so," Sinclair said. "She isn't as worldly or as experienced as you, your lordship. She does not deserve to be treated in such a way."

He doubted she was as innocent as Sinclair believed, but that was a comment he didn't voice.

The less he thought of Ellice, the better.

Chapter 10

For two days Ellice waited for her mother's explosion. She readied herself for the lecture to come.

How could you have done such a thing! My own daughter to shame me in such a way. Eudora would never have acted in such a disgraceful fashion!

Or: *What have I done, to be treated like this by an ungrateful child? What sins have I committed, to be humiliated in front of the whole of Scotland by a daughter who transformed herself to a harlot?*

Without even thinking about it, she had changed herself from being demurely proper to acting just like Lady Pamela, hadn't she?

She'd become surprisingly brave, but had no defense against her mother's tirade.

Gadsden had looked at her with those glorious eyes and that stubble of beard and she'd nearly swooned in his arms.

To her surprise, her mother didn't say a word about harlotry or wickedness. Oh, but she said a great deal about helping to save the village.

"Whatever could you have been thinking of, being out in the weather, and with the maids, of all people? What will they think of you?"

She didn't know. Nor did she care. She felt curiously distant from the opinions of others, but she did note that the maids smiled more easily at her. Even Brianag unbent enough to thank her for her efforts to save Kinloch.

Gadsden was still at Drumvagen. The river hadn't subsided enough for the bridge to be passable. She vacillated between hoping the water level would soon drop to praying that it wouldn't do so anytime soon.

Even her mother noticed her mood.

"What has gotten into you, child?" Enid said on the morning of the second day after the scene in the gazebo.

Would she always think of time that way, she wondered: the day before the gazebo and afterward?

"I've never seen you so unsettled. Are you certain you're not ill?"

"No, Mother."

"If you are, do not go to see Virginia. That's all she needs, to come down with your cold."

"I assure you, Mother, I'm well. Truly," she said, leaving the room to see Virginia for the first time since she'd given birth.

The baby was large, loud, and greeted everyone but his mother with a squalling cry. As far as Virginia, she was still pale, her eyes shadowed and her lips nearly without color. When Ellice handed her a cup of tea, a restorative blend Brianag swore by, Virginia's hand trembled as if she were still weak.

"I'm not to stay but a moment," Ellice said, "but I wanted to see you."

"Who told you not to bother me?" Despite her wan appearance, there was a spark of humor in Virginia's eyes.

"Brianag."

"Not Macrath?"

She hadn't seen Macrath since the night he'd come to the

gazebo, yet another person she avoided assiduously. In Macrath's case it wasn't difficult. He was either at Virginia's side or in his library. As long as she avoided those rooms, she was relatively safe.

"I'm surprised," Virginia said. "He's very protective of me. More so since Carlton was born."

The baby snuffled in his cradle beside the bed as if knowing he was the topic of conversation.

Virginia stretched out her hand toward her son. "My milk has not come," she said. "It's the first time I've not nursed my child."

"You had a very difficult time."

Did Virginia know how close she'd come to dying?

She sat with Virginia for five minutes more, talking of the baby and the flood. Before Macrath came back, or Brianag arrived to chastise her, she stood, kissed Virginia on the cheek, and left for the nursery.

To give Mary a respite, Ellice took the children to the large parlor on the first floor. Brianag called it the Tartan Parlor because every upholstered surface was in a bright red and black plaid. Even the curtains were tartan, framing a view of the rear of the house, the barn, and Macrath's laboratory.

Brianag had placed bouquets of heather in clay jars on the tables. Ellice liked the fragrance but preferred roses from the sheltered garden at the rear of Drumvagen.

She was not about to mention that to Brianag. As Enid's daughter, she was naturally suspect and considered in the enemy camp.

Macrath's suggestion, a few years earlier, for the Dowager Countess of Barrett and Brianag, housekeeper to Drumvagen and wise woman of Kinloch Village, to pen a book between them had been considered odd. No one, least of all her, had expected the *The Lady's Guide to Proper Housekeeping* to succeed as well as it had. Macrath told her they'd received orders from as far away as Australia.

They'd been at each other's throats within months of the publication of the book. The only respite had been the days of worrying about Virginia. Now that life was almost back to normal, her mother and Brianag were fighting again.

Even now she could hear them.

"Of course the Scots would want to know how an English-woman manages a household," her mother said. "The Scots always look to the English."

Brianag was not to be outdone. She muttered something in that unintelligible Scots of hers, followed by, "Only if they want to know how to ruin something."

Macrath had urged them to work on another book in the futile hope that activity would keep their antipathy at bay. So far they couldn't be in the same room for more than five minutes.

How could they be so shortsighted?

If she had the opportunity they'd been given, she would have leapt at the chance. She would have done anything Macrath wanted in order to get her book published. As it was, her manuscript remained a closely guarded secret. She and Virginia—and now the Earl of Gadsden—were the only ones who knew of its existence.

"Glib i the tung is aye glaikit at the hert," Brianag said, her voice just this side of a shout.

"What is that supposed to mean?" her mother said. "Would it be too absurd to hope that one day you would speak the Queen's English? Even a Scot can learn that."

When a door slammed somewhere, she closed her eyes. Who had made a grand exit now?

Alistair was drawing, an occupation Ellice fervently approved of, since she had to rescue Fiona every other minute. What the little girl didn't try to eat she wanted to climb.

The first notice she had that Macrath entered the room was Fiona's screech in her left ear. Since she was holding the child at the time, she wasn't prepared for a high-pitched squeal or for Fiona to suddenly lunge forward with her upper body, arms outstretched.

Ellice nearly fell on her face.

Thankfully, Macrath was there, plucking the little girl from her arms and into the air, which prompted yet another squeal.

"I've come at the right time," he said, smiling.

She nodded, struck dumb by surprise. He didn't seem angry at her. Nor were his eyes narrowed in disapproval or disappointment. Perhaps his relief over Virginia's health had made him more sanguine about her lapse of decorum. Or it was possible he'd forgotten.

She doubted either, but perhaps he wasn't going to tell her mother how wanton she'd been.

"I never got a chance to thank you for your efforts for Kinloch," Macrath said.

"I'm afraid you're going to have to replace all your bedding, and the muslin as well."

"A cheap enough price to save the village."

She nodded again. Evidently, she wasn't going to be reprimanded for the scene in the gazebo.

"Go and get some air," Macrath said. "We'll survive without you for a few hours. The day is a beautiful one."

"If you're sure."

"I am," he said, placing Fiona on his shoulders. His daughter squealed in delight as she left the room.

"Ellice."

She turned at the door.

"We're having a farewell dinner tonight. Gadsden is leaving in the morning."

"He's leaving?" she asked, feeling a curious constriction in the area of her heart.

"The water is subsiding. The bridge is passable and the roads clear enough."

She nodded again.

"I know you've been avoiding him, but I'd appreciate your presence at dinner."

For a third time she nodded, incapable of speech. Escaping the parlor, she rushed up the stairs to her suite, where she grabbed her manuscript then flew down the stairs and out Drumvagen's front door, heading toward the crofter's cottage.

Virginia had found her in the gazebo once, when she'd gone there to find some peace and to write. She made the cottage available and ensured that a table and chair were delivered along with a lamp to use on those gray days.

Many rainy afternoons Ellice sat at the table beside the window, watching the raindrops fall from the thatch, thankful for the tranquility Virginia had given her.

Now she opened the cottage door and, with the sigh of one to whom a reprieve had been given, studied the interior. Other than the floor being muddy along the edge of the walls, and signs that the thatch needed repairing again, the cottage had survived the storm well.

The interior smelled of damp, though, and she opened the door and the windows to air out the space.

In the last two days, whenever her imagination threatened to catch her up and lift her away from the real world like a gust of wind, she'd stop herself and concentrate on the task at hand. Nor would she allow herself to write, and that was the most grievous self-punishment she might have devised.

She had no one to whom she could confide her deepest thoughts. If her sister were alive she might have spoken to her. Or perhaps not, for fear Eudora would go to their mother. She certainly couldn't waylay one of the maids, pull her into her room and regale her with all the thoughts she'd had over the last two days.

Her only confidante was a blank page. Her self-punishment, therefore, only lasted a few hours.

Once her pages had been arranged on the table, she sat, picked up her pen and began to write.

He was leaving.

Of course he was leaving. He was returning home. He'd never think of her again. Never smile at her.

He is on my mind so much I would think myself enchanted, one of the Scottish creatures Brianag is either threatening to summon or promising to vanquish.

I was captured by the moment, by the sheer passion of it all. I was no longer Ellice Traylor but someone else. Not as exciting a personage as Lady Pamela, but someone close. My own version of Lady Pamela, perhaps, without the auburn ringlets and the magnificent green eyes.

How I wish I were different. Not as plain brown as I am. I wish my hair and eyes were a different color. I would have a smaller mouth, a less forceful chin, a face in a round shape. My jaw is too square and my features forgettable. What would a man say about my nose?

She has a nose. There, that's it. That's all anyone could possibly say. Would a man ever kiss the tip of my nose like Donald did to Lady Pamela? Would he ever wax eloquent as to the shape, about the way it tipped at the end? No.

Her lashes were full and thick, however.

Did a man ever notice eyelashes? She doubted it.

What would he think of other physical attributes? Would he admire her breasts? They were rather large, compared to the other females of her family, an announcement her mother had made in exasperation after she tried to button one of her mother's older bodices.

No other woman of her acquaintance. so said her mother, was ever so blowsy, or so possessed of a music hall shape. At the time, she'd been humiliated and strangely apologetic—it wasn't as if she could have altered anything about her body, after all.

Now, however, she wondered if writing about Lady Pamela had freed her. She was beginning to think of her body in different terms. She no longer wanted to be reed thin with a flat chest. No, she quite liked her breasts, her hips, and was proud of her narrow waist.

It seemed to her that a man would pay more attention to a fine figure than he would a tiny nose.

What would the Earl of Gadsden say?

She put her pen down and pressed her hands against her heated cheeks.

Macrath had known she was avoiding him. If Macrath knew, then Gadsden must know, too.

She'd dreamed of him. Her imagination, unfettered in her sleep, had featured him. He'd been gloriously naked and her hands had explored the whole of him, delighted to discover that the handsome man was even more magnificent without clothes.

Drumvagen might be set into the Scottish wilderness, but it had furnished her with a great deal of knowledge she otherwise might not have had. She listened to the maids discuss their love lives with a frankness they never would have had they known she was eavesdropping. Then, there was the sight of the handsome Scots lads bathing in the sea.

The books she read from Mairi's library had strengthened her imagination, adding details otherwise missing from her personal experience.

She picked up her pen again and sat back in her chair. She was safer inventing someone scandalous like Lady Pamela than revealing her own thoughts. Let Lady Pamela pant in ecstasy. No one would know that she yearned for fulfillment as well. Lady Pamela might wonder about a certain earl, but no one would know that Ellice's thoughts were similar.

She could almost feel his kiss, the press of his mouth against hers, and that yearning she felt for it to lead to something more.

Oh dear. The Earl of Gadsden was proving to be a very dangerous character, one she couldn't control.

She had the oddest feeling that he was staring up from the page and smiling at her, amused at her discomfiture.

Perhaps it was a good thing she was never going to see him again after tonight. The disappointment she felt at the thought would simply have to fade, that's all.

She stacked her pages carefully, rewrote the title page so it was pristine, and wrapped the twine around the manuscript.

A loose stone in the half wall at the end of the cottage led to a space that had been a safe of sorts in the past. She debated leaving the manuscript there, then chose to take it with her. For now, she had some privacy in her suite.

She didn't doubt that her mother would search her rooms, however, if Enid thought she had something to hide.

Closing the cottage door, she took the stepping stones to the road.

Tonight she would have to say good-bye to him. She would no longer have to avoid him for fear of doing something foolish, like throwing herself into his arms.

As she was returning to Drumvagen, Ellice heard the rumble of carriage wheels and stepped to the side of the road.

The vehicle slowed and the door opened.

"Can we give you passage the rest of the way?" Logan asked. "Or are you set on walking?"

"I'm not, no," she said as he opened the carriage door. She didn't wait for him to get out but stepped inside, closing the door behind her and settling in beside Mairi.

"You're the first person to come down this road in days," she said.

"Have you come to see the baby?" she asked at the same time as Mairi said, "Is everything all right at Drumvagen?"

They smiled at each other.

"Everything is wonderful at Drumvagen," Ellice said. "Virginia is recuperating. Carlton is healthy and looks just like Macrath, and Fiona and Alistair are well."

Logan sat back after giving the driver instructions to continue.

When she'd first met Mairi at Virginia and Macrath's wedding, she thought the woman was striking but not as beautiful as Virginia. After being married to Logan, however, Mairi had begun to change. She rarely frowned, and when she did it was often followed by a smile. She was more relaxed, the look on her face one of deep contentment.

She was in love and anyone around her knew it, especially when she glanced at Logan. When he looked back at her there was no doubt of his feelings. Love for her shone through his eyes, softened his smile, and even seemed to change the air.

Would anyone ever look at her with such adoration?

"What have you there?" Mairi asked.

Ellice glanced down at the manuscript in her arms. Here was her chance. Here was what she'd wanted from the very beginning, and it was as if Providence, having tossed her to the Scottish hinterlands, was making amends.

"I've written a book," she said. Before she lost her courage, she thrust the manuscript at Mairi.

Mairi took the book. "Have you?"

"Would you read it?" she asked. "I haven't asked anyone else."

Only one other person had read it and he'd been shocked. Was that a good thing?

"You want to publish it?" Logan asked.

Ellice nodded.

"Of course I'll read it," Mairi said. "Shall I give you an honest assessment or a family one?"

She looked at Mairi and considered the question. Did she want kindness? Or did she want to be a better writer? How could she bear it if Mairi thought the book without merit?

"An honest one," she said, hoping she was brave enough to hear what Mairi thought.

Mairi nodded, her attention on the title page.

"*The Lustful Adventures of Lady Pamela*?"

To her horror, Mairi untied the string. She'd expected the other woman to read it in her spare time, not in the carriage. Not while she was watching.

Logan must have sensed her panic because he leaned over and patted her arm.

She had hidden in a carriage in order to go to Edinburgh for this exact purpose—having Mairi read her book. Yet now that the moment was here, she was terrified. Would she have frozen in the same way if she'd made it to the city and presented it to Mairi?

Not once had she thought she'd be afraid, but she was.

Mairi would immediately see how many mistakes she had made, how many rules she'd broken. How awful the story was and how improbable the characters.

"If your eyes get any wider," Mairi said, "I'll think you're going to faint. Are you?"

"Must you read it now?" she asked as they approached the rear of Drumvagen.

Mairi glanced at her, then Logan. "No, of course not."

She felt somewhat better when Mairi tied the string around the pages and placed them in the valise at her feet.

Mairi would read the book and think it terrible but not know how to convey that to her without words that wounded.

It's truly terrible, Ellice. What were you thinking?

No, Mairi wouldn't say something like that. Instead, she might return the manuscript to her and say something innocuous like, *I applaud all your work, dear Ellice. It's not what we normally publish, however.*

Yes, she could see Mairi saying something like that.

The earl had thought her shocking, while Mairi might well think her incompetent.

Mairi would know every secret thought she had, every wonder and deeply held belief. She'd see her behind every one of Lady Pamela's actions even though that wasn't exactly correct. True, she'd become Lady Pamela, but it was like putting on a mask and being someone else for a time. Parts of her were there in the character but most of it was dreaming and letting her mind wander free.

How much would Mairi think was her, and how much was simply imagination?

Why hadn't she considered those thoughts earlier?

Regardless of what Mairi thought, however, she was proud of the book, of the effort she'd put into it, of all the times she'd revised and thought, changed and reconsidered. This was her accomplishment and Lady Pamela was her creation, good or ill.

The Earl of Gadsden had already made his opinion known. What on earth would Mairi say?

Chapter 11

Sunlight glittered off Drumvagen's windows and set the brick of the house to sparkling. The breeze smelled of damp earth, green growing things, and a faint hint of heather. Ross had rolled up his sleeves and was working beside the other men, as indistinguishable as one blade of grass from another.

The Water of Kinloch had returned to its banks, but the ground was so saturated that a day's rain could bring a flood again. Instead of disposing of the sandbags, Ross and the other men lined them up at the highest point the water had reached. The villagers would keep the sandbags there until it was certain they weren't needed again.

For two days he'd helped remove debris from the front of Drumvagen and down the road to the bridge. Branches and whole trees had to be carted away, along with the bodies of some farm animals caught in the current.

When he could, Macrath helped, but he spent most of his time with his wife and newborn son.

The activity kept Ross busy, made him think of precautions he could take at Huntly, and helped him avoid Ellice Traylor.

He was not as successful in banishing thoughts of her.

She'd burred in like an insidious weevil and refused to leave. Worse, he remembered her literary creation, Lady Pamela. A woman too close to Ellice.

Should authors mirror themselves in their characters? He pushed that thought away and concentrated on dragging more branches from the road.

Today they'd finish clearing up the last of the debris. Tomorrow he would leave for home. He was eager to return, be about his life, the election, and put aside memories of this interlude at Drumvagen.

A carriage approached just as they were dragging the last trunk into the grass beside the road. Slowing, it entered the circular drive in front of the house. Curious, he glanced over as he worked, only stopping when he recognized the woman emerging from the carriage.

Mairi Harrison was a striking woman with brown hair and blue eyes that reminded him of Macrath. Ellice was the second person to exit the carriage, followed by Logan Harrison, the former Lord Provost of Edinburgh, an imposing man with a grin that made people underestimate him.

Logan caught sight of him, did a double take, then smiled broadly, striding across the grass to shake his hand.

"I never expected to see you here," he said. "What brings you to Drumvagen?"

"A whim," Ross confessed. "I wanted to see the changes Macrath had made."

"That's right, your father once owned the place." Logan turned to look at the towering edifice of Macrath's home. "What do you think of it?"

"He's made it a home," Ross said.

"It is, at that." Logan grinned, clapped him on the shoulder and said, "Come, have a whiskey with me. Unless you need me to change and join you."

Ross glanced to the staircase and the two women talking as they mounted the steps.

To anyone else, Ellice looked like a normal young woman, plainly dressed yet winsome. He knew better. She possessed the imagination of Ovid and was more than willing to thumb her nose at society.

She kissed too well for a virgin.

"We're mostly done," he said, directing his attention to Logan again. "I've a favor to ask of you."

Normally, he wouldn't have phrased the request so baldly, but he was aware that he might not get this opportunity again.

"About your election?" Logan asked. "Mairi would be pleased if you solicited her approval. She's all for women having the vote. Until that happens, she's determined to be an influence."

"No, not about the election, although I would gladly accept your help and hers."

He turned and began walking, Logan accompanying him. At the end of the drive, in a spot overlooking the sea, he stopped.

Logan remained silent, evidently a man who'd learned the value of patience. Ross wondered if the trait had been developed from his political life or if he'd always possessed it.

Now that the moment was here, he wasn't sure how to explain so that Logan would understand.

His friend owned a chain of bookstores. Blackwell's was so successful that Logan had recently opened a large store in London. The fact that he and his wife owned a publishing company put Logan in a perfect position to ensure that the books published by Gazette Press were successful.

He could just imagine what would happen if *The Lustful Adventures of Lady Pamela* ever saw the light of day.

Would people buy such a book? Or would they be horrified by its contents? He'd been horrified, yet fascinated as well, and so intrigued that he'd read every word.

The book would be a phenomenal success.

His friendship with Logan had been formed in politics; they rarely discussed personal matters. He would have to make an exception now.

"My father was a wastrel," he said, staring out at the ocean, deeply blue this afternoon. "He was, using an exceedingly kind term, a skirt chaser. I've seven illegitimate brothers and sisters."

Logan didn't comment.

"I've spent the last five years attempting to eradicate what I can of my father's memory or at least replacing it with something better."

"I've knew your father owned Drumvagen at one time. The rest? I dismissed those tales."

"I wish I could have. Prior to my father's ascension to the title, the earls of Gadsden were known for their library, for Huntly, and for their generosity. My father changed that. Now the name is associated with debauchery, licentiousness, and wenching."

Logan didn't say a word. Nor did he ask the question some brave fools eventually asked: what about your wife?

Ross wasn't going to expose that part of himself. Not even to save his political life.

"Is that why you're standing for election?" Logan asked.

He shook his head. "No. That's for me. Not him." He was damned tired of being chained to his father. "I want to be a representative peer. I believe I could be an asset to Scotland in Parliament."

"Your chances are good," the other man said.

Ever since leaving office, Logan had acquired a reputation of being a kingmaker. It was said that if you wanted to succeed in political life, see Logan Harrison. He'd put you in touch with people who could help you, groom you, advise you. If he liked you, he'd stand behind you politically and ensure your success.

He hadn't traded on his friendship with Logan, but now that same relationship might prove deleterious, especially if Ellice succeeded in convincing him and Mairi to publish her book.

"You've still got your share of competition, though," Logan said, then named two men who also wanted to be representatives in Parliament.

Ross nodded. He knew both men well. Only one of them concerned him.

"The Earl of Dunfife is a neighbor," he said. Or as close a neighbor as Huntly could boast.

"A fine man," Logan said.

"With a fine reputation," Ross said. "There are no ghosts in his past. His father was an honor to his name."

Logan didn't speak, an indication that he agreed.

"In order to have a prayer of winning the election, I have to ensure that not a whisper of gossip is uttered about me. Not a speck of innuendo can be attached to my name."

"Is that a problem?" Logan asked.

"Normally, no, but Miss Traylor has written a book."

"I just now learned that."

Ross glanced at him. "Has she asked you to publish it?"

Logan nodded.

"If you do," Ross said, "it will be the end of my political career."

Logan frowned. "Why is that?"

"It's a story of debauchery," Ross said. "But I don't care about that. Except that I bear a resemblance to the hero. In addition, the heroine lives in a place that's reminiscent of Huntly. If you publish the book, people will wonder at the connection. There are too many coincidences, Logan."

Logan didn't say anything. Nor did he comment for the next minute.

"I'm asking you not to publish it," Ross said, aware that he was pulling on the bonds of friendship.

"When Mairi believes in a cause, nothing on heaven or earth will stop her," Logan finally said. "If she wants to publish Ellice's book, you'll need to convince her."

His chuckle didn't need to be deciphered.

If Mairi Harrison wanted to publish the book, Ross knew he might as well give up any thought of preventing another scandal.

"**W**ell, what do you think?" Logan asked.

For the last hour Mairi hadn't said a word. She sat on the bed in the room Macrath had set aside as theirs, turning page after page, transfixed by the manuscript Ellice had given her. She hadn't even looked up when he brushed her hair back from her nape and kissed her there.

That surprised Logan. It was the first time he'd been unable to tempt her away from a task.

She glanced up, her cheeks pink.

"Oh, Logan." Her blue eyes were sparkling.

"That good?"

"If we published this, she would be the most scandalous woman in all of Scotland, maybe even the world."

"That good?"

She nodded. "But it's shocking. Terribly so. We might be considered scandalous by publishing it as well."

"You could always counter that you're giving a woman author a voice."

She smiled at him. "There is that." Fumbling through the pages, she held one up. "But listen to this. This is what I mean.

" 'His fingertips were hot, touched with the fire of passion. He expected them to glow, so heated were they. He wanted to stroke them over her skin, mark her in some way so that any man who came after him would know her as his. When she bathed, she'd see the remnants of his touch and it would warm her.'

"Or this," she said, looking through the pages. When she found the one she wanted, she cleared her throat and began to read again.

" 'He was the apex of joy, a man created for her delectation. His arms were thick and muscled, as were his legs. His chest was a pillow for her cheek, his buttocks soft and round, playthings for her hands. Her fingers teased in that spot behind his heavy testicles, cradled them in her palm, then paid homage to the hot and hard length of his cock. That, too, was hers, in the way it grew at her touch, shivered at her look, and when she kissed it, wept with joy.' "

"Ellice wrote that?" Logan said. "Our Ellice?"

She nodded, her eyes shining.

"You're going to publish it, aren't you?"

"Yes," she said, a delightfully impish smile appearing on her face. "I like the idea of being shocking." She tilted her head and regarded him. "Have you any objections?"

"Would it matter?" he asked.

She nodded. "Yes, it would. I'd be disappointed. I'd try to convince you otherwise, but if you objected, I wouldn't publish it."

"Gadsden isn't going to be happy."

"I doubt it will affect him as much as he thinks."

"He has a reason for being adverse to scandal," Logan said.

"A pity women don't have the vote," she said. "I'd vote for Gadsden if he's anything like Donald."

He crawled up on the bed beside her, gently pushing her until she was on her back beneath him.

"Scandal delights you, does it?"

She smiled at him again.

"A touch of it from time to time."

"Shall we be scandalously late for dinner?"

She dropped the pages and reached up, winding her arms around his neck.

"Please," she said, and smiled into his kiss.

Chapter 12

"He's a widower," her mother said, frowning at Ellice's dress. "Tonight's the last chance you'll have to impress him. Not that you've done so until now, Ellice. Tromping through the countryside like a hoyden, getting buried in mud, sewing bags, of all things."

As her mother bustled around her, inspecting every inch of her very boring person, she stared at herself in the pier glass.

He was a widower.

Did he still mourn his wife?

What had she been like?

Of course, she would have been beautiful, with radiant blond hair and bright blue eyes. Or perhaps clear green like the emeralds in the brooch Macrath had given Virginia last year. She'd have been soft-spoken with a voice that sounded like a gentle breeze over the glen. Her laughter would have charmed the birds and her most common expression would have been a smile.

People loved the Countess of Gadsden for her generosity of spirit, for her kindness in the midst of their pain. She would have remembered people's names and those of their children. Each one of her staff adored her.

Had she died giving Ross a child?

Her death would have sent Ross hurtling into despair. Had he sat beside her casket with tall white candles lighting the night, unable to part from her, unwilling to say good-bye one last time?

Had he stroked her cold hand with his fingers, wanting to impart his warmth to her, wishing to give her life? He would never love again. Never look at the dawn without knowing that his beloved was gone.

But he'd kissed her, Ellice thought, not once but twice. He'd kissed her so passionately she'd almost begged him to take her.

Had his wife been a sickly creature who could give him no ease? Or was she really not dead but chained in the attic? A wild woman whose very presence in life made him a prisoner as well?

Had he visited her at midnight, praying outside the attic room that she had somehow changed, that circumstances had rendered her the beauty he'd known in earlier days?

Had he made her, Ellice, his Jane Eyre? Was the Earl of Gadsden a man to be pitied for his impulsiveness?

Or on viewing her, had he been instantly enchanted to the extent he had to kiss her?

What foolishness. He might address Lady Pamela in such a manner, but never her.

"You have been on my mind since the first moment I met you," he might say.

"Have I?"

She smiled fondly at him, but not too fondly lest the man think he had a hold on her heart. She was, after all, a famous beauty, and not to be tied to one man for long.

"Lady Pamela, allow me to escort you to the terrace."

She looked around at the dancers, knowing that although she didn't seem to be the focal point of their attention, each one of them would see the instant she left the ballroom with the earl. Did she care? Her reputation was such that a man was only enhanced by hints of a dalliance with her.

"I think not, Gadsden," she said, still smiling. "If I were to go with you, I'd no doubt kiss you. Then what would you think of me?"

"That you were the most ravishing creature I've ever met. I haven't been able to stop thinking of you. I smell your perfume in an empty room. I hear your laugh when I'm alone. You're in my dreams and my every waking thought."

"Hush, Gadsden," she said, admonishing him with a look. "People will think you've developed a tendre *for me."*

"What man would not?"

Would he act in such a way? Or would the Earl of Gadsden be disapproving of Lady Pamela, too?

"I've heard of your exploits, madam, and I am not like your stable of males."

"Aren't you?" Lady Pamela smiled, a pitying expression wrapped in a bit of compassion. Few men could refuse her once she turned her wiles on them.

She followed him to the terrace, bored by the sight of the dancers and the endless recitation of praise and compliments from the men who clustered around her. No, this man interested her. His gray eyes were as distant as a Highland storm. his lean face aesthetically perfect.

He was her foil, her opposite. A male beauty with cold eyes to offset her own heated gaze.

His glance swept over her, hesitated at her breasts, traveled the curve of her hips and seemed to measure the length of her legs.

What would he think of her unveiled? Would he believe her a magnificent beauty or would he, unlike her other lovers, remain aloof?

She stepped toward him, hesitating only inches away.

His glance hadn't changed but there was a hint of a smile

at the corners of his beautiful mouth. His bottom lip was slightly fuller than the top, a succulent pillow for her tongue.

"Tell me, Gadsden," she said softly. "Why have you come tonight? Why here? Why this place and this time?"

"I had business with our host. It seemed opportune."

"Not to see me?"

"Why would I wish to seek you out, madam?"

"To renew our acquaintance, perhaps? To see if that first kiss was as delicious as it was? Or did you simply imagine it?"

"Are you threatening to kiss me, Lady Pamela?"

"I want to," she said, her gaze on his mouth. "I want to very much. I want to moisten your lips with my tongue and taste you."

Was it her imagination or had his cheeks deepened in color? His eyes weren't so cold now. Nor were they reminiscent of London fog. Instead, they were steam.

"Are you listening, Ellice?" her mother asked.

No, not the least little bit.

Why should she listen to a litany of her flaws when she knew them all so well? She never stood up straight. She always looked down at the ground when she walked. She jutted out her elbows and didn't stand with grace. She never backed up until she felt the chair behind her and then gracefully sank to the cushion like a feather. Instead, she sat like a stone falling to the ground.

When she did laugh, it normally ended in an unladylike snort. She cried much too often when touched by a scene, a flower, a sunset.

"Well? What do you have to say?"

About what? To admit she hadn't been paying any attention would be to summon another lecture. But it seemed her mother didn't need her participation in this conversation.

"Granted, he's only a Scottish earl, but he's more elevated in rank than anyone else who ever visited Drumvagen."

She stared at her mother. Words simply wouldn't come.

"He's fantastically wealthy," Enid said, fluffing the back of Ellice's skirt. "That's always a blessing."

Her mother walked around her, then stepped back to finish the inspection.

"Have you nothing more festive than dark blue?"

Her mother was serious in her matchmaking. She'd never before suggested that her wardrobe might be dull, especially since she herself had given orders that most of Ellice's dresses be blue. Ellice had one black dress, but if she never had to wear mourning again, she'd be happy.

She shook her head.

"We'll just have to make do, then," Enid said. She narrowed her eyes. "Perhaps a brooch might brighten you."

Enid's eyes narrowed as she tucked a tendril of her daughter's hair back into place.

"I once despaired of you, child. You had no manners at all. You said the most dreadful things to anyone whenever you wished."

She jerked at Ellice's bodice, straightened the white collar, and retreated once more to frown.

"But you've matured, I'm happy to say. You've learned how to guard your tongue."

Ellice remained silent.

"Tonight, however, you need to charm the man. I meant to speak to Macrath, find out his interests." Once more her mother frowned. "Eudora would take this opportunity to be gracious and charming. She would not squander the moment."

"Eudora was perfect," Ellice said, the words limp.

"Of course she wasn't perfect," Enid said. "But she had a great deal of charm. You might emulate her. Anything but be silent and mousy."

She *was* silent and mousy. Whatever could she say to that?

"I do wish I'd thought to increase your wardrobe. Perhaps Virginia has something we might borrow."

"No," Ellice said, shaking her head. "I look fine. Clean, presentable enough for such fine company as the earl. Besides, I don't want to bother Virginia."

"A pity she will not be able to attend dinner. She could easily direct the conversation to your abilities."

What were her abilities? She played the pianoforte passably well even though it didn't interest her. She loved to read and could spend the rest of her life in a library. She'd written a book, and her imagination was such that she could transport herself from the wilds of Scotland to anywhere.

Thank heavens and all the saints for her imagination. She wasn't just Ellice Traylor. Parts of her were Lady Pamela, a very accomplished and seductive, sophisticated woman.

Even the name sounded grand. *Pamela.* She elongated the syllables in her mind. The name sounded like a brook babbling in the midst of summer, trickling over stones on its happy way to the sea.

Everyone wanted to be Lady Pamela's friend. Or love Lady Pamela. No one ever told Lady Pamela that her dead sister was so much more talented.

She smiled now, turned to her mother, and wished Enid's frown would ease.

"I won't embarrass you, I promise," she said, hoping it wasn't a lie.

"You've always been a bit graceless, child. Eudora always put you in the shade. Perhaps I'm being foolish thinking you might charm the man. You've been given little practice, having never attracted anyone."

Somehow Ellice managed to smile.

A week ago her mother had been set on matching her with anyone. Tonight it was an earl. Who would it be tomorrow? A coachman? The solicitor who visited Macrath from Edinburgh?

She should tell her mother that Gadsden thought her shocking. He'd never consider her as a wifely candidate. But once Enid dug in her heels, there was no moving her. She was better off simply acquiescing to Enid's plans.

Perhaps she should warn Gadsden.

"My mother thinks I should charm you."

His eyes would give her that frozen glance. "Does she?"

"I can't, of course. It's much too late for that. But I felt it only fair to warn you that she has thoughts of a match between us."

His eyes narrowed.

"After all, I'm the daughter and sister of an earl. You're an earl."

"Does she know you're also a harlot?"

"Is that really fair? I've given you no indication that I'm without morals."

"You kissed me."

"You kissed me first."

"You liked it," he said.

"If I hadn't, I would have started screaming. You would have been set out into the storm and no doubt contracted pneumonia and a host of other diseases. The fact that you're so hale and hearty is credited, therefore, to me."

Her cheeks warmed. Perhaps it wasn't wise to think of him right at the moment.

"Shall we go?" she asked in a subdued voice.

Her mother nodded, gliding before her to the door.

Ellice reluctantly followed, hoping the dinner went better than she expected. Her mother would be cloyingly charming. The Earl of Gadsden would be unaffected and cold. Logan would be amused. Mairi would be direct and slightly shocking, and Macrath would be watching everyone.

No, it couldn't possibly be anything but a disaster.

Chapter 13

Just before dinner, Ross met with Brianag, arranging for the servants who'd tended to him to be given a small monetary gift in envelopes he'd prepared. Despite being unexpected guests in a difficult time for the inhabitants of Drumvagen, he and Harvey had been treated like family.

Brianag, still basking in the glow of saving the mistress of Drumvagen from a breech birth, accepted his thanks with a regal nod. No smile was in evidence, but her square face looked oddly right without expression, like she was carved from stone. Most statues didn't smile, either.

As Ross headed for the stairs, Carlton announced his presence. The nursery was not, as in most houses, on an upper floor, but located next to the master suite. Close enough to the guest room that he was aware of the baby's schedule.

He descended the stairs, hearing the Sinclairs' older children giggling in the corridor. Looking up, he was startled to catch sight of the former Lord Provost of Edinburgh playing horse with his nephew.

Logan was on his hands and knees, Alistair gleefully holding onto his hair with both hands and spurring him on with cries of, "No, Uncle, not there! There!"

How long had it been since Huntly was filled with the

sounds of children? Or had it ever been? Was the house too large to be tamed in such a way? He pushed the thought aside, along with the strange discomfort of it.

He entered the family parlor. The room had a warm welcome about it, but that was true about every room in Drumvagen. Flowers dotted the parlor, the colors teal and gray selected with comfort and tranquility in mind. The knickknacks were of the humorous sort, a porcelain shepherdess looking down in exasperation at a smiling sheep, a china dog with a goofy expression on his face.

On each wall there was a separate family portrait. From where he sat in the parlor, he studied a painting of Macrath and his wife along with two of their children above the mantel. Carlton would no doubt be added soon.

Would he ever have children? Another thought he pushed away.

On the next wall there was a portrait of a woman resembling Sinclair and a red-haired man, both of them strangers.

The third wall featured a portrait of Logan Harrison and Mairi. He studied the artist's rendition of her with interest. She stood behind Logan in the reverse of most contemporary paintings in which the husband stood behind a seated wife. Her eyes glittered with amusement as her fingers were gripped by one of Logan's larger hands.

He could only wonder if she'd been counseled to restrain herself in the sitting and the artist had captured that moment.

A maid entered, bobbing a curtsy and offering a smile. Was the room warm enough? It was. Was he needing anything else? He wasn't. The family would be with him soon, he was told. He wanted to ask if that meant Ellice as well. Or would she find a way to take a tray in her room again?

For the most part, he socialized whenever he was forced, no more than that. He'd been on display all his life. When he could, he retreated to his library, to a world he chose.

But he had a feeling this night would prove to be fascinating.

The first person to appear was the Dowager Countess of Barrett followed by Ellice.

He'd met the countess the night before at dinner. She was an impressive woman, but not for her demeanor or even her personality. No, her power lay in the ability to change Ellice from a startling, almost shocking female to a meek, subservient creature who walked behind her, kept her eyes carefully averted, and managed to stare at the carpet.

The countess herself wasn't all that different from dozens of other women he'd met. They were certain of their place in society and therefore felt as if they had the right to dictate aspects of it.

They were the doyennes, the arbiters, given their power by the acquiescence of society. He understood the need to be charming when he encountered them at a gathering or, like tonight, a private dinner. Together, they were like a coven, witches with the ability to alter destinies.

With a glance, a girl might be considered ruined. Or another woman with a sullied reputation could be accepted back into society, all her past sins forgiven if they decreed it.

Their influence wasn't felt all that much in politics, at least not on the surface. But some of these women had husbands, either happily married to them or chained by obligation. As wives, they had the ability to make a remark, drop a hint, or even encourage.

For that reason, but mostly because he was a man reared to be polite, he made obeisance to Enid Traylor, bowed slightly over her hand, and conversed with her, the conversation almost a word-for-word repetition of the previous evening.

No, he hadn't known her husband. His condolences on her loss. No, he hadn't known Lawrence, either. Or her deceased daughter. He did know her youngest daughter but that was a question she oddly didn't ask, and from Ellice's panicked glance—the first time she deigned to look at him—he wasn't to say anything about the depth of their acquaintance. No confessions about the gazebo or, previously, in the Great Hall.

When his host arrived with apologies for his tardiness, he came bearing tales of his children and explanations why Virginia would not be attending dinner.

Ross hadn't expected to meet the elusive Virginia so soon after she'd given birth. Since the birth had been difficult, he was surprised she was doing as well as she was.

"She'd be up and about if she had her way," Macrath said.

His smile was genuinely happy, not simply painted on to hide his true emotions. If Macrath felt regret or sorrow in his life, it wasn't evident in the man's clear gaze or his relaxed pose.

When a fire was lit, Ross was grateful. Spring didn't mean warmth in Scotland. In the midst of summer the wind could carry the chill of winter with it. With the dampness in the air, the fire was welcome.

Macrath possessed an inventive mind. He'd developed a refrigeration system that was changing the way food was brought to market. Now, according to him, he was experimenting with ways to bring the convenience of those same large systems into each household.

"I foresee a time when each home will have a similar unit," he said. "A woman won't have to send the servants to market. Instead, she'll have access to fresh food in her own home."

"Wouldn't that change society itself?" he asked, a question that began a rousing discussion.

From time to time he looked at Ellice. Other than that one panicked glance, she ignored him, evidently interested in the flooring beneath her feet, her own nails, or her mother's whispered comments.

He suspected that the Dowager Countess was giving her

instructions. *Sit up straight, girl. Smile more. Can you add nothing to the conversation?*

He'd been witness to enough of those mother-daughter moments to identify one when he saw it.

What he couldn't understand was where Ellice had gone. For two days she'd avoided him. But now she was here yet not.

The young woman who sat on the settee in front of the window wasn't the same one who hid in his carriage, kissed him in the Great Hall, or was his partner in saving the village. Nor was she the author of the most erotic book he'd ever read.

The demure and withdrawing figure she portrayed was as skilled an act as the role of a girl just barely out of the schoolroom.

She was neither, but something more, an experienced woman who'd nearly lured him into danger twice. Yet anyone looking at her now would think him a fool for admitting that.

Ellice was a temptation and he was not a man often tempted.

Oh, he liked women, and he enjoyed the company of a few. One, a widow in Edinburgh, invited him for dinner often enough that his needs were met.

He wasn't his father, after all. He was not a rutting beast, someone who thought only of his hungers, not his responsibilities.

Ellice challenged him on an elemental level. She fixed those heated brown eyes at him and pierced him to the core.

He wanted to kiss her again, and that was only one sign of his insanity. He was too curious about her.

Ellice lowered her head, looking up at him through her lashes, startled to find Gadsden glancing at her again.

He and Macrath stood near the fire, engaged in conversation about ice machines and servants.

However, he kept looking at her, enough that she was disconcerted.

Did she have a wart on the end of her nose?

Was he thinking she was the ugliest woman he'd ever met? Or was he wondering how he could have found himself ever kissing her?

Pompous man. She was the sister of an earl and the daughter of an earl. An English earl, not one of the trumped up Scottish earls. She was certainly good enough for him. The question was if he were good enough for her.

Her family stretched back five hundred years. How many years did the Earls of Gadsden trace their lineage?

No doubt he thought himself better than her because he was as handsome as sin.

She caught herself. Dear heavens, she sounded just like her mother. She'd be better served by listening to Lady Pamela. She had a saying that it wasn't beauty that snared a man, but pleasure. Give a man pleasure and he will be your slave for life.

She could give the earl pleasure, enough to sot his wits. He'd be drunk with joy around her. He'd kneel at her feet, head bowed, and she'd knight him with a gentle touch on his shoulder, head, and shoulder.

"Do you swear to be my vassal, Sir Gadsden, forever to obey my slightest whim?"

"I do, my lady," he'd say, looking up at her worshipfully. "Give me but a command and I shall execute it."

"Then I command you to swear your fealty. To announce to all and sundry that you are mine."

He wouldn't even balk at that, only smile at her in that way that made her toes tingle. "I shall, my lady."

Then he would slowly raise the hem of her dress, a white tunic banded with gold, cinched at her waist with a gold, ruby-encrusted belt.

Inch by inch the hem would be crumpled in his large hands

as he unveiled her for his eyes. Her knees would receive a soft kiss for being such lovely knees. Then her upper thighs where he would rub his cheek against her tender skin, acquainting her with the feel of his unshaven face. Then higher, where he rested his face against the curls of her mound, his breath heated and fast.

"I don't see how delaying dinner will ruin Brianag's cooking, Macrath," her mother was saying. "The woman's veal tastes like leather anyway."

Ellice blinked rapidly, conscious of two things: her face was fiercely hot, and her mother was about to embark on another battle in the Drumvagen War.

Before Macrath could say anything chiding, and before Brianag could hear or be told about Enid's criticism and respond in kind, she stood.

"Let's just go into dinner, shall we? Why wait on Mairi and Logan?"

Ellice marched to Gadsden's side, grabbed his arm and smiled grimly up at him. "Will you take me into dinner, your lordship?"

Everyone in the parlor stared at her. She'd just disobeyed every rule of etiquette she'd ever learned.

"I'm desperate," she whispered, turning so her back was to her mother. "Please, just pretend that you're starving and can't wait to eat."

He had no idea of the repercussions from her mother's words. If Enid was allowed to continue her complaints, one of the maids would tell Brianag. They were nearly as fearful of Brianag as Ellice was.

As it was, the two women had put aside their differences for the few difficult days of Carlton's birth. But the respite was over. War had already broken out and she'd do anything to keep the peace, at least tonight, even if it meant acting foolish.

To her great surprise he didn't say anything, merely placed his hand atop hers.

Inside the dining room, she guided him to her chair. While she waited for the others, she smiled with a determination that hurt her cheeks.

Macrath escorted her mother. After everyone had been seated and he sent a frowning glance toward Ellice, he gave orders for dinner to begin.

If Logan were here, he would sit beside her. To her left was her mother, who was accorded the position of honor at Macrath's right hand since Virginia was absent. Mairi would, if she ever appeared, sit at the earl's left hand.

Ellice had been allowed at the dinner table since she was thirteen, expected to contribute to the general discussion and offer topics of interest.

Not one word came to mind.

Mairi would have regaled them all with tales of Edinburgh. Logan would have commented on her stories, adding a more sober opinion. The two of them would have contributed to the conversation. There wouldn't have been the awkward silence with only the four of them at the table.

The earl was still looking at her from time to time. She wanted to put her soup spoon down and dare him to tell her why she was the object of his attention.

Did no one of his acquaintance ever act impulsively?

"Have you lived in Scotland long, your ladyship?" Gadsden asked.

Please God, don't let her say something insulting about Scotland. Or Brianag.

"A few years," Enid said. "An interesting country, Scotland."

"Have you ever visited England?" Ellice interjected. "You sound very English."

Her mother frowned at her.

"I was educated there," the earl said. "No doubt the reason for my accent."

"Virginia had an English nurse," Macrath said. "That's why she sounds more English than American."

"I didn't know your wife was an American," Gadsden said.

Macrath nodded. "I forget it most of the time myself. She seems almost like a Scot now."

"What is being a Scot like?" Ellice heard her mother ask. *Oh, no.*

"A certain independence of spirit," she answered before the men could. Or before the girl serving the venison could hear, take notes about Enid's snide remarks, and carry them to Brianag.

"An ability to carry on despite circumstances," she continued. "Perhaps a belief in otherworldly phenomena."

"Do you think we all believe in ghosts?" Gadsden asked.

She glanced at him. Now was not the time to recall the feeling of her breasts pressing against his chest, of his fingers on her skin, his lips trailing kisses along her throat.

Or her earlier image of him unveiling her, inch by inch.

Her cheeks warmed.

"Do you believe in ghosts?" she asked him.

"Not the incorporeal ones," he said. "Only those of memory and mind."

"Are you a haunted man?"

He didn't answer her, merely sat there, his gaze steady on her. To her surprise neither her mother nor Macrath said a word. Or perhaps they did and she didn't hear anything.

She was caught by his gray eyes, snared and netted until she could almost imagine she was at his feet, head bowed, swearing allegiance to *him.*

He'd raise her up with both hands on her arms until she stood before him, clad only in her gauzy tunic. A slave brought to the man who declared himself her master.

"Please forgive us," Mairi said as Logan pulled apart the sliding doors into the dining room. "Logan would have been here early but for me. Our tardiness is all my fault."

Ellice blinked, looked away, forcing a smile to her face as Mairi entered the room like a gust of wind.

"It's actually all your fault," Mairi said, looking at Ellice.

Her eyes widened. "It is?"

"Your book." Mairi glanced at her brother. "It's magnificent. I can't wait to publish it."

"You like it?" Ellice was very careful not to look in the earl's direction. She could almost feel the anger rolling off the man.

"Like it? I love it. It's earthy, spell-binding, and enchanting. In one sitting I nearly read it through. It's like a fairy tale wrapped in an erotic binder. You'll be the toast of Scotland."

"Or the scandal," Logan added.

"Oh dear, you've read it, too?" Could her face get any hotter?

Her mother looked at Mairi, then Logan, and finally at her. "What book?"

She hadn't considered explaining *The Lustful Adventures of Lady Pamela* to her mother over venison and vegetables. Not with witnesses and especially not with the Earl of Gadsden glaring holes in her.

She could almost feel his gaze searing her skin.

"I've written a book," she said, staring down at her plate. How could anyone possibly eat at a moment like this?

She wanted to jump up, hug Mairi, then do a little dance around the dining room. At the same time, she wanted to fold her arms over her head and wait for the inevitable storm of protest and censure.

Dear God, her mother would want to read the book.

She sent a look to Mairi. She probably looked like a rabbit just before it was shot.

"Ellice has written the most wonderful book," Mairi said. "It's a little different from what we normally publish but we'll talk more about it later."

Somehow, they had to stop her mother from reading the book.

The image of Enid on the settee, intent on each page, was enough to chill her to the core. She would never again be able to meet her mother's gaze.

"How have you learned such things? No daughter of mine would ever think to remark on a man's limbs, let alone his . . . cock," she said, her voice choking on the last word. *"You weren't raised in such a manner, Ellice. How could you have written such filth?"*

No doubt she'd get the same reaction from a good many people. Yet perhaps there would be just as many who were enchanted by Lady Pamela's courage and daring.

"Don't you think so?" Gadsden asked.

Ellice looked at the earl across the expanse of snowy linen.

"I'm sorry. I wasn't paying any attention," she said, giving him the truth. "What were you asking me?"

"I apologize for the manners of my daughter, your lordship," her mother said, sending a narrow-eyed glance at her.

She was going to be chastised about the whole evening, wasn't she? Her mother was probably planning the lecture now.

"I was saying," the earl said, "that it must require a bit of an imagination to dream up a book, especially one of such a carnal nature."

Oh dear heavens, must he use the word "carnal"? Her mother's face was turning red.

"Whatever does he mean, child? What have you done, Ellice?"

At the moment she didn't have an answer for her mother.

Someone had placed a noose around her neck and she was being strangled. Any moment now she'd feel her feet leave the floor to dangle uselessly beneath her.

Ross thought dinner at Drumvagen the most interesting social experience of his life.

Mairi was as he remembered, one of the most charming

women he knew. He thoroughly enjoyed the conversation among Mairi, Logan, and Macrath, and wished he had the occasion to meet with them more often.

Another interesting dynamic was that of the housekeeper and the Dowager Countess. When Brianag came into view, Enid made a show of being unable to cut her meat. When dessert was offered, she pushed away her plate, looking disgusted. Brianag countered by slamming the platter of Scottish candy in the middle of the sideboard and muttering something that sounded suspiciously like an English oath.

At first, Ellice barely breathed. She didn't look up, smile, converse, or otherwise attempt to be personable. She was simply there, and despite her efforts to remain invisible, his attention was drawn to her again and again.

Now she had a panicked look on her face and wouldn't look in her mother's direction.

The countess didn't know about *The Lustful Adventures of Lady Pamela,* that was evident. Otherwise, Mairi would have continued her praise for the manuscript. How was she going to explain the book to her mother? Or to anyone else, for that matter? Yet she'd neither asked him for anything nor had she accepted his offer of money.

Ellice was an odd and unsettling woman, one he'd do well to forget as soon as possible. She was a contradiction, one who incited him to be someone he wasn't. She smiled at him and he forgot who and where he was. He'd kissed her in the Great Hall and again in the gazebo and now he was torn between compassion and curiosity.

No, he most definitely needed to leave Drumvagen tomorrow.

First, he needed her to agree not to publish that damnable book.

Chapter 14

Ellice had never considered that it would be so uncomfortable sitting across from the Earl of Gadsden with her mother seated next to her.

He watched her constantly, his gray eyes daring her to remember the moments in the Great Hall. Or when he'd held her in the gazebo, her weariness forgotten beneath the surge of passion she felt.

As if she could forget.

She wanted to kiss him now, so much that she bit her lips, concentrated on her plate and tried to pretend he wasn't sitting there, looking at her.

He was impossible to ignore.

She could just imagine the reaction of the others if she threw herself over the table, dragged the earl's head down and kissed him like she wanted.

Her mother would scream.

Mairi might applaud.

Logan would smile, while Macrath would look shocked.

What would Gadsden do? His lips tilted up on one corner when she glanced at him.

She wanted to kiss the smile off his mouth, sit on his lap and hold his head still so she could rain kisses all over his face. Then, when his eyes grew soft, she'd place her lips over his mouth, breathing against them softly.

"Kiss me, but slowly," she'd say. "As if you don't know how."

"Will you school me in kisses, Ellice?"

She would smile against his lips, empowered by the Earl of Gadsden in thrall to her.

She could barely eat anything. She knew they were having venison because her mother kept commenting about it. Greens were on the menu along with some sort of aspic. She didn't like her food to shake, but rather than offend Brianag, who supervised the cooking and the cook, she tasted some of it and managed not to wrinkle her nose at the sour taste before putting her fork down.

The earl ate with precision, taking a small bite, chewing it well. She watched as he swallowed, wondered what it was about his throat that fascinated her.

Lady Pamela would have fed him.

She would have held a bit of Scottish candy just out of reach of his mouth until his tongue darted out and licked it.

"Do you like that flavor?" she'd ask in a husky tone. "Or would you prefer the chocolate?"

"The chocolate, I think," he'd say. "But place it between your breasts."

She would have bared herself right there at the table, opening her bodice, the busk of her corset, and pull down her shift until it rested below her breasts, raising her nipples. Then she would have placed a tiny piece between her breasts, as a lure, a treat, a tease for his lips.

"You mustn't touch me," she said. "Only the candy."

His eyes gleamed silver.

"What if I want a true sweet? Your nipples are tastier than any candy."

She would shake her head slowly from side to side, her smile teasing.

She had to get out of here.

Ellice knew she was going to be lectured for what she did next, but it would be worth it to escape the dining room.

She stood and addressed the table. "If you'll forgive me," she said, "I'm feeling tired." With no more explanation than that, she escaped.

As she walked quickly down the hall, she placed both palms against her hot cheeks. She really must stay out of his presence. Something about the Earl of Gadsden inflamed her.

He resembled her hero too well, that's why. That was all it was. Nothing about the man attracted her otherwise.

She didn't know him. He'd never once told her the name of his favorite book, what type of music he preferred, if he liked dogs, or if he was an avid hunter. Did he dance?

She sincerely hoped not since she was clumsy on the dance floor. What did she care if he danced? She was not going to be dancing with him.

All she knew about him was that he didn't like her book and wanted to ensure it wasn't published. Hardly reasons to feel kindly disposed toward him.

"You've got to stop her."

Ellice turned to see him standing in the middle of the corridor, his napkin still clutched in one hand. Dear God, had he made a scene following her?

His cheeks were bronzed, his eyes a flat gray.

"You've got to stop the publication of the book."

"Why, because you decreed it?" She turned into her room. The more distance she put between them the better.

"I thought you understood."

She turned to face him. "I understood that you don't want it published. I do."

"There you are," he said, his lips curving in a smile. "I wondered where you disappeared. I much prefer this Ellice to the one in the dining room."

She blinked at him, surprised.

"It's your mother, isn't it? Are you reminded of who you should be around her? Not the person you really are, of course."

She frowned. He said the most outlandish things at times. At least she kept the brunt of her imagination on the page.

"Go away, your lordship," she said, opening the door to her sitting room. "Go bedevil some other poor woman."

"No other poor woman has written a book like yours. Change the hero."

She turned to him again.

"What?"

"Give him red hair and a lisp. Make him limp from the wars. Give him a rakish scar. Do not make him an earl with gray eyes and black hair."

"People won't associate my book with you."

"Why wouldn't they? You even made Lady Pamela's home sound like Huntly."

She walked into the sitting room, unsurprised when he followed. She'd need a net and a bevy of men with spears to keep the Earl of Gadsden away at the moment.

"Next, you'll be wanting me to change Lady Pamela's name." She turned and faced him. "Your wife's name wasn't Pamela was it?"

"Cassandra."

A lovely name, perhaps she'd use it in another book. She could just imagine the earl's irritation when she did that.

"You really have nothing to worry about. Donald isn't a widower." She tilted her head and regarded him. "I'm sorry that she died."

His only response was to continue to stare at her.

"Am I not supposed to be sorry?"

"It was five years ago."

"Don't you miss her?"

He didn't answer.

"Five years is hardly long enough to mourn someone you loved greatly, is it? You should always carry a bit of her in your heart. Perhaps until the day you die."

"What rot."

"You didn't love her." She shook her head at him.

"Change the hero. Better yet, have it published anonymously."

"If I hadn't been in your carriage, you would never have read the book or even known about it."

"Ignorance is bliss, you mean?"

She nodded, backing up to the settee in front of the fireplace. Unlike the parlor, there was no fire in this room and the air was damply chilled.

"You would never have known about it. No one else will make any connection to you. You aren't, your lordship, as important to everyone else as you think you are."

He advanced on her one predatory step at a time

"You don't understand. Someone would read it and speculate. The gossip would start and the rumors begin. People would wonder."

"You're the Earl of Gadsden. People wouldn't talk about you."

"Because I'm the Earl of Gadsden, people *will* talk about me."

She didn't understand that comment at all.

"Very well, let's say you're correct." She held up her hand to forestall his comment. "Just for a moment, we'll pretend. Even so, the election is a few weeks away. My book won't be published that quickly. You'll be elected long before anyone sees the book."

"Do you always get your way, Ellice? Do people merely bow down before you?"

She laughed at the thought that she had influence over anyone.

Reaching out, he gripped her arm, pulling her to him so fast she didn't have a chance to protest. He didn't kiss her, though, merely held her close, her breasts pressed against the wall of his chest. He was an imposing man when viewed across the room. Up close he was almost overwhelming.

"Shall I simply forget the looming scandal because you smiled at me?" he asked, bending his head.

She closed her eyes, waiting for his kiss.

He brushed his lips over her forehead as he released his grip on her arm. The message was clear. She was free to go, to escape him. She needn't wait to flee as the minutes ticked by. She had no reason to worry about a purloined kiss.

She opened her eyes and tilted her head back. His eyes were direct and unflinching.

"Do you really not miss her?" she whispered.

He didn't answer, only bent his head, his mouth hovering over hers.

I'll change the hero's appearance. The words never came. Not after his mouth greeted hers again.

Colors swirled behind her lids as the room spun. She reached up and grabbed his shoulders for balance.

She forgot how to breathe.

Her heart pounded faster as fire raced through her.

Of its own volition, one hand moved to rest against his heated, bristly cheek. She would forever feel him against her palm, know the contour of his jaw, the silky touch of hair at his temple.

He pressed against her until the settee was at her back.

She could have pulled away. She could have simply turned her head, breaking the kiss. She could have closed her eager mouth, bid her tongue to cease tasting his lips.

She could have clenched her hands into fists and beat against his chest in protest.

Instead, she sighed or moaned, the sound an audible indication of the delight she was experiencing.

Her lips had never been so sensitive. Her mind was silenced, thought replaced by wonder. She wanted to taste him, fill herself with him.

When he placed his hands at her waist, she wanted to be naked for him. Instead of silk, let him feel her skin. Let him know every inch of her so that he might identify each breast, a hip, her inner thigh.

Let him be the author of her pleasure.

"Oh dear God in heaven," her mother said.

"See, I told you," Brianag replied.

She jerked away, staring up at Ross with blinking eyes. She didn't have to turn to see disaster on the threshold. She knew without looking that her mother was there, wearing an expression of such horror that one would have thought someone had died.

Brianag was there, too. Did she wear a look of triumph on her face? She'd finally bested the Dowager Countess of Barrett by revealing her daughter as a strumpet.

Ellice gripped Ross's jacket, hoping her knees would support her. Hoping, too, that he could simply look at the women and they'd disappear. Poof! They'd magically be sent to France. Would that be far enough away?

She pressed her forehead against his chest, still breathing hard, still adrift in the languor of budding passion.

Why hadn't they closed the door?

Why hadn't they gone to his room?

Perhaps she should feel some degree of shame that she wasn't condemning herself for kissing him. She wasn't that much of a hypocrite. She'd thoroughly enjoyed it and wanted to do it again.

A great many times, in fact.

He placed his hands on her shoulders and gently pushed her away. She didn't want to go, but she reluctantly did, looking up at him to discover a wry smile on his face.

Their gazes caught and clung. In his, she glimpsed a shining bit of humor. What did he see in her eyes? Longing? If she could have taken him to her bed at this moment, she would have.

She would pray for her immortal soul later. Right now she had to face her mother.

"I think you and I need to talk," Macrath said.

Oh, dear. Not only did she have to explain to her mother, but now Macrath.

She peeked around Gadsden to find Macrath staring at the earl's back.

Could this get any worse?

"My girl is ruined," her mother said, clenching her hands together and beginning to weep. Her face crumpled like the linen handkerchief she wadded in one hand. "Ruined by a Scottish reprobate." She sent an accusing look at Macrath. "You promised we would always be safe here. Is this what you call safety, Macrath Sinclair?" Her gaze shifted to Gadsden. "If this is a friend of yours, I hesitate to think what your enemies might be like."

The Dowager Countess of Barrett drew herself up, calling upon decades of intimidation of servants and tradesmen, not to mention her husband and children. Her eyes were hard as stones as she regarded Macrath.

He wasn't the type to flinch under such scrutiny. Instead, he faced her eye-to-eye.

Holding her handkerchief in a death grip, she lowered her voice until Ellice could barely hear her. Her face was splotchy and red, her lips thinned. There wasn't a trace of tears in her eyes, only fierce determination.

"I won't have it, Macrath. I won't."

"Leave it in my hands, Enid," he said. "You and Ellice are both members of my family now. I'm sure it's not as bad as it looks on the surface."

Ellice closed her eyes. Her mother was going to explode.

Only Brianag had been the recipient of her infamous rages until now. Macrath, by trying to mollify her, had pushed Brianag aside and now stood front and center before Enid, target number one.

"Not as bad? Not as bad?"

Brianag, standing tall behind the two of them like a totem, looked vastly pleased with the situation. Her wide mouth, normally curved down at the corners, was now curved in a smile. But the look in her eyes warned Ellice that she was in for dire treatment. She'd embarrassed Macrath Sinclair and for that there would be punishment.

Her clothes would be laundered with a double measure of starch. Her bedsheets would be shorter than usual. Her rooms would be filled with dust, her food cold and inedible.

No doubt Brianag would also make some sort of sign in the air and curse her with a garbled Scottish oath, uttered in a language Ellice couldn't translate.

Yes, she was most definitely in disgrace.

But that wasn't the worst of it. No, that came when her mother refused to be calmed, when she turned once more and leveled such an intent look on her that Ellice felt singed by it.

In that instant she realized how much of a disappointment she was to her mother. She wasn't beautiful, talented, poised Eudora, who had died in the smallpox epidemic.

"You cannot imagine how bad it is, Macrath," Enid said. "Ellice is odd enough. Finding a potential husband has been next to impossible, not to mention she lives in the midst of the Scottish wilderness. Now you've rendered her unsuitable for marriage, or do you think gossip doesn't travel?"

She sent a fulminating look at Brianag. "Before dawn the whole of Kinloch Village will know that one of your guests"—she spat out the word—"had his way with my daughter."

"He didn't—" Ellice began, only to be silenced by a look from her mother and Macrath.

"You must make him marry her," her mother said, addressing Macrath while frowning at Gadsden. She sent another glare at Ellice. "If not, she's ruined for polite society. If not, she'll be known as the Whore of Drumvagen."

Ellice closed her eyes and prayed that this was all her imagination. She was very much afraid, however, that her imagination had deserted her and this situation was only too real.

Chapter 15

She was going to be sold to white slavers. Macrath was going to stand on the shore and wave as the ship carried her away to a life of debauchery and degradation.

Her mother would march away from the sand, muttering words like, "She should have been more like Eudora."

"She's no better than I thought her," Briunug would say

The Earl of Gadsden would stand behind Macrath nodding in approval of his actions.

Or if she wasn't sold to white slavers, she'd be sent to America, to work in one of Macrath's factories. Or Australia where the seasons were upside down. She might like that, having winter when Scotland was in the middle of summer.

Perhaps her mother would simply disown her and she'd never again be known as the Earl of Barrett's daughter. *Oh, her? She has no identity, no name. No one claims her. What a pity. She shunned all that anyone would be overjoyed to have—a family and a good name.*

Worse than all her imaginings was the very real chance that Macrath would listen to her mother and insist on marriage. After all, he'd caught her and the earl twice now.

Why should she be considered a scandal when Virginia and Macrath had done far worse?

When she first came to Scotland, there had been no explanation why their cousin had suddenly ascended to the earldom. No one had ever come out and discussed the matter with her, but it was plain enough that her nephew looked exactly like Macrath. In addition, he'd been renamed Alistair.

Yet *she* was the scandalous one?

If forced to marry her, Gadsden would only resent her, just like her brother Lawrence had resented Virginia. Their marriage had been horrid.

Or if Gadsden didn't resent her, he would insist that she not write anymore. How would she bear that, not being able to communicate what she thought or felt? She might as well be encased in a brick, an object without the power to hear or speak.

When he deigned to speak to her, the earl would go on and on about his dead wife's accomplishments. She would have been a jewel in the eye of society, while his new wife, in comparison, was a stye.

Nothing she'd do would be right. He'd probably write letters to her mother, and the two of them would commiserate with each other through their correspondence.

She's clumsy, he'd write.

She's always been such. I've tried, I truly have, to make her as graceful as Eudora.

She sits in silence at the dinner table and doesn't say a word.

Her mother would write back and answer, *She lives within her own mind too much, dear Gadsden. She's always been so. I've despaired of ever having a decent conversation with the girl.*

She was very much afraid that what she imagined could too easily come true.

"I've come to offer moral support."

Ellice turned her head to see Mairi entering her sitting

room. She'd been sitting in the dark ever since Macrath told her to remain where she was—his exact words. She hadn't moved from the corner of the settee.

Mairi lit the lamp on the table and came to sit beside her.

"You look distraught."

"Macrath was very irate," she said. "So was mother. I've been horribly shocking."

"When I was horribly shocking, I had a great deal of fun. Are you enjoying it, too?"

Surprised, she glanced at the other woman.

"Do you think you're the only one?" Mairi asked with a smile. "I was not the demure miss I should have been with Logan. Something about the man simply lured me."

"I don't think it's the Earl of Gadsden," she said. "I think it's my character. I imagine all sorts of predicaments and adventures. Before I know it, I'm neck deep in them."

"I never knew you to be that adventurous before."

That was true. She hadn't been. In fact, she'd been the pale, almost ghostly person the earl seemed to despise.

"Perhaps it *is* him," she said. She would prefer to blame her lack of character, and fall from grace, on anyone other than her own failings, but fairness prompted her to amend the statement. "Or how I am around him."

"I think that's closer to the truth. Perhaps we can call it the Logan effect. I was relatively sane until I met Logan. Then I started doing all sorts of odd things."

Mairi smiled at her, which eased the ache in her chest somewhat.

"What do you think will happen?" she asked.

Mairi sat back, staring into the cold fireplace. "I think Macrath will have a lengthy conversation with the earl and impress upon him that being a peer does not give him the right to act the cad. You, despite your flaws," Mairi added, "are still an innocent."

"The earl doesn't think so, not after reading *The Lusty Adventures of Lady Pamela*."

"There is that," Mairi said. "We do want to publish it, you know."

"Then you like it?"

Mairi nodded. "I do. It's funny and profound and poignant. Above all, it's exciting."

She noticed that Mairi didn't ask if the adventures of Lady Pamela were based on real life. As a publisher, she would know that not everything that seemed real was.

"Will Macrath truly make him marry me?"

Mairi sighed. "He could. Perhaps we should enlist Virginia's help there."

"We mustn't disturb her."

"Nonsense, she's bored senseless in her room. When I visit her, she wants me to tell her everything that's happening."

"She'll be disappointed in me."

"Virginia's just like the two of us. We've all acted the fool around men."

"Why aren't they foolish around us?"

Mairi laughed, reached over and hugged her. "They are, my dear, they are. They just hide it better."

He was being flailed alive by politeness.

Sinclair led him to his library, offered him whiskey, invited him to sit, remarked on the full moon, and was a conscientious host.

All the while, they watched each other warily.

Any moment now, Sinclair would to come out and say what he really thought, and it wasn't too hard to guess what that was.

"The first time would have been ludicrous, Gadsden, but this has become a habit."

The comment was almost a relief.

"One regrettably instituted by Miss Traylor."

"You're saying that she held you down and kissed you? It didn't look like coercion from where I stood."

"It wasn't," he said. "I shouldn't have followed her into her room."

"Why the blazes did you?"

"There's something about the woman that irritates me like a burr."

"Or an itch?"

Surprised by the question, he glanced over at the other man.

"Like an itch. I take it you've had a similar response?"

"Her name is Virginia," Sinclair said, smiling, "and she's my wife."

Ross sipped his whiskey and placed it on the table between them before speaking.

"I've been married before."

"I know," Sinclair said.

"The marriage was not an amicable one."

"I suspected as much."

"How do you know that?"

One of Sinclair's eyebrows arched upward at the question.

"You never talk about her. I've mentioned my wife every time we've met. You never add to the conversation. Oh, yes, my wife did the same. Or she loved violets. That sort of thing. You don't remember her."

"Oh, I remember her." Ross picked up the glass and stared into it, wondering what Sinclair would think if he drank the whole thing and requested another. He always wished he were intoxicated when discussing Cassandra. The better to tolerate the humiliation, perhaps.

"You're standing for election soon," Sinclair said, enough of a warning.

"Yes."

"Do you not think your chances would be greater if you were married?"

Ross put his glass down. "I doubt I would be a good match for Ellice."

Sinclair smiled. "Technically, she's the Lady Ellice Traylor, but she hasn't gone by her title since leaving London. As to not being a good marriage, why not? You're an earl. She's the daughter of one. She would probably be happier living closer to Edinburgh. Your chances of winning an election would be better as a married man."

Sinclair leveled a look on him and went on. "I know for certain that you're disposed to one another. I've found you in two compromising situations in a matter of days. You talk about scandal, Gadsden. It doesn't take but a whiff of scandal to ruin a woman's chances for a good marriage. Even here at Drumvagen."

He knew that to be true, just as he knew he'd been in the wrong.

"Have you read her book?" he asked.

Sinclair shook his head.

"I think you need to read it to understand what I'm about to say. I think she's a dangerous woman, Sinclair. I'm not sure if I would be saving her from scandal or pitching myself head first into it."

Sinclair folded his arms and regarded him steadily. What was the man thinking?

"I can't do a thing about my sister publishing the book," he said.

A sister who did anything she wanted, Ross thought, and Ellice, whose penchant for scandal was only slightly less than his father's. Add to that the termagant of a housekeeper and an adopted mother-in-law and Drumvagen was an asylum.

"Have you no control over the females in your life?"

To his surprise, Sinclair grinned at him. "Little or none," he said. "Perhaps that's why I'm so damn happy."

Was there something to the man's reasoning? Huntly was a peaceful oasis, but he hadn't been happy for a great many years. Content, yes, but not happy.

What would marriage to Ellice be like? The fact that he was asking the question bothered him.

Sinclair leaned back in his chair, steepled his fingers and regarded the ceiling.

"Enid isn't going to forget. She isn't going to see you leave in the morning and think, 'Oh, well, he didn't want to marry. No matter.' The woman is as tenacious as a bulldog." His gaze moved to Ross. "I don't know what kind of influence she still has, if any, in England. But she is the Dowager Countess of Barrett. If you make her mad enough, she'll start writing people and they might listen to her."

"If she went around saying that I ruined her daughter, you mean."

Sinclair shook his head. "I doubt she'd word it that way. But a hint about your mental stability, your character, in the right places might well harm you."

"Blackmail, in other words."

"Not mine," Sinclair said. "I'm not altogether sure you would be a good enough husband to Ellice."

That comment had him sitting back in his chair. "Why is that?"

Sinclair didn't look away.

Was he going to mention Cassandra? If so, he had to applaud the man's bravery. No one in the last five years had the courage to look him in the eye and mention his wife.

"You don't care about her," Sinclair said, startling him. "You would agree to marriage for a selfish reason."

"Marriage is inherently selfish," he said.

Sinclair smiled again. "You really have to meet my wife."

"Perhaps not all marriages," he amended. "But most. Most in my circle of acquaintances. Bonds are made for a great many reasons and hardly any of them are for love."

Sinclair nodded. "Perhaps I was better off growing up on the streets of Edinburgh."

Surprised, Ross regarded his host. Macrath Sinclair's reputation was that of a genius at business and invention. He was one of the new industrialists whose talent had enabled him to create a far-flung empire. He'd never once considered that Sinclair had done it on his own, without family resources.

"But Ellice is a woman," Sinclair said. "Who was reared in London. She no doubt expected to marry at a certain age, like most women do."

Ellice was not like most women. Why didn't anyone realize that?

"If she doesn't marry you, it's conceivable she'll be gossiped about to the extent she'll be unable to marry anyone."

Ross stood, walked to the window, staring out at the night.

"Yet you don't think I'm good enough for her."

"I don't," Sinclair said. "Not because you're not a good man, Gadsden. But because you don't care about her."

He did, but not in the way Sinclair meant. She annoyed him, irritated him, and amused him. More, he wanted her, and it appeared as if her desire was as great as his.

"An arranged marriage wouldn't be out of the ordinary," Ross said. "But I would want some time to get to know her better. As you said, it's only been a few days."

How had he gone from protesting a union with Ellice to suggesting it might be a good idea?

"Is that calculation talking?" Sinclair asked. "Are you thinking that you can postpone the marriage until after the election? Then you could extricate yourself from the situation."

He turned and studied Sinclair. "You think I would do that? Hardly the actions of an honorable man."

Sinclair smiled at him.

"But then, my actions have hardly been honorable, have they?" he asked.

"If I were in the same situation, I'd be considering a variety of options. I'm not above lying in certain circumstances. But I'll ask you not to in this one. Ellice is a young woman who's not been treated all that well by life. She lost her father young, then her brother and a beloved sister. She was uprooted from her home in London to Drumvagen. She deserves to be treated with care. If not that, compassion."

"You don't mention love."

Sinclair smiled. "Love is not your choice," he said. "Love is like lightning. You never see it coming. If it strikes you, you know it instantly and it will forever leave its mark. Sometimes," he said, picking up his glass once more, "you feel like you're dying from it."

"I don't love her," he said. He wasn't certain what he felt around Ellice, but it wasn't love.

He didn't want to write sonnets to her. He didn't want to bring her flowers or sit and wonder at her beauty. No, he wanted to toss her onto the nearest flat surface or kiss her until he was finally done with the need to kiss her. He wanted to shout at her, another indication that what he was feeling was most definitely not love.

He turned and faced the window again.

He was standing for election, and even Logan had hinted that marriage would be an asset. As a widower, he was tired of the hopeful mamas and properly schooled ingenues who seemed to follow him from one event to another. He had no heir, unless you counted an obscure cousin who seemed perfectly suited to managing his own estates and didn't covet Huntly at all. His mother would be pleased.

"I'll marry her," he said.

"But will you be a good husband?"

He glanced at Sinclair again. "Yes," he said. As good a husband as he knew how to be. That would have to be enough.

When Mairi knocked on the door of Virginia's sitting room, it was answered by Mary, who smiled at her and nodded down to a sleeping Carlton in her arms.

The room smelled of baby and roses, a combination that was strangely fitting. Macrath had gardeners create a rose garden on the back lawn, large enough that Virginia could walk among the paths. Some of the bushes were already blooming. Soon the whole of Drumvagen would smell of roses.

Ellice and Mairi stood aside as the nurse carried the baby to his bed, where he would be tucked in and watched over by Mary.

Virginia wasn't in her bed but seated in a chair beside the fireplace, her feet propped up on a large footstool.

Mairi and Virginia were sisters-in-law, and Ellice was Virginia's former sister-in law. But as Virginia smiled and greeted the two of them, Ellice had the feeling that the skeins of marriage that bound them were only incidental to the love they felt for each other.

Virginia stretched out her arms to enfold Mairi in a hug, laughing when Mairi remarked on how well she looked.

"I feel absolutely wonderful. It's your brother who has me confined to this cage," she said. "If I had my way, I'd be all over Drumvagen."

"Which is probably why he insists you rest," Mairi said, sitting on the edge of the footstool.

Ellice had thought Virginia looked radiant while carrying her child, but she was doubly so now. Her black hair skimmed her shoulders and gleamed in the lamplight. Her skin was as perfect as one of her mother's Royal Doulton porcelain plates. A soft rose glow brushed her cheeks, graced her lips with color. Her eyes, so pale a blue that they were always startling, were soft and held a look of contentment.

She was a madonna in the glow of the lamp. A woman other women aspired to emulate. Kind, graceful, and beautiful, Virginia was all the things she wasn't. Macrath loved her desperately and it was evident to anyone that she felt the same for him.

"Our Ellice has gotten herself into a bit of a problem," Mairi said, glancing at her.

She sat on the nearby chair, feeling like a puppy who was being chastised by older dogs.

"The Earl of Gadsden," Virginia said.

Surprised, Ellice nodded.

"A very attractive man, I hear."

"One who bears a striking resemblance to her hero," Mairi said. "After reading the book, I can understand why the man is desperate to halt its publication."

Virginia placed both hands on the arms of her chair and scooted into a more comfortable position.

"Now that I hadn't heard about," she said, glancing at Ellice.

"He wants me to change Donald's appearance. Make him so he doesn't have gray eyes and black hair."

"Or have his physique?" Mairi asked.

Ellice nodded, even though the earl hadn't mentioned Donald's figure.

"I don't see how I can," she said. "Lady Pamela remarks on his gray eyes several times."

"You could make them blue," Virginia said. "Like the Sinclair eyes. They're very striking. Regardless, I need to read this book of yours."

"Only after I finish it," Mairi said. "But that's not the reason we're here. We've come to get your wise counsel."

"You make me sound like an oracle," Virginia said.

"Should I be peering into a bowl of water or something? Shall we summon Brianag?"

Both Ellice and Mairi said, "No!" at the same time, resulting in laughter.

"We have a situation," Mairi said, and went on to explain the embarrassing circumstances, glossing over the part where Ellice had been bent over the settee. What she didn't say was that Ellice was only a moment or so away from willingly surrendering her virtue to the earl.

Virginia looked from Mairi to Ellice.

Ellice decided it was wiser to concentrate on the music boxes in the nearby cabinet than to meet Virginia's eyes.

"What we really want," Mairi said, "is for you to convince Macrath that there's no reason to marry Ellice off."

Was that what she really wanted? Oh, most definitely not.

"I kissed him," she said, and looked away. "Besides the scene in my sitting room. I kissed him two other times."

Both women glanced at her, surprised.

"I'm only mentioning it because Macrath was a witness to one of those occasions, which might have something to do with his decision."

"Macrath feels very protective of you," Virginia said. "If marriage is the best answer, he will insist on it."

"There's another alternative to marriage," Mairi said. "If your book was published and sold well, you could have your own establishment." Mairi's mouth firmed, her chin jutted forward, and for a moment she looked just like a figurehead on a ship: all challenge and pride.

Did she want her own establishment? She wasn't sure about that, either. She wanted a home of her own, one that wasn't occupied by her mother or Brianag. One where she could sit and write for hours if she wished. One where there was peace and happiness, but an atmosphere she created, not one she borrowed.

"How do you feel about the Earl of Gadsden, Ellice?"

She glanced at Virginia. She wasn't used to exposing her emotions in speech. People had rarely asked her to do so. Now, it seemed almost impossible.

She might be able to write about Lady Pamela seducing Donald, but to explain how she felt about Gadsden to the two women who sat waiting expectantly for her to speak? No, she couldn't possibly.

He excites me. He makes me feel alive. I want to ravish him. When I'm around him, I want to touch him everywhere.

"You don't dislike him, surely?"

She shook her head. No, that was definitely not the feeling she had around him. He occupied entirely too many of her thoughts. But thinking of him was better than not thinking of him. How did she explain that?

"Could you imagine yourself being his wife?"

Her gaze flew to meet Mairi's.

"I never could," Mairi said, "Not Logan's, I mean. It was such an impossible thing that I never allowed myself to envision it. Do you?"

Ellice shook her head again.

That was not quite true, though, was it? If she married Gadsden, it would be the result of her own choice, wouldn't it? After all, she was the one who decided to kiss him, not once but twice. She had dreams of him. Her imagination had furnished her with all sorts of images, things she'd like to do to him, not to mention what she wanted him to do to her.

"Macrath will want what's best for you."

She nodded again.

"I can't see myself remaining at Drumvagen for the rest of my life." She looked at Virginia. "It's a lovely place."

"But it's not your place," Virginia said, smiling softly.

Ellice nodded.

Now she glanced at Mairi. "I don't want to have my own household. I don't want to be alone."

How did she tell them that contrary to any good sense,

she wanted the Earl of Gadsden? The idea of being able to be close to him anytime she wanted was heady, making her pulse race even now.

A knock on the door made them look at each other. The visitor could only be Brianag or her mother, neither of whom she wanted to see.

Mairi opened the door to Enid, who entered the room as if she were the queen and the rest of them merely her lowly subjects, none of whom deserved an iota of attention.

"There you are, child. I've been looking for you."

Ellice had the strangest feeling that she was about to be beheaded. Either that or sent to the Tower.

Her mother's face was more florid than usual, her lips smiling instead of thinned, and there was a look in her eyes that spoke of hard won triumph.

"You're to be married, child. To the Earl of Gadsden."

Ellice clamped her lips shut to hide her relieved smile.

Chapter 16

Ellice didn't know whether to be overjoyed or terrified.

She stood outside Macrath's library, fist raised to knock on the door. It was a very solid oak door with carved panels and a shiny brass handle. None of the hardware at Drumvagen ever creaked or groaned. If she pressed down on the handle it wouldn't squeak. The hinges wouldn't betray that she'd opened the door.

Everything would change the minute she walked over the threshold.

Stepping back, she dropped her hand. She couldn't marry the man; she barely had the courage to see him.

"The earl will attend you in the library, Ellice," her mother had said. "Be on your best behavior child. Do not embarrass the family."

Be more like Eudora, in other words.

She was to be married by default, because she was shocking. Because she was brave and outlandish and had the entire family talking about her.

The Earl of Gadsden was going to marry her. A man who wouldn't have ordinarily looked at her but for the intervention of Lady Pamela. How very odd that a character in a book had aided her more than any real person.

The door opened suddenly and Macrath stood there. She was still trying to think of something to say when he bent and kissed her on the forehead.

"You two need to talk, I think," he said, abruptly leaving her.

There was nothing more to do but walk through the doorway.

The earl stood in front of the window, with its view of the clear, moonlit night. Was he intrigued by the glow of the moon reflected on the ocean?

As she entered, he turned to face her. Without speaking, he walked past her to close the door, then came to stand in front of her in the middle of the room.

He was the most handsome creature she'd ever seen. Not even Donald had as perfectly sculpted a face. His eyes were steam now, his mouth thinned a little, the muscles in his jaw flexed.

She wanted to place her hand on his cheek and soothe him in some way.

Instead, she kept her hands clasped in front of her.

"We are to wed," he said, his voice as cold as winter at Drumvagen.

She held herself tight, merely nodding at his words. Couldn't he have pretended a bit of interest or enthusiasm?

"Because of my schedule, I would appreciate some flexibility on your part. I'm standing for election as a representative peer in a little while. I'd prefer to wed shortly."

What, exactly, was shortly?

He answered in the next breath.

"I realize that three weeks is not very long, but it will have to suffice."

She nodded. She'd never been one of those girls who dreamt of her wedding. If it was to take place, then why not as soon as possible?

"I've another favor to ask of you."

She waited, silent.

"The weddings of the Earls of Gadsden have always been held at Huntly. It's a tradition I'm loath to break. Would you mind being wed there?"

She shook her head.

"Have you nothing to say?"

"Is my conversation truly needed at this point? It seems as if all I need to do is simply be there."

Some of the steam left his eyes.

"If you object, then we can talk about alternatives."

She shook her head again. "I don't object to being wed in three weeks. It seems to me if I'm to be married, why wait? It's not as if I'm going to France for a trousseau."

He looked as if he wanted to say something, but she held up her hand. "As far as being wed at Huntly, that doesn't matter to me, either. One place is as good as the next, isn't it?"

If he was going to treat the whole matter with sang froid, then so was she.

"Why does your mother think you're odd?"

She hadn't expected that question. She glanced at him, then away.

"I'm not my sister. My sister was perfect. I'm not." He might as well know the whole truth now. "I don't care very much about what other women seem to," she said. "I haven't any interest in fashion. Jewels bore me. I don't like gatherings all that much. I'm a lamentable dancer and I sing like a tortured owl. I'd much rather be reading or writing."

His face changed, so subtly that if she wasn't watching him so closely she wouldn't have seen it.

"About your writing . . ." he began.

"No," she said.

"No?"

"No. If you're going to forbid me to write, I shall not marry you. I don't care what inducement Macrath offered."

"Perhaps he didn't offer any inducements."

"He had to," she said, "for you to agree."

When he didn't say anything, she frowned at him.

"I am serious. This is the one thing about which I care. We can marry in the desert for all it matters to me. This evening if you wish. But you will not forbid me to write."

"Will you publish your book?"

That's when she knew.

"Is that the price for marrying me?" she asked. "Macrath agreed that my book won't be published?"

"Actually, he didn't," he said.

Her heart swelled. She should have known Macrath had more character. Now she felt terrible for even thinking it.

"But it's what you want," she said, certain of it.

"I'd be a fool to say no."

She felt like she was standing on a fulcrum and could topple either way. Before she fell, however, she was going to take as much advantage of the situation as she could.

"Then agree," she said. "I want a contract between us. If you will let me continue writing and agree that I should be permitted to act independently, I will agree that *The Lustful Adventures of Lady Pamela* will not be published."

One eyebrow arched upward. "A contract?"

"You do not strike me as the type of man to dishonor his word. Are you?"

"No."

"Then, yes, a contract."

"Why must it be in writing?"

"Why shouldn't it be?" she asked, moving to sit at Macrath's desk. She pulled out a piece of paper and one of Macrath's pens. She readied her writing instruments and waited.

"Am I to dictate the terms of this contract?" he asked, sitting on the chair beside the desk.

"I think it should be a mutual decision as to the wording," she said.

"Very well. I, Ross Forster, Earl of Gadsden, hereby agree to allow Ellice Traylor, soon to be the Countess of Gadsden, the time and place to write, what she will, when she will, where she will. However, she will not attempt to publish said writings without my express permission."

That was hardly fair. Instead of saying anything, she wrote what he'd dictated, adding her own paragraph beneath it.

Ellice Traylor, soon to be Countess of Gadsden, has the ability to renege on this contract if the Earl of Gadsden does not materially agree to its provisions. He is to allow her the independence she wishes, including the ability to refuse his dictates. In exchange, she will agree not to publish any of her works.

"Independence?" he asked, reading what she'd written. "What, exactly, does that mean?"

She bit the end of the pen, considering the matter. "If I don't wish to eat a certain dish, you will not cause to have it served."

"Anything in particular?" he asked.

"Brains," she said without thinking. "Tripe. Anything featuring eyeballs."

"Agreed."

"You will treat me with respect."

He didn't say anything for a moment.

"What does that mean?" he finally asked.

She looked over at him. "Do I need to explain that, your lordship? I would think an earl of your reputed stature would know the meaning of respect."

He stood and walked away, intent on the window and the blackness beyond. Could he even see anything or did the window solely act as a mirror?

"You're a very annoying female. I trust you will not continue to be so after our marriage."

She put the pen down. "I'm very certain to be exactly the same way as I am now," she said.

He glanced at her.

"Are you always so honest?"

She thought about it then ruefully shook her head. "No, but I feel compelled to tell you the truth. Why shouldn't I? You'll discover it yourself soon enough."

He waved his hand toward her. "Very well, put your clause about respect in the blasted contract."

She waited until he returned to the chair beside the desk before continuing.

"I will have access to Huntly's library. You do have a library, do you not?"

He sat back, his eyes boiling once more. "You've never heard of Huntly's library? There's nothing more famous in all of Scotland."

She shook her head. "That's wonderful. See, that's an inducement for marriage right there."

He frowned at her.

"You will allow me the use of the library," she said. "Nor will you cavil at my purchase of books."

"What does that mean?"

"If I want to order a book from an Edinburgh bookseller, you will not argue with me about the expense."

"At least wait until you see if it's already in the library," he said.

"Agreed."

This next clause would be more difficult, she was certain of it.

When he looked at her, she warmed. Her body seemed to glow, heating in places that ached to be touched.

She needed some way to counteract his effect on her.

"If I do not want your attentions, I have the right to refuse them," she said, holding her pen over the document.

Did he notice her hands were trembling? If he did, did he care?

"No."

"No?" she asked, surprised.

"You have no right to refuse me. I am your husband."

"Not yet."

"Perhaps not ever," he said.

She placed the pen on the desk, sat back in Macrath's chair and looked at him.

"Your lordship, I would be just as happy unmarried as I would be married. I have no reason to want to marry you. You, on the other hand, have some reason to want to marry me."

He stared at her, holding her gaze as if he would mesmerize her.

She was, for the first time in her life, in a position of power, and recognized it. The sensation was indescribably wonderful.

She could stand and walk from the room without a second thought. Granted, she might be disappointed not to marry him, but not for the reasons he probably thought.

Wealth didn't concern her. Prestige didn't excite her. What she wanted from him were his kisses and his body, and although she'd been more than direct during this meeting, she didn't know how to say that to him.

"No," he said.

"Shall we compromise?" she asked, feeling magnanimous and recognizing the earl's stubbornness.

Evidently, she'd lighted upon something that was important to him.

"Three times," she said.

"I beg your pardon?"

"I can refuse you three times."

"In the course of our marriage?" he asked.

"No, in a month."

"No."

"Very well," she conceded. "Six months."

"No."

"Then a year?" she asked.

"Three times in one year?"

She nodded.

"I agree."

She wondered if she would ever want to use those three refusals. He was eminently kissable.

For example, she wanted to kiss him now. Lean over the desk and press her lips lightly against his to seal their bargain.

The urge to do so was so strong that she couldn't ignore it any longer. She put the pen down, stood, and before he could move, kissed him.

His lips were so soft they felt like pillows. Then they hardened as his hands reached up to hold her face still.

He stole her breath and made her heart race.

When she drew back, they looked at each other. His eyes were steam again, but not with anger. Passion bronzed his cheekbones.

"You will not bed any man but me."

Her eyes widened. "I beg your pardon?"

"This independence of yours. It won't consist of different bed partners."

"Isn't that in the wedding vows?"

"I'll have you put it in your contract."

She hadn't the slightest idea how to word that. She ended up writing: *both parties will be faithful, each to the other.*

Sitting back, she stared at the paper and cleared her throat.

"I'll make two copies," she said, "and we'll sign both. That way, each of us has a copy."

He didn't say anything, just kept looking at her in that heated way. If he didn't look away, they wouldn't have to wait until their wedding night to consummate the marriage.

Macrath's desk would do well enough.

"I don't need a copy."

"It's only fair that you get one."

"Finish that one and I'll sign it."

She nodded, wishing he wouldn't stare at her mouth so. She brushed her fingers over her bottom lip, still feeling his kiss.

Would she get any sleep tonight? Or would it simply be better to write another chapter of Lady Pamela's adventures? Perhaps she meets a brigand who robs her coach, and engages in a torrid kiss. Something that weakens her knees and heats her until she felt like she was melting inside.

He didn't move away as she wrote. Instead, he sat there watching her. His arm rested on the edge of the desk, his fingers lifting one by one. Each time they flexed her attention was caught.

At this rate she'd never be finished, and she wanted the contract to be precise, not filled with ink blotches.

She bit her lip, concentrating, wishing he'd go and sit on one of the chairs before the fireplace. Or stand at the window and watch the full moon. Anything but sit there so close she could smell the sandalwood soap he used.

Night had brought a shadow of a beard to his face. He no longer looked every inch the earl, but more a coach robber, someone who would march her out to the glen and kiss her until she fell to her knees.

He would show no mercy to her. Instead, he would make her beg.

"Please," she'd say, "don't kiss me again. I can't bear it."

"What is it you can't bear, my dear captive?" He'd leer at her, exposing perfect white teeth. "My kisses or the passion that courses through you?"

"Either, both, whatever you will," she said weakly, secretly wishing he'd cover her body with his kisses.

"Will you give me the book?" he asked.

She blinked at him, pulled back from the imaginary glen with difficulty. Her lips felt full and her eyelids heavy.

"What?"

His eyes narrowed. "Will you give me the book?" he asked again. "Consider it a wedding gift."

"Because you don't believe me?"

"Perhaps I want to read it again."

She shook her head. "No," she said. "I'll keep it."

His lips thinned but he didn't protest.

"I'm leaving early," he said, standing. "I'll say good-bye now."

Did she get a good-bye kiss? Would that be entirely proper? Or wise, for that matter? She could certainly see that kissing him farewell might be acceptable, but there was the matter of Macrath's desk.

Was every other woman in creation made weak by desire?

She wanted him, and although she'd written about desire—Lady Pamela was suffused by it often—she'd never understood that it could strip your senses from you. She was all throbbing parts and moist, hidden places.

She wanted her breasts kissed.

He would see her naked, and for the first time in her life she anticipated being as bare as a babe.

No, desire was a heady thing and not to be underestimated.

No wonder Lady Pamela had only to crook her finger and all manner of men followed. Donald was the only one who could do that to her.

The Earl of Gadsden was her Donald and had been from the very beginning.

"You haven't signed it," she said, pushing the paper toward him.

He grabbed the pen from her hand and scrawled his signature across the bottom.

"Are you certain you don't want a copy?"

"Yes."

He strode toward the door.

She liked watching him move. He really was a magnificent specimen of man.

Just think, he was going to be her husband. He was going to come to her room, to her bed. All those feelings she'd poured into Lady Pamela were going to be hers instead. She was going to tremble at his touch, scream in pleasure and delight.

No, she really wasn't going to sleep tonight, was she?

What sort of ravening beast was he?

He left Sinclair's library, standing with his back to the door, wanting to return, tumble her to the floor, kiss her until the damn urge left him and then bury himself in her.

She wasn't a virgin, no matter what Sinclair thought. No virgin would have sent him such a look, her chocolate brown eyes nearly melting with heat.

He was breathless with need, pained with it to the point that even walking was difficult.

She didn't know how close she came to be ravished, and he'd never ravished a woman in his life. Nor had he ever been tempted to, not until Ellice Traylor looked at him with wide eyes, caught her bottom lip with her teeth, and frowned down at the page in front of her.

Her chastity wasn't a problem as long as he didn't touch her until he was sure she wasn't with child. He owed it to the earldom to produce a legitimate male heir. His own celibacy wasn't the issue; he'd gone for months without bedding Cassandra.

He could do it again.

He could do it again as long as he didn't study Ellice too closely, read what she'd written, or engage her in conversation. He would be wise to ignore the shape of her lips as well.

Ellice waited until the morning before visiting with Mairi. She wasn't afraid of what Mairi would say. At least that's what she told herself. Mairi would fuss, she knew that much. The other woman might even accuse her of sublimating her own desires for that of a man. That would be partially true and an accusation for which she had no defense.

The truth, stark and unremitting, was that she very much wanted to marry the Earl of Gadsden. Oh, marriage itself wasn't that important. If she could have stolen away with him to a cottage in the woods, she would gladly have done that as well. But society being what it was—and her mother being like *she* was—there would simply be too many ramifications for that behavior.

She might as well marry if she was going to be a licentious creature.

She knocked on Mairi's sitting room door, surprised when it was answered by Logan, barely dressed.

Taking a step backward, she tried to keep her gaze away from his half unbuttoned shirt and that expanse of golden chest.

What would the earl look like naked?

Once she was no longer a virgin, she would be free of this surge of lust whenever she thought about him.

Logan smiled, called for Mairi, and stepped away.

She deliberately didn't look after him.

Had she called on them too early? They hadn't been at breakfast or she would have talked to Mairi then.

Had they been engaging in . . . her thoughts ground to a

halt at Mairi's appearance. Her friend's cheeks were flushed, her lips swollen.

Dear God, had she interrupted them? Please don't let her have come at the wrong time. Perhaps they'd already made love and that glow was how a woman looked afterward. She made a mental note to give Lady Pamela the same rosy glow and lambent look in the eyes.

"I'm sorry," she said.

What did one say in such a situation? The etiquette books never seemed to mention a circumstance such as this. What about her mother? Enid was penning a book on polite manners. Perhaps she should ask her.

She swallowed a giggle at that thought.

"You wanted to see me?" Mairi asked, frowning.

"Yes, I'm sorry." She decided to come out and say it. "I won't be publishing my book," she said, "and I wanted you to know."

"You've changed your mind?"

"Yes."

"Why?"

"I just have," she said, hoping Mairi didn't take the question further. But this was Mairi, after all, and once she was intent on a matter she was like a hound after a rabbit.

"Come in," she said, stepping aside.

Ellice really didn't want to enter their sitting room, especially since it was obvious to her now that they'd just finished doing . . . what did one call it? In *The Lustful Adventures of Lady Pamela* she'd called it sex, making love, rogering, and in one passage, tossing her skirts over her head. None of those descriptions seemed apt at the moment.

"I can't stay," she said, almost feverishly. "I must go. I just wanted you to know."

"Are you all right, Ellice?"

"Yes," she said. "Yes, I am."

"Are you certain you wish to be married? Is that something you want, Ellice?"

At Mairi's frown, she felt a surge of disappointment. Why wasn't Mairi happy for her? Or perhaps Mairi only saw it as coercion. She mustn't think that.

"Yes, it is. I made him sign a contract," she added. "It promises me independence."

"Have you?"

"In exchange, I won't publish the book."

"Are you very certain this is what you want, Ellice?"

She nodded. "The wedding will be in three weeks. You will attend, won't you?"

"I wouldn't miss it," Mairi said.

Ellice stepped back. "Thank you." There, that was done. Now all she had to do was escape.

"Is she that innocent?" Logan asked, coming to stand beside her.

Mairi frowned, watching as Ellice nearly raced down the corridor to her own set of rooms.

"I wouldn't think so, not with the book she wrote, but she seems to be, doesn't she?"

"Perhaps naive is the word I'd use."

"And impulsive," Mairi said. "That can be a rather dangerous combination."

"Being impulsive seems to run in the family," Logan said, smiling at her.

"We're not related," she said, "but I know what you mean." She frowned. "I hope she realizes that no contract in the world will guarantee her independence."

"Women have a way of getting what they want," he said, nuzzling her neck.

She laughed, swatted at him with one hand while she wrapped the other around his neck.

"Then I hope that Ellice learns that lesson as quickly as she can."

Logan drew back. "Pity the Earl of Gadsden if she learns it as well as you."

Laughter filled the room.

Chapter 17

Macrath and Virginia were fighting.

Or perhaps it would be fairer to say that Virginia was all for fighting but Macrath was being stoic.

The situation was so odd that all of them were speechless, watching as Virginia stormed down Drumvagen's curved staircase, her maid Hannah following.

The children, Virginia had announced a few minutes earlier, were going to remain at Drumvagen for the two days they would be gone. Brianag was going to supervise their care and act as lady of the manor, if Ellice had her guess.

Macrath was standing in front of the door, refusing to move.

"You aren't going."

"Of course I'm going," Virginia said, halting in the middle of the stairs and sending a barbed look toward her husband. "Ellice is getting married at Huntly. I wouldn't miss it."

"You nearly died."

"I didn't nearly die. You've been listening to Brianag." As if the woman had been waiting offstage for her name to be announced, the housekeeper strolled into the massive foyer.

"Very well," Virginia amended, "perhaps it was a difficult birth and unexpected, but it's been weeks, Macrath."

"You're not well enough."

Virginia blew out a breath. "Of course I am, Macrath. I'm well enough to take strolls around Drumvagen. I'm well enough to walk to the village. I'm well enough to spend the night walking Carlton when he's fussy."

She frowned at him. "Nothing, not even you, is going to keep me from Ellice's wedding, Macrath."

"It's nearly four hours by coach."

She raised her eyes heavenward. "During which I shall be sitting, you foolish man. Would you keep me wrapped in bunting?"

"I would do anything to protect you."

Virginia's eyes softened. She came down the rest of the way, stepping into Macrath's arms. In full view of the rest of them, she kissed him. Not the kiss of an invalid, or a mother, but the kiss of a passionate woman deeply in love.

When they parted, he looked down at her.

"You're not going to relent, are you?"

She shook her head.

"You're not going to listen?"

She shook her head again.

"Nothing I can say will change your mind?"

"Anything you say is important to me, Macrath."

"If I told you I would worry less, would you still insist on coming?"

She smiled at him. "Yes, because you really would rather I stay in my room, take my meals from trays, and be protected from the world."

"I nearly lost you, Virginia."

"Oh, Macrath." She put her hand on his cheek. "I'm truly well, my darling."

He looked past her to where the rest of them were standing. Mairi, Logan, Enid, and Ellice returned his look. Did he know that they were all on Virginia's side in this matter? It seemed he did from the sigh that left him.

Turning to Brianag, he said, "Keep my children safe."

"Dinna get up to high doh," she said in return.

Ellice rolled her eyes. Half the time she didn't understand the housekeeper, and today was no exception.

An hour later they were off, Logan and Mairi traveling in their own carriage and Virginia and Macrath in one of the Drumvagen vehicles. Ellice and her mother took pride of place at the head of the line, almost as if they led a funeral cortege.

Instead of a rolling catafalque following them, however, there was a wagon containing Ellice's clothes, her collection of books, even her grandmother's lace doilies, a present from her mother and one she didn't know how to refuse.

Evidently, she was going to her bridegroom with all her earthly possessions, since her rooms were now bare. She couldn't rid herself of the notion that she'd been banished from Drumvagen, as if the house knew she'd been critical of it.

She wished she could have traveled with anyone else. Her mother was going to take this opportunity to lecture her on how to be a good wife, how to be a good manager of staff, how to be a good countess. Enid considered herself the arbiter of all things great and good, and the four hours to reach Huntly would be endless.

Ellice had already been informed that being a Scottish countess did not rank as high as being an English one, so despite the fact that her mother had been pushed back to being a Dowager Countess, she still outranked her, or so Enid insisted.

The only way she would have outranked her mother was to marry a duke. Then, no doubt, Enid would have claimed that a Scottish duke was no more important than an English earl.

One way or another, her mother was always going to be more important.

How odd to find some measure of compassion for Brianag.

"This house of his is supposed to be large and imposing," Enid said with a sniff. "I've heard of it, of course, but I doubt it's the equal of some of our grand homes in England."

Her mother always made the demarcation between Scotland and England, no matter that they were supposed to be one country. Brianag did the same. Ellice had made the mistake of saying something like that to Brianag once. For weeks afterward there was a foul smell in her room that she couldn't locate, almost as if a dead fish had been placed beneath a floorboard.

At least she would no longer have to see the housekeeper every day. Only on visits, if she were allowed to make any back to Drumvagen.

Huntly was outside of Edinburgh, between the city and Drumvagen, close enough that she could easily visit any number of shops if she wished, or even go see Mairi and Logan. She would very much like to do that, as well as renew her acquaintance with Fenella, Mairi and Macrath's cousin. The woman had married the previous spring and was with child.

In the normal course of things, she would be a mother. She might give birth to numerous children until Huntly was a home as filled with raucous laughter as Drumvagen.

She and the earl would be parents.

Would they have a marriage as distant as her own mother and father? Or one as close and warm as Virginia and Macrath, Mairi and Logan?

"Did you love my father?" she asked, turning her head to survey her mother.

Enid's eyes widened.

Had she broken every rule of polite behavior by asking? Today might be the very last opportunity she had to ask. Besides, after today her mother couldn't march into her room to criticize her for another failing. Nor could she hold Eudora up as a paragon of all the virtues. An angel who, no doubt, was instructing the angels on being angelic.

"It's because it's your wedding day, of course, Ellice. You would be thinking of such things."

"Did you?"

"Love isn't important, child. Not when so many other things are pressing."

What could be more important than love? She didn't ask the question, but her mother answered nonetheless.

"Family," Enid said. "Connections. The future. Respect. Honor."

She'd never thought her mother all that fond of family. She avoided their cousin who'd inherited Lawrence's title and entailed estates. She always seemed surprised that Ellice was her daughter. As for the rest, she didn't know what connections meant. The future? The continuation of the line, perhaps, something that Lawrence hadn't cared about. Respect and honor? That was the answer to her question.

Her mother hadn't loved her father. She had honored him by wearing mourning from the day he died until now. Perhaps she respected him by never challenging his dictates, by accepting his rules.

Didn't she ever want to feel love?

No, that was certainly not a question she was going to ask.

But she did skirt the edge of it when she said, "How can a woman live with a man without loving him?"

Her mother smiled. "You have a great deal to learn of the world, Ellice."

She turned back to the scenery, wondering if she truly did. Or was that simply her mother's way of waving her hand in the air and dismissing all the uncomfortable thoughts her question summoned?

Perhaps it had to do with how you defined love. She wanted a passionate romance like those she'd been around at Drumvagen. She wanted to look across the room, see her husband, and feel her cheeks warm. She wanted to rise late because she'd been bedded. Or not attend a function, in favor of fevered lovemaking with her husband.

Could she accept another brand of love, that of friendship? If she could laugh with her husband, tell him stories of her day and have him want to listen to her, that might be enough. If what they felt for each other in their bed wasn't as torrid as she wished, she would allow her imagination freedom in her writing.

Or was love simply defined as acceptance? Was she to see her place in life as the wife of the Earl of Gadsden and come to realize that caring for her and giving her a home was an example of his kind affection for her?

What balderdash.

She couldn't imagine ever thinking of the earl as simply a friend. Yes, they might come to like each other, to share themselves, to care about one another. But sparks flow when they were inches apart, and the world exploded in a bright sizzling light when they kissed.

How could their lovemaking be anything less than wondrous?

Or would they only feel passion without affection?

Lady Pamela had felt that before meeting Donald. She'd known her share of conquests, men who wanted physical pleasure above all. Those men cared nothing for her thoughts, for her wishes or dreams. A pair of upturned breasts, silken thighs, a bottom they stroked with their hands—Pamela was wanted, but as parts, never a whole.

She couldn't allow the earl to think of her in such a way.

Her thoughts trailed away as she became aware of the silence in the carriage. Her mother was never silent.

She turned to find Enid staring out the carriage window, her mouth agape.

Ellice looked beyond her to what had captured her attention.

"Is that Huntly?" she asked, the words pushed past the constriction in her throat.

"I believe it is," her mother said. Nothing more was forthcoming. No criticism or remark about how Huntly was not as grand as some of the houses in England.

Ross was wrong. She'd never imagined anything remotely like Huntly. The house wasn't just one building, but a series of connected structures, each the size of Drumvagen.

The framework was a C, the main building comprising the backbone of the letter. Two sprawling towered buildings were at either end of the C and connected by curved wings. A massive cobbled courtyard lay in between, a pattern laid out in the bricks.

Greeting the visitor was an impressive domed building fronted by ionic columns. Behind the house, and visible because of the elevation of the road they were on, was a large circular lake flanked by woods. They might be close to Edinburgh, but the impression was of an estate—a palace—in the middle of the country.

A palace waiting for a princess, and she was as far from a princess as anyone could possibly be.

"Stop the carriage," she said.

Her mother glanced in her direction but ignored her. Since her mother normally ignored her, Ellice simply said it again. "Stop the carriage."

"Don't be foolish, child."

"I'm not being foolish," she said, panic nearly swamping her. "I can't live there."

"Of course you can."

No, she really couldn't.

She'd heard people talking about Huntly, but why hadn't they said more?

She'd thought Huntly was the size of Drumvagen, something large but manageable. Not once had she considered that the Earl of Gadsden would be as wealthy as a pasha, ensconced in his palace.

No, she couldn't possibly marry him.

"I'll tend the children," she said. "Virginia will never have to employ a governess. I'll teach them. I'm good at reading and writing."

"What has gotten into you?"

"I'll scrub the floors. I'll work for Brianag. I'll even do the laundry."

Her mother reached over and patted two fingers against her cheek. "Don't be foolish, Ellice."

She'd go to Mairi and tell her that she'd changed her mind. Publish *The Lustful Adventures of Lady Pamela* far and wide. With any luck the book would be a success and she'd be able to live on her own, with maybe one maid and a cook, since she hadn't the slightest idea how to cook. Bread and jam wouldn't be substantial enough to live on day after day.

"Eudora would know how to handle the situation. Your sister would have been poised right now, not a silly girl uttering nonsense."

That was hardly fair.

Eudora would never have found herself in this situation. If the earl had offered for Eudora, it was because he wanted a porcelain statue for a wife, not because he'd nearly taken advantage of her.

However much her mother wished it, Eudora had not been a saint. Nor had she been given to physical demonstrations of affection. She didn't like to be touched, and the idea of marriage—as she once said—seemed distasteful to her.

While Ellice had not only imagined her downfall with great gusto but chronicled it as Lady Pamela.

Perhaps her mother should read her book. Then she'd know exactly who she was and how different she was from Eudora.

Her mother wasn't going to help. Nor was she going to utter reassurances.

You'll do fine, my child. You're the equal of this place and that man. You're a Traylor and can acquit yourself well to any situation.

No, she wouldn't say any of that.

Lady Pamela would have sailed out of the carriage, removed her gloves, looked Huntly up and down as if it barely met her expectations and addressed the majordomo. *Have my bags brought to my quarters. I'd like to be shown them, please, before meeting with the earl.*

She would want, of course, to be at her very best before seeing the man who offered her a palace in exchange for her presence in his bed.

That thought brought Ellice up short.

He'd nearly ravished her. She'd nearly ravished him.

Wasn't that the most important thing? Not how large and imposing Huntly was or the extent of his wealth. No, the man she kissed hadn't been the owner of an estate as much as a man with talented lips, who murmured promises against her ear, kissed her throat, and had her sighing in bliss.

She would think of him and only him. Not this surprising home that terrified her.

Ross sat in the library of his home, intent on chores he'd given himself before his bride arrived.

Huntly's library was a masterpiece of design, crafted by the second Earl of Gadsden.

When approaching Huntly, the library was to the left, a separate building attached to the main structure by a curved wing. Square, with an octagonal cupola, it had two floors, the second accessible by a intricate wrought-iron staircase.

Except for the staircase, the building was identical to the

one his mother occupied on the other side of the courtyard. Huntly's architect had a penchant for order and balance. If there was a columned entrance on one side of the ballroom, it was duplicated on the other side. The double doors leading to his suite in the family quarters were matched by the double doors of the countess's suite.

Even the floor was marked off in geometric perfection, the tile patterned to lead the eye to several sections inlaid to appear like stained glass, their theme the flowers that grew in Huntly's gardens.

The walls were covered in crimson silk. On the far wall, opposite the window, were a dozen paintings, each one framed in gold.

The window behind his desk gave him a view of the land he'd inherited: perfectly manicured lawns giving way to woods, rolling hills, and the river in the distance. Nearer the house, the third Earl of Gadsden had dammed a tributary, creating a lake fed by dual waterfalls.

From where he sat he couldn't see the rest of Huntly, but it was in his mind's eye, just as it had been from the moment he realized it was going to be his.

He was simply one more in a long line of men whose duty was to care for and guard their home. Not a glen or a mountain, but a structure built by men who were experts in their fields. One look at the plaster carvings on the ceiling and you knew you were in the company of an artist. Studying the perfection of a brick wall made you realize the skill of the masons. The stained glass had taken months to finish, each step done with care and talent.

Huntly's order suited him, eased him, made him feel as if the chaos of his personal life was transitory, measured against the perfection of his heritage.

Each time he entered the library he felt a surge of joy, not for his possessions as much as his good fortune. Even deep in his studies or investigations, he never failed to appreciate exactly where and who he was.

He was petitioned throughout the day for this or that. If his farm manager didn't need to see him, the gillie did. He met with his majordomo daily, as well as the housekeeper since his mother had abdicated any responsibility for Huntly. He approved bills, discussed economies, allowed hunting on part of his land and fishing in the river.

Standing, he stretched, went to the window and admired the view of the lake.

The trees around the perimeter needed to be trimmed this spring. An army of gardeners worked at Huntly, their role a simple one. Keep the magnificent estate looking that way. No leaf should be out of place. No tree should be unpruned. The gardens should be blowsy with flowers, all the topiary animals kept manicured.

Those travelers on the road stretching through the glen should be able to glance toward Huntly and be in awe.

He was only the steward for Huntly, the role he'd been reared to perform since childhood. Was that why his father never remained long at the house? Because he knew that Huntly wasn't truly his home but more a responsibility?

His father had managed to escape the duties of his office due to the work of Melrose Bishop, a factor who'd retired a few years ago. Without his tireless work when Ross was a boy and his father out trying to populate Scotland, Huntly would have probably been in disrepair. As it was, the three-hundred-year-old house was as perfect as man could make it.

Ross didn't employ a secretary simply because he enjoyed the minutia of his life. He wanted to know everything there was to know about Huntly, the farms, the properties he owned. Besides, a secretary would have been a distraction. He already had enough of those.

"It's almost time, Ross."

He glanced at the door as his mother entered the room.

Tall and slender, she was dressed for his wedding in a dark blue dress, the bell-shaped skirt so wide she could rest her arms at her hips. A gold broach adorned with pearls was at her neck, and pearls dangled from her ears.

Although of middle years, she was attractive, her black hair untouched by gray, the glint in her blue eyes hinting at a woman of a much younger age.

For the last five years, she'd occupied the building opposite the library, on the other side of the cobbled courtyard.

The Countess of Gadsden had the entire structure to herself, and she filled it with every sort of excess. She considered herself a collector. Jeweled reticules, gloves of all lengths and types of fabric, bonnets and headdresses, shoes of every fashion and country of origin—all these occupied every spare inch of space.

The last time he saw her home, he'd been overwhelmed by the clutter.

His majordomo had informed him last month that she was now acquiring kilts, arranging them on straw figures in the upstairs drawing room.

His father had settled a substantial sum of money on her during their marriage. Ross often wondered if it paid for her silence. Or if her collecting had eased any pain she might have felt about her husband's indiscretions.

Since she didn't draw from the Forster coffers for her acquisitions, there was nothing he could do.

He heard the rumble of wheels and glanced out the window overlooking the courtyard. Instead of the contingent from Drumvagen, it was a wagon, emblazoned with MCMAHON'S EMPORIUM on the side in red and gold letters.

His mother's face changed, her smile broadening.

"Ross—" she began, but he forestalled her.

"Brass andirons in the shape of horses, Mother? Or Egyptian headdresses?"

"Oh, I don't know, Ross. Isn't that the fun of it?"

He wouldn't know, not having a penchant for buying things unseen as she did.

She looked at the wagon, then at him, then back at the wagon.

"You'll try to be there when Lady Ellice arrives?" he asked.

"Of course," she said, her smile broadening.

Without another word, she left him. In moments, he saw her swiftly crossing the courtyard.

Twenty minutes later four carriages from Drumvagen arrived. He moved to stand in the same spot he had when Cassandra had come to Huntly.

He'd been a boy then, or as much as he'd ever been one. His hands had trembled and his stomach clenched.

Today he was no longer that boy but he still felt mildly ill at ease. His chest was oddly hollow, the sound of his heart beating too loud.

What would Ellice think of his home? Cassandra had known all about Huntly, of course. He'd later thought it was half the reason she'd married him. His family's wealth had been a quarter. And the remainder? He'd often wondered.

At least the fourth Earl of Gadsden wasn't standing on the steps beside him, but neither was his mother. Evidently, whatever she'd purchased had taken precedence over good manners.

Two footmen, both dressed in Huntly livery, strode to the carriage. One footman stood just beyond the door to extend his arm to help Ellice exit, the other opened the carriage door.

There, a foot. Now the hem of her dress.

She looked up then, her eyes finding him as if she knew he'd be standing there. She took the footman's assistance, stepping down onto the cobbled courtyard.

Not once did she look away from him.

Her eyes were on him all the way across the expanse of

courtyard and up the steps. She didn't pay attention to her mother, who had also exited the carriage, or the others, who had begun to disembark as well. She did not look around her and seemed unimpressed by the magnificence of Huntly. Instead, her gaze was for him alone.

He felt his heart stutter.

"Lady Ellice," he said, stepping forward and extending his hand. "You've made the journey safely, I see."

She wasn't carrying a reticule and was simply dressed. Her pale blue dress was adorned with embroidered flowers, little touches of decoration that made him wonder if she did needlework, before he remembered. She'd stuck herself badly when sewing the bags during the flood.

Perhaps her mother had done the embroidery, but then, he couldn't see the Countess of Barrett focused on such a task. She would spend her time in more ambitious pursuits, like most of the mothers of females he'd met in Edinburgh and London.

Cassandra's mother still claimed a relationship with him, stating that he was her "dear beloved Cassandra's sweet husband." He had no doubt that the woman knew the entire story, and the charade she played had a mercenary cause.

Ellice clasped his hand and he wondered at the chill he could feel through her gloves.

"It was short in one way and interminable in the other," she said, not looking away from him.

He found himself caught in the warmth of her eyes.

"Why was it long?" he asked. "Was the journey difficult?"

"My mother insisted on lecturing me about all my many duties."

"Did she?" he asked, ignoring the rest of his guests, now milling in the courtyard. He was being rude, but was too intrigued by his bride to look away.

"I am to be docile," she said. "And conformable. I'm to

pay attention to everything you say as if you're the wisest man on earth. I'm never to disagree with you. Or challenge any assumptions you might make, even if they're glaringly wrong."

The last was said with a roll of her eyes.

He smiled. "I take it you won't be that kind of wife."

She sighed. "I don't see how I could," she said. "Are you to be applauded for drawing breath just because you're male? Is everything you say simply precious because you're a man?"

"I don't believe so, no. On the same front, however, are you to be treated with cotton wool because you're a woman? Should you be protected from life itself because you're too fragile?"

She blinked at him. "I shouldn't think so. It's never been my experience that women are treated that way."

"Good," he said, taking her hand, placing it on his arm and turning to the rest of his guests.

She studied him as if she found him more fascinating than Huntly, the first time anyone had ever done so. She didn't exclaim in wonder over the marble steps or the gilt adorning the tower spires. She didn't ask about the stained glass in the dome or inquire as to the architect or how long the house took to complete.

She simply watched him.

He greeted the others with the first real smile he'd felt for days.

Chapter 18

Huntly had a guest wing, an entire wing set aside for nothing but guests.

"But it's not as if we have all that many visitors nowadays, Lady Ellice," the maid said, curtsying once more. "The housekeeper tells stories of how there used to be balls and things here at Huntly and hundreds of people staying for a week or two."

Her mother and the others had been whisked away to their quarters by the housekeeper, a short older woman with graying hair and a sweet smile. She didn't glower at Ellice. Nor did she issue pronouncements in a near unintelligible Scottish accent or threaten things under her breath.

Instead, she'd introduced a bright-faced young maid with a gap-toothed smile, glorious red, curly hair, and green eyes.

"It's a great privilege to serve you, Lady Ellice," the girl said. "I'm Pegeen. My mother was Irish and my father a Scot. I've twice the Celt, my mother always says."

She curtsied again, then opened the door to admit a series of footmen with Ellice's trunks. The girl smiled at each man and thanked him softly.

"Begging your pardon, miss, but have you no maid of your own?"

She shook her head.

The girl's eyes widened. "Now, that's a surprise," she said. "Here I was thinking you'd come with as many servants as the first countess."

"Did you know the first countess?"

If it was possible to turn someone to ice with just words, she'd just accomplished it.

Pegeen stared at her, too much white showing in her eyes.

"I shouldn't have mentioned her, Lady Ellice. No one said you didn't know."

"Of course I knew," she said. "You're speaking of Cassandra."

The girl sagged, shoulders slumping. "Yes, Lady Ellice. Of course, no one called her that. Except for the earl, I mean."

The girl's face took on a rosy color.

"And here I am, talking too much. I never talk too much, miss. Not really."

"It's all right," Ellice said. "You're probably nervous. So am I."

She looked around the sitting room, with its corbeled ceiling painted with a scene of clouds and rosy-cheeked, diaphanous clad damsels smiling down. The two settees in front of the fireplace were upholstered in a deep blue that matched the striped wallpaper of ivory and blue. Three-foot-high porcelain urns sat on either side of a gilt-etched white marble fireplace.

The mahogany tables were waxed to a sheen, the air laden with the scent of lemon oil and rose petals.

Three windows draped in blue velvet overlooked the broad lawn and beyond to the woods she'd seen from the carriage. The view alone was something out of a painting, a creation that could have been entitled: Bucolic Scene in a Fairy Tale.

The room was large enough to hold an assembly, perhaps even a ball. She doubted that she'd ever curl up in one of those settees, light the lamp on the table, and spend the evening reading.

The room was too beautiful, too large, and simply too much.

"I take it these are the countess's rooms?"

"Yes, miss," the girl said.

Have you anything smaller? Something more intimate? Something that doesn't scare me to death?

What would the poor girl do if she said that? No doubt scurry off the housekeeper, afraid she'd lose her job.

Ellice kept silent, following Pegeen as she went to the side of the room, opening double doors to reveal the bedchamber.

This was even worse.

A massive four-poster easily double the size of her bed at Drumvagen stood on a dais on the opposite wall. She could run and dance and skip to the bed and it would take her a matter of minutes to get there.

Why must one room be so large?

A secretary sat along one wall, looking small and curiously out of place.

"His lordship had it moved here," Pegeen said. "He had the armoires moved to your dressing room."

"Dressing room?" she asked, feeling a surge of warmth about the addition of the desk.

A moment later she stood in front of another set of double doors. When Pegeen pushed them open, Ellice gaped at the contents. Four armoires sat there, two facing two, with a vanity and dressing table between them at the far end of the room. The wall was mirrored. Not simply a gilt-etched mirror but the entire wall.

Had Cassandra been so concerned about her appearance?

"Did you know the first countess?" she asked.

"Me?" Pegeen shook her head. "No, miss. She was gone before I came to Huntly. But I've heard stories of her every day since. She liked the color yellow, I understand. It flattered her blond hair. Her eyes were blue, but not a normal blue. Someone said they looked like the sea just after a storm, kind of blue and green mixed together."

Her hair was brown.

Her eyes were brown.

She could just imagine the stories told about her. Oh, the second countess? Brown, she was, just like the color of earth after a storm. You know, when you're turning clods of it beneath a plow.

What was she doing here?

She should find the stables, bid one of the coachmen take her back to Drumvagen posthaste, please. No, not there. Her mother would find her and she'd be returned to this palace where it was so obvious she didn't belong. Even Pegeen, evidently a sweet girl, was looking at her in confusion.

She'd never use the dressing room in a thousand years. She wasn't so enamored of her brown looks that she'd stare into the mirror, enchanted.

Pegeen suddenly dipped into a curtsy. Before she could tell the girl that such obeisance wasn't necessary, a voice said, "I thought they might have brought you here. Forgive my rudeness. I should have been at the door to greet you but they were delivering a new shipment of tartan and I wanted to see if they'd finally gotten the red and black I wanted."

Before she could completely turn, Ellice was enveloped in a powdery, perfumed hug.

A moment later she was released to find her assailant smiling at her.

The woman was tall and slender, dressed in a glaringly pink silk dress with panniers. To complete the look, she was wearing a powdered wig adorned with a chain of pearls.

The stranger looked as if she had stepped out of a book on Versailles.

"My dear girl, how overwhelming everything must be for

you. I felt the same when I first came to Huntly all those years ago. It seems like a palace, doesn't it?"

She nodded.

"And you've no idea who I am, of course," she said, her smile broadening. "I'm Ross's mother and soon to be yours."

Not one word came to mind.

"I have my own home," the countess said, pointing toward the window. "You must come and visit, after the honeymoon, of course. But I did want to greet you, however tardily."

"Thank you." There, proof that she could talk, after all.

The other woman laughed. "You must think I've lost my senses, my dear. A selection of costumes arrived today and I just had to don one. I've been of a mind to have a masked ball at Huntly to welcome you."

Ellice blinked at the countess.

"Doesn't that sound delightful?"

She pasted a smile on her face even though she couldn't imagine a worse idea. A ball? She was going to be a hostess for a ball? She could barely dance. No, she couldn't dance. She was clumsy. Nor did she hold any fondness for dancing. Her hands got damp and her toes turned numb.

"Now I must leave you, my dear, and dress for the wedding. Ross is all for having the ceremony as soon as possible. Is there a reason for such haste?" Her soon to be mother-in-law stared at her stomach.

"No," she said, clasping her hands over her waist.

"Oh, well, there's time. But not too much," the countess added, wiggling a finger in front of Ellice.

Once again she was rendered mute.

She could only stare as the countess edged sideways out the dressing room door.

Ellice's breath was tight, her stomach cramping, and she felt curiously dizzy.

She followed the candlelight procession of twelve pipers to a building set on a knoll overlooking the river. Evidently, when the Earls of Gadsden wed, the pipers played.

Even if the earl married an English girl?

She hadn't asked that question and now it seemed a huge oversight.

Some of the great homes of England had a private chapel. Huntly had a cathedral, complete with buttresses, a soaring ceiling, and stained-glass windows now dark against the night. When light flooded them, they would no doubt be as magnificent as the rest of her new home.

The only thing out of place was her.

The broad oak doors were flung open and someone intoned something in Gaelic, a greeting tantamount to a welcome to the family.

Thank heavens she wasn't required to respond. She didn't think she could speak.

The pipers parted, their skirling music accompanying her entrance. Her family was seated to the left of the aisle while the right was filled with what she thought were Ross's guests. But then Pegeen smiled at her and she revised her assumption. Perhaps the crowd was made up of Huntly's staff.

The Gadsden crest was emblazoned in blue and green on a wall hanging beside the altar—as if the Forster family took second place only to God.

According to Pegeen, the crypt was located to the right and was where the previous earls and their countesses had been laid to rest. Not for them the cold earth of Scotland. Instead, they had fitted space in the east wall, each crypt adorned with a brass plaque.

Did Cassandra's ghost waft from its resting place to stand there watching her? Did she resent the presence of the living or did she simply recall her own wedding?

How had Cassandra died? A strange question to ask in the

middle of her wedding. Even odder that she hadn't considered it before now.

Had she died in childbirth as Virginia almost had? Or had it been an accident of some sort? Had she been killed riding, taking a hedge at breakneck speed, as reckless as Lady Pamela?

Did Ross mourn her still? Was he remembering the glorious Cassandra right at this moment?

What a pair they must have made. She, so beautiful, and he, as handsome as any man Ellice had ever seen, especially now.

He was dressed in a dark blue and black kilt topped with a black jacket. He was staring straight at her as if to summon her with his gaze.

What other choice had she but to continue walking toward the altar?

At her arrival at Huntly, she'd pretended to be Lady Pamela. Perhaps it wouldn't be amiss to do the same now.

What would Lady Pamela do? She would smile. There, she could do that well enough. She would hold the Book of Common Prayer between hands that were dry, not damp and trembling.

She wouldn't feel as if she were going to be sick any minute.

Ross's eyes were silver in the candlelight. They sparkled at her as she neared him. Behind her the pipers still played.

Lady Pamela would smile and approach him, hand off her prayer book to someone standing behind her, turn and place her hand on Ross's arm, all without a trace of fear.

She managed most of it but she couldn't banish the trembling.

When it came time for her to recite her vows, she did so in a firm, clear voice. No one was more surprised than she. Evidently, she had more Lady Pamela in her than she realized.

She signed her name in a passable rendition of her usual

signature, stepped back and accepted the congratulations from her family and her new mother-in-law.

Her mother frowned at the woman, but all her mother-in-law did was smile back at Enid.

There was a battle brewing there, but that wasn't entirely unexpected.

Ellice, with an incipient headache, a feeling of unreality, and a desperate desire to maintain her composure, was escorted back to Huntly and into a massive dining room by her new husband.

He was a man she didn't know, a man who intrigued her, charmed her, and excited her, but still a stranger, and one who would soon climb into bed with her.

She didn't know if what she was feeling was terror or excitement.

Ross had the curious feeling of déjà vu as he walked into the dining room with his bride at his side. A few years ago he'd been a new bridegroom, but it was Cassandra who accompanied him then.

His father and mother had welcomed them along with Cassandra's large family.

A strange thing, to think of her with fondness now. The girl she'd been, innocent and artless, had been replaced in his memories by another woman, one who was so desperately in love she was willing to shock the world.

This time he was determined to be wiser. This time, if any suspicions arose, he wouldn't shut them off. This time he'd be certain of the woman he called his wife.

Certain was not a word he would use in conjunction with Ellice.

She confused him to the point that he wondered if she did it deliberately. One moment she was a bright-eyed beauty with a mouth that lured him. The next, she was a fragile-looking female with hunched shoulders and downcast eyes.

Which one was she, truly?

Ellice had trembled during the ceremony, reminding him of a leaf in a gale. She bit her lips and took deep breaths as if mustering her courage.

Twice, she looked as if she were about to faint. He'd put his hand over her cold one, smiled into her eyes, and she responded with the helpless glazed look of a dying fawn.

If he didn't know better, he would have thought Ellice Traylor Forster, Countess of Gadsden, was a virgin. A terrified virgin, one who kept shooting wide-eyed glances in his direction. Her laughing brown eyes were filled with fear. Her easy smile had vanished, replaced by lips thinned in nervousness.

The Ellice he'd come to know had disappeared again.

Perhaps it was better if she stayed gone for a while.

He found himself wanting to reassure her somehow, to tell her that he had no intention of bedding her until he could ensure that she wasn't with child. His heir must be his and there mustn't be any doubt about it.

Instead, he remained silent and escorted her to the place of honor at the table. Their guests stood, waiting for her.

"You have to sit," he said, whispering to her.

She shot a panicked glance down the table and nodded.

Her mother frowned at her, and he suddenly wanted to shield her from the woman's disapproval. His own mother was smiling at Ellice. No doubt she considered his marriage a sign of progress, an indication he was able to put Cassandra and her betrayal behind him.

He'd forgiven Cassandra. He couldn't forgive her lover. Not yet and perhaps not ever.

Ellice finally sat, and he lifted a hand in a signal that the meal should begin.

The dining room was suddenly filled with servants bearing trays of steaming meats and vegetables, tureens of turtle soup, and platters of salmon in dill sauce.

He turned to Ellice, to find her staring down at the wineglass now being filled.

Reaching over, he placed his hand over hers.

She jerked, turning to stare at him.

If he hadn't been so conscious of the glances of the others, he would have leaned over and whispered something reassuring to her. Or perhaps he would have teased her, asked why she looked so uncomfortable when he knew for certain that she wasn't a virgin.

Certain—there was that word again.

Was she dreading the night to come? Or simply this dinner in front of her family? Did she regret their marriage?

Withdrawing his hand, he smiled down the table, made a comment about the duck to Sinclair, and asked Logan Harrison a question about Edinburgh.

All in all they weren't a large group. He hadn't invited any friends to attend, simply due to the nature of the ceremony. This wasn't a love match. Nor was it an arranged union as his marriage to Cassandra had been. This was an attempt to prevent a scandal, no more or less.

Why, then, was he feeling like a villain?

Chapter 19

"**A**re you certain you understand, Ellice?"

Ellice folded her hands together on her lap, stared at the blue and white carpet beneath her slippered feet and nodded.

Her mother's heavy French perfume was making her nauseous. Or maybe it was simply this meeting her mother had insisted on, one she'd dreaded.

"I understand," she said.

"I know such frank talk can be embarrassing, but no daughter of mine will meet her husband ignorant of her duties. A man does not require much to be excited to that state. A glimpse of your breast or bottom will be sufficient that he is able to perform."

Dear God, please silence my mother. Do something.

God ignored her.

"You must indulge in the act as often as he wishes. You must submit, my child. That's what men want."

She could only say a hurried prayer of thanksgiving that her mother hadn't yet read her book.

Lady Pamela knew that submission was the last thing men wanted.

Her mother sighed. "I've thought of this conversation a great deal, my child. I always thought I would give advice to Eudora first."

Thankfully, her mother seemed to have forgotten the carnal nature of *The Lustful Adventures of Lady Pamela.*

"Can you not feel your sister near? I can and have all day."

All she'd been able to think of was her own anxiety. Huntly was a behemoth; the wedding ceremony had been an awe-inspiring event even on such short notice, and the dinner following had been fit for royalty.

How could she possibly be the Countess of Gadsden?

"She would have fit in well here, don't you agree?" Enid asked, looking around the sitting room.

As opposed to her, who was a poor substitute for the lovely Eudora?

Eudora would have been proper, wouldn't she? She wouldn't have been overwhelmed by Huntly. She would have been a regal countess. Perhaps she would have been majestic in her greeting of her bridegroom. When her husband entered, she would open her wrapper and give him a glimpse of the curve of her breast. She might even have bent over and let him look at her bottom.

Everything else would have been done in the darkness. She would have lain still and proper and silent, obeying her mother's dictates to the letter.

Ellice was tempted to ask her mother if a woman was not supposed to feel passion. If she was brave enough to do that, Enid's eyes would widen. Her face would take on a rosy hue and she would be rendered speechless.

Or worse, Enid would harangue her for hours about her lack of decorum, her demeanor, and the fact she wasn't Eudora.

She wished Virginia and Mairi had come to her room, but her mother specifically requested time alone with her daughter. The other women would have told a different story, she was sure of it. They would have spoken of love and eagerness. Light the lamps, sing songs of joy, and prepare yourself for bliss.

A far cry from the endurance her mother counseled.

"Thank you, Mother," she said, careful to keep her head bowed and her voice low.

"I will see you in the morning, my child. Then we must away to Drumvagen and leave you and your husband time to yourselves."

She could only imagine what that meeting would be like. Would Enid question her? Would she ask if she'd lain as still as a board? Or would she just assume that no proper woman would feel anything?

She walked her mother to the door, kissed her on the cheek, and thanked her again. Once alone, she turned and faced the sitting room, overpowered by its sheer size. Was there no place at Huntly that was cozy and intimate? No room that was small, enclosing, and warm? Or were all the rooms designed to house an army or to impress?

Entering her bedroom, she gathered up her yellow silk wrapper, climbed the three steps to the bed and waited.

She was not afraid. She would be like Lady Pamela, eagerly anticipating the arrival of her lover, imagining the delights in store for both of them.

Ross kissed like a demon. Was he as skilled in other ways?

She lay back on the counterpane, staring up at another scene painted on the ceiling. This one was of nymphs and cherubs, all scantily clad and portrayed as smiling in the clouds.

He would be taken with her beauty, enough that his fingers would tremble as he reached out to rid her of her wrapper.

You are so magnificent, he would say. *Even my dreams of you were paltry compared to the exquisite reality.*

You dreamed of me?

How could I not? You are my heart's wish. My soul's partner.

No, that was Donald, not Ross. Even though he looked like her hero, that's where the similarities ended. Ross was not in love with her. He'd married her to prevent a scandal.

She rose from the bed and walked to her secretary, wondering if she might ask that it be moved into the sitting room. Was that acceptable? Or must every one of her requests be filtered through the earl?

Sitting, she opened the drawers one by one, surprised to discover a thick supply of paper and new pens. Someone had thought of everything, even the rocking blotter she would use to dry the ink.

She had left her manuscript behind at Drumvagen. After Mairi returned it to her, she'd taken it to the cottage and hidden it in the stone safe. Now she wished she had it with her. She would have read about Lady Pamela's fearlessness, imbuing herself with some of the woman's courage.

Ross had married her because of the manuscript. He'd brought her to this palace and ensconced her here as its princess.

She didn't want to be a princess. She wasn't even sure she wanted to be a wife.

What did she want? Oh, that was the question, wasn't it?

She picked up a pen and a blank sheet of paper, finding solace from the world in a place she imagined, among people who were more real to her than her absent bridegroom.

When she looked up at the mantel clock, Ellice was startled to find that three hours had passed. Time always flew by when she was writing. Tonight, however, she'd expected to be interrupted by a knock on the door or even Ross's precipitous appearance.

He hadn't come.

She stared down at the page before her, placed her pen on the stand and sat back.

He hadn't come.

Was she supposed to go to him?

He hadn't said, and that was a bit of information her mother hadn't imparted, either.

She knew where his rooms were, or could at least guess. The double doors at the end of the corridor were a match to hers. Surely that meant they led to the earl's suite.

Should she go to him now?

She stood, pushing back the chair. Another thing she'd ask for, a more comfortable chair. Something with a bit less gilt and a better cushion. A footrest as well, perhaps, could she ask for that? She'd also request pens like the ones she had at Drumvagen and more paper so she didn't run low.

She brushed down her wrapper, wishing it hadn't wrinkled so much. In addition, there was an ink spot in the middle of her chest. She might as well have an arrow pointing to it. Plus, there was another stain in the area between her thumb and forefinger.

Perhaps other people could write without getting ink all over them. She'd never mastered the knack.

She went to the dresser, pleased to find that she had another wrapper and nightgown, this one in a color she liked even better than the yellow. It reminded her of the sky at sunset, when the orange of the sun faded to a pale salmon shade.

Dragging a brush through her hair, she stared at her reflection. Her eyes looked tired. Her face was too pale. Would he even want to bed her, looking as she was? She certainly didn't have Eudora's regal appearance. Nor was she a blond beauty like Cassandra.

She was just herself, flaws and all. Her shoulders were too rounded and she had a habit of hunching them, no doubt from hours sitting at her desk. One of her teeth slightly overlapped the other. Virginia said it gave her an endearing appearance. Perhaps Ross thought it ugly. Her hair was dull brown in the lamplight. Sometimes her eyes looked almost black but to-night they were simply brown.

She looked away from her reflection, wondering if he would come to her at all.

Or did he regret this marriage already? Was he mourning his first wife on the night of his second marriage?

Lady Pamela wouldn't tolerate being pushed aside, but Lady Pamela wasn't a transplanted, uncertain English virgin, either.

Still, the longer she stood there, the more she glanced at the clock, the greater her annoyance.

She'd kissed him and he'd been affected. Even a fool knew that. He'd felt the same passion she had. Why, then, was he ignoring her now?

Was she supposed to remain meekly in her room, waiting for him? Hoping he would appear and then be abjectly grateful when he did manage to show?

No, she wasn't going to be that kind of wife. Not ever, and certainly not from the beginning.

Lady Pamela would never tolerate such behavior.

She went into the bathroom, washed her hands and face, surveying herself once more in the mirror. Walking back to the secretary, she found her slippers, fluffed her wrapper, and made it to the door before she stopped.

Returning to the dressing room, she donned her cloak. The earl's suite was some distance from hers, and she didn't want to be seen in her nightwear by any of the servants.

The sconces in the corridor were turned low, no doubt in deference to the hour.

She approached the earl's suite and knocked on one of the double doors. She waited a while, then straightened her shoulders and knocked again, but was still met with only silence.

Had he fallen asleep?

Warmth suffused her, but it wasn't passion as much as embarrassment.

Was it terrible, my child? She could just imagine her mother asking that. How would she answer?

No, Mother, he fell asleep. So much for deathless passion.

You must simply try harder to interest him, my child.

She could stand naked at his door, but if he wasn't going to answer, there was little she could do.

"Your ladyship."

She jerked, startled, then glanced to her right to see a footman standing there.

"His lordship is not in his suite," he said, bowing slightly.

She was torn between asking where he was and simply thanking the man, turning and walking back to her room.

Thankfully, she didn't have to ask.

"He has gone to his library, I believe, your ladyship."

She nodded just as she'd seen her mother do. An almost regal gesture that implied, yes, I've heard you, and I'll either act on your information or I shall not.

She didn't know what to do.

"Where is the library?" she heard herself ask.

So much for decorum and dignity.

She knew, because of her mother's training on staff, and not because they'd employed any in London, that a footman was not supposed to smile. Nor was he to look at her with a compassionate glint in his eye.

She didn't bother to chastise him for his familiarity. A little kindness didn't seem amiss right at the moment. All she did was listen intently to his directions, nod again, and pretend she wasn't the least discomfited by the idea of having to search out her own bridegroom.

Huntly was too large.

She walked down to the end of the corridor and turned left, following the instructions. She came to a large anteroom, for lack of a better name, at the convergence of two wings, the one she'd come from and another, according to the footman, that housed the kitchen, pantries, and laundry.

Above her a ceiling was lined with skylights. During the day this one spot would be bathed in light, a bright and pleasant place to stand. Now it was dark with not a hint of moon or stars. All she could see above her were fast moving clouds.

The house wasn't a house but a giant creature of myth and magic into which she'd crawled. Perhaps it was a giant reptile that stretched, serpentine, over the hills and around the carved lake.

The heart of it would be the kitchens, the tail and wings all these impossible corridors. The brain, if a creature could be said to possess one, might be her destination—Ross's library.

Who would build something so large? Of course it had been done to impress. *My dear, have you any idea of the Gadsden fortune? Simply look to Huntly and you'll see.* Not only was the house larger than any other structure she'd ever seen, including the British Library, but the upkeep and maintenance must cost a fortune.

She'd seen gardeners crawling about the place like industrious ants. How many maids were employed here? How many footmen, standing guard in the shadows?

The cathedral had amazed her with its beauty, but the courtyard stunned her. She'd never considered that an expanse of that size would be cobbled, and in a pattern that could be seen for miles.

Finally, she was at the front of the house, with its enormous foyer and dome. Here she saw two more footmen standing beneath the sconces. She nodded to them as if she'd expected them to be there. Perhaps they wouldn't challenge her.

A draft blew the hem of her cloak, revealing her bare legs. She hurried on her way before they realized that the newly made Countess of Gadsden was wandering through Huntly in her nightgown.

Scottish servants gossiped as well as those from London. She'd heard the Drumvagen maids herself. Granted, they were too wise to ever speak of Brianag, but she'd heard them talk about her. According to them, she was a sweet thing with a vacant look in her eyes.

She wasn't particularly fond of that word—sweet. She didn't want to be sweet. She wanted to be compelling, fascinating, or unique. After meeting her for the first time, people would want to continue their association with her.

Oh, Ellice? What a fascinating woman! Did you hear her story of exploring Huntly on her wedding night? My dear, she's witty and bright and charming down to her toes.

Would she ever tell anyone about this? Would she write how the shadows of this narrower corridor were causing her to walk slower, wide-eyed, and wishing she'd never thought to seek out Ross? Here, there were public rooms, the footman had said. Not the ballroom, of course, since it was on the second floor and could only be reached by the sweeping grand staircase she passed five minutes earlier.

She missed the sound of laughter, children's voices, the endless quarreling tones of Brianag and her mother. She missed noises because Huntly was suffused with the quiet of the grave.

If she shouted, would the sound echo?

She stopped, wondering about the source of the lemon scent. Was it coming from the pierced potpourri jar on the occasional table beside the window? Or from the wax that polished the wood?

The draft carried another scent, of growing things and newly blossoming flowers. Was there a garden just outside an open window?

The parlors and sitting rooms she passed were named for women: the Sarah Parlor, the Caroline Sitting Room, and more she couldn't remember. She stopped before one open door and stared inside at the shadow draped furniture. She could barely make out a portrait over the fireplace. Is that how you could tell which room you occupied? Was there a

Cassandra room here at Huntly? Would she, herself, be immortalized by appending her name to a chamber?

She left the room, grateful that the sconces had been left lit down this curving corridor. Perhaps that's why footmen were stationed throughout Huntly. Not to guard against intruders as much as fire. As large as the house was, one wing could cheerfully burn to the ground before the inhabitants in the other wing realized it.

Here there was another junction. The one to the left would lead to the building occupied by the now Dowager Countess. The second corridor would lead to the earl's library even farther away.

Had he wished to escape her so much?

Another door stood open, and she peered inside, expecting a duplicate of the first parlor she'd seen. This room wasn't spacious at all. Instead, it was half the size of the other rooms and could easily fit into her new sitting room.

Windows, draped against the night, stretched along the far wall. A small fireplace sat in front of two chairs and a table. The room didn't boast a rotunda or a corbeled ceiling or a cupola with glass inserts. Other than a settee, two chairs, and a small table, there was no other furniture.

In another house it might be considered a perfectly adequate room. At Huntly it looked like a miniature of everything she'd seen.

She loved it immediately.

Here, too, was a portrait above the mantel, but she couldn't make out the features of the woman. She suddenly wanted to see her. Wanted to know, also, why this room had been picked for her.

One of the gas sconces was located right outside the room. She turned the key at the base of it until the globe burned brightly. The light didn't illuminate the entire room, but it shone enough that she could see the woman in the portrait.

Thankfully, it wasn't Cassandra. Cassandra was supposed to have blond hair and blue eyes. This woman's hair was brown. Her eyes were brown as well, carrying a look of such warmth that Ellice felt touched by it. Her face was oval, her skin a perfect porcelain with a touch of rose on her cheeks. Behind her were several full bookshelves, a window that looked out over Huntly's lake, and a curved iron staircase.

She stood looking up at the woman, wishing the light were enough to read the brass plaque beneath the painting.

"Are you lost?"

She closed her eyes and pretended for a moment. Ross's voice was warm, not caustic. His question was not whether she was lost but if she knew whose room this was.

Pretense worked at Drumvagen, but it had no place at Huntly.

She turned and faced her husband. He was fully dressed, although not in the kilt he'd worn at the ceremony and banquet. Instead, he'd changed into a white shirt and black trousers. His hair was mussed as if he'd thrust his fingers through it. His eyes were polished marble.

He was a formidable man even if she could ignore how handsome he was.

"Who is she?"

He glanced up at the portrait. "My grandmother," he said. "Mary."

She wanted to ask him so many questions. Why were the rooms named for women? Why had Mary been relegated to this small space? But she asked the one question she was not truly prepared to hear the answer to, instead.

"Why haven't you come to me?"

He only raised one eyebrow.

"Am I supposed to chase you and demand that you perform your conjugal duties?"

"Is that what you're doing, chasing me?"

Yes, it was, and how humiliating to admit it.

She folded her arms, steadied her lips—she refused to allow them to tremble—and regarded him as stonily as he was staring at her.

"You didn't have to marry me, you know," she said. "I would have been just as content to remain unmarried."

"So I gathered."

"But once you married me, you can't simply put me in a room and forget about me."

"I can't?"

She shook her head. "No. You can't."

"Go back to your room, Ellice. I have no intention of bedding you tonight."

Well, that was certainly to the point, wasn't it?

"Why not?"

She waited for him to answer her, to tell her something pointed and hurtful. He couldn't forget Cassandra on this night of all nights. Or she wasn't pretty enough or attractive enough or desirable enough.

Instead, he simply turned and walked away.

She stared after him. Was she supposed to chase him? Did he expect her to follow, weeping, and beg him to treat her with kindness? Or, at the very least, remember that she was his bride?

Lady Pamela would have simply stood at the doorway, watching him leave.

Ellice didn't do that. She walked out of the room and turned left, intent on her room. If he asked, she'd tell the kind footman that she'd indeed found the earl.

But she wished she hadn't.

Chapter 20

She returned to her chamber without, blessedly, seeing another servant. To her surprise, she fell asleep with ease, waking in the morning to her mother's knock.

The Dowager Countess entered the room as if a fierce gust of wind propelled her. She did not, however, ask questions about Ellice's wedding night. Nor did Enid's eyes ever meet hers, almost as if her mother were embarrassed by the whole situation.

Instead, Enid began to give her another lecture, this one about remembering who she was, her family's antecedents, and the fact that the Scots, however civilized they might appear to be now, had been bare-assed and carrying clubs when the English were making laws. Not that her mother would ever say the words "bare assed," but she implied it with a wrinkle of her nose and pursed lips.

Ellice nodded, torn between two feelings, both of which she was familiar: love and frustration. She loved her mother but she wished her gone. Let her lecture Brianag, who was more equipped to deal with the irritation Enid fostered. Let her yell at the gorse and pontificate to the heather, just not at *her* for a little while.

Breakfast was a formal affair, with Ross entering the cavernous dining room after all the overnight guests had been seated at the twenty-foot-long table. He inquired as to their sleep, then thanked them again for attending the ceremony at Huntly.

At every plate there was a small gift-wrapped box. Inside was a gold enameled box featuring a lid painted with a rendition of the great house. Engraved on the inside was the date of their wedding.

She hadn't known anything about the gifts but suspected that her life would be marked by thoughtful tokens like that, especially to strangers.

How Ross treated people who were close to him—or supposed to be close to him—was another matter entirely. Would he continue to be so distant to her?

The man who sat opposite her was pleasant, approachable, and personable to his table mates. He smiled. He laughed a time or two. He asked questions of Macrath and complimented Virginia. He endured Mairi's probing, and exchanged more than one look with Logan. He was unfailingly polite to her mother, even when she made a disparaging comment about the size of Huntly.

"I imagine it's cold in the winter," she said. "A house as cavernous as this can't be heated properly."

"My grandfather was an inventor of sorts," he said. "He designed a series of flues that carry heated air into the larger rooms. Perhaps you'll visit in the winter so I can show you how comfortable Huntly truly is."

Her mother only inclined her head in a queenly gesture.

Ellice wondered if people would notice that Ross hadn't looked at her once. Nor had he spoken to her.

Were they supposed to be shy around each other? Or circumspect in public? If what should have happened last night had actually happened, how would they have acted?

She would have looked around this morning for some

salve to put on her skin, perhaps, because his kisses had been so intense. Her lips would have been swollen, her cheeks abraded by his night beard.

Would she have been flushed with color at the thought of sharing a table with her relatives after having been thoroughly rogered the night before? She would probably have stared at the tablecloth, as she did now, or noted the trembling of her fingers as she brought the cup to her lips.

She stared at his hands, wondering what it would be like to have his fingers on her bare skin. He'd touched her face with such tenderness. Surely those fingers would be just as gentle on her breasts.

They might have even been late to breakfast, and instead of coming in separately, would have arrived hand in hand. He would have led her to her chair, bent over her, brushed her hair back to place a kiss against her cheek. In plain sight of everyone, he would have whispered an endearment to her.

" . . . wind was so fierce. Is it ever so?"

She blinked, brought herself back to the table. Her mother had said something and was now intently regarding Ross.

"I'm sorry that it kept you awake."

"I didn't say it kept me awake, only that it was annoying."

Perhaps it was for the best that everyone was leaving this morning. Her mother was acting every inch an autocratic English countess and Ross's smile was tight.

She doubted her ability to be a peacemaker. She'd never been accomplished at the role before. Her mother always brushed her words aside, and Ross would probably not even notice her, let alone what she said.

When Macrath thanked Ross, explaining that they needed to return to Drumvagen because of the children, she wanted to stop him. Or ask if she could ride back with them. Drumvagen had never felt like her home but it was certainly more so than this British Library of a house.

Instead, she bit back her panic, stood, and walked with Ross to the rotunda where everyone's bags had been delivered. They took their place on the steps as a half-dozen footmen placed everything in the three carriages, the empty wagon waiting to join the procession. Two maids appeared, dressed in dark green, each carrying a basket of food and drink for the journey.

Another example of effortless courtesy delivered to almost strangers.

Her mother-in-law had not made an appearance this morning. Instead, Ross had conveyed her apologies.

"My mother is awaiting a shipment of wool from the Hebrides," he said.

"Evidently, a shipment of wool is of greater importance than being polite," her mother had whispered.

Ross overheard them, smiled and said, "To my mother, yes. For that, I apologize as well."

Her mother swept her into an uncharacteristic hug. "Remember your upbringing, child."

Ellice was frankly surprised not to hear about Eudora at their parting, as in: *Eudora would not need my warnings, child. She would be the perfect countess.*

She nodded to her mother, kissed her cheek, and tried not to reveal her relief when Enid finally entered the carriage.

Virginia hugged her as well. Her comment, "Be happy, my dear sister," almost made her cry.

"Demand your happiness," Mairi said, and that swept her from near tears to laughter.

Macrath enveloped her in a hug, then said something that troubled her. "You'll always have a home at Drumvagen."

Did she need one?

Logan, however, was the one who left her staring at him. "He needs you."

She couldn't imagine anyone who needed her less than the Earl of Gadsden.

She stood and watched as the vehicles, her mother occupying the head carriage in sole and regal splendor, pulled away from the steps of Huntly, out into the courtyard, and beyond to the road to Drumvagen.

The two of them stood there silently until the carriages were out of sight.

"We need to talk," he said.

She wanted to deliver a scathing announcement to him, something about being uninterested and supremely bored about any conversation he wished to initiate.

Instead, she only nodded.

To her great surprise, he took her hand, but instead of turning back and entering the house, led her across the courtyard.

She stopped in the center of a brown circle, tugging on his hand.

"What is this pattern?"

"It's a Celtic knot. Evidently, my great-grandfather didn't want anyone to forget he was a Scot. You'll see it in various places throughout Huntly."

"I would bet my family goes back as far as yours," she said. "Perhaps even farther," she added, to tweak his nose. "But I wasn't constantly reminded of my ancestors' presence."

"Perhaps because you weren't the heir," he said.

She held his gaze as long as she could. Normally, she didn't have any difficulty appearing placid and agreeable. Why was she finding it so difficult with him?

Because he was handsome? Was she that shallow a woman?

Because he was charming when he wished to be, like now? Was she that needy to crave kindness from a man who was more a stranger than a husband?

She was very much afraid that the answer to all those questions was yes, she did have an appreciation for his form and his face, and yes, she was feeling adrift at the moment.

Still, was it fair to call him a stranger? She'd been closer to him than any other man in her life. Probably any other person.

"No," she said, slipping her hand free of his on the pretense that she needed to lift her skirts. "I think it's because they hadn't built anything like Huntly."

She stopped in the middle of the courtyard and turned in a full circle.

"It really is magnificent," she said. "Like living at the Vatican. Or Versailles, from what I've heard."

"If you think this is impressive, wait until you see the family entrance," he said.

Surprised, she turned to him.

"The formal entrance is on the other side. A road stretches between the lake and the house, and that's where guests usually arrive."

She hadn't seen a road, but then she'd barely seen anything but her room. Or the corridors she'd walked last night.

Yes, they really did need to talk.

"My ancestor had a great appreciation for large buildings. He said why build anything unless you can guarantee people will notice it and it'll be around for centuries?"

"He didn't build the Coliseum, by any chance?"

He smiled. "Are you well traveled, Ellice? Or just well schooled?"

"I'm not well traveled. Coming to Scotland was as far as I've ever been. Nor am I excessively schooled. My father barely noticed us, the two girls, being concerned mostly with my brother's education. However, I read a great deal, and it's said that an armchair education is sometimes the best one."

He frowned at her.

"Females do read, your lordship."

"I am aware of that, your ladyship."

She blinked at him. How very cold his voice could be sometimes.

Looking ahead, she picked up her skirts and made her way over the cobbles.

"Why are we going to your library?"

"It's actually Huntly's library more than belonging to any one man. I thought we might have some privacy there."

"I cannot imagine that it's the only place at Huntly to find some privacy. What about your chamber or mine?"

He didn't answer her.

"You're going to lecture me, aren't you, and you want an official place to do it? My first lecture as a married woman." She frowned and dropped her voice. " 'My dear Ellice. You mustn't cavort around Huntly in your nightgown. If I'd wanted to come to you I would have. Have you no propriety, no sense of decorum?' " She shook her head, resuming her normal voice. "Is that it?"

He still didn't answer, but his face now wore a frown as fierce as the one she pretended.

"Oh dear. Am I allowed to guess what my punishment will be? Are you going to show me your library—Huntly's library—only to take it away from me? For your sins, Ellice Traylor, I ban books from you." She lifted her head and stared up at the sky. "It doesn't matter, you know, I've brought my favorites with me."

"It's Forster," he said.

She glanced at him.

"Your name is no longer Traylor. It's Forster."

"But the rest is right?"

He shook his head. "You really don't require anyone else's participation in your conversations, do you?"

"No," she said. "At Drumvagen, I often talked to the sheep. Or a goat or two. The horses were great listeners, but the cattle were less so. They made noises, while the horses only snorted from time to time."

He stopped. "Are you jesting?"

"Why would I jest about such a thing?" she asked, stopping as well.

"Why were you talking to the livestock?"

"Because no one else wanted to hear what I had to say."

She hadn't meant to phrase it quite as baldly as that. But Virginia always had the children, Macrath had his inventions. Her mother and Brianag were either conspiring on their book or feuding about it. The maids were involved in their work.

He strode ahead of her to open a large glass-paneled door, then stood aside and allowed her to precede him.

She expected an anteroom or a foyer. Instead, she walked inside to find walls lined with impossibly high bookshelves. Not one space remained on any one of them. Not one more volume could be slid into those shelves.

She looked up, not at all surprised at the soaring ceiling. Huntly was graced with a dozen of these, all painted with murals to astound and amaze. This one was of men reclining on clouds, unfurled scrolls covering their nakedness. No semiclad nymphs joined them, however, making her wonder if Ross's ancestor was inclined to believe that females didn't read.

"I should have talked to you last night," he said.

"Yes," she said, still with her head tilted back. "You should have." She'd much rather stare at the gods, if that's what they were supposed to be, than Ross when having this conversation. "You might have spared me the embarrassment of seeking you out to rid myself of my virginity. Evidently, you had other plans for our wedding night."

He didn't answer, and she was forced to look at him.

His expression was one she couldn't read, and it took her a moment to realize that's exactly what he intended. There was no emotion in his beautiful gray eyes. Instead, they were flat, like disks of silver. His face was still, his mouth neither smiling nor turned down.

She'd changed him to stone with her words.

People would come from miles around to see the Stone Earl. They'd poke him with their fingers and get into his face to see if he blinked. He never would, of course. Nor would he act as if he saw them.

Perhaps she could charge a goodly sum, just for pin money, of course. Just think of the paper and supplies she could purchase. All without having to ask anyone for funds.

"What is the Gaelic word for stone?" she asked.

He blinked at her. "I haven't the slightest idea."

"Why not?"

"I don't speak all that much Gaelic."

"Why not?"

"Because I was educated in England."

"Why?"

"Because it was simpler to ship me off to England."

Perhaps he wasn't stone at all, because there was fire behind the smoke of his eyes.

"Why did you ask?"

She waved her hand in the air. "It isn't important."

"You can't be a virgin," he said.

"I can't?"

He shook his head.

"Why can't I?"

He didn't answer, only moved farther into the room. She had no choice but to follow him, stop and stare upward at the ceiling once more. In this part of the library, they were directly below the tower. She'd thought it only an ornament, an addition to the roof. But she could see the sky from here and the bright morning sun streaming into the room.

A curved iron staircase wound, snakelike, from the tile floor all the way up to the tower, passing two levels of books.

"How many books do you have?"

"Do you think I'm an idiot?"

"Not with all these books," she said, fingering one shelf of particularly beautiful books, their gilt bindings catching the light.

"Ellice."

She turned to look at him. No, he was definitely not stone now. Still, she was going to look up the Gaelic word.

"You can't be a virgin," he repeated.

"Do you want me to be experienced?"

Once again he didn't answer.

"You really have to stop doing that," she said.

"Doing what? Questioning you? Refusing to believe any foolishness you utter?"

She took a deep breath, released it slowly. "No, not answering when you don't want to. It gives everyone the impression you're autocratic and haughty."

"You're not making any sense."

"Do you want me to be experienced?" she patiently asked again.

He glared at her. She'd never been the recipient of such concentrated anger. She stared right back at him, wondering why he was so enraged with her.

She just wanted to kiss him.

Was now the right time? What better time was there?

She walked to him, placed her hands on his shoulders and stood on tiptoe, pointedly ignoring his raised eyebrows.

Slowly, giving him time to move away, she placed a chaste kiss on his lips. Close-mouthed, very friendly but entirely lacking in passion.

"Do you want me to be experienced? I can pretend, I think. Shall I be an East End prostitute? Or someone more refined?"

He carefully removed her hands from his shoulders and took a step back.

"I'm a virgin, Ross, and it amazes me that you would think otherwise."

"I've read your book."

She took another deep breath.

"Have you never heard of imagination? Is every writer supposed to have done the deeds he writes about?"

"In the case of *The Lustful Adventures of Lady Pamela*, yes."

"Is that why you didn't come to my room?"

"I have no intention of raising another man's child, Ellice. I've had my fill of scandal."

That was pointed, wasn't it? She couldn't very well counter that she hadn't been scandalous. After all, she'd hidden in his carriage. She'd left an undergarment behind, and even worse—at least to his mind—she'd written a book filled with passionate encounters.

"Carnal knowledge is everywhere, your lordship. Everywhere." She was close enough to poke him in the chest with her finger. When she did, he grabbed her hand and held it still.

Pity, she liked touching him, even when she was annoyed. Would he feel the same? If she couldn't convince him she was a virgin, she'd never know.

"Am I in quarantine?" she asked. "For how long?" She suddenly understood and nodded. "Until you're certain I'm not with child. What a pity my little visitor hasn't come. We could have dispensed with that foolishness."

"I don't share the same view as you, Ellice. I don't think it's foolishness."

She blew out a breath.

"And I never thought I'd have to claim my virtue. I haven't been locked away in a room, although I'm sure my mother would have wished it." She smiled. "The better not to do something that shamed her." She shook her head. "Not in your way, Ross. But in hers. I must always be perfect. I am not perfect. But I am a virgin."

He looked as if he wished to say something, and she pulled

her hand free while, with the other she pressed her fingers against his lips.

"I observe. I watch. I see," she said. "People think no one can see them, but they do. The laundress is in love with her husband and they're always groping each other. Hannah, Virginia's maid, goes around with a smile on her face all the time. I've seen her and Jack kissing when they think no one notices. I'd have to be blind not to notice Macrath's glances at Virginia or her smiles back to him. Take Logan and Mairi. They had a love affair that nearly scorched Edinburgh. What about all the animals at Drumvagen? Am I supposed to pretend I don't notice them? The dogs mate and the males all get this look of ecstasy in their eyes. A mare might scream when a stallion mounts her but I don't think it's in pain."

He drew back.

"Yes, it's passion, your lordship," she said, throwing her hands in the air. "I've written about it. So throw me in a cell. Close the door and lock it. Consign me to purgatory."

An idea was occurring to her, one so shocking that it really should have sent her scurrying back across the courtyard.

Lady Pamela would have done it. The fact that she was as far from Lady Pamela as she could imagine wasn't important at the moment.

She unfastened the brooch at her throat, put it in her pocket and began working on the buttons of her bodice.

"What are you doing?"

Really, what a foolish question.

"I'm undressing," she said.

"Stop it."

She shook her head. "There's only one way to solve this issue. I say I'm virtuous. You would have me be Salome." She glanced at him. "Do I need to tell you who Salome is?"

"I know who she is."

How interesting that his eyes didn't move from her fingers. She was down to her waist and her dress gaped open to show a very pretty corset cover embroidered with clusters of violets.

Should she be frightened? She wasn't. Instead, she was determined. She hadn't been frightened of him even when he'd nearly taken her over the settee. That had been the single most erotic moment of her life, in real life or in writing.

She wanted to replicate it, right this minute.

The room was bright. The air smelled of lemon and leather, or maybe that was him. His desk was large, the expanse of it nearly equal that of a bed. Granted, it might be a bit harder than a mattress but she doubted she would notice after he touched her. Was he going to touch her?

"Ellice—" he began.

"No," she said. "I'm not going to hear any more protests from you. You would think you're the frightened virgin, not me."

"Are you frightened?"

She stopped in the act of removing her bodice and considered the question.

"No, actually, I'm not. I'm just annoyed."

"Annoyed?"

She frowned at him. "If you make love the way you kiss, I doubt I'll be disappointed. But why should I have to beg you to bed me?"

She fussed with one button on her cuff, finally got it loose, and tossed her bodice to a gilded chair sitting against the wall. When it caught, then slid to the floor, she shrugged.

"I would think a virgin would wait until it was night for me to come to your chamber."

She sighed, removed her skirt, then began working on the tapes of her bustle and petticoat combination. She hadn't had a maid since living in London. Her mother had refused to ask Macrath for extra servants to tend to them, so she'd learned quite well how to dress and undress herself. She'd also become adept at mending her own garments as well as turning cuffs and collars, but she'd tell Ross about those skills some other time.

"Perhaps I should," she said, "but I doubt you would come to me. I'd wander all over Huntly trying to find you again."

She stepped out of her skirt, letting it fall to the floor. Placing it on the chair, she wiggled out of her bustle, placing it atop the mound of her clothes.

"The sooner my virginity is gotten rid of, the better, don't you think? I won't wander throughout your home like a virtuous ghost, sad that she never had a chance to be wicked, and you won't have to beat me back when I get too eager."

He shook his head.

"Besides, it's in our contract."

One of his eyebrows arched.

"I don't believe it is."

She nodded. "It is. I have the right to refuse you three times a year. You have no right to refuse me. If you wanted to have that clause in our contract, you should have negotiated that point."

After unfastening the busk of her corset, she moved to raise the hem of her shift. Before she could, his hands reached out and grabbed hers.

Smiling, she leaned toward him.

"Kiss me, then," she said, wondering at the sound of her own voice. She sounded sultry, passionate, almost as if she were a purring kitten.

"This isn't wise."

Ah, the words of a man who was justifying his surrender. She bit back her smile, looked up at him and told him the truth.

"I'm a virgin, husband. But an impatient one. I've wanted you to take me since our first kiss. If you discover that I'm not a virgin, then banish me to Ireland. Send me to America. Do anything you want."

"What the hell do I do with you otherwise?"

Bed me. That answer sounded too stark. "Hold me in your arms every night," she said. There, an answer that pleased her and seemed to melt the Stone Earl.

He reached for her and she smiled.

Chapter 21

He was an idiot to believe her.

He was an idiot to be captivated by her artless invitation to passion.

He was a hundred times an idiot to be thinking of bedding his wife on his desk, but that's exactly what he was about to do.

A caution slid into his mind. If she were truly a virgin, he should be slower, gentler. If she were a virgin, then she was touched by some amazing and dangerous talent: the ability to deaden his mind, his instincts, and everything but his loins. That part of him was working quite well.

He touched his mouth to hers and it was like he was numb to everything but her.

He kissed her and reason fled from him.

She made breathy little sounds when he deepened the kiss. He framed her face with his hands to keep her still. Her lips trembled and it both surprised and aroused him.

He didn't know what it was but for the moment he was in thrall to it. He would figure it out later when she was in another room, perhaps, or he could think again. When the smell of her perfume, something that reminded him of faint spicy blossoms and spring, wasn't wreathed in a cloud around him.

Maybe it was magic. Was she one of the creatures from the many Scottish tales his nurse had told him as a child?

She was English so that couldn't be it. Unless she was some kind of secret weapon they'd reared to strip the sensibilities from the Scots.

She had her hand on his chest, somehow burrowing beneath his shirt. Where had his jacket gone? One of her hands was at the nape of his neck, sliding through his hair.

When the hell had a virgin ever been this eager?

When the hell had he ever been wanted this much?

He cupped her breast on the outside of her shift, feeling the nipple pebble against his palm. He wanted to touch her skin, test whether she was as responsive in other places. Would she moan when he mouthed her breasts?

The morning sun danced on her hair, transforming the brown to gold and reddish glints. An errant sunbeam angled over her face, dusting her long lashes with light, accentuating the perfection of her nose, her cheekbones, and the beauty of her complexion.

He wanted her in that moment, but it was a need that went beyond the flesh. He wanted her to belong to him, to cleave unto him, to match her steps with his, to laugh at the same time he did. The sensation was so odd and so unexpected that he drew back.

She blinked her eyes open, arousal making her smile a tempting thing.

He wrapped his arms around her, shelved his chin on her hair, and waited out the strangeness.

Her arms reached under his, her hands pressing against his back. How small her hands were, yet she held him within her palms, if she only knew it.

He bent his head, smelling oranges in her hair, wishing he were a wiser man or a less needy one in that instant.

"Have I done something wrong?" she asked in a thin voice.

How unsure she sounded, and yet she was the most powerful woman in the world.

"No," he said. "No, you've done nothing wrong."

He pulled back and studied her face, wishing he could tell her of that odd moment he'd experienced, when he suddenly and inexplicably felt bound to her in some way beyond law or ceremony.

She would be his friend, but even that explanation sounded foolish.

She, who was so quick and talented with words, might have a way to describe what he felt, but he didn't. So he could only show her in gestures. A soft and delicate kiss, one that made her eyelids flutter down to shield her eyes. The tender touch of his fingertips on her shoulders encouraged her to wrap her arms around his neck. His palms trailing over her back caused her to sigh and press closer.

He had no choice but to pick her up in his arms, holding her encapsulated in the sun's bright beam, her cheeks and lips pink, eyes lambent.

"I've no wish to bed you here," he said softly. "But I don't think I could walk across the courtyard in this state."

She shook her head. "I'd much rather not wait. If you don't mind."

He had no control over his smile. It burst forth, along with his amusement.

What a damn fool he was over her. If he was cuckolded and shamed, it was his own fault. Let that be a lesson, then.

He could not trust himself around Ellice.

He sat her on the edge of his desk, sweeping his arm behind her to clean off the surface. He heard the alabaster inkwell fall and didn't give a flying farthing. The blotter with its tooled Moroccan leather fell against the wall. His favorite pens rattled along the floor.

She wiggled, and it wasn't until she was pulling off her

shift that he realized what she was doing. She sat there naked but for her stockings and shoes, a picture even more erotic than anything she'd written.

Lady Pamela had nothing on the Countess of Gadsden.

He slid one garter down her shapely leg. Who knew that his wife was a curvy little thing? He wanted to palm her breasts but kept his eyes on his hands, now smoothing down her stockings. He realized he'd forgotten her shoes, then unlaced them to let them fall before finishing with the stockings.

She was gloriously naked and all she did was blink up at him, her mouth slightly swollen and needing a kiss. Her hands were at her sides, not attempting to cover up one magnificent inch of her skin.

Her breasts were beautiful, larger than he'd thought, with large coral areolas surrounding turgid nipples. He bent and placed his mouth over one, hearing her gasp.

His tongue flicked over the tip. Her hands crept up to burrow in his hair. This moment in the sun when he suckled her was the single most erotic scene of his life.

In her silence and her welcome she granted him a freedom he'd never known. Here there was no judgment and no one to be compared against.

For her, he wanted to be a better lover than he'd ever been. He wanted to bring her to pleasure with his hands and his mouth, with his cock and his words. He wanted her to shiver and tremble and scream in pleasure.

First, however, he would be as naked as she, as exposed and vulnerable.

She didn't look away once, but sat there intent and quiet, looking her fill.

When he finished undressing she almost unmanned him.

"You're more beautiful than I imagined," she said, her eyes sweeping over him.

"You imagined me naked?"

She nodded.

She continually surprised him, but no more so than in that next minute when she widened her legs, placed her hands on his chest, and urged him closer.

"Shall we be about this business of making me a wife?"

"Why so quickly?" he asked.

"Because I can't wait any longer."

The insides of her thighs glistened with her arousal. He placed both hands there, gently spreading her open with his thumbs. Her eyes closed, her breathing escalated, and she bit at her bottom lip.

For all his wish to be slow, he doubted he'd be able to, not after touching her and feeling how swollen and wet she was. His thumb gently circled one spot, causing her eyes to open and fix on him.

"Ross."

Just his name, but it was as great an entreaty as he'd ever been given.

He pulled her forward with both hands on her hips, then gently kissed her.

The kiss turned heated within seconds. Her tongue dueled with his as her hands swept over his back, cupping his buttocks and pulling him forward.

She was a damn demanding virgin.

"I don't want to hurt you," he said.

She pulled back. "It's going to hurt?"

"Did no one ever tell you?"

She shook her head. "It isn't something that comes up in polite conversation, is it? And my mother certainly didn't say anything. In fact, she didn't say much of anything that I could use."

The image of the Dowager Countess of Barrett giving her daughter seduction advice was not one he wanted to have in his mind.

"I'll be as gentle as I can."

"I'll try not to scream," she said.

He didn't want to hear that, either, so he kissed her again.

Lowering her back to the desk, he rose over her, kissing her breasts, drawing one hard nipple into his mouth.

Before she could worry about it, he slowly entered her, feeling her so tight that he wondered if he would be any type of lover at all. He felt a slight constriction, then pushed forward.

Ellice hadn't lied. She was a virgin, one with a magnificent imagination, eyes that bore right through him, and a body to tempt him.

Her eyes were clenched shut and she was biting her bottom lip again. Slowly, he withdrew, and just as gently entered her again.

Her nails were gouging into his shoulders.

Once more he left her and entered.

She opened her eyes. "When is it going to hurt?"

"It doesn't?"

She shook her head. "It pinches, but I suspect that's because you're so large."

He felt a smile begin again.

"And it itches a little, as if I want you to do more than what you're doing."

Was she coaching him now?

"What do you think I should be doing?" he asked, startled by the combination of humor and lust.

"Going faster, I think," she said. "I do wish you would."

"I can do that," he said. This time he surged into her, until the hair at his groin mingled with hers.

She groaned softly.

When her eyes opened, he asked, "Was that painful?"

She shook her head. "Not at all. It felt very nice."

Well, hell. Nice was not a word he would use to describe

what he was feeling. The top of his head was about to blow off.

He paid more attention to her breasts, cupping one while he gently suckled the other. Then he kissed her again, thumbing her nipples, keeping up the stroking rhythm. Her breathing was keeping time. Each time he surged within her, she would gasp. Each time he withdrew, she made a strange little sound and her hands gripped his arms tighter.

"Is it nice?" he asked against her ear.

"Yes," she said, but that one word seemed to cause her a great deal of trouble.

"How nice?"

She groaned when he began to move a little faster. If he were truly blessed he'd be able to bring her to satisfaction before his own.

But it would be a tight race.

"Oh, Ross."

"Very nice?"

She made a noise in the back of her throat.

She pulled her mouth away from his, her eyes flying open.

"Ross, oh, Ross."

In the next instant, she wrapped her legs around him and raised her hips. Her whole body trembled, her channel gripping him, milking him until he had no choice but to surrender.

Chapter 22

"**I** think I screamed," she said.

"Only in the most ladylike manner."

"It was very, very nice. The nicest thing in the world, actually."

His smile startled her as he helped her sit up.

She looked at the floor, surprised she hadn't noted the vibrant colors in the Turkish carpet. Or the expanse of windows through which they could easily be seen. Nor had she fully grasped how very large the library was, or how small they seemed at the moment, two naked people, one of whom was smiling.

She, on the other hand, was trying very hard not to cry.

His hand cupped her chin, raised her head. She blinked up at him, refusing to let him see how emotional she was at the moment.

He didn't say a word, but his smile vanished. Slowly, he lowered his head and kissed her. She was nearly overwhelmed by the tenderness of it, enough that one tear fell soundlessly down her cheek.

"I hurt you," he said, the words echoing in the silence.

She shook her head. "Oh, no, you didn't."

"Then why are you crying?"

Was there a way to say how she felt? She was so much more adept at putting her thoughts on paper. Then, she had a chance to change her mind, reassess, and correct. When speaking, she had to be correct from the first.

"What is it, Ellice?"

She shook her head, looking away from him.

"Ellice?"

She finally turned her head. They exchanged a long look, one that made her weepy again. She wanted, almost desperately, to wrap her arms around him, rest against the wall of his chest until she felt more capable of facing the world again.

Bending, he grabbed his clothes, retrieved a handkerchief from somewhere and handed it to her. He dressed as she blotted at the evidence of their passion. She knew, without being told, that she should feel embarrassed and vulncrable.

Strangely, she didn't. Instead, her skin was warm, her body still pulsing with delight.

His eyes were soft as wool when his gaze touched her.

The blood startled her. She must have made a sound, because he glanced at her, then at the cloth in her hand.

"It's nothing to worry about, I understand," he said. "It's merely proof you were a virgin."

"And now I'm not."

"No, you're not."

When he brought her clothes to the desk without a word, she donned her garments, slower than she'd pulled them off her body.

She'd dared him and he'd taken her dare, teaching her about passion. She'd been right about a great many things but wrong about so much.

Passion had made her insane for a little while. Was it supposed to do that? Was she supposed to lose her wits? All she could think about was him, touching him, making him touch her, take her. Everything else was meaningless.

The sky could have fallen and she wouldn't have cared.

He hadn't donned his jacket, merely stood there in his shirt and trousers. He dragged a chair to sit in front of her, grabbed her stockings, and began to roll each one up her leg.

"Are you a lady's maid, too?"

"It will speed things along if I help you dress. Women always have more clothing."

"Do you think I'm with child?"

His head jerked up and he stared at her. She smoothed her foot over his trousers and he grabbed it, held it in his warm hand. Who knew that her foot could be so sensitive?

"You haven't asked about your staff," he said, which wasn't an answer and at the same time was. The idea of her being with child was not something he wished to discuss.

The thought scared her a little. Was she prepared to be a mother? Would she be as terrible at the job as her own mother? Or was that too harsh a criticism? Enid had always been devoted to her children. The loss of Lawrence first, then Eudora, changed her.

"I have a staff?" she asked, which was an easier subject than motherhood at the moment.

He nodded. "A secretary, the maids that are assigned to your suite. Your own cook, if you wish, and of course your personal maid."

She stared at him. "I haven't the slightest use for any of those people, especially a personal cook. What foolishness."

If she hadn't been so close to him, she probably wouldn't have seen the way his eyes darkened, the center black part widening. She was captivated by the beauty of his eyes, enough to simply sit there and study him.

When he frowned at her she realized she'd been doing that for a few minutes at least.

"You have to have some staff. You're the Countess of Gadsden."

She sighed. "Very well, but no secretary and certainly no personal cook. The girl I met yesterday will do fine as a lady's maid. Pegeen, I think her name is."

"She's assigned to the public rooms," he said. "She has no experience at being a lady's maid."

"And I have no experience at being the Countess of Gadsden, so we'll suit each other perfectly. But how did you know about Pegeen?"

He slowly rolled the stocking from her foot to her knee, smoothing it as he went, taking such care that her leg trembled from his touch. She really wished he wasn't as good at dressing her, or touching her for that matter. The former made her wonder at his experience with women, while the latter made her regret she was getting dressed and not the reverse.

"I'm the earl," he said. "I'm supposed to know how many people are employed at Huntly and who they are."

"How many?"

"One hundred sixty-seven."

Her eyes widened. "Do you know where each of them works?"

"Not all of them," he said, tightening the garter above her knee. "But Pegeen is memorable because she has red hair and green eyes."

At that moment she'd give anything to have red hair and green eyes.

"I'm sorry I'm so plain," she said, watching as he fastened her left shoe.

She had to stand to don her corset properly, but she wasn't about to interrupt him. She hadn't been dressed since she was a child and never considered that a man, her husband, might do so.

"What utter rot," he said, beginning to roll up the second stocking.

She frowned at him. "What is utter rot?"

"That you're plain."

"My eyes are brown and my hair is brown."

"Your eyes are the color of warm chocolate," he said, tilting his head to study her. "Your hair isn't brown, but auburn with gold and red threads in it like the finest tapestry."

Her heart turned over.

"I haven't your beautiful gray eyes," she said when she could speak. "Perhaps our child will."

He didn't look away but his hands continued to caress her leg.

"Pegeen it is, then," he said, finally breaking the spell that stretched between them. "But if you change your mind about the others, let me know."

"A personal gardener," she said, forcing a smile to her lips. She wanted, almost desperately, to kiss him, but she already knew where that would lead. She didn't want to be taken on the desk again. There were enough beds at Huntly to test all of them at least once.

"If that's what you wish," he said, not batting an eye.

"A personal farrier, perhaps."

"Someone to shoe your personal horses?"

She nodded. "I don't ride. I think you should know. Not that I have anything against it. It's just in London there was never the time or the inclination, and one doesn't just ride for pleasure at Drumvagen."

"What does one do for pleasure at Drumvagen, other than talk to the animals?"

"One writes," she said, genuinely smiling this time. "Or one tends to children or goes on long walks."

"A very placid existence."

"Very placid. So placid I might have been bored without Lady Pamela."

He finished with her stocking, garter, and shoe, then helped her stand.

"Lady Pamela is most definitely not boring."

"I was teasing about the gardener," she said. "I wouldn't change a thing about Huntly."

"It's yours to change," he said. "Within reason."

"So I can't dig up the courtyard and have the Celtic knot replaced with an English symbol?"

"I think my ancestors would emerge from their crypts," he said.

"Can I change the countess's chambers?" she asked, serious now. She donned her corset over her shift and tightened it.

"What would you change about it?"

"All those mirrors," she said as she finished dressing. "I'd have them removed. And surely no one needs all those armoires. I'd have the secretary moved to the sitting room."

"Done," he said. "What else?"

Surprised, she glanced at him. He was looking at her with a small smile.

"A larger desk?" she asked. "Not appreciably bigger but a little."

"I'm sure we have something in another room that will suit."

She nodded, a little bemused. No one had ever listened to her so carefully or granted her wishes with such alacrity.

He brushed her skirt in the back, surveyed her once, as she did the same to him. He offered her arm and she took it, allowing him to lead her from the library as if there was nothing untoward about their visit there.

She noticed the alabaster inkwell on the floor and bit back her smile.

He was besotted.

What else could he call it? Whenever he looked at her, he wanted her again. She talked about children, his children, and he wanted to push her back down on the desk and make her scream in pleasure. She teased him and he desired her.

She confessed to not liking to ride, and he wanted to place a kiss on each pink cheek, enfold his arms around her and protect her from every fear she had, every lack in her life.

He wanted to assign each and every one of the hundred and sixty-seven of Huntly's staff to her beck and call.

No, he was most definitely besotted.

When they crossed the courtyard with her hand still on his arm, he took it in his instead. As they entered the house and he greeted one staff member after another with a nod, he still held onto her hand. And when they stopped in front of her suite, instead of relinquishing her, he pulled her down the hall, opened his doors, and brought her to his room.

He stood silent, watching her look around, feeling a sense of wonder at her surprise. The sitting room was as massive as hers, but the furniture was upholstered in the Forster tartan. The bedroom was dominated by a bed hewn from an oak from Huntly's forest over two centuries ago.

But it was the bath where he led her, a series of rooms to rival or exceed anything at Huntly.

The first chamber was occupied by a simple tub made of copper, a design of vines pressed into the back and sides. The stone dais on which it sat was beige with veins of copper and green.

The second part of the bath, reached through an arched door, was their destination.

The room they entered was hewn from the same beige stone, a bowl carved in the center. Thick copper pipes jutted out from one wall. He bent, turned one faucet, and hot water began to fill the tub.

She hadn't said a word since they entered the room. He'd expected, at the least, a dozen questions. Instead of waiting for her to ask, he gave her what information he could.

"It's built over a hot spring," he said, adjusting the cold water.

"What's that smell?" she asked. "It reminds me of medicine."

He smiled. "The water's thought to have medicinal properties. It's from the mineral springs."

She stepped forward, stretched out her hand, then drew it back in surprise. "It's really hot."

He reached her, began to unfasten her buttons.

How wide her eyes were and how silent she was. As if she were stunned at the force of their passion or his actions of the last fifteen minutes.

Little did she know he felt the same.

He'd never cared for a woman like he was doing now. He'd never coaxed her hair free until it fell below her shoulders then returned the pins to her so she could make sure it was up, out of the water.

He'd helped a woman undress before, holding her steady so she could step out of her skirts and the rest of her clothing, but he'd never done so with such tenderness. Nor had he ever cautioned himself to restrain his libido.

His wife was only one interlude away from being a virgin.

When she was down to her shift, the rest of her garments placed on the stone bench at his back, she finally spoke.

"Will you be joining me?"

He smiled. "No, not this time," he said. "I want you to soak so you aren't sore."

Her cheeks grew pink as he watched. She could dare him to take her, then blush when he mentioned she might be sore? What a contradiction she was. She had imagination enough to create Lady Pamela, yet she was every inch an innocent. She was a virgin, yet the most passionate woman he'd ever known.

How many other contradictions would he discover about Ellice?

She raised her arms as he slipped the shift over her head. A tiny smear of blood on her thigh held him still for a second. He wanted to enfold his arms around her, take from her any of the pain he might have caused. At the same time, he felt oddly proud that he had introduced her to passion, that in his arms she'd shivered and cried out.

He took her hand and gently led her down the three steps into the half-filled tub. She sat, making no effort to cover her breasts. Instead, she closed her eyes, inhaling the mineral smell, a scent that had always reminded him of camphor and newly sprouted leaves.

Reaching to the shelf to his left, he grabbed a washcloth and towel. Leaving the towel on the bench, he dipped the washcloth in the water, then squeezed it over her shoulders.

He wanted to touch her in some way. The foolishness of that thought made him drop the washcloth and step back. When the tub was full, he turned off the faucets.

"Take as long as you like," he said, deliberately not looking at her.

Only then could he leave the room.

Chapter 23

Ellice stared at the closed door, hoping Ross would return. When he didn't, she released the breath she was holding, sinking back against the polished stone.

Why did she feel like weeping at the moment? As if all the hurts stored up inside for years now sought to be released?

She was a bride. More, she was a wife. The wife of a very surprising man, one who rendered her speechless.

She'd imagined their passion but not the tenderness. What kind of man gently dresses a woman and then as sweetly undresses her? He almost started to bathe her. Why had he stopped? Why, for that matter, hadn't he joined her?

She lay her head back, feeling the tendrils of steam against her heated cheeks. The mineral water was heavily scented but not unpleasantly so. As she relaxed she could feel herself drift off into a pleasant hazy almost sleep. She felt this way when writing sometimes, as if she were in a place between reality and imagination.

Should her heart ache when thinking of Ross? Should something open up in her chest? She wanted to ease him in some way, hold him close, and in a way she never expected, protect him.

How could she protect the Earl of Gadsden? Why did she feel the need to?

Had he loved Cassandra very much? Had she bathed here with him? She wanted the answers to both questions and yet she'd never ask. Sometimes, an answer was worse than knowing for sure. At least now she could pretend that no, he hadn't loved Cassandra, or if he had, what he was feeling for her was so much more. Or that Cassandra was cold and unfeeling and that's why Ross had wished never to marry again.

She wanted to make sure he didn't feel that way now.

How did a wife seduce a husband? The same way she had this morning as a virgin, but with greater skill and more anticipation, knowing the pleasure she'd feel.

The tub was large enough to nearly swim in, certainly to stretch out each limb. She did, keeping her eyes closed, enjoying the buoyancy, the tingle as the mineral water loosened her muscles and soothed her skin.

She wasn't sure how long she remained there, but it was long enough for the tub to cool. She was looking for a handhold when the door opened and Ross stood there. He must have bathed as well because his wet hair curled at the neck. He'd changed his clothes, too. Now he wore black trousers and another shirt, almost snowy in its whiteness.

Without a word he came to the edge, holding out a hand. Once out of the tub he handed her the towel, not looking at her. She smiled and wrapped it around her body, knowing in a way she didn't understand that he desired her.

She wanted him after just looking at him.

She stepped in front of him and dropped the towel. At the same time, she reached up and placed her arms on his shoulders.

"Thank you," she said. "That was a lovely experience."

He didn't speak but he did put his hands on her waist, fingers splayed.

"Will you lead me to your bed?" she asked. "It must be softer than your desk."

"Ellice—" he began.

She silenced him with a kiss. When that was done and both of them breathless, she drew back.

"I'm feeling wonderful, Ross. Truly. The only thing that would make me feel better is if you showed me your bed."

She laughed as he grabbed her, lifting her into his arms, and strode out of the bathing chamber with her.

"Thank you, Mr. McMahon," the Dowager Countess of Gadsden said. "You've been very kind to bring me the new shipment."

"'Tis my pleasure, your ladyship. I thought there'd be people still here and all, what with the wedding."

"Oh, it was a small celebration. Perhaps we'll have a ball or something later in the year. We've not entertained at Huntly for some time, I'm afraid."

She stepped aside, allowing Mr. McMahon to enter her home.

"You're very physically fit, Mr. McMahon," she said, watching as he carried a rolled carpet with the strength of a much younger man. His arms bulged and his jacket seams didn't look as if they could stand the strain.

"All in a day's work, your ladyship."

She knew he wasn't married, that he lived with his sister and was content enough with the arrangement, all information she'd gleaned from previous visits.

"I've had Cook make some apple tarts," she said, having recently discovered that he particularly liked them.

He set the carpet down in the parlor. "You tell me where you'd like this first, your ladyship."

"Right there is fine, Mr. McMahon," she said. She'd have to find room for it later and send for a few footmen to help her.

At the moment she was more interested in luring him to the settee with promises of something sweet along with a little conversation.

"Tea?" she asked, sitting and smiling up at him.

He was really the most remarkable man. Not as handsome as her husband, true, but handsome men were a bother. No, Jack McMahon had something about him, some power of presence she noted in only the very important or the very wealthy.

She had no doubt he was on his way to being very wealthy. She'd spent a fortune with him this last year. But it was more than that.

He was short yet powerfully built, with broad shoulders she couldn't help but admire. His physique reminded her of those employed in Huntly's stables and gardens, earthy men who were used to getting their hands dirty and felt the ache of sore muscles each night.

What a pity he didn't have someone to care for him.

The birds began to chatter, so loudly she couldn't be heard over their noise.

He smiled, the expression changing his appearance in a way that was always magical to her. His face, square and broad, was close to being plain. But his wide and engaging smile brought a twinkle to his hazel eyes and a lightness to his features.

He would never be handsome but he was most certainly arresting.

"Come now," she said, picking up the teapot. "You have time for tea, surely? And a tart or two?"

She wanted to wave her hand in front of the tarts so he could smell the cinnamon and apples topped with a dollop of cream.

"Your ladyship . . ." he began, but she smiled at him, ignored his protests and poured him a cup.

She stirred a little cream into it, just the way he liked it, and placed it on the table before patting the seat cushion beside her.

He came and sat.

"Tell me about Edinburgh," she said. "I want to hear what's new in your shop and how your sister is faring."

She placed a tart on a small plate for him, put it on the table, and began eating her own pastry.

Today she would call him Jack, and if she were very, very fortunate, he would want to know her name as well. Small victories that flushed her face and made her heart race.

Ellice lay sprawled across the bed, staring up at the ceiling.

She was going to die of passion, she was sure of it.

How did the poor dear perish? So young, you know.

Oh, didn't you know? She expired from passion. She was rogered to death. But they cannot rid her of her smile.

Shocking.

She turned her head to where Ross lay in a nearly identical pose. His manhood, which should have been flaccid after all that work, twitched a little at her look. She really did want to touch it, to smooth her fingers over it, but perhaps it was better if she waited for a while.

After all, they had years and years of this.

Would she survive it?

"I never thought it would be like this," she said once she found the strength to speak.

Ross turned his head and regarded her, his gray eyes soft as a kitten's fur. "Like what?"

"Like feeling your soul leave your body."

His lips curved in a smile. "Is that what it's like?"

"You felt the same. Don't try to pretend you didn't," she added, a little smugly. She'd heard his shout at the end. The very proper Earl of Gadsden had nearly screamed his release.

His smile deepened but he didn't concur. That was fine; she didn't need his agreement to know what she knew.

She really should reach down and pull up the sheet, but

she didn't mind being naked around him. How very strange since she'd always been so modest. Now she could very easily traipse to the bathroom and glance over her shoulder with a cheeky smile. He'd be watching her, of course, his cock twitching a bit more.

Stretching out a hand, she very nearly touched him before some imp of wisdom cautioned her that it wouldn't be wise. He must have thought the same because he reached out and grabbed her hand, bringing it to his lips where he kissed her knuckles.

He really needed to stop making gestures like that. He would bring her to tears.

She rolled over, propping her head on her hand. How glorious he was. She liked it when his hair was mussed and his beard showing through. He looked almost like a ruffian. A brigand who insisted on robbing her, but only of pleasure.

She scooted up to place a kiss on his cheek.

"I'm very pleased," she said, wondering if it was wise to be so honest with a new husband.

She only had Virginia and Mairi as a guide, and they never seemed to withhold anything from Macrath and Logan. She would begin that way, too.

"Are you?" he asked.

She nodded. "Very much. You're a magnificent lover."

Were his cheeks deepening in color? She could almost imagine it. No, the Earl of Gadsden would never blush.

"You should have told me."

His bark of laughter made her smile.

"I don't think that would have been entirely proper."

"Oh, I think so," she said. "I can imagine the conversation, can't you? 'Lady Ellice, I have so many acres, so much income, and by the way, I'm a great lover.' You should have," she added, placing another kiss on his cheek. "I wouldn't have cared about the acreage or the income."

"You wouldn't, would you?" His frown surprised her. "Why wouldn't you?"

She thought about it for a moment. "Perhaps it's because I know what it's like to be both wealthy and poor. I wouldn't choose to be poor, but I can endure it. Besides, I know how fleeting wealth can be."

"You needn't worry," he said. "The Gadsden wealth isn't fleeting."

"Well, if the coffers ever run low, you could always invite the queen to make Huntly one of her palaces."

One edge of his smile quirked up. "It's not really that big."

"It's the British Library," she said. "It's quite the largest place I've ever seen. I think you could rattle around in here and get lost."

"I would send a hound after you."

"Do you have hounds?"

His smile broadened. "We've all manner of animals at Huntly. Hounds and cats, sheep and cattle. We probably have a few of anything you'd like."

"Does it never disturb you?"

"What, the size?"

She nodded, reaching out and tracing a pattern on his arm. "And the loneliness," she said, startled at her own words.

He didn't say anything for a moment. "It doesn't feel lonely right now."

"So you never get lost."

"Never," he said. "Although there are parts I haven't visited in years. For example, the north wing off the servants' wing. It's where we store old furniture. I haven't been there in at least three years."

She shook her head. "See? That sounds unbelievable to me, that there might be places in your own home you haven't seen for such a long time."

"And my mother's house," he added. "I try never to go there unless absolutely necessary."

"Truly?"

He nodded. "If you ever saw it, you'd know why."

She waited but he didn't explain.

"So you spend most of your time in the library?"

"How did you know that?"

"A process of deduction," she said. "When I went looking for you, the footman said you would be in the library. This morning, you took me to the library. I think it's probably the place you spend most of your time."

"Even people who know me well don't know that," he said, reaching out and pushing a tendril of hair back from her cheek. "You're very astute, Ellice."

"I'm your wife," she said. "Shouldn't I know secret things about you?"

"I broke my toe once," he said, sticking out his foot. "It looks a bit strange."

She reached down, cupped her hand over his toes. "You have lovely feet and you know it. And very hairy legs," she added, ruffling the hair there. "I shan't need a blanket in the winter. You Scots have very cold winters."

Suddenly, she was flat on her back and he was over her, smiling.

"I promise you'll be warm in my bed."

She wrapped her arms around his neck and pulled his head down for a kiss.

To her surprise, he wouldn't continue with their love play, merely tucked her in at his side, wrapping his arm around her and shelving his chin on her hair.

They talked for hours, it seemed. He told her about growing up at Huntly, being sent away to school in England. She told him of Lawrence and Eudora and the smallpox epidemic that had so changed the tenor of their London days. He confessed that he grew tired of women always talking about the color of his eyes. She came up with a dozen colors they might be called other than simply gray.

When the conversation led to his plans for the library, she lay her head on his shoulder, her hand on his chest, realizing how much it meant to him.

"I'd like to make it available for any Scot to explore if he wished. There are valuable books there, volumes I suspect are among the rarest in the world."

"Would you have people come here?"

He shook his head. "I'd donate them," he said. "As long as I'm assured that there would be a proper place for them." He smiled. "Something like the British Library."

Her stomach rumbled and she laughed.

"We've not eaten," he said, his tone surprised.

They looked at each other. Night had fallen and they'd spent the day together, entranced with one another to the exclusion of anything else, even food.

The servants hadn't knocked on the door. Her new mother-in-law hadn't disturbed them. They'd been in their own world.

"Do you like sandwiches?" he asked.

"At this point, I think I'd eat anything. Other than rabbit. I'm not excessively fond of rabbit."

"Or anything with eyes," he said, charming her by remembering. "I've an appetite for beef, some bread, mustard, and ale."

At her look, he smiled. "I have a schoolboy's tastes. It's what I lived on in England. I still crave it from time to time."

Huntly's staff must have been prepared for his cravings because within a quarter hour they were seated in his sitting room with a large tray on the table between them. She was dressed in one of his blue silk dressing gowns and he wore a black patterned one.

She tucked her feet beneath her as, one by one, he took the domed lids from a succession of plates, each smelling better than the one before. When he came to the cake, a delicious looking confection filled with nuts and fruit, she glanced up at him.

"I want cake," she said. "Before anything healthful or beneficial."

"Cake it is, then," he said, cutting a piece and handing it to her.

She closed her eyes after the first forkful. The taste was heavenly, light and airy yet filled with nuts and chopped apricots.

When she opened her eyes, it was to find him watching her.

"I love cake," she said, embarrassed. "I love sweets."

"What about rabbit cake?"

"Oh, that would pose a problem for me."

He smiled and she felt it down to her toes.

Her body was still thrumming with delight, her lips swollen from his kisses. Her husband was the most handsome man she'd ever seen, and she had cake.

Could anything be more wonderful than this moment?

Chapter 24

He was well on his way to being an absolute idiot.

The world was a glorious place this morning. The birds were particularly noisy in their greeting to the day. The sky was a cloudless blue, the color of delphiniums.

He'd never before equated the color of the sky to a flower.

This morning he would show Ellice some of the rare volumes in the Forster collection. He hoped she would be impressed at the illuminated scrolls or the Bible he suspected was one of the first Gutenberg volumes. Would she be interested in the Latin poetry he'd found? One of his ancestors had evidently collected erotic poetry.

Perhaps he could read it to her one evening. She could counter by reading a chapter of *The Lusty Adventures of Lady Pamela* aloud.

He smiled at the thought.

He knocked at her door, but when she didn't answer, he opened it, calling her name.

Where was she?

He should have checked his suite first. She enjoyed the bath so much that she'd used it often in the last week. Would it be possible to create a hot springs bath in her quarters? Better yet, perhaps she could simply move into his suite, an idea that had never occurred to him before this moment.

He stopped in the middle of the sitting room. She'd been here only a week and already made changes to claim this space.

The room smelled of lemon wax and the perfume she wore, something delicate and unassuming, not truly mirroring the complex woman she was. She should wear something hinting of roses, or more exotic blooms, a scent that teased the senses.

She hated the mirrors, so he had them removed. He found another desk in the attics, one more suited for a study, but she'd been overjoyed when first viewing it. There was enough space in the sitting room, and that's where it rested, beneath the window looking out over Huntly's glen.

He wished this view was of the lake. She would have liked the sight of the birds soaring over the trees or the pale light of dawn reflected in the water.

A robe rested on the back of the settee. Had she taken it off as she walked into her bedroom? He fingered it, willing himself to feel a residual warmth of her body, but the silk was cool to his touch.

The room felt empty. How could she be here and he not know it?

Gone was the silent wraith who looked wide-eyed at him in the presence of others. This woman dared him and challenged him.

A book sat upside down. He tilted his head to inspect the spine. She read poetry. He made a note of that. Another book was on the settee. A depression on a pillow meant she'd rested there for a while. He placed his hand there, shook his head at himself, and moved away, smiling at the sight of her slippers at the entrance to the bedroom.

The desk was strewn with paper. He hesitated, wondering if she had the pages in a certain order. He picked up one, began to read, realizing as he did so that the maids assigned to her room might glance over her work.

He didn't remember this chapter.

Frowning, he pulled out her chair and sat.

No, he definitely didn't remember this part of the book. She had changed from third person to first, as if the recollections of her adventures were spoken in Lady Pamela's voice. By the second page he realized he wasn't reading from her book at all but something of a diary.

He wanted to call back the action of his hand the minute he picked up the third page and began to read. This was not something Ellice had written for anyone else's eyes. He told himself that even as he was captured by her words.

When he touches me my skin begins to glow. I feel heated from inside, as if the whole of my body recognizes him. Here is the origin of my contentment. Here is the source of my pleasure. He alone can bring me to fulfillment, make me cry out in wonder, weak with bliss.

My body erupts, even in sleep, imagining him touching me. His hand stretches out and touches my breast, cupping it gently, teasing me. My nipples elongate at the thought of his mouth. My head arches back for him to trail kisses down my throat.

My lips swell to cushion his.

"How beautiful your back is," he said, and I want to thank the God of all creation for making it so. Thank you for narrowing his experience of women that he would think me beautiful. Thank you for giving me enough foolishness that I would hide in a stranger's carriage and end up with this man as my husband. My lover to whom I can go every night and with whom I can satiate myself.

He put the page back down on the desk, wishing he'd never sought her out. She was a drug, an opiate, and it was all too clear that he was becoming addicted. If she were here, he'd probably sweep her pages away and mount her again on a desktop.

What had happened to him? He wasn't a fool, yet nothing labeled him one more than sitting here imagining loving her again.

He was well on his way to behaving just like his father, as unprincipled and hedonistic.

That thought was a blow to the chest.

"I never knew a cocksman like your father," a duke once said to him. "The man could shag his way across the Empire. He once told me that gambling was a waste of money and drinking gave him tremors and a headache. But loving a woman, that was the best of all sins."

He was his father's son, wasn't he?

For the last week he'd spent all his waking time with his wife. They'd explored the attics, and acted out one of the scenes in her book. They'd talked for hours about anything. He'd told her about his joy in coming home to Huntly and his excitement in going off to school.

He'd introduced her to everyone at Huntly, from the footmen to the grooms to the undercooks to the chef he'd purloined from a duke in London.

"Do you know all their names?" she'd asked.

"Of course."

"But there are a lot of people here."

"Yes, but they work for me."

"I should learn their names as well, shouldn't I?"

He hadn't gotten the opportunity to answer her. She'd reached up, pulled his head down and kissed him.

One day, they'd gone to the lake, and he'd taken her out in the boat, the afternoon transfixed by laughter. She had a sense of humor he'd not expected, able to laugh at herself.

"You were alone too much," he said, after she told him about London.

She looked surprised at his comment.

"It was a difficult time," she said.

"You were still alone at Drumvagen. Did no one notice?"

He was angry on her behalf. Had she been invisible to everyone?

What the hell had he done?

He'd become ensnared with a woman. His every waking thought had been of her.

Where had his ambition gone? He'd done nothing in the last week to advance his career or solidify his chances in the coming election. He hadn't written any letters, planned any events, or scheduled meetings.

He'd been adrift in lust, as unrestrained as his father.

He had goals and aspirations, duties and responsibilities. He was damned if he was going to be in thrall to a woman, any woman, even his wife.

He was not going to be like his father. There was more to his existence than his bodily desires. He had greater plans for his life than to be led around by his cock.

He left the pages where they were, striding out of the room before she returned. At least he hadn't mentioned the idiotic notion of her sharing his room.

"I wonder how Ellice likes married life," Mairi said to her husband in their carriage. "The first week is always the most challenging."

"Is it?" Logan asked, making no effort to hide his smile.

"You snored. I hadn't known that. Plus, you're difficult to wake in the morning. You would burrow yourself under the pillow if you could."

"And you learned that all in the first week?"

She nodded. "Plus the fact that you love sweets." She eyed him. "What did you learn about me?"

"You steal my side of the blanket," he said, "and you get cold at night."

She looked over at him. How could it be that she loved him even more than that first week?

"I'm still disappointed," Mairi said, plucking at her gloves. "I wanted to publish Ellice's book."

The crunch of wheels on the gravel was strangely comforting, perhaps because it was proof that they were finally heading home.

Macrath, especially protective of Virginia, had insisted on all of them returning to Drumvagen immediately after the wedding. His solicitousness had gotten to the point where the two women often exchanged a glance and a shake of the head.

Mairi reflected on her brother. Didn't Macrath know that women gave birth every day? True, there were some tragedies, but Virginia hadn't been one of them. He simply had to stop wrapping her in batting and treating her like crystal.

Not that Virginia wasn't capable of fighting that battle. But she and Logan had remained at Drumvagen for a week anyway, to give Virginia some moral support.

Spring was in the air, in the gusts that carried the scent of new roses and grass. Even the sea air smelled sharper, as if waking to a different season, one filled with boiling clouds and tumultuous storms.

Drumvagen stood impervious to any of nature's tantrums, the gray brick sparkling in the sun the four towers tall, proud, and as stubborn looking as Macrath himself.

Mairi had grown to love her brother's home, but she missed Edinburgh.

Her cousin, Fenella, and Fenella's husband Allan, had managed the paper for the last two weeks, but it was time to return to business. She missed the smudge of ink on her fingers, the smell of paper, and the ever present click and clank of the new rotary press.

"I think Ellice allowed herself to be purchased," she said now, staring out the carriage window at the sunny day. "She traded that manuscript for a marriage."

Logan glanced at her.

"If she did, she got the better end of the bargain, Mairi."

"You like him," she said, surprised.

"I like him," he affirmed. "I always have."

"He's asked for your help, hasn't he?" Mairi asked. Even though Logan had retired from political life, he was still influential. A word from him would go a long way to ensuring a man's future, even a pompous earl's. "How silly of him to think a book might do him damage."

"I think it's entirely within the realm of possibility," Logan said. "Especially given what I know of his father. Ross called him a wastrel. The man was a bit more than that."

"Oh?"

"He was a satyr, or as close as I've heard. His exploits were legendary, fueled by a fantastic fortune. For years, Ross has done what he could to offset his father's reputation."

"Has he had ambitions to be a representative for that long?"

He smiled at her. "Perhaps. Or perhaps it was simply that he hated what people thought of the Gadsden name."

"Or maybe he wanted people to respect him," she said. "Men won't follow those they don't respect."

"And where did you come by that knowledge?"

"From you." She could tell she surprised him. "People have always respected you, Logan. If you respect Gadsden and support him, his chances of being elected are better."

"He has some fine ideas for the future."

"How does he feel about women?"

He glanced at her.

"I'm a newspaperwoman, my darling Logan. Of course I want to know. I am surprised, however, that he would want to go to Parliament. Doesn't Huntly keep him busy enough?"

He smiled at her, which immediately made her wish she'd been more tactful. Logan was often amused at her blunt way of speaking, and there were times when she wished she had kept her mouth shut as well. Questions and comments just flowed from her brain to her lips at the most inappropriate moments.

"Gadsden's started several scholarships, plus he's working on cataloging the Huntly library. I understand the original Latin works are priceless."

"One would think, with his love of books, that he wouldn't try to censor one."

"I doubt the Latin works are as worrisome as *The Lustful Adventures of Lady Pamela*."

She shook her head, sinking back against the seat.

"I can't believe that Ellice, our Ellice, would have written such a thing. I haven't given up, however. I'm still determined to publish it."

"I said the same to Ross."

"Did you?"

He nodded.

At first she found it a little disconcerting that he knew her so well. Now it was a source of endless comfort and occasional humor.

"He wants to win the election," Logan said. "He's very ambitious in that regard."

She shot him a glance. "Like becoming Lord Provost was your ambition?"

He nodded. "Once I became Lord Provost, I realized that I wasn't suited for a life under constant scrutiny. I wanted my privacy. Then I found another ambition, one as important."

"Expanding Blackwell's."

He smiled. "Marrying you."

She reached over and kissed him for that comment. Pulling away, she was gratified to see that he was breathing hard as well. She straightened her bodice and reached for the hated bonnet on the other seat.

"Why do you even bother?" he asked. "You carry the blasted thing more than you wear it."

"Just in case I need it," she said.

She answered a similar question at least once a week. Perhaps one day she would have the courage to leave her bonnet behind. She'd become an arbiter of fashion, Mrs. Logan Harrison, who despised hats, refused to wear them, and began the Women's Hatless Brigade.

Perhaps she could write a series of columns on unnecessary garments that women felt compelled to wear. While she was at it, she might consult with Dr. Thorburn again about the dangers of corsets.

She didn't know if the readers of the *Edinburgh Women's Gazette* would be shocked by such a frank topic.

For that matter, what would people say if she dared to publish Ellice's book?

She grabbed his hand, wrapping hers around it. They'd been married for two years, and for two years she'd been happier than she'd ever dreamed of being. Sometimes she was afraid of such joy because life wasn't especially joyous. But then she reasoned she'd been given Logan because of her earlier losses. Providence's way of balancing the scales.

That wasn't to say they always saw things the same way or that there was little discord between them. Sometimes they disagreed about little things, and when that happened each had to decide whether it was worth the argument. At other times, however, she didn't have a problem with getting face-to-face with Logan and arguing like a Jesuit priest at the top of her voice. Nor did Logan object to being just as loud.

He was a lion, a comment she'd made to him several months ago, one which had stopped him in his tracks.

"You aren't a blond," she said, "which might make you look more like a lion. But your hands are large, like paws, and you have this stance with your feet apart and your arms braced just so as if you're protecting your herd."

"Pride," he said. "It's called a pride, and I thought you always likened me to a bear."

"No," she said, shaking her head. "A bear isn't proud or regal enough."

He smiled at her then, and whatever comment she'd been about to make had simply flown from her mind.

He could make her forget everything with that smile, and it disconcerted her every time it happened.

She wasn't about to tell him he possessed a secret weapon.

Would Ellice be as happy with her earl as she was with Logan? She said a silent prayer for the girl and the man, only because Logan liked him.

Whether he was worth Ellice was the question.

Chapter 25

What had she done wrong?

She'd evidently said or done something, because Ross had ignored her for a week. In that time, she'd seen him twice at dinner. Once, he left the dining room the minute she entered, leaving the footmen standing there with stone faces as she and the maids stared after him with wide eyes.

The second time, Ross remained in place, but when she attempted to speak to him looked straight through her.

"What have I done?" she asked. When he didn't answer, she asked another question. "Have you been ignoring me because I've been writing?"

His head jerked up, his eyes as sharp as steel.

"I promised I wouldn't take my book to Mairi," she said, feeling betrayed. "But my contract says I can write. You promised."

She hadn't waited for him to answer. That night she'd been the one to leave him. For the last few days she'd taken a tray in her sitting room.

The marriage that had begun with such delight was now a disaster.

The man she'd seen only a glimpse of, tender, kind, and passionate, had disappeared, replaced by the cold and distant earl she'd first met.

How could she possibly make it better if she didn't know what she'd done? At least at Drumvagen she had no doubt which flaw of hers had irritated her mother.

She hadn't seen her mother-in-law for days. At first she thought it was because the woman was giving her and Ross time alone. But Pegeen told her that the countess had a penchant for avoiding people at Huntly.

"We can go for days without seeing her, your ladyship. At Huntly you could go a year without seeing anyone. I've a friend who works on the second floor of the countess's house. I rarely see her. Even the laundry is separate."

Drumvagen was filled with people. Some days she'd had to escape to the cottage in order to be left alone. At Huntly, she could skip through the corridors and no one would notice. She might as well dance naked in the courtyard, for all the attention Ross paid her.

Pegeen was the one person she saw every day. The voluble maid was a delight to be around, for short periods, at least. Pegeen had a great deal to say, however, and was evidently intent on saying it all as quickly as she could.

Ellice had become adept at sending her on errands just to get a little peace and time to write.

She was determined not to hide in her rooms, however, so when she was finished writing she explored Huntly with Pegeen as her guide. She lost count of how many rooms there were. If Pegeen hadn't been with her, she was certain she would still be wandering through the wings, corridors, and rooms.

Most of the public rooms were housed in the main building, with the family rooms in the wing to the right. Other rooms, such as the Earl's Study, the Chart Room, the Map Room, and the Persian Room, were located in the wing to the left.

Behind the curved wings, where they couldn't be seen, stretched two more sections. To the right were the kitchen, laundry, and storage rooms. Directly opposite, and similarly hidden from view, were the stables, farm offices, and dairy barns.

Four separate gardens were accessible through various rooms. The Flower Room, so called because of its mural of endless rows of flowers, was adjacent to a magnificent rose garden. The Tiger Room, a bit horrifying since it held the heads of various beasts mounted on its walls, led to the spice garden. A walled garden, accessible through the magnificent Red Drawing Room, was so secluded and silent it felt like the interior of a cloister. The fourth garden was a maze of hedges. When she entered it from the Receiving Room, she immediately felt small and insignificant next to the six-foot-high greenery.

Huntly's ballroom was the largest room she'd ever seen, even considering the British Museum. What looked like an acre of polished wood floor stretched between walls either covered with tall windows or plastered with gilt and ivory. Six crystal chandeliers hung over the space, sunlight bouncing off the prisms and hurling fractured rainbows over the walls.

The State Dining Room was five times as large as the smaller Family Dining Room, but that room was not intimate by any means. Thirty people could sit at the table.

Everywhere she looked there was something to marvel at, from the gold cupids holding bouquets of flowers in the corner of the conservatory or the Viewing Platform located at the very top of the house. After climbing the hundred steps, she and Pegeen stood against the railing, marveling at the view of the river and beyond.

She could even see to Edinburgh and the castle sitting atop the highest rock.

Huntly's setting reminded her of Drumvagen, since it was adjacent to a river and set amidst woodland. But Huntly was set on a rise, making it appear even more majestic than its size alone would dictate.

Although the view of Huntly was easily accessible to anyone traveling to Edinburgh, she'd never seen the house. If she had, she would probably have wondered at the inhabitants. Who were they, that they could live amidst such splendor?

An ordinary person, as it turned out.

She toured the kitchen, so cavernous that voices echoed against the vaulted ceiling. The laundry operated every day instead of just a day or two during the week, with vats kept boiling to accommodate the vast number of sheets, towels, aprons, and napkins used at Huntly. Uniforms were laundered twice weekly, and delicate clothing, such as her dresses, would be done on an as needed basis by a woman skilled in such a task.

"Unless you take on a lady's maid, your ladyship," Pegeen said. "Someone from London or Edinburgh."

"I see no reason to do that," she said. "Together we'll muddle on."

"About that, your ladyship," Pegeen said. "I'm to tell you about all your appointments. You have to see the dressmaker, to add to your wardrobe. The housekeeper has asked for time. So has the majordomo, the head gardener, and the stable master."

"Why do I have to meet with the stable master?"

Pegeen's eyes widened at the question. "To arrange for your mount, your ladyship. Surely you want to pick your own horse."

"I don't want a horse."

"Then you need to tell him that, begging your pardon, your ladyship. He'll be disappointed, though. He's been looking through the mares, trying to pick the best one for you."

She pushed that thought to the back of her mind. But the

dressmaker? When she asked about that appointment, Pegeen's mouth firmed.

"Yes, your ladyship, I took it upon myself to summon her. You've only ten dresses. The Countess of Gadsden needs a substantial wardrobe. The earl concurs," she added, as if knowing that Ross's agreement would be the trump card.

From the look on Pegeen's face, half triumph, half determination, Ellice suspected she wasn't going to win that war.

But there was really no need for her to meet with the gardener and the majordomo. When she said as much, Pegeen laughed gaily.

"But you're in charge, your ladyship. They look to you for guidance."

"Surely they look to the earl."

The maid shook her head. "Not since he married, your ladyship. Everyone assumes you're responsible for the house."

As well as the hundred sixty-seven staff?

She was suddenly grateful for her mother's tutelage. From the time she was a little girl she'd been taught how to manage a household. Granted, she doubted her mother had ever envisioned her managing a house the size of Huntley. Surely the lessons were the same, only on a grander scale.

Still, the idea of managing Huntly was overwhelming.

"Why doesn't the Dowager Countess handle all this?" she asked weakly.

"Oh, she did," Pegeen said, guiding Ellice to another corridor. This one was floored with delicate blue and white marble.

A perfect floor on which to roller-skate. What a pity she'd left her skates behind in London. Whatever would the staff say to see her sailing through the corridor, squealing with glee?

Perhaps she could order a pair.

"Until the earl died," Pegeen explained. "Then the countess moved to the East Building and there she's been ever since. She's as far removed from Huntly as she can be and still be in the house."

"The East Building?"

Pegeen nodded. "It's the main building on the right when you enter Huntly's courtyard."

"Across from the library," she said, nodding.

"You've seen the library, your ladyship? Is it as glorious as I've heard?"

"You've never seen it?"

Pegeen shook her head. "Oh, no, your ladyship. It's forbidden to enter the library. The earl doesn't even allow anyone to clean in there."

"I've only seen one part of it," she said, praying a blush wouldn't appear on her cheeks.

She described the tower to Pegeen, the view of the lake, and the shelves and shelves of books, along with the wondrous curving stair.

As they were exploring, she caught a glimpse of her reflection in one of the paneled mirrors of the room in which they were standing. The Reception Room? The Greeting Room? How was she ever to memorize all the rooms, let alone manage their care?

Dark circles beneath her eyes revealed her problem sleeping. She was remaining awake until all hours, anticipating Ross's arrival, only to fall into an uneasy sleep. In the morning she awoke feeling curiously ashamed, certainly lonely, and most definitely uneasy.

Was this going to be the pattern of her days?

Her face looked sad, and nothing she did, from practicing a silly smile to making faces at herself, would alter the look.

Perhaps it was simply the expression in her eyes.

At least at Drumvagen she hadn't known what she was missing. She hadn't been kissed into delirium, coaxed to surrender, and given delight as a reward.

She thought to remain awake at his side, watching him as he slept. She wanted to know more about his library. She wanted to ask him more about his childhood or the future he'd envisioned for himself.

Instead, he ignored her.

For all his neglect, he had the mirrors in her dressing room removed. He replaced the delicate secretary with a massive desk equal to the one in Huntly's library.

What had she done?

She scoured her mind for anything she might have said to offend him. Something had happened and she didn't have any idea what it was.

She needed to ask him, straight out. She needed to discover what she'd done and then she would correct it if she could.

What if he was simply missing Cassandra? What if he was regretting marrying her and not remaining a widower?

What could she do about that?

Virginia wanted to throw something at her husband.

She'd adored Macrath from the instant she met him, but he was annoying in the extreme lately.

Two months had passed since Carlton's birth, yet he still had barely kissed her. They'd never gone so long without being close to each other.

After Fiona was born, he didn't miss a night cradling her in his arms. Sleeping together was one of the most comforting aspects of being married, especially sleeping in Macrath's arms.

Yet for the last two months he'd studiously avoided her. During the first month, he'd slept in the sitting room, even going so far as to have a cot moved in and kept behind the settee.

She'd come out on many a morning to find him hunched

into nearly a ball, trying to keep his feet from hanging over the end of the cot. Nothing could make it wide enough for his shoulders, however.

"This is ridiculous, Macrath," she'd said, standing over him one morning. "You'll come back to our bed now. I'm fine and I'll be even better with my husband sleeping beside me."

But just because he was sleeping beside her didn't mean he was touching her.

When she cuddled next to him, he stiffened, moved to the edge of the bed and remained there until she rolled over.

"It's not another woman," she said, frowning at him now. "You'd not do something so foolish."

He turned in the act of stropping his razor and looked at her. The lower half of his face was covered in foam, but she could see his look of incredulity well enough.

"Are you daft?"

She nodded. "Over you? Most definitely."

He smiled, then continued with his shaving. She loved watching him shave. She loved watching him doing anything. Each of his movements was deliberate, as if he thought about every action before performing it.

"Have I lost my looks, then?" she asked, deliberately trying to sound Scottish. She amused him, mixing her American and English accent with her adopted homeland.

He didn't smile. He didn't even look at her.

A woman knows when she's desired, and she didn't feel that way at all.

She wanted to touch him. The need to do so was so strong she reached for him in the night. Each time it was the same. He moved away.

He finished shaving, rinsed his face and blotted it dry. In a moment he'd put his shirt on, say something conciliatory, and kiss her on the forehead, placing his hands on her shoulders to restrain her if she tried for a deeper kiss.

She wasn't going to tolerate it.

"If you don't want me, Macrath, I'm afraid you're going to have to say it to my face. I want the words."

He looked at her over the towel.

"Yes, Carlton's birth was difficult, but it's over and done."

The midwife—and Brianag, the traitor—had been insistent that she not bear another child. She was not satisfied with their opinions. She was going to see Dr. Thorburn when she was next in Edinburgh.

Even so, there was no reason her husband couldn't touch her.

She cinched the belt on her robe tighter, went to stand behind Macrath and wrapped her arms around him. She turned her head, resting her cheek against his back, ignoring his rigid posture.

"I won't break, my darling," she said. "A kiss, that's all I want."

"Virginia."

"Macrath."

He slowly turned. "I almost lost you once, and I told myself it would never happen again."

At first she thought he was referring to childbirth, but when he touched the small scars on the corner of her eyes she understood he meant the smallpox epidemic that had swept through London years ago. She'd nearly died, but Macrath hadn't been responsible. Nor could he have done anything to save her since he'd been in Australia at the time.

"I nearly lost you again, my love," he said softly.

She shook her head. He'd always been able to bring her to tears with his words. "You think it's your fault?"

"If you hadn't been with child, you wouldn't have nearly died in childbirth. If I hadn't bedded you, you wouldn't have been with child."

He was such an intelligent man that when he uttered a stupid comment it was a surprise.

She didn't quite know what to say to him so she wrapped her arms around his neck and pulled his head down for a kiss.

This time, however, he stepped back, removing her arms, smiling gently at her.

"I love you too much," he said.

When he left their bedroom she could only stare after him. Something must be done.

Chapter 26

She took the shorter way around to the library by cutting across the courtyard. Halfway to the building she wondered if Ross would reject her. Would the scene of such initial joy also be the place where he rebuffed her?

She halted halfway there, turning and staring at Huntly's edifice, once again reminded of the British Museum. Perhaps she was just one more exhibit. Statue of Lonely Countess, circa 1875. Mark the female's lost look, the distance in her eyes, the frozen tears on her cheeks.

Lady Pamela wouldn't tolerate such treatment. Lady Pamela would demand her rights as a wife. She would seduce Ross until he was captivated. He'd come crawling back to her on his knees, begging for one more chance.

"Please Ellice, forgive me, but smile at me, I beg you."

She would turn and look at him, groveling at her feet. Perhaps she'd pity him for the sincerity of his apology. Perhaps she wouldn't because of all the despair he'd caused her in the last week.

The sad and unchangeable fact, however, was that while she might yearn to be Lady Pamela, she wasn't. She was simply Ellice Traylor Forster, the Countess of Gadsden, and a more miserable creature she couldn't imagine.

Changing her mind about the library, she turned and was heading back across the courtyard when a wagon pulled out from behind the East Building. Her mother-in-law stood atop the back steps, a gauzy shawl around her shoulders, her hair coming loose from its bun. A bright smile wreathed her mouth and made her blue eyes sparkle as she waved with the tips of her fingers at a departing wagon. The Dowager Countess turned on the steps then, looked down and saw Ellice. "My dear," she said, "you've come to visit. How lovely!"

She was well and truly trapped.

Rather than explain that she was feeling abjectly sorry for herself and not wishing any company, she pasted a smile on her face.

"I haven't come at a bad time?" she asked, grabbing her skirts with both hands and mounting the wide steps behind the building.

She concentrated on her footing. When she looked up as she was climbing steps she sometimes grew dizzy. Her mother said it was because she'd ruined her eyes reading so much. Ellice had bitten back a comment that she'd rather read than concentrate on the infinitesimal stitches in needlework. That was a truly eye-ruining exercise.

However, needlework was more proper than writing, wasn't it?

Why was the world divided into what she should do and what she most wished to do?

"Did you have some more wool delivered?" she asked the older woman at the top of the steps, remembering when the countess couldn't say good-bye to her family because she was expecting a shipment. Was she involved in trade?

"Oh, no," the countess said, laughing gently. "That was a shipment of brass pots. Quite lovely things from India. Do you want one?"

"Um, no, but thank you."

"Mr. McMahon brought them. He'd just acquired a few and thought I would like them."

"Did he?"

"He's the most wonderful merchant," the older woman said, leading her into the house.

As her mother-in-law was extolling the virtues of Mr. McMahon—more than any merchant surely deserved—Ellice looked around, eyes wide. What had Ross said about it? She couldn't remember, only that he didn't like coming here. She could well imagine why.

She wondered if she looked as surprised as she felt. She tried, very hard, to rearrange her features so they wouldn't give anything away, but it was so difficult, given the cluttered condition of her mother-in-law's home.

Had the older woman taken up residence in the East Building because of all her possessions?

She could barely navigate the hallway because of the crates and baskets stacked there. When she followed her mother-in-law into the parlor, she couldn't help but stare.

Where another person might have had a few tables and lamps, her mother-in-law had ten. Bird cages hung from the ceiling and were stacked in the corner, each and every one of them filled with a canary or budgie. Three carpets, one atop the other, stretched over the wood floor, and wherever there might have been a spare inch of space there was instead a copper or brass pot filled with ferns.

Upholstered chairs were stacked on top of each other in the corner.

"There's no room to set them out," her mother-in-law said. "I need another two parlors, I'm afraid."

"How many do you have?"

"Four in all. This part of Huntly was designed to hold different branches of the family. Wasn't that clever of Ross's ancestors? Unfortunately, however, the family has died out in the meantime. All that's left is Ross." She smiled brightly. "And you, of course. You may be the answer to a mother's prayer."

Was she supposed to fill Huntly with children? Would any one woman be up to that task?

"Ross says I have too many things," the countess said, looking around her.

Ellice fervently agreed with her husband. She grabbed her skirts with both hands and made her way to the settee. Grabbing an armful of pillows, she deposited them on a facing chair, cleared off the space of small brass cups, and sat on the green velvet.

Dust and feathers floated in the air. Didn't the countess find it difficult to breathe? The smell wasn't obnoxious, though, because of the potpourri containers on the table, pierced brass fixtures emitting something that smelled heavily of cinnamon.

The first question that came to mind was why the countess owned so many things. The second thought was that it was none of her concern. Still, she was curious. Did the woman really like all those birds? She counted to thirty before giving up.

"Who feeds them?" she asked, looking at all the cages.

"I do," the countess cheerily said. "Every morning. I do need help cleaning the little darlings' cages. That is a chore in itself. But I take great pride in their health. I think how a person treats an animal to be a mark of character, don't you?"

She nodded. She'd never been able to abide a person who was cruel to any animal.

"I'm so glad you came to see me," the countess said, leaning forward to grab an oversize bell on the table. When she shook it, the noise woke all the birds at once. The resulting cacophony prevented Ellice from hearing what the other woman was saying. The noise didn't seem to disturb the countess at all, who kept talking.

When the squawks and screeches subsided, she smiled. "I've rung for tea. I haven't had a visitor in so long that I have forgotten how to be polite. Oh, except for Mr. McMahon," she added.

"Did Mr. McMahon bring you the birds?" Ellice asked.

"Oh, yes. He brings me everything. He owns the most wonderful emporium. I must simply take you there one day. Do you like Edinburgh?"

"I've only been there a few times," Ellice said. "But I found the city to be fascinating."

"It is, of course, if you like cities. I find that all those people are a bit frightening."

Ellice just smiled. She was finding the conditions of her mother-in-law's home to be more frightening than any crowd of people.

"How are you settling in at Huntly?"

What did she say that could be complimentary and yet not a lie?

"It's very large."

"It's an elephant of a house," her mother-in-law said, surprising her. "Ross loves it, of course, but visitors have a tendency to gape. When I first came here I thought I'd never learn all the rooms or find my way."

"Did you?"

Her mother-in-law laughed. "No, which is why I'm living here. I know this house very well. I don't get lost, and if I want to go to the parlor I don't have ten to choose from."

Perhaps she could find a place to spend time as well, somewhere not as imposing.

"I've often thought the house was built to impress, but then the family history is impressive. Did you know that the family fought on the Royalists' side during the civil war? At one point there was even talk of a Forster being sentenced to death. But during the Restoration, the family fortunes turned. James Forster became a knight and the Lord Clerk Register of Scotland."

She smiled at Ellice. "A great many Forster men have been in service to their country."

"Is that why Ross wants to be a representative peer?"

"What a very astute question. I quite like you, my dear."

She also felt a sense of kinship with her mother-in-law. If that feeling could extend to her husband, she'd be happy at Huntly.

Ross, however, wasn't speaking to her. He didn't even remain in the same room.

She pushed the thought away as two maids emerged from a doorway she hadn't seen.

For the next several minutes she and her mother-in-law occupied themselves with tea and scones. She hadn't eaten much that morning and now found herself famished.

She took a sip, a mixture of black tea and something more fragrant, perhaps chamomile. This, too, was overlaid with the scent of cinnamon.

Across the room, three shelves were filled with an assortment of stuffed birds. Evidently the countess didn't see the odd juxtaposition of dead birds in the same room with dozens of live ones. She counted at least three pheasants, two quail families, and a half-dozen hawks. In addition to the birds there was a creature that looked like a mad chipmunk, rearing up on his hind legs, claws extended like he was trying to escape the glass dome surrounding him.

"Now," the countess said a few moments later, "let me answer your question about Ross."

Placing her cup on the tray before her, her mother-in-law turned and regarded her. Her blue eyes were soft but held a world of pain. A strange thought to have amid the excess surrounding them.

"I'm not a very clever woman," the countess said. "But I am a kind one. I've found that kindness is a greater asset than cleverness."

Since Ellice had always been surrounded by clever people who were also kind, she didn't know what to say. Thankfully, her mother-in-law didn't seem to expect a response.

"How much do you know about Ross's father?" she asked.

"Nothing," Ellice said, realizing it was true. Ross never talked about his father.

"Ours was an arranged marriage, something planned from my birth. No one knew that I was madly in love with Thomas from the moment I saw him." She plucked at her skirt with one hand. "Love is a very strange emotion, don't you think? It makes you miserable and fills you with delight at the same time."

The older woman glanced over at her. "Do you love my son?" Before she could formulate a reply, the countess shook her head. "No, don't answer that. It's none of my concern. All that I hope is that you, too, are a kind person, Ellice. He so needs a little kindness."

Once again she didn't know what to say.

"I wasn't clever enough or beautiful enough to keep Thomas. Oh, he did his duty by me. But once he had his heir, he looked to other women."

The countess closed her eyes, took another deep breath, then opened them again.

"You don't know any of this, do you?"

Ellice shook her head, placed one hand on the velvet cushion beside her, fingers absently stroking the softness.

"Perhaps the greatest kindness I could give you is to leave you in ignorance," the countess said.

Ellice stood then and walked to the far end of the room and the windows overlooking the courtyard. "Everyone is leaving me in ignorance, I'm afraid." She could see the library from there. Was he working inside or had he left Huntly? Was he visiting Edinburgh?

"You'll find that I'm invariably nosy, my dear. It's one of my failings. Why do you look so sad?"

She turned, facing her mother-in-law. "Do I? I haven't the slightest idea why, your ladyship."

A lie, and it seemed the older woman knew it.

"You have a mother," the countess said. "So I will not ask you to call me that. But could you not call me Janet?"

Ellice nodded.

"Now, tell me why you're so sad."

"Did he love her very much?"

Janet didn't answer her. Instead, she sat back, sipped at her tea and studied the far wall. Finally, she looked back at Ellice.

"Come and sit, my dear. We must have a very difficult conversation, you and I."

She didn't want to return to the settee. She wanted to leave this room with its overpowering clutter and this woman with her glistening eyes.

But she had vowed to be a woman of courage. Slowly, she walked back and sat, waiting for the countess to speak.

"Cassandra was an exceedingly kind woman," she said. "A beautiful woman as well. She was clever, too." Janet smiled. "There were times I almost wished to hate her. A beautiful, kind, and clever creature. It hardly seems fair, does it?"

"I have been surrounded by women like that all my life," Ellice said, thinking of Virginia and Mairi.

She didn't want to hear about the paragon of virtue who was Ross's dead wife. How, though, did she silence the countess? She was at fault for voicing a question she shouldn't have asked.

"I thought, at first, that it was a blessed marriage," the countess said. "Ross felt for her what I felt for his father, a sort of uncomplicated adoration."

She smiled, and Ellice thought it was a strangely sad expression.

"Lovers are allowed to be fools for a certain amount of time, I think. Perhaps a year. Certainly not longer and in some cases much sooner. In my case," she said, glancing at Ellice, "it lasted much longer. But it was a willful blindness. My son was never a fool, Ellice. He's not given to much emotionality. I credit his father's overemotionality for that."

Janet held out the teapot. "More tea?"

Once their cups were refilled, her mother-in-law seemed reluctant to continue.

"My mother says she loved my father but they never seemed to talk to each other," Ellice said, staring into her cup. "My brother never pretended to love his wife, but now she's madly in love with her husband and makes no pretense about it."

"And you? Have you ever been in love?"

There was that question again. How would she describe her feelings for Ross? A delirium, perhaps, one that was keeping her confused. He'd introduced her to the joy of passion and then ignored her.

Janet placed a hand over hers.

"Ross deserves love, my dear Ellice. Of all the people I know, even me, he deserves love most of all. And someone to trust."

She looked away, disturbed by Janet's gaze.

"Because he lost Cassandra?"

"No, my dear girl, because he never had Cassandra. He loved an illusion, a woman he created from wishes. She was never who he wanted her to be."

"But she was clever and kind."

"Yes, but she didn't love him."

She looked over at Janet. The other woman nodded.

"She made him miserable," Janet said. "Just as his father made me miserable. You shouldn't make people who love you miserable, even if you don't feel the same."

"She didn't love Ross?"

"Oh, no, my dear. She loved my husband."

Chapter 27

Ellice stared at her mother-in-law. For a moment she forgot to breathe.

Words backed up in her mind, gated by surprise and something like disbelief. Surely Janet was joking. But the older woman wasn't.

"What happened?" she asked, dreading the rest of the tale.

"Only a handful of us know," she said. "Not out of respect for the parties involved as much as for Ross." She inclined her head and smiled. "And perhaps for me. Not that it matters anymore in my case. But it was a sordid story, all the same. A man old enough to know better, a girl half his age, and passion, of course."

Janet took a sip of her tea, made a face and put it down. Although she took a biscuit, she didn't eat it, instead stared at it as if surprised to find herself holding it.

"I think Thomas fell in love. I think it surprised him as much as anyone. As far as Cassandra, it was easy to see how she would have been swept up. My husband was a very attractive man."

She glanced at Ellice. "Ross is his likeness, of course. But where Ross is more serious, his father was always filled with laughter. He wanted to experience life with open arms. He was interested in everything, knew everyone's name, was probably the most popular man in Edinburgh at one time."

Ellice set her cup down beside Janet's, wondering if the older woman's hands were trembling, too. Was this story as difficult to tell as it was to hear?

She was filled with questions but restrained herself, sitting back and folding her hands in her lap. The fewer interruptions, the faster the tale would be told.

"Thomas was enchanted with Cassandra from the first. He welcomed her into the family with his usual boisterous joie de vivre. She was, I think, charmed by him, but most women were."

She looked away, staring into the air as if seeing the two of them in her mind.

"I don't know when it changed. I've spent enough hours going over things. When did his smile become less avuncular and more possessive? When did she stop seeing him as father-in-law and start viewing him as a lover?"

She shook her head. "It's not anything I've asked Ross. In the last five years we've been very polite with each other. We deal well with day-to-day issues, but I don't discuss his father and he doesn't discuss Cassandra."

Janet folded her hands together, studying them where they rested on her knee.

"They ran away together, of course. Thomas left a very civilized note. They were going to live on the Continent. He wasn't concerned about a divorce. He didn't believe in marriage all that much anyway. To the rest of the world, to people who didn't know him, he'd be Cassandra's husband."

She smiled again. "I knew him better than that. In a few months he'd want to resume his identity as the Earl of Gadsden. It was as much a part of him as his teeth or hair. In time, he'd be annoyed at society's censure. He'd want to either marry Cassandra or give her up for another toy."

She placed her cold hand over Ellice's. "I think Cassandra would have felt differently. Thomas thought himself a proletariat despite being firmly in the aristocracy. Cassandra was neither, just a decent woman in an indecent situation."

"You're very fair," Ellice said. "More than I would be, I think."

"Oh, my dear, that's because Cassandra and I shared the same failing. We were both wildly in love with the wrong man."

"What happened?"

"Ill fortune. Fate. Circumstances." Janet pulled back her hand and waved it in the air. "Pick one. Pick them all. Their carriage overturned on a rainy night outside Paris. Cassandra died instantly. Thomas lingered for three days before succumbing to his injuries. We didn't know until a week later that they were dead, and since it happened abroad we were able to alter the story a little. They hadn't run away together. They were simply traveling to meet Ross."

She finally understood the urgency Ross felt at keeping her book unpublished. Or at least changing the names and the circumstances.

She couldn't ask the questions she most wanted answered. How had he felt about Cassandra's betrayal? Had he loved her so desperately that he couldn't believe in love again?

Was he still in love with her?

She didn't like the feeling she was getting, a sour taste at the back of her tongue, one that translated to a sudden coldness of her limbs.

"So you see, my dear, my son deserves a woman who adores him for his own sake. Not for his wealth or even his looks. But for the person he is."

She met Janet's eyes. "And if he never feels the same way?"

"Then you will have to live like I have, my dear. But it's not been a bad life for all that. Loving someone, even if they don't return it, is better than never feeling love at all."

She wasn't sure she agreed, but Ellice picked up her cold tea and pretended to drink, the better to keep herself from asking questions Janet couldn't answer.

The afternoon was a bright one, the sun streaming into the library, dancing along the stone floor, inspiring Ross to turn more than once and gaze out at the lake in the distance.

Anything but think about how inept he felt.

He hadn't been able to finish the letter about his new acquisition of two Egyptian scrolls. He kept getting stuck on the second sentence. Nothing he wrote made any sense. He sounded like a bumbling fool. Or worse, a pontificating, bumbling fool.

He'd thrown away a dozen pieces of stationery, rejected an equal number of pens, frowned at his inkwell, polished the silver dome of it with a piece of soft cloth he found in the bottom desk drawer, and was generally out of sorts.

If he didn't know better—and there was every possibility that he didn't—he'd have thought his brain was directly connected to his libido.

For a week he'd stayed away from Ellice. He'd been cordial but cool, determined and distant. He hadn't returned to her room. Nor did he invite her to his.

He certainly didn't discuss what he'd read, even though he wasn't able to dismiss it from his mind all that easily.

She might have been surprised at passion, but he was surprised by her. She'd asked him questions about the election that were more politically astute than he'd expected. She seemed truly interested in his plans for Huntly's library. She'd laughed with him over some of his childhood exploits and confessed her own.

She wasn't the least impressed with Huntly. In fact, it was possible she disliked his home, which disturbed him. He wanted her to be happy here.

He repeated that thought, knowing it was at odds with his treatment of Ellice for the last week. He wanted her to be happy. He wanted her to be pleased. He wanted her smiling and laughing.

He wanted her in his bed.

For years he'd remained largely celibate. Why, now, was he feeling nearly desperate?

Last night he woke after a particularly graphic dream and wanted to go to her. Laying there, fists clenched in the sheets, he'd willed himself to banish all thoughts of his wife. Finally, he fell back to sleep at dawn.

Now he was staring at another draft of his letter to a scholar of antiquities like a schoolboy just learning to write.

What would she think of the scrolls? Or his plans for a gazebo near the lake? Why did he want to discuss his day with her, or ask her opinion of his speech before the election?

This morning she'd knocked on his door. Charles, one of the footmen, had told him when he'd returned to his chambers after breakfast.

"Did she say anything?" he asked, feeling like an idiot for soliciting information from one of his staff.

"No, your lordship."

Perhaps he should travel to a friend's house, go to Edinburgh to garner support for the election. Or even travel to London. He could see his legal firm there as well as his factors. The Forster fortune was due to varied global interests. Although his father had rarely concerned himself with ensuring its continuation, he was involved on a daily basis.

Society might consider it plebeian for him to involve himself with trade. He thought it even more so not to care and watch an income vanish.

Luckily, there was no chance of the Forster fortune disappearing anytime soon.

His wealth was one of the reasons he avoided remarrying. He didn't want to be the sweetest apple on the tree, the man sought after not for his character or any other trait but for his income.

Ellice hadn't known about his wealth. She hadn't even been aware of Huntly.

He should at least show her more of his home. She would want to see the source of the hot springs, the newborn hound puppies, the dairy operation. He'd take her walking along the lake, show her where he fished as a boy. Perhaps he'd even take her to the bench where he sat so many hours after his wife left him.

He should tell her about Cassandra.

The notion of being that vulnerable wasn't appealing.

He pushed back his chair, stood, and stared out the window at the glittering lake.

When he was a boy home from school, he'd been at the lake most days. His mother thought him fishing but he'd equally enjoyed swimming, a forbidden pastime since he was the heir and too precious to put himself in danger.

He'd reasoned then that what people didn't know wouldn't get him in trouble.

He'd been daring when riding, too, but the stable master reported his antics. Gone was the excitement of mounting the new stallion bareback. Instead, he was relegated to a sway-back mare that plodded along despite any encouraging words.

Even his school years were constricted. Within that frame-work, the boy he'd been had been molded and pressed into the shape and form he was now, standing at a window and yearning to be what he could never be again.

Perhaps the word was free.

Ellice made him feel free.

From the very first he'd been someone else around her, a man tied to his impulses and his emotions.

He turned away from the window, returning to his desk and the letter that had defied him for an hour.

Ellice didn't think she could feel any more wounded than when she'd left her suite a few hours ago. That had been a selfish pain. She wanted to weep for the young man who'd loved his wife, only for her to run off with another man. Not any man, though, but his father. Weren't fathers supposed to protect and shelter their children, not cause them unalterable harm?

"Does he still love her?" she asked, hearing her voice quaver.

Janet patted her hand. "I wonder, sometimes, if he ever did. Or if he simply married her because it was a duty required of him. Of course, the fact that she was a lovely girl was very nice as well."

She didn't think Cassandra was a lovely girl. How could a lovely girl have done such a thing to Ross? Never mind the scandal. What about the hurt?

The birds chittering behind her were a vocal audience to her silent thoughts.

Janet was a better person than she. She doubted she could have viewed a philandering husband with as much kindness.

Was that why Ross had not come to her? Because of lessons he'd learned about husbands and wives? A wife was supposed to endure whatever behavior a husband doled out? He could have a mistress or a dozen, carouse and bed his way through the Empire, and she'd welcome him home with open arms?

What foolishness.

That behavior was not acceptable, would never be acceptable, and Ross needed to know that.

Nor was ignoring her for a week the least bit acceptable.

"Thank you for the tea," she said primly. "And the story. I understand some things much better now."

"Perhaps it's better for Ross not to know I've told you," Janet said. "I'm sure he'll tell you about Cassandra when he feels the time is right."

She managed to smile at her mother-in-law, the habit of the last five years of restraint coming to her aid. She said nothing about Janet being too understanding and too kind.

Instead, she stood, bent and kissed her on the cheek, left and made her way to Ross's library.

A glimpse of something yellow and fluttery caught his eye.

Ellice was coming down the steps of the East Building, where his mother lived. As he watched, a breeze caused the tendrils to come loose from the bun at her neck and brush her face.

Her face was strangely immobile, as if she deliberately withheld her expression. She was no doubt disgusted by what she'd seen. She couldn't know that ever since his father left, his mother had taken to acquiring things as a way to deal with the pain of his abandonment.

He left the library, intent on intercepting Ellice.

Let her think what she might about him, but her judgment of his mother should be kind, one based on compassion.

She stopped at the base of the steps, one hand stretched across her waist, the other fisted at her side.

Her eyes were as flat as stones.

He approached, stopping in front of her.

"You've seen her house," he said.

She nodded.

"She spends money the way an addict takes opium," he said. "Thankfully, she has enough to do what she wishes."

Ellice blinked up at him.

"I hope you don't judge her too harshly. She feels my father's loss keenly. I don't think she knows how much she's accumulated. I keep sending footmen to the attics with the bigger pieces and she keeps filling up her house."

"You think your mother buys things because of your father?" she asked.

He nodded.

She shook her head. "I think she buys things because of Mr. McMahon."

He frowned at her. "Who's Mr. McMahon?"

"A merchant who supplies each and every item she's acquired. Including the birds."

He stared down at her, surprised.

The idea that his mother would be interested in another man was ludicrous. She'd been devoted to his father, and when he deserted her, she was devastated.

That had been five years ago, however.

Could Ellice be right? He made a mental note to visit this McMahon character. He didn't want the man to take advantage of his mother.

"You didn't tell me everything I needed to do," she said unexpectedly. "You didn't tell me that I would barely have time to write. That was not well done of you, Ross."

"What do you mean?" he asked, frowning at her.

"Dresses," she said, throwing her hands up. "And horses. I have to choose a horse. I have to approve the staffing recommendations of your majordomo and the days off for the maids and the gifts to the poor, not to mention inspect the food storage, approve the plans for the new garden, and plan the clearance of the debris on the riverbank and the lake."

She scowled at him.

"I'm sorry," he said, surprised at her litany. "I've been doing all that, but they were my mother's duties before my father died. I guess the staff thought you would assume her position."

She looked away then back at him. "If I don't, I look like a layabout."

"No, just unprepared."

Her scowl deepened. "Well, I'm not that, your lordship. If Huntly is my home, I'll be its chatelaine."

"What do you mean, 'if'?"

She folded her arms and regarded him with a stony stare. Her chocolate brown eyes now had the appearance of a curiously earth-colored shale he'd seen in the Highlands.

"I don't feel like a wife, your lordship. How can I feel like a countess?"

He didn't know what to say to her.

"Why haven't you come to me? What have I done?"

"Nothing."

"Surely not nothing," she said, frowning at him. "I must have done something to scare you away from my bed."

"I've been busy."

"Too busy to bed your wife?"

"Have you always been so candid?"

"Have you always been so guarded?"

What would she say if he told her the truth?

"I want you in my bed but not my heart," he said, daring himself. "If you're in my thoughts they'll only be libidinous ones. I do not want you to disturb me during the day when I'm writing a position paper or my correspondence."

Her eyes widened.

"I do not want you to bother me otherwise. I will not be concerned about your happiness or your contentment. I will not *worry* about you, Ellice."

"In other words, be your countess but not your wife."

"If that's the way you choose to interpret it," he said. He turned before he was tempted further to pull her into his arms. "I'll come to you tonight."

"Will you?"

He glanced over his shoulder at her.

"You'll find a locked door," she said, following that surprising statement up with a scowl. "I'll not be ignored for a week then used when you have a craving."

He grinned at her, more amused than he'd been in a week.

"Very well, Ellice," he said. "That's one."

Chapter 28

"**I**'ll come to you tonight."

If he had said it in another tone, she would have smiled, gone to him and kissed him, and asked if they had to wait until tonight. But in that particular voice, as if she were a servant who had stolen a silver fork, and with that look in his eyes, dismissive and sharp, she wasn't inclined to welcome him.

That's one.

He evidently remembered their contract. She returned to her rooms, took the document out of her papers and studied the terms she'd written.

Ross Forster, Earl of Gadsden, hereby agrees to allow Ellice Traylor, soon to be Countess of Gadsden, the ability and the time to write, what she will, when she will, where she will. However, she will not attempt to publish said writings without his express permission.

Ellice Traylor, soon to be Countess of Gadsden, has the ability to renege on this contract if the Earl of Gadsden does not materially agree to its provisions. He is to treat her with respect at all times, given the nature of their relationship. He is not to ridicule her or belittle her in any manner.

In exchange, she will agree not to publish any of her works.

Why had she ever thought of this foolish contract?

As it was, she might as well have gone to bed early. She remained in her sitting room, waiting for his knock, but he never came.

Her righteous indignation lasted until the next morning when she discovered that Ross had left Huntly.

"What do you mean, he's gone?" she asked as she stood above Pegeen, who was hemming one of her new dresses.

"His lordship left this morning," the maid said from her position on the floor.

The seamstress had provided the dress in a matter of days. Rather than wait for the woman and her helpers, Pegeen was pinning it.

Ellice made herself stop moving. The sooner the task was done, the sooner she could remove the dress and put on one of her older garments.

"Did he say where he was going?"

Dear God, had he gone to Drumvagen? Was he armed with a dozen excuses why this marriage could not continue? Could such a thing even happen? Could he wave his hand and she would magically be Ellice Traylor again?

She'd heard of annulments, but surely he couldn't accomplish such a thing.

"I'm sorry, dear Ellice," Macrath would say. *"He said you didn't suit."*

"I didn't suit?"

Virginia's face bore an expression of pity, her eyes filled with tears. "I'm so sorry, Ellice. He wasn't pleased."

"What did I do?"

"You refused him. The Countess of Gadsden can never refuse the Earl of Gadsden. If so, she magically isn't a princess anymore."

"What utter rot."

Pegeen looked up. "I beg your pardon, your ladyship?"

She shook her head. "Nothing, Pegeen. I'm just indulging in a little wool gathering."

Pegeen smiled around the pins in her mouth and returned to her task.

She didn't take attendance on him. But wasn't he supposed to be attentive to her? What if she needed him? What if something dreadful happened and he needed to be with her?

"Was she taken ill?" he'd say.

"Suddenly," the doctor said. *"She called for you but you weren't there."* The man turned and looked at Ross, eyes narrowed, mouth firmed. *"Where were you, sir, that you denied your wife comfort in her hour of need?"*

"With another woman, of course. Her breasts are larger and her hips wider. She didn't refuse me."

"We'll have you out of this in just a minute," Pegeen said.

She nodded, feeling her face warm.

Had he been with another woman? Surely not. Not with his dislike of scandal.

Or perhaps this was his way of paying her back for daring to say no.

Had Cassandra ever told him no? If she'd run away with Ross's father, it's possible she did. How could a woman love one man and lay with another?

Was that why he was so adamant about not being refused her bed? Was it a test of some sort? If she lay with him, then she wasn't in love with someone else.

Did men actually think that way?

She should have simply told him that she knew about Cassandra. She had no intention of living in Cassandra's shadow, and was a vastly different person than his first wife.

As far as she was concerned, Cassandra wasn't a paragon of virtue and wasn't to be pitied simply because she'd fallen in love with the wrong man.

She had fallen in love with the wrong man, after all, and no one pitied her.

Her thoughts ground to a halt.

In all her thoughts of him she never imagined that it would strike her like this.

She knew only too well that love wasn't a gentle emotion. She'd seen it all around her, tumultuous and passionate. But she'd never considered that she would come to love such a stubborn, autocratic, foolish man.

Above all, a foolish man who didn't want to *worry* about her.

Ross left Huntly at dawn, telling himself it was better to remain away from his wife for a while. Although Huntly was less than an hour away from Edinburgh, he maintained a small town house in New Town, and that was his base of operations for the next three days.

The election for representative peer would be held among the nobility of Scotland, so it was to them he turned. He visited with the Duke of Campbell, the Earl of Donsett, and a half-dozen others to gauge his chances.

Logan Harrison had thought Ross would win election, and by week's end he was comfortable in that opinion as well.

The taste of victory wasn't as sweet as he'd expected, however, and that disturbed him almost as much as his longing for home.

Each night, as he stood at the window of his second floor bedroom, looking out toward where Huntly lay, he wondered at his feelings. What did he most want? His home or his wife?

Three days later he finally concluded his business and left for home with only one stop in between.

McMahon's Emporium took up one city block, the shop so large it rivaled any store he'd visited in London.

As Ross entered, he noticed that a wagon was leaving and wondered if it was heading for Huntly.

His mother's contribution to Mr. McMahon's fortune had been immense, enough that he was irritated by the time he met the man.

Jack McMahon, however, was not the man he expected. He was short, nearly bald, and had a genial expression similar to a Buddha statue he'd once seen.

He couldn't imagine this man taking advantage of anyone, which was a clue that McMahon was probably a master at it.

"I expected you long before now, sir," he said, surprising Ross as he led the way into his office.

Here, too, Ross was surprised. The emporium was crowded from floor to ceiling with items from around the world, the air perfumed with heavy spices. This space was clean and free of clutter. On McMahon's desk was one stack of paper, an inkwell, a blotter, and a lamp. Behind him, a bookshelf was filled with a selection of leather-bound books, ledgers from the look of it.

Instead of taking his place behind his desk, McMahon sat on one of the chairs in front of it, gesturing to Ross to join him. Without asking, he turned and poured a measure of whiskey from a decanter on the credenza behind him into two glasses, placed one on the desk in front of Ross and began to sip from his.

"You expected me earlier?" Ross asked, ignoring the whiskey.

"Indeed I did, sir." McMahon stared down into the amber liquid. "She's your mother and all." He looked up at Ross, his hazel eyes earnest. "She's a lovely woman, your mother. I've thought so from the very beginning."

"Have you?"

McMahon nodded. He stood, walked around to his desk and opened a bottom drawer. He took out a metal box, leaned over and placed it on the desk in front of Ross.

"It's all there. Every bit of money she's paid me in the last year."

McMahon sat back in his desk chair, reached for his glass but only studied it.

"A man should be honest, sir, in his dealings with others. I'd never cheat a soul who walked into my shop. I feel the same about my competitors."

Ross remained silent.

"I've never lied to my sister or to my mother, may she rest with the angels. But as for me, sir, I've not been as honest with myself."

McMahon leaned back in his chair, his gaze fixed on the ceiling.

"I tell myself that I only see the countess because she gives me tea and asks about my sister and my shop." His head tilted forward, his gaze meeting Ross's. "But that's not the reason."

He moved the glass an inch to the left, then an inch to the right. Finally, he glanced at Ross with a sad smile.

"I stayed away for a whole week once, I did. Made myself do it. Sent the lads to Huntly." He nodded as if he'd asked and answered a question to himself. "But I was miserable, I was. I was lying to myself, and a man should be honest to everyone, especially himself, don't you agree?"

Ross found himself nodding.

"Did she ask you to come?"

Ross shook his head.

"I'm glad of that, I am. But it couldn't last. She, such a great lady, and me just a merchant."

He took a sip of his whiskey and met Ross's gaze. "I won't be back, your lordship. I'll promise you that."

Ross didn't move to pick up the strongbox or open it. Instead, he had the uncomfortable feeling of having barged into a situation he should have ignored.

He'd grown up knowing his father was unfaithful. At first he'd been incensed on his mother's behalf. Later, he was angry at her for tolerating his father's behavior.

Through it all, she'd probably been lonely.

Why had he never considered that? Why had he never thought that Mr. McMahon offered her something no one else could—male companionship.

He stood.

"Mr. McMahon," he said, "I've no objection to your visits. Or to my mother's purchases. The one thing I would ask of you is to limit the number of those purchases. Is there any way I could convince you to take back some of what my mother has bought?"

McMahon's smile was sudden and amused. "Aye, that I could do. Those birds alone will drive a man barmy."

Ross reached over and pushed the strongbox toward McMahon with one finger.

"I don't believe you tried to cheat my mother."

"She's a lovely thing, she is," McMahon said, staring at his clenched hands. "I got in some jeweled reticules that reminded me straight away of her."

"I'm sure my mother would appreciate seeing them."

McMahon looked up at him, his eyes not unlike one of Huntly's hounds. "Are you sure, your lordship?"

Ross extended his hand.

"I am. While you're at Huntly, however, I'd appreciate your saying nothing about this meeting."

As he made his way back to Huntly, the merchant's words were like a whisper from his conscience.

McMahon had known he was lying to himself. When was he going to admit the same? Avoiding Ellice hadn't stopped him from thinking about her, wanting her, lusting after her, and even missing her. Avoiding her had only proven one thing: his marriage wasn't what he'd planned on it being.

He'd expected to marry Ellice and banish her to the back of his mind while he was about the business of his life, just as he had with Cassandra. If he won the election, he would take Ellice to London if she wished to return to the city. If not, she could make her home at Huntly and he'd represent Scotland in the House of Parliament.

Neither of them would take a lover. Instead, they would meet periodically to assuage any physical needs. In that way they would manage a life together.

His plan had been doomed to failure the minute they married. Ellice refused to retreat to the place he'd carved out of a busy life for her. Instead, she marched up, front and center, and demanded his attention.

Avoiding her was not working.

There was only one thing to do: admit when he'd been bested.

Virginia smiled, extracted the items Mairi had sent her, and couldn't help but laugh when she assembled everything on the top of her bureau.

Between Brianag, Dr. Thorburn, and her sister-in-law, she was armed for battle.

Battle it would be, she suspected, but one she was determined to win.

She adored Macrath, but he was being the most obstinate man. He had a core of stubbornness and it had helped make him who he was. She never considered that she might come face-to-face with it and have to wage war for her own happiness.

They were both miserable and both determined that the other not realize it.

She'd lain next to him for years now. She breathed in tandem with him. She'd borne his children. He was part of her, just as she was part of him.

He might as well surrender now. She was going to win. She took another look at the items she'd accumulated and grinned.

"**T**his was my grandmother's favorite room," he said.

Ellice turned to see Ross at the doorway.

Carefully, she tucked her writing beneath the blank pages, put her pen away, and waited for his further comments.

He didn't say anything as he entered, merely smiled up at the portrait. He carried something in his right hand, a parcel fastened with twine that also served as a handle. She looked at it curiously, but he didn't mention it.

"I like her," she said. "I've grown accustomed to her looking down at me."

"I think she would have liked you," he said, surprising her. "She was from England, too."

She glanced at the empty chair, hoping he would sit. When he did, placing the parcel beside the chair, she felt her smile bloom. What a silly girl she was, to be pleased that her husband sat with her.

"I think, sometimes, that she was a bit surprised to find herself here at Huntly, especially married to my grandfather. He was larger than life. He liked to fish, so he created a lake and had it stocked. He wanted to expand Huntly, so he added the buildings that are now the library and my mother's home."

"If he liked to climb mountains, would he have created one of those, too?"

He chuckled. "According to my grandmother, he would have. I never knew the man, only learned of him from others."

"I don't remember my grandparents," she said. "But I do recall my father. He was a tall, quiet man. He never spoke much to me or to anyone. He liked the garden and that's how I remember him, sitting there staring off into the distance. I used to wonder if he were wishing to be somewhere else."

"Where would he have been?"

She smiled. "Anywhere but London, I think. When he could, he escaped to the country. My mother didn't like the country."

"Yet she lives at Drumvagen, which is as distant from a city as you can be and still be in Scotland."

"Circumstances change," she said.

He didn't respond, which was a disappointment. She wanted him to say something about their changed circumstances.

Instead, he stared up at the painting. "She once told me that I reminded her of him, that I was not only his namesake but had aspects of his character."

He didn't say more, and that's when her sense marched away in a huff, allowing idiocy to brush off a chair, sit, and send words to her lips.

"You left Huntly," she said.

He nodded.

When he didn't continue, she frowned at him. "You've been gone three days."

He smiled, a curiously annoying expression when she was trying to get an answer. He knew he was being irritating, too, if that gleam in his eyes was any indication.

"I only know because my maid told me. Otherwise, I wouldn't have noticed."

His smile broadened. "You missed me."

"Most assuredly not."

He stared at the cold fireplace, decorated now with a bouquet of flowers.

"Where did you go?" she asked.

"To Edinburgh," he said. "To see about my chances for election." He glanced at her. "A great many people congratulated me on my wedding."

"Did they?"

He smiled, stretched out his legs and crossed his ankles.

"I also went to see this McMahon person," he said.

She waited impatiently for him to continue.

When he didn't speak, she reached over and touched his sleeve, a gentle push to encourage him to talk.

He turned to look at her.

"Did you meet him?"

He nodded.

Was she going to have to pull each word from him with tweezers?

"What was he like?"

"A very nice sort," he said. "I've encouraged him to continue calling on my mother."

That was a surprise.

"I think you women do it on purpose."

Her eyes widened with the change of subject. "What do we do?"

"Confound us. Make us question everything we've ever known. Why are you here?"

"I'm writing."

He shook his head. "Not that. Why here? Why not on the terrace? Or the Ladies Library or the Yellow Parlor? Why here? It's the smallest room at Huntly."

"Why did your grandmother like it?"

"She hated Huntly. Do you?"

"Hate Huntly?" she asked, playing for time.

He stretched out his hand and, surprised, she reached out with hers. He gripped her fingers.

"What can I do to make it more of a home to you?"

Should she tell him? Did he really want to know?

"Don't ignore me. Don't leave without telling me. Don't stay away so long. You were angry because you thought people ignored me at Drumvagen, and you've done the same here at Huntly. If you're angry at me, tell me why. Otherwise, I'm apt to imagine the most horrible scenarios."

"What have you imagined?"

"You've become dreadfully ill and don't want to concern me. You've fallen in love with a maid. I bore you."

"You most certainly don't bore me."

"But there's a chance you might be in love with a maid?"

He shook his head.

"Tell me your health is perfect, please, or I really will be worried."

"My health is perfect."

He hadn't released her hand, was staring down at it with such an intent look on his face that she knew he wasn't seeing her palm but something else.

Before he could speak, she said, "You don't have to be concerned about me. I don't want you to worry about me. I don't want thoughts of me to take you from your duties. Truly."

He frowned at her. "Why not?"

Was he trying to be contrary on purpose?

"It's enough that you come to my room," she said, confessing all. "I've missed you."

He looked away then back at her. What was he trying not to say? She waited, hoping the words wouldn't be unkind.

"I brought you a present," he said, reaching down for the package and handing it to her.

"A present?"

Her fingers trembled as she unwrapped the parcel. Impatiently, she pushed aside the paper, staring at his gift in silence.

The dark wood was etched with a gilt pattern on the edge, the polished surface sloped and opening up to reveal a storage space for pens and paper.

"It's a lap desk," he said. "I thought you could use it if you're somewhere else other than at your desk. Like here, for example."

No one had ever given her a more perfect gift.

He stood, studying her in silence.

Reaching out, he held her chin gently, looking down into her face.

"I missed you, too," he said.

"You didn't come to my room," she said, wondering at her own courage.

His smile was slight. "You refused me. Don't you remember?"

I wouldn't now. Words that were too difficult to speak and so they cowered behind her smile.

He dropped his hand and turned away, leaving her sitting there staring after him.

Chapter 29

When the knock came, Ellice opened the door, clad in a pale pink nightgown.

She'd brushed her hair, leaving it unbound.

He stood there studying her, his eyes darkening. Without a word he entered her sitting room, pushing the door shut behind him. The click of the latch was as loud as a rifle shot.

He'd come to her, just as she hoped.

"I have two more refusals," she said.

"Yes, you do," he said, walking toward her slowly.

She didn't move.

When he was close enough to feel the warmth of his body, he stopped. She wanted to lean into him, press her cheek against his and feel his arms around her.

"It's in the contract."

"Yes, it is. I could say to hell with the contract, Ellice." He bent toward her, fingering the bow at the top of her nightgown.

Slowly, he pulled on the bow until it slipped free, becoming two short pieces of ribbon. Her neckline gaped open, but since the material was diaphanous, it hardly mattered.

"I could say to hell with you, your lordship," she said softly.

"Then you should say it now. Before matters proceed any further."

Lady Pamela would joust with him, her words teasing.

What matters would those be, your lordship?

She might even be amused, the sparkling cascade of her laughter echoing through the room.

She wasn't Lady Pamela. She was only Ellice. This handsome man was her husband and he'd come to her.

But it wasn't marital duty that made her turn and lead the way to the bedroom. Excitement marked each step, her blood pounding through her body with such speed she felt lightheaded.

He followed her, stopping in the bedroom doorway, his eyes boring into her.

She crawled up on the bed, sat, and waited for him.

"If you don't want the nightgown ripped, I'd dispense with it," he said.

How very proper he sounded. He could be speaking about the weather. *Do you think it will rain this evening? Oh, by the way, I'm going to ravish you.*

His eyes glittered in the light. Should she ask him to extinguish the lamp?

Or should she be as nonchalant and wicked as he?

Leave the light burning, your lordship. I want to see your magnificent body.

For a moment she thought she'd said the words aloud because Ross removed his robe, tossing it to the chair in the corner. The silk clung for a moment then slid to the floor. He didn't look as if he cared.

She certainly didn't, not when he was standing there naked, light gleaming on interesting places on his body.

His chest was broad, the dusting of hair there making her want to run her fingers through it, play with his nipples, trace every line of muscle down his stomach.

His hands rested on his hips. Only one part of him moved, and that seemed to twitch as she pulled her nightgown off and tossed it to the floor.

She could feel his gaze on every inch of her flesh.

Slowly, he walked to her, a smile beginning to curve his lips.

As he reached her, she rose up on her knees and put her hands on his shoulders.

She loved him.

She loved this man with his silver gray eyes and his seductive mouth.

Emotion thrummed through her, her pulse racing so loud it was the only sound she heard. Words trembled on her lips but when he bent his head to kiss her, they vanished.

She planted both hands on his chest, fingers splayed. She wanted to touch him everywhere, where his chest tapered to a slim waist, to his hips, to the nest of curls at the base of his erection.

She wanted to stare and study, mark each play of muscle and bone and note where God in His perfection had created this man.

The ridged muscles of his stomach contracted when she ran a finger down them. Even Lady Pamela, with all her experience, would have been impressed at the size of his cock.

Her hands gripped him. How had he become so perfect, so hard in places and soft in others?

"Ellice."

She looked up just as he grabbed her, tumbled with her to the bed.

"Now," she demanded.

"Now?"

For this night he was hers. There was no past, no uncertain future, only the night with the rain drumming on the windows and the sound of the storm masking any sounds of passion.

She could make sounds of delight at the touch of his mouth on her breasts.

When he turned her on her stomach and kissed her from her heels to her neck, she could moan as loudly as she wished. At the scrape of his teeth on the tender flesh of her buttocks, she could yelp and turn, only for him to grin.

He growled deep in his throat, the animal sound startling her. She lay before him, thighs spread wide.

He stared at her as if he'd never before seen her, and perhaps he hadn't, not like this, weak and powerful in surrender.

Laughing, she reached for him, wrapped her legs around his and, in a move that startled even her, turned with him on the bed.

She rose above him, moving until she was astride him. Not as perfectly as she wished, though. Sliding down his body, she dipped her head and licked him.

He thrust upward, his hands reaching for her.

"No," he said. "I'll not last."

"I don't want you to last," she said, feeling victorious and joyful.

He grabbed her and abruptly reversed their positions again. Now he was rising above her, dominant, powerful, his eyes dark, his breath fast.

He pinned her to the bed and kissed her, stripping her of breath and turning his name into a low, throaty moan.

She arched toward him, demanding touch, recognition, a soft stroke of a finger. He kissed her still, murmuring against her lips when she pouted.

Locking her arms around his neck, she wiggled beneath him, teasing with her body. His erection nestled in the juncture of her thighs and she widened her legs. He pressed forward and she closed them, trapping him against her.

Finally, finally, his hand cupped one breast, a talented thumb flicking against her nipple. A moment later he bent his head to suckle at her breasts.

"Now," she said. "Please."

Grabbing her hands, he held them over her head and entered her slowly. He stilled her with a kiss, pushing forward until he filled her.

When the pressure and pleasure built, she was nearly insensate with it, tossing her head from side to side.

He whispered words of encouragement to her, of praise, of teasing. She couldn't reciprocate because passion had stripped her of every thought. She was only feeling, becoming a glowing ember of need.

She gripped his arms with nails transformed to talons.

He left her and entered her again, his eyes still on hers.

When her lids fluttered shut, he said, "Look at me, Ellice."

She tried, she really did. But her lids kept falling as pleasure rippled through her. Just when she thought she could feel nothing more, he began to increase his pace, strokes that pushed her over the edge.

The storm swallowed her screams of pleasure.

She heard his exultant laughter as she jerked her hands free, gripped his buttocks and pulled him to her, riding out her climax with his.

His pulse was still racing as he lay at her side, drawing her to him. Her eyes were melted chocolate as her lips curved in an exhausted smile.

"You don't have to do a thing you don't wish to do," he said.

Her smile faded.

"About Huntly," he said. "It's not necessary that you do anything."

She nodded and closed her eyes. He thought she'd drifted off to sleep but she spoke a few minutes later.

"I'm your wife," she said. "It's my duty."

He pressed his lips against her forehead. Her breath had finally calmed along with his heartbeat.

"I didn't marry you to be Huntly's chatelaine."

"No," she said, blinking her eyes open. "You married me to prevent a scandal."

Had he?

The answer occurred to him instantly.

Not entirely.

He'd been captivated by her from the first moment she emerged from his carriage. He'd been charmed by her smile, and she'd triggered his curiosity. He'd watched her cheeks blossom with color and been aroused by her writing. Her laughter enchanted him.

He looked down at her, thinking that he could drown in the deep dark pools of her eyes.

"Stop it," he said.

"Stop what?"

"You're looking at me with that look, the one that makes me want to love you again. Or do you think I behave like a rutting boar all the time?"

"I've never seen a rutting boar," she said, beginning to smile. "Do they kiss well?"

She lay back on the bed, covering her face with the sheet. A moment later she peeped up at him, her cheeks and lips pink.

"I'm sorry about Cassandra."

He froze.

She sat up again, placing her hand on his chest. Her soft fingers were warm on his skin, tapping lightly, as if to call his attention to her words.

He didn't want to talk about Cassandra.

"I know I shouldn't have spoken of her, but it's a little difficult since she was your wife and now I'm your wife, and of course I understand about the book now and I do wish you could have explained it to me before your mother did."

He stared up at the painting on the ceiling. Angels at every age frolicked among the clouds.

"No wonder you weren't all that fond of marriage."

"Ellice."

Just that, just her name, spoken in such a soft tone that it halted her in mid-commiseration. He didn't need her compassion. Nor did he want it.

"Did you love her very much?"

He glanced at her. Did she want the truth, unadorned and as smudged as it was? Or should he fancy it up, polish it until it was bright, and then give it to her?

He decided for the unvarnished version. Let her see him as he was, not as she imagined him.

"I thought I did," he said. "She was all I could have wanted in a wife. She was sweet, gentle, and kind. She never said a bad word to anyone or about anyone. She was unfailingly polite."

She didn't speak, didn't pepper him with questions. Instead, she let the silence sag between them.

"I was tired of her company within a month," he confessed, turning his head to look at her. "I found more and more things to do that would take me away from Huntly. I visited the farms, our property near Glasgow, anywhere I didn't have to endure my wife's endless sweetness."

To her credit, she didn't look away. Had she always been so courageous? Perhaps she had, or she wouldn't have hidden away in his carriage.

"I don't think anyone would ever call me sweet," she said, her well-kissed lips curving into a half smile. "I doubt many people would remember me at all."

"Why do you say that?"

"I'm imminently forgettable."

"I didn't have any trouble remembering you."

Now she regarded him with soft eyes.

"I have often asked myself if she would have turned to my father if I'd been a better husband."

"She might not have," Ellice said, brutally honest in this as in all things. "Or she might well have and suffered more guilt for it."

He shook his head, amazed at her ability to turn something on its head. He'd never considered that he might have spared Cassandra further grief by not being an attentive husband.

"So, you think she was destined to fall in love with my father all along?"

"Love is like a river, don't you think?"

"A river?"

She nodded. "It finds its own level. You can put up barricades but it will flood if it wishes. Sometimes, it even changes course."

"And you think love is like that?"

"Yes. Because we find ourselves in love sometimes despite our wishes or our wants. We feel helpless in the face of it."

Had she loved someone? he wondered. Did she love him still?

Her smile was infinitely kind. "She hurt you because she chose someone else. I grew up being told that someone was always better than me. Cassandra leaving you was the same thing."

He couldn't speak. With her smile, she'd taken away his power of speech, this strange woman with her kind eyes and her unbridled imagination. She couldn't be right and yet he suspected there was some truth to what she was saying.

He was left floundering for words again. How did she so effortlessly do it?

"You worry too much about scandal, Ross. Scandal will always touch you because people will always gossip. You can be a saint and they'll find something wicked or nasty to say. People will always say something bad just because of who you are."

"Thomas Forster's son."

She shook her head at him. "No, Ross. You're the Earl of Gadsden. You're handsome as sin, you own a fabulous house, and you're wealthy. They envy you."

She pressed her hand to his chest. "Perhaps you should be more like your father."

"I beg your pardon?"

"I think people admire your father, not because of his wildness as much as his disregard of what the world thought of him. I think everyone secretly wishes to be as brave."

"It wasn't courage, Ellice. It was selfishness."

"Or love."

He stared at her.

"What would you do for love, Ross?"

He didn't know how to answer her. Thankfully, she didn't seem to want one.

Her head rested on his chest, her arm extended around his waist. His hand threaded through her hair. In these quiet moments before sleep, he realized that Ellice brought something different and unusual to his life. A feeling of peace he'd never had before, as if being here, being with her, was what he'd been destined for all along.

A strange thought to have before sleep overwhelmed him. Ellice Traylor Forster was his destiny. Did she feel the same about him?

"I need to go to Edinburgh," Macrath said, removing his shirt as he walked toward the bathing room.

Lately, he'd been very careful to not undress in front of her. As if she could forget what he looked like naked.

Virginia sat on the chair in their sitting room, taking care not to let him know how appreciative she was of the view. Quick glances would have to do for now.

"Will you be gone long?" she asked.

"Not long," he said. "I may stop by Huntly to make sure Ellice is well."

She was nearly swamped by love. On their wedding day, he'd taken Ellice and Enid as his own, caring for them, fussing over them, loving them.

"She's still on her honeymoon," she said. "Would that be entirely proper?"

He entered the bathing chamber. She sat listening to running water, his comments about the hot water, and the accompanying splashing.

Standing, she walked to her armoire, opened it and retrieved the basket she'd packed and stored there.

"Perhaps not," he said, moving from the bathing chamber to her side, a towel wrapped around his waist.

Her heart stuttered at the sight of him and that one lone droplet traveling down his chest.

She wanted to lick it off.

"What is that?" he asked.

"A compromise," she said, placing the basket on the bed. She crawled up on the end, removed her wrapper and smiled at his indrawn breath.

Good, he'd noted that her décolletage was very low. Had he also noticed that her nipples were erect?

Reaching over, she opened the basket, folding back the top.

"This is a packet of herbs Brianag mixed for me," she said, holding it up. "I take it in a tea every evening. I will continue to take it every night for the rest of my life if necessary." She glanced at him. "It's ghastly."

He hadn't moved. Nor had he grabbed his pillow and the coverlet to sleep on one of the settees, as he'd done often enough in the last two months.

"The sponge and acidic solution are from Dr. Thorburn. He's found that it's very successful in preventing pregnancy. I've already used one," she said. "It's quite easy."

He didn't say a word, so she moved on to the next item.

"These are for you, I understand." She stared at the bulge beneath the towel. "I don't know how you're to put them on, but I haven't spent much time reading the instructions. Do you speak French?"

"What are you doing, Virginia?"

"I'm seducing you," she said, looking directly at him. "I understand your fear. I do, Macrath. I also know that I can't live the rest of my life without your touch. I'll go mad. Maybe I'll even take a lover."

"That's not going to happen," he said, his cheeks taking on a bronze color.

"Then you will simply have to ensure I'm satisfied."

She took out another jar.

"I'm supposed to use this before we love," she said, opening the jar and smelling the contents. Something minty and not unpleasant. "This," she held up a brown bottle, "is to be used after we've loved."

"Anything else?"

She peered into the basket. "Just a few more things. I'll gladly take all of them."

"What happens if you get pregnant?"

"Then it will be a child ordained by God," she said. "Especially in view of all these preventatives."

"What if I lose you?"

She slid from the bed, coming to stand in front of him.

"What if nothing happens? What if we're happy? Macrath, you took chances when everyone told you it was foolish. You decided what you wanted and went after it, keeping your own faith, deciding it would happen."

"This is a little different."

"No," she said, slapping her hand against his bare chest, "it's exactly the same thing. I want you and I refuse to admit any barrier to that."

He looked past her to the bed and the assembled products. "You'll be safe?"

"I'll be safe."

"Promise me."

She understood what he was asking. He was asking for absolutes, and there were none in life. Oh, perhaps one. She absolutely adored him.

Standing on tiptoe, she kissed him lightly on the mouth. "I promise."

She didn't get a chance to say another word before he grabbed her.

Chapter 30

Dawn came to Huntly with none of the power of a Drum-vagen morning. Instead, the sun peeked over the crest of the hill almost in apology for disturbing the great house. Pale pink and blue streaks sat against a sky not yet wakened from night. The birds greeted the day with soft chirps; the morning breeze was gentle on her cheeks.

Ross had left her a few minutes ago.

"I'll be back in a few hours," he said. "After three days away, I'm certain there are a variety of details I need to address."

She'd nodded, kissed him, and watched as he left her bed and room.

Unable to roll over and sleep, she rose and walked to the terrace door. Carved balusters and railings painted white surrounded a pale pink tiled floor. Four white ceramic pots in each corner held miniature yews, and two iron benches sat opposite each other in the middle of the space. She sat facing east, the view overlooking the expanse of lawn.

Would she ever become accustomed to the size of Huntly? Or to the wealth it represented?

She didn't care about the Forster fortune. All she truly cared about was Ross. From the beginning, he'd treated her differently. She wasn't invisible to him. He made her feel singled out. Not anyone else, just her. She felt safe with him, in a way she couldn't explain. Yet no one else had the power to hurt her like he did. His opinion mattered. His judgment counted.

She was in love. Why hadn't she told him how she felt?

Cassandra had hurt him, perhaps more than he knew. Was he capable of loving anyone again?

He needed to trust her, first. Perhaps if he did, he'd feel free enough to love.

She was going to have to do something, a grand gesture like one Lady Pamela would make. Something that would ensure he trusted her. Something to make him understand exactly how she felt.

She rang for Pegeen then sat down at her desk and wrote a note. Before the maid arrived, she peeked out her door, motioning to one of the ever-present footmen stationed there.

"Yes, your ladyship?"

"Will you make sure my husband gets this? He should be in the library."

The man surprised her by shaking his head. "We're not supposed to enter the library, your ladyship."

"Even to take him a message? He won't mind," she said. "I promise." She smiled at the man, but it didn't seem to reassure him one bit.

Another change she'd make at Huntly. Why wish to share the treasures of the Huntly library with the rest of Scotland when they were forbidden to the staff?

After explaining what she needed to the stable master, he nodded and provided one of the carriages, along with a driver she recognized.

Harvey nodded when she told him their destination.

She entered the carriage, settling herself in for a few hours of travel. The quicker they made it to Drumvagen, the better.

Ross had removed his father's portrait from the public rooms five years ago. The only place the fourth Earl of Gadsden remained was the Earl's Gallery, a light and airy room in the north wing. Several portraits of each of the previous earls stood in the sunlight, staring out at the floor-to-ceiling windows on one side of the room.

One day, someone might stand here and wonder about the man, note the handsomeness of his features, the rigid pose featuring him standing in the Red Parlor, one hand on his hip, the other at his side. Studying his eyes, the fourth earl didn't look restless, but rather, empty.

Had his father been lonely? The thought had never occurred to him before. He'd always considered his mother's point of view but never his father's.

His marriage to Cassandra had not been one of kindred minds and hearts. He'd been busy with his life, intrigued by his studies. When he thought of Cassandra, he realized that she didn't figure in the important moments. He couldn't see her in his memories.

He'd ignored her until she was no more important to him than a doorstop, a realization that didn't sit well.

He couldn't imagine doing the same to Ellice. He couldn't even stay away from her for a week.

Had Cassandra been as miserable with him as his mother had been with his father? Another thought he'd never had until this moment.

He'd not been guilty of infidelity, but he'd matched his father in inattentiveness.

But Cassandra had found someone to notice her, hadn't she?

Before leaving Huntly, his father had left him a note.

Forgive us, if you can, Ross. We don't do this to hurt you but to find some measure of joy together.

Had she found that happiness? Had both of them? Had those short weeks together given them the joy they wanted, payment enough for their actions?

He would never know, but for the first time, he hoped they'd found it together.

Walking to the window, he stared out at the lake.

The day was glorious. The morning sun bathed Huntly in an otherworldly glow, as if he'd been given a sight of heaven.

His life had changed. He hadn't planned it, but it had altered the moment he'd gone to Drumvagen. A woman with sparkling brown eyes had forced him to confront himself, and now he couldn't avoid what he'd discovered.

When had it happened? At Drumvagen in the Great Hall when she'd stood there with her arms folded, nearly daring him to kiss her? Or when she'd emerged from the carriage, voluble and fascinating? Or that dawn in the gazebo when he'd wanted to hold her in his arms and comfort her?

Somewhere along the way, he'd fallen in love with his wife.

Everything now paled in importance to that fact.

"You don't come here often," his mother said from the doorway.

He turned, surprised to see her there.

She walked into the room, glancing around. "Neither do I."

She moved to stand in front of his father's portrait. After studying it for a moment, she joined him at the window.

"Why have you?" she asked.

"A moment of memory," he said. "Or perhaps honesty."

"You have to let it go, Ross. You've spent a good deal of your life trying to make up for your father's scandal. But there comes a time when you have to stop thinking about the past and focus on the present and the future."

"As you have?" he asked.

"As I have," she said, nodding.

She stood with her hands clasped in front of her, a proper

countess in so many ways. But there had always been a bit of a dreamer about his mother, a tender soul in a life not especially easy, for all its wealth and privilege.

"I have," he said. For the first time, it was the truth. He had given it up.

Even more importantly, he understood.

Maybe the fourth Earl of Gadsden had been as stunned as he was now, realizing that his life, his emotions, even his thoughts, were no longer his own.

What would he have done if Ellice had been married to someone else? If he'd found himself as adrift in lust and love as he felt now? He would have let nothing stand between them, not writ or rule or another human being.

Would he have thought of anyone else but himself and her? Would he have considered the ramifications of his actions?

It's quite possible that he wouldn't have cared. That scandal could have surfeited him, and it wouldn't have mattered as long as she was by his side.

Was love that selfish?

He'd used that word in describing his father, thinking that the man was self-absorbed, caring only for his own pleasure without regard to anyone else.

But as he stood there, Ross knew he would have done the same if the woman had been Ellice.

"Ellice is a lovely girl," his mother said, startling him. "I wondered about the haste of your wedding. I thought you were making a mistake."

"You never said anything."

She glanced at him with a smile. "When have you ever listened to me, Ross? You consider me a foolish woman occupying her days with buying trinkets."

Perhaps he had, once, but not since meeting McMahon.

"But now, I'm glad you married her. Overjoyed, in fact. I no longer need to worry about you."

"There was no need to worry about me in any case, Mother."

"Of course I did, you being so afraid of feeling anything."

"What do you mean?"

"Oh, Ross, I've watched you the last five years. You've been very proper, very contained, but I'm afraid it's because you were afraid to be vulnerable again. You didn't want to be hurt the way Cassandra hurt you."

He stared out at the lake, not knowing how to respond.

"Then Elise came into your life. You're half startled, half delighted she's the way she is."

He glanced over at her.

"I've watched you with her. It's almost magical, the effect she has. You've laughed more in the last weeks than I've ever heard you. You smile more. You aren't buried in the library at all hours."

Had he changed that much? Yes, he had. He was—and for a moment he fumbled for the word—happy.

"Life is so much more magical when love is the filter through which you view it," his mother said. "I'm not saying loving your father was comfortable. This time, I'd prefer to have my love returned."

"Mr. McMahon."

She wound her arm around his. "I hope so, dear."

Had he ever known his mother? He was beginning to think not, just as he was wondering if life had been a giant mirage he'd never understood until now.

"Did you ever consider that it's because of your father that the two of you married?"

He frowned at her. "What do you mean?"

"If you hadn't been beset by nostalgia, you wouldn't have gone to Drumvagen. You and Ellice wouldn't have met."

He'd never considered that, either.

"Are you in love with her, Ross?"

"Yes," he said without having to consider it.

"Then why has she left?"

He turned to her. "What do you mean?"

She sighed. "I saw the carriage leave an hour ago, dear."

"The carriage?"

Could he do nothing but ask questions?

"Ellice was in it, along with Pegeen."

"You're wrong."

"I'm not, you know. Wherever has she gone?"

He couldn't think. Nor could he put two words together. He left his mother standing there and flew down the stairs, his destination the stables.

She couldn't leave him.

"She's gone to Drumvagen, your lordship," the stable master said.

"Ready a coach," he told the man. "With the fastest horses I own."

The man nodded and bowed his way out of Ross's sight.

Was he that terrifying? Perhaps he was.

Ellice had left him.

He walked to his room, readying himself for the journey. If Macrath gave her safe harbor, he'd reason with the man. If that didn't work, he'd fight for his wife. He'd damn well lay siege to Drumvagen.

She couldn't leave him. Not now.

He felt like he'd been asleep before meeting Ellice. She made him wonder what she was thinking. She brought him amusement, and he'd not felt humor for a very long time. She forced him to examine himself. She challenged him to be a better man.

He wanted to share his future with her. He wanted to confide in her, tell her those thoughts that kept him awake for hours, those insecurities plaguing him.

How could he do all that if she left him?

What would you do for love, Ross?
Anything, for her.

"**I**t's a lovely place, isn't it?" Pegeen said, peering out the window. "A bit small and all, after Huntly, but a charming house."

She had never thought Drumvagen small, but compared to Huntly, it certainly was. Drumvagen could be placed in Huntly's courtyard. But the house was noisy and filled with life, one thing that couldn't be said about Huntly.

She had the driver go around to the back. When the carriage, a beautiful vehicle with pale gray velvet cushions and ebony lacquer exterior, finally stopped, she motioned for Pegeen to precede her.

Closing her eyes, she said a quick prayer that this task could be accomplished with a minimum of fuss. She wanted to talk to Virginia, first, while avoiding her mother.

That thought died a frustrating death the minute she stepped from the carriage.

"Oh, will you stop, you harridan!"

She sighed.

Macrath didn't tolerate their arguing within Drumvagen, so Brianag and her mother tried to keep their battles either out of earshot or outside. Evidently, Macrath was in the house, which was the reason they were in garden.

"It's not the province of a gardener to decide a lady's garden. It's for a lady to give the gardener instructions."

Brianag said something incomprehensible, followed by her mother's near scream.

She glanced at Pegeen, whose smile lightened her mood. Perhaps the two women were amusing if one didn't have to hear them often.

She looked toward the kitchen door. Could she make it

before either women realized a strange coach was in the drive?

No, she couldn't.

"Child!"

Suddenly, she was enveloped in a flurry of fragrant black silk, her mother's embrace nearly choking her. A moment later Enid stepped back and examined her, from the top of her head to her shoes, peeping out from beneath the hem of one of her new dresses.

At least she had the foresight to look like the Countess of Gadsden.

"Where is your dear husband? Why are you here? Is something wrong? Why have you come back to Drumvagen?"

In the next instant her mother had placed her hand over her mouth, her eyes widening.

"Don't say you've left your husband, Ellice." Before she could answer, her mother continued, "I won't have it."

Time seemed to slow as Ellice took a step back.

Pegeen, at her side, had the wisdom to retreat.

The breeze smelled of roses. Would she always smell them and think of Drumvagen? For that matter, would she always recall this exact moment?

Her heart beat a steady rhythm, but so loudly it echoed in her ears. Her mouth was dry and her movements slow as she lowered her hands to her sides, raised her head and straightened her shoulders.

Perhaps it was the time she'd spent as a wife, or being a countess in her own right. Perhaps it was being away from Drumvagen and her mother's eternal meddling, chiding, and criticism. Or perhaps it was simply that she'd had enough and this point had to be reached sooner or later.

"I will not be spoken to in that tone," she said to her mother.

Enid's mouth gaped open. For only a moment, however, until she began to protest.

"You've gotten snippy since your marriage, haven't you? I'll not take that behavior from you, child. Your sister would never have disrespected me in such a fashion."

"Enough!" Ellice held up her hand, her gaze never once leaving her mother.

"When have you ever respected me, Mother? I'm only a poor substitute for Eudora." She took a deep breath. "I'm not Eudora," she said. "I'm not your beloved daughter who died. I'm the one who lived. I'm tired of hearing about what my sister did or would have done. I suspect that Eudora would have silenced you long before now."

She grabbed her skirts and walked around her mother, heading for the kitchen. At the door, she stopped and turned.

"Must I die before you begin to value me as well?"

Without looking back, she made her way inside, hearing Pegeen behind her.

With any luck she could finish her task and leave Drumvagen before her mother got over her shock and planned her retaliation.

A few minutes later she was in the nursery.

"I've offended my mother," Ellice said to Virginia, placing her reticule on the table.

She'd left Pegeen in the kitchen. No doubt the girl was being plied with questions about her, Huntly, and Ross. Pegeen, however, was canny enough to survive any interrogation.

Without thought to grace or manners, Ellice dropped into the chair, waiting as Mary gathered up the two older children for a walk. The baby was asleep in the cradle beside Virginia.

When she apologized for interrupting, Virginia shook her head. "They'll not suffer for the lack of me. Besides, it's little enough time I get for myself. I'll take your visit as the treat it is. Tell me why you're here, but first, what did you say to your mother?"

"I told her that I wasn't Eudora and I was tired of being compared to her," Ellice said, both hands on the arms of the chair. She looked upward. Drumvagen did not have nearly the plaster adornments of Huntly. On every ceiling at Huntly there was either a god or goddess looking down at her or a gathering of cupids—what was more than one cupid called?—or a magnificent painted scene.

Although it was almost restive to find nothing on the ceiling at all, it was also disconcerting.

"What did she say to that?" Virginia asked, nodding when one of the maids entered with the tea things. Say what she would about Brianag, the woman always furnished refreshments without being asked.

"I left before she could say anything. But she gave me a fulminating look. No one can scowl in a ladylike way like my mother."

Virginia leaned forward, selected a nut and chocolate biscuit, one of Cook's best treats, and nibbled on the edge.

"I'm so very tired of her being disappointed that Eudora died and I didn't."

To her surprise, Virginia didn't look the least startled by her words. She only smiled, poured the tea and handed Ellice her cup.

"Enid is one of those people who will take advantage of every iota of tolerance," Virginia said, taking another of the chocolate and nut biscuits. "If you don't say anything, she will assume you don't care. You must make your wishes known each and every time she says something. Until, of course, she finally learns that you mean what you say."

"I always thought you and mother were in perfect agreement."

Virginia laughed. "I doubt we were ever in perfect agreement over anything," she said, to Ellice's surprise. "The only thing we did well, evidently, is hide it."

"But you get along now, don't you?"

Virginia nodded. "But it took some time until your mother understood she wasn't to criticize Macrath or Drumvagen, or me, for that matter."

"She doesn't," Ellice said, realizing it. "I've never heard her say anything bad about you or Macrath. Although she does occasionally criticize Drumvagen, but that's only to Brianag and only to annoy her, I suspect."

Virginia sighed. "Ah, the only two devils in my perfect heaven. But for the two of them, peace would reign at Drumvagen."

The far off sound of a child's scream of protest made her smile. "Almost," she said.

Virginia offered her the plate of biscuits, and Ellice took one, staring down at it.

"But you didn't come to Drumvagen to have an argument with your mother."

"I came for two reasons," she said. "One of them was to talk to you."

Virginia didn't ask why, merely sat silent.

"Marriage is exceedingly complicated," Ellice finally said. "Exceedingly."

"Men are even more so."

"I concur," Virginia said.

"Even Macrath?" Ellice asked, surprised.

"More than most."

That made her feel marginally better, although she wasn't sure why.

"I don't know if I like Huntly, even though it's a lovely place."

"You need to make it yours," Virginia said.

She returned the biscuit to the plate. "How?"

"When I came to Drumvagen, it was already built. Macrath had done everything he wanted in his home. Each door, each window, each painting, was exactly the way he wanted it. It took some time, but I had to make my mark here as well."

"The Rose Parlor," Ellice guessed. Virginia had turned what had once been a lovely rose suite into a sitting room and small library. The two rooms had been renamed the Rose Parlor.

Virginia nodded. "And a new conservatory we're having built."

"Very well, I might learn to live at Huntly. How do I learn to live with a husband?"

"You've been married less than a month," Virginia said, her eyes soft. "It's a difficult time."

"It's a hideous time," Ellice said, blowing out a breath. "I adore the man and he barely tolerates me."

"Why do you think that?"

Reaching forward, she picked up the biscuit again and took a bite from it. She chewed slowly and deliberately so she wouldn't have to speak.

She didn't want to tell Virginia about the interludes of passion followed by being ignored. Certain things should not be shared, even among women who loved each other.

"He has never said anything to me," she finally explained.

"Men don't, as a rule. They say things that make you guess it's 'I love you.' Women, on the other hand, are more direct. We prefer the words."

Ellice nodded.

She wasn't sure Ross could ever love her, not the way she wanted. Not the way she'd always dreamed of being loved. She wanted to be herself, seen as who she truly was, and have the man she loved know and cherish that woman.

"Does he know how you feel about him?" Virginia asked.

"How do you hide that sort of thing?"

"It's very possible he doesn't know," Virginia said. "You need to make sure he does. Then fight for him."

"Even if I have to fight him?"

"Oh, yes," Virginia said, laughing. "Especially then."

She smiled, an easier expression now than fifteen minutes ago.

"What's the second reason you've come?"

She told Virginia, finished her tea and stood.

"I'd better be going," she said. "I want to be back at Huntly tonight."

She kissed Virginia on the cheek, thanked her, and was making her way to the door when Virginia spoke again.

"About Enid."

She stopped and turned.

"I think it's time you stood up for yourself. I wish you'd done so years ago."

That, too, made her feel better. With a lighter step, she made her way to the cottage.

Chapter 31

"Where is my wife?"

Virginia frowned at the Earl of Gadsden, not at all surprised to see him so shortly after Ellice left the house.

"Do not refer to Ellice as if she's a hat you've misplaced, your lordship."

He surprised her by nodding. "You're right," he said, running his fingers through his hair. "You're right, of course. Do you know where she is?"

"Yes."

He frowned at her. "Are you going to tell me?"

She tilted her head and studied him. "I'm not entirely sure," she said. "What did you do to her?"

His face took on the appearance of stone.

"What did she say?"

"Absolutely nothing, but Ellice would not have." She regarded him with a frown. "I've known Ellice since she was fifteen," she said, reaching for the pot.

He shook his head and she shrugged, pouring herself a cup of tea. She didn't care if the Earl of Gadsden was impatient; he was simply going to have to hear what she had to say.

"I've always found her to be a reasonable girl. One who tries to accommodate people. Perhaps too much. She surrenders her own happiness to keep peace."

Virginia sat back and sipped from her tea. She enjoyed this brew. In an hour or so Brianag would bring her the nightly tea she drank. She was determined to acquire a taste for it as well.

"I thought marriage would bring her happiness," she said, studying him. "Why isn't she blissfully happy, your lordship?"

She smothered a smile at his look.

"If you'll pardon me for saying, Mrs. Sinclair, that is none of your business."

His frown was back, just a gentle lowering of his brows, but his eyes had turned icy.

"Is there nothing about her that you like?"

He surprised her by smiling. "Your husband has a theory about wives and what it means when you talk about them," he said. "Is that why you're asking me about Ellice?"

She shook her head. "No, I'm just trying to decide if I'm going to tell you where she is."

"I like a great deal about her, Mrs. Sinclair. She admires my library. She's fond of my mother. My mother is well on her way to adoring her. She seems to make my staff happy. They smile a great deal around her. She's a little messy, but so am I. She thinks about things I never would. I never know what she's going to say. Or do," he added.

"Is that such a bad thing?"

He sent her such a fierce glare that she was almost intimidated. However, she'd been married to Macrath long enough that she wasn't cowed by a stubborn man.

"No," he said, finally. "It isn't. It's startling and different and uncomfortable at times but it isn't a bad thing at all."

She took another sip of her tea.

"Will you tell me where she is?" The ice was gone from his eyes. "Please."

"You don't know why she came to Drumvagen, do you?"

Once again he gave her an impatient look, a quick glance from his gray eyes that said he would just as soon dispense with any further conversation and find his wife.

"She's at the crofter's cottage," she said.

He frowned. "The one on the way to Drumvagen?"

She nodded. "You can follow the road or cut through the glen," she said. "Either way, you'll find her there."

He made his excuses with enough haste to border on rudeness.

She chuckled as he left, imagining their confrontation. Ellice would give as good as she got, which is exactly what she should do. Being in love was no excuse to be a carpet for a man.

The more stubborn the man, the more obstinate the wife needed to be. After all, it was only fair.

She smiled, thinking of the skirmish to come.

In the crofter's cottage, Ellice moved the stone out of its place and withdrew the wrapped manuscript of *The Lustful Adventures of Lady Pamela* from its hidey-hole.

She took it to the table, sat there with her hand on it, staring down at the stack of pages.

Would he understand?

Ever since her marriage, Lady Pamela had begun fading in importance. Where once the character had given her courage, and sometimes even hope, now Lady Pamela was a barrier between Ellice and her husband.

The door abruptly flew open, so strongly that it banged on the wall behind it.

She stood, facing a force of nature. Not a storm or a gale, but Ross Forster, enraged.

"You're not going to leave me," he said.

Startled, she could only stare at him.

"I'm not?"

"No. I'll tear Drumvagen down, brick by brick with my bare hands if I have to, but Sinclair will not give you shelter. You are not going to leave me."

"What makes you think I was leaving you?"

His eyes weren't cold now. Instead, she had the strangest thought that she might catch fire if she met his gaze any longer.

"You're here, aren't you?"

"I left you a note. Didn't you get it?"

"What note? What did it say?"

"That I had an errand at Drumvagen and would be back at nightfall." She took a step toward him. "I'm not Cassandra, Ross."

"I know that," he said, frowning at her. "I was never once annoyed at her. She didn't anger me. She certainly didn't say things that made me want to clamp my hand over her mouth. When she wrote, they were thank-you notes and letters to her sister."

"Never lustful literature."

"Never lustful literature," he said, surprising her with his smile.

"You truly thought I left you?" she asked, still surprised. Or maybe she was more startled that he'd come after her.

"Were you afraid of another scandal?" she asked, retreating one step. "Is that why you're here?"

He ran his hand through his hair. "No. I don't care. Let people talk about me all they want."

Her eyes widened.

"I find I care about damn few people nowadays," he said, crossing to her. "I can count them on the fingers of one hand. You. My mother. You."

"You counted me twice."

"You matter twice as much as anyone."

She was not going to cry. Instead, she needed to tell him what she felt.

"I love you," she said. "I've loved you for a very long time. Or, at least it feels that way. You make me tingle just looking at me. I want to smile when you're around me. I'm miserable when I don't see you."

He took another step but she held up her hand.

"But I'll not have the type of marriage we've had for the last two weeks. I won't be ignored. I won't be shuffled off into a corner of your life. That's not the kind of love I want."

"What kind of love do you want?" he asked gently.

"Once I might have said like Donald and Lady Pamela. But they're imaginary. I want you to adore me like Macrath adores Virginia. Like Logan adores Mairi. I want to make your life better for being in it."

He came to her, bent his head until his lips were against her temple. "You've changed me, Ellice. You've made me whole. I won't live my life without you."

He rested his forehead on hers.

" 'Life has no meaning without you in it. Without the glory of the dawn in the shine of your hair. Without the blue of the skies in your eyes.' "

"I wrote that," she said, pulling back. "I was a bit over-blown there, wasn't I?"

He smiled down at her. "Not at all. Donald is a man in love. Men in love say things that sound a bit overblown to anyone else."

"Do they?"

He nodded again. "Things like your eyes are as soft as velvet sometimes. And sometimes as hard as stone. I can always gauge your mood by how your eyes sparkle or if they don't. If you're amused or sad or a dozen other emotions. The rest of your face can be perfectly still, but you can't hide your eyes."

She looked away, never knowing that she revealed herself so easily to him. Or that he'd cared to look.

She didn't expect him to grab her, haul her up against him and kiss her soundly. She should have known that she would surrender all too soon despite any wish to seem cool and unaffected. Lady Pamela might be a great actress; she never would be. The minute Ross touched her, she melted.

When he finally released her, she took two cautionary steps back and added another one for good measure.

He stood there, a handsome man with eyes that had always transfixed her, especially when they were as heated as they were now.

She turned and grabbed the manuscript and thrust it at him. "Here," she said. "It's why I came to Drumvagen. I wasn't running away. I wasn't leaving you. I came to get the book to give it to you."

"Give it to me?" He stared down at the oiled-paper-wrapped package in his hands.

"It's a gesture, Ross. A grand gesture."

"What do you expect me to do with it? Destroy it?"

"It doesn't matter," she said. "Not as much as you do."

He looked as if she'd struck him.

"I would never destroy it," he said. "It's your work. Your creation. Besides, it brought us together." His smile was wry. "My mother thinks my father had something to do with our marriage. If I hadn't visited Drumvagen, I would never have met you."

"Or if I hadn't hidden in a carriage," she said.

"Or if the storm hadn't come and trapped me here." He placed the manuscript back on the table.

"Or you hadn't been so kissable," she added.

"And you, such a temptation."

They smiled at each other.

"Despite all my flaws," she said, determined to be completely honest with him, "I'm good enough."

A vertical line formed between his brows.

"What do you mean, 'good enough'? Of course you're good enough. You're beyond good enough. You're Ellice."

She blinked at him.

"That's perfect for me."

She couldn't speak.

"I love the way you laugh and the way you're touched by something beautiful. I love your curiosity, your questioning, your imagination, your temper."

"I don't have a temper."

He only smiled and reached for her.

"I love the way you've brought life to Huntly. To me. I love you."

Could you cry and smile at the same time? It seemed she could, especially when he pulled her back into his arms.

He bent his head and kissed her tenderly, sweetly, the gentleness making her want to weep again.

When the kiss was done, she lay her cheek against his chest, sighing in happiness.

"What are you looking for?" she asked, glancing up to find him staring out the cottage window.

"A storm," he said. "Macrath once told me that love is like lightning. That it strikes when you least expect it."

"Have you been struck by lightning?" she asked, breathless.

"Yes," he said. "I find I have."

That deserved another kiss. When they parted, he looked down at her, his finger delicately stroking the path of one tear.

"I love you, Ellice Traylor Forster. Come home with me."

She should have told him that home wasn't London or Drumvagen or even Huntly. Home was in his arms. But he kissed her again and every thought flew out of her mind.

Epilogue

A year later

Mairi lumbered into the dining room, frowning at her husband when a smile lifted the corners of his mouth.

"You try being as big as a carriage," she said. "You wouldn't be amused."

Logan pulled out a chair for her, glanced at the mound of her stomach, and moved the chair even farther from the table.

"You have three more months," he reminded her. "I can't wait to see how large you get then."

Mairi rolled her eyes. "You're entirely too large," she said. "Our daughter is going to be a mammoth child."

"Or our son," he said, the argument of long duration.

Virginia laughed, and when Mairi frowned at her made no effort to contain her amusement.

Macrath's three children were alternately angels and devils, depending on their moods. Mairi and Logan's offspring were no doubt going to be the same, especially given the stubbornness of their parents.

Macrath glanced at Virginia and then away, no doubt in an effort to keep from laughing as well.

Ellice watched them all, feeling a surge of joy that they were family, one not related by blood as much as choice.

They'd all converged on Drumvagen at Virginia's request. Tomorrow they would leave for home again, but not before making plans for another reunion. Perhaps their next meeting would be in Edinburgh when Mairi's child was born.

Reaching beneath the table, she grabbed Ross's hand. They weren't seated in proper dinner party style, not as they would be when they entertained at Huntly.

To her great surprise, she was quite a good hostess. All she really had to do was remember people's names and find something about them to compliment. Since she knew how it felt to be uncomfortable and out of place, she was very good at that.

Over the last year, ever since Ross had been elected a representative peer, they'd entertained at least every week, especially when they were in Scotland. In London their home was in a lovely town house in a fashionable square, not far from where her mother now lived.

The Dowager Countess of Barrett had no qualms about taking vast sums of money from her son-in-law, who, thank Providence, had no reservations about spending it on her.

Ross had purchased a large town house for Enid and settled a generous annual sum on her as an allowance. That amount, along with the funds she'd earned from her book on housewifery hints, was enough to ensure she lived in luxury.

Her mother was overjoyed to be back in the most civilized city in the world, as she called it. As a Dowager Countess and the mother of a countess, not to mention the author of a best-selling book, Enid was feted and very popular.

Life at Drumvagen had settled back to a peaceful place with Enid remaining in London and Brianag resuming as resident martinet.

As far as her own home, Ellice had made Huntly hers in small ways, but it was Ross who'd done the most. Not only had he allowed Huntly's staff to tour the library and read any books they wished, but one day he'd blindfolded her, leading her laughing through the house. Once they arrived at the Yellow Parlor, he removed the blindfold and showed her the shiny brass plaque on the door.

"The Lady Pamela Parlor?" she asked. She couldn't see for blinking back her tears, especially when she entered the room to find that the painting of flowers above the mantel had been replaced by the new portrait of her he'd recently commissioned.

She looked beautiful. More, she looked happy.

Tonight he would look the same after she told him her own news. Mairi wasn't the only one who was going to be huge in a few months.

Her mother-in-law would be pleased, but then Janet often looked happy lately, especially after her trip to Italy. She'd been gone for months, finally arriving home with tanned cheeks, a perpetual smile, and plans to visit Spain next summer. Coincidentally, they'd learned that Mr. McMahon had made a recent buying trip to the Continent.

When Ross would have spoken to his mother, Ellice discouraged him.

"Let her have her secrets," she said.

Now it looked as if her family had their own.

Mairi glanced at Ross, who looked at her, then at Logan. Before she had a chance to ask what they were about, Virginia said, "Oh, do tell her."

Mairi nodded.

Logan reached down, handing a parcel to Ross, who passed it to her.

From its heft and size, she could tell it was a book. The smell of the leather was strong even through the paper. Slowly, she unwrapped the package to see a blue leather-bound book with gilt-edged pages. The title was inscribed on the front in elaborate gold script.

THE LUSTFUL ADVENTURES OF LADY PAMELA
By Ellice Forster, Countess of Gadsden

She stared at it, spellbound.

"Nothing's changed," Ross said. "Not Donald's appearance or the house. It'll make people wonder if it's based on real life or not."

"You used my name." She traced her fingers over the incised gold letters.

"Why should you do all that work and not be recognized for it?" Ross said. "It's a very good book, Ellice."

She shook her head. "You daft man. They'll drum you out of Parliament."

"Nonsense," he said. "I'm a very good representative peer. If I lose the next election, they didn't deserve me anyway."

"You won't lose," Logan said, smiling.

Ross stood, gathered her up in his arms, smoothing his fingers over her tears.

She looked at them all: Macrath and Virginia, Mairi and Logan, and her own beloved Ross. Her imagination was silent because there was nothing more wonderful than this moment and these people.

Macrath Sinclair looked around the table before his gaze rested on Virginia, the woman responsible for filling his heart and his home with people he loved. Each of the people at this table had brought something to his life, and he hoped he enriched theirs as well.

Logan Harrison placed his hand on the mound of his wife's stomach beneath the table. Even here, in the soft light from the candles, he could see that their babe was insistent and active. Mairi glanced at him and smiled, used to his touch.

Virginia blinked away her tears. Upstairs, her children slept, each one healthy and happy, members of a clan the man at her side had created, heirs to the empire he founded. Once, fate had seemed pitiless, but now her life was filled with joy.

The summer storm that had been threatening all day blossomed over Drumvagen's roof. Thunder raced from cloud to cloud almost in celebration. Lightning created a show of fireworks and wind whistled in appreciation.

The house, built to shield and support a family, stood resolute beneath the onslaught.

Ross bent his head and kissed Ellice. She dropped the book on the table, wrapped her arms around his neck and enthusiastically kissed him back to the accompaniment of fond laughter.

Author's Notes

Huntly was modeled after an estate not far from Edinburgh. As is common when I borrow a location, I've changed enough details that it would probably not be recognizable to those familiar with the house and all its wonders. Drumvagen, as well, was inspired by a house in Scotland.

Memoirs of a Woman of Pleasure, or *Fanny Hill* as we've come to call it, was published in 1748. *The History of Tom Jones, a Foundling,* also known as *Tom Jones,* was published in 1749. In 1899, Kate Chopin wrote *The Awakening,* a novel that detailed her heroine's attempt to obtain sexual independence. Of course the book created a scandal, just like *The Lusty Adventures of Lady Pamela* might have.

Catch up with the rest of Clan Sinclair!
Keep reading to get a taste of
Virginia and Macrath's story in

THE DEVIL OF CLAN SINCLAIR

and Mairi and Logan's story in

THE WITCH OF CLAN SINCLAIR

The Devil of Clan Sinclair

Prologue

*London
September, 1868*

Please let him be there. If he hadn't come to the Duke of
Bledsoe's ball, she didn't think she could bear it.

He must have been invited. She'd done enough hinting to
the duke's daughter that she'd be very, very pleased if Macrath Sinclair was invited, along with his sister Ceana.

She'd waited so long already, a whole day, since seeing
him. She'd told herself that all she had to do was be patient
a few more hours. That refrain had sung through her mind
all during the time her maid had dressed her hair, when the
gown needed a few last minute stitches to keep one of the
silly bows in place, and when her gloves were handed to her.
Only one more hour, she'd thought as she was inspected by
her father and Mrs. Haverstock, turning in a slow circle so
her appearance could be judged.

To her surprise, neither her English chaperone nor her
father had said a word. Nor had her father frowned, his usual
expression in her presence. He only nodded, a sign to precede
him into the carriage, Mrs. Haverstock following.

The carriage wheels had been too slow. Her heartbeat had

been too fast. Hours, decades, eons later they were finally at the Duke of Bledsoe's home, only for it to take forever before the carriage got to the head of the line and they could leave the vehicle. Because of the crush of people, there was another interminable wait to climb the steep stone steps, and yet another to enter the ballroom.

Would he like her hair? Her maid had done it in an intricate style tonight. What about her new scent from Paris? She'd thought about him the moment she uncapped the flacon, wondering if he would think the rose scent too strong. Would he think her high color attractive? She couldn't help herself; the thought of seeing him after an absence of twenty-four endless hours reddened her cheeks.

Dear God, please let him be here. Please. She'd promise a dozen things, only let him be here.

She heard Mrs. Haverstock behind her, greeting friends. Moving away, she scanned the crowd for a sight of him.

Thank you, God. There he was. There, just beyond the pillar in the ballroom. Standing there, looking out at the crowd as the music surged around him.

She made herself wait, watching him. He was so handsome in his elegant black evening dress. He stood on the edge of the ballroom, a man with the studied gaze of a person twice his age. His stature was of someone who knew himself well, who'd gone through his own personal battles and won his wars.

Several women stopped, their looks intent. Suddenly, she felt a fierce possessiveness, and wanted to clamp her hands over their eyes to stop their acquisitive looks.

He was hers.

He turned in her direction, his eyes lighting on her. There it was, the smile she'd been anticipating. Slowly at first, dawning with merely a quirk at the corners of his lips, growing as she walked toward him.

She wanted to race to him, throw herself into his arms, press her hands against his chest and feel the solidness of him. Otherwise, she might believe she'd dreamed him, conjured him up from a lonely girl's prayer and a wishful woman's yearning.

He was as perfect as any daydream could create him, but he was no illusion. He was Macrath and she was enthralled.

"Are you well?" she asked on reaching him. A full day, nearly twenty-four hours, had passed since she'd seen him last, and anything might have happened in the interim.

The smile she'd watched from across the room was now directed solely at her. How wonderful, that an expression could have such warmth, like the sun spearing directly into her.

"I am well, Virginia," he said. His voice, warm and low, held a roughness that chafed her senses. "And you?"

She was just now starting to heal. The last day without seeing him had been unbearable. She was shriveling up inside for lack of one of his warm smiles. Without seeing his beautiful blue eyes and hearing his Scottish accent, she was not quite herself.

How did she tell him something like that? It seemed like he knew, because his smile faded and he reached out one hand to hold hers.

She could hear people around them, but it was like a bubble surrounded Macrath and her. No one was important. Nothing else had weight.

"You're beautiful," he said.

She smiled, pleased he thought so. Few people did. She was too retiring to be noticed most of the time.

When she just shook her head, he said, "You're the most beautiful woman in London."

"You're beautiful as well," she said. She didn't mean handsome, either. He was a gift from God, a creation of masculine beauty.

Even his laugh was glorious.

"Will you dance with me?" he asked, still holding her hand.

He seemed as loath to relinquish it as she was to step back. Prudence dictated that she do so, at least until Macrath spoke to her father, but prudence could go to blazes for all she cared now.

She was gloriously, madly, spectacularly in love with Macrath Sinclair and she didn't care who knew.

"I'd rather go into the garden," she said, daring to tell him the truth. She wanted another kiss from him, another stolen embrace.

"It looks to rain," he said.

"Do you care?"

"Not one whit."

"I don't either. Besides, it's forever raining in London."

"You'll find that Scotland is the same in some months."

"I won't care," she said. "It will be my home."

"Soon," he said, the look in his eyes growing more intense.

Perhaps she should thank Providence that the weather was souring. Otherwise, she might make a fool of herself in the garden, demanding kiss after kiss.

"Virginia," a voice called, breaking the spell.

She blinked and turned her head to see her father standing not far away.

Her stomach dropped, and she looked up at Macrath with apology in her eyes.

"I'm sorry," she said, "but Father's calling me."

"I understand. Shall I accompany you?"

"It's best you don't," she said. "I've no doubt done something wrong."

"When I meet with him tomorrow, I'll tell him the press of business demands a speedy marriage. We'll be in Scotland before you know it."

She would be with him wherever that was: in a corner of the garden, in a vestibule in the ballroom, in a hallway, a servant's stair. The location didn't matter, as long as she was with Macrath.

She squeezed his hand, then turned and reluctantly walked away, glancing back with a smile. Her father led her to an anteroom and closed the door.

"I'll not have you making a fool of yourself over that Scot," he said.

She held herself stiffly, as she did whenever he issued a dictate. The slightest indication that she disagreed with him would only make the punishment worse.

Now, she concentrated on the floor between them, hoping that he wouldn't see her inability to look him in the face as disrespect.

"I'm sorry, Father," she said.

Docility was better than rebellion. Easier, too, because she'd once tried to debate a point with him and had been severely punished for doing so. Her governess had taken great delight in using a birch rod. The lesson being that few things were worth physical pain.

Macrath was, and she wondered if her father knew it.

"People will look at me and wonder at the lack of control I have over a female in my own household."

She'd heard a variation of that comment all her life. Ever since coming to England, however, it had grown more difficult to listen to him, and maintain some appearance of humility while doing so.

"I'm in love with Macrath, Father," she said, the first time she'd ever admitted such a thing to him. She glanced up at him to find his eyes had narrowed. "You've agreed that Macrath could call on you tomorrow," she hastened to say.

After that, her future would be assured. She would be Macrath Sinclair's wife.

"I've already picked out your husband and it's not that Scot."

Her hands were still clasped in front of her. She bowed her head again, her gaze on the crimson patterned carpet. She'd think of anything but her father's words. Her mind, unaccustomed to joy, had forced her imagination to produce something more familiar, her father's derision.

"You're going to be a countess, daughter. How do you feel about that?"

She was going to be sick.

Slowly, she lifted her eyes, unsurprised to find him smiling.

"But you agreed to meet with him," she said.

"It's done, Virginia. We've just now finalized the arrangements. You're to be married within the month to the Earl of Barrett."

Turning, he extended his hand and a woman stepped out of the shadows. "Your future mother-in-law, Virginia. The Countess of Barrett."

She gave the woman barely a glance, intent on her father. She said the one word she never said, one tiny word she'd learned had no power in the past. Perhaps it would work now.

"Please."

The world halted, stilled, hung on a breath of air.

"There's no fussing about it; the deal has been struck."

"But you agreed to meet with Macrath."

He scowled at her. "I won't tolerate your rebellion, Virginia." Turning to the woman, he said, "I'll have her chaperone take my daughter home, your ladyship. Perhaps a few weeks of contemplating her future will make her grateful for it."

The woman merely nodded.

"There won't be any entertainments until after your wedding," her father said.

Did it matter?

She'd be confined to her room, but she didn't care. She'd sit and stare out at the world, her body in one place, her soul and heart in another.

Virginia only shook her head, unable to speak, flooded by a sense of despair so deep she was certain she was bleeding inside.

Chapter 1

London, England
July, 1869

The ferns near the window wiggled their fronds as if they wanted to escape the room.

Virginia Anderson Traylor, Countess of Barrett, wiggled on the chair and wanted to do the same.

She sat in the corner of the parlor, swathed in black. Her hands were folded on her lap, her knees pressed together, her head at the perfect angle.

How many times had she thought about this scene? In the last year, at least a dozen or more, but in her imagination she'd always been surrounded by weeping women rather than sitting a solitary vigil.

She stood, unable to remain still any longer. She'd been a good and proper widow for nine hours now. For the last four, she'd watched over her husband's coffin alone.

Her thoughts, however, had not been on her husband.

A dog howled, no doubt the same dog that howled for three nights straight. Ellice, her sister-in-law, thought he'd announced Poor Lawrence's death.

The parlor where she sat stretched the length of the town

house. Two fireplaces warmed it in winter, but now it was pleasantly temperate. The room had been refurbished with the infusion of money she'd brought to the marriage. The wallpaper was a deep crimson, topped by an ivory frieze of leaves and ferns. Four overstuffed chairs, upholstered in a similar crimson pattern as the wallpaper, squatted next to a tufted settee. A half-dozen marble-topped tables, each adorned with a tapestry runner, filled the rest of the available space, their sharp corners patiently waiting to snare a passing skirt.

No doubt Enid meant for the room to be the perfect showplace in the Earl of Barrett's home. What her mother-in-law had accomplished, however, was a parlor reeking with excess. Even the potpourri was overpowering, smelling so strongly of cloves that her nose itched and her eyes watered.

The coffin was crafted of polished mahogany, wider at the shoulders and narrow at the feet, with three brass handles on each side. A round brass plaque over where Poor Lawrence's heart would be was engraved OUR BELOVED.

Not *her* beloved, and he hadn't shown much love toward his family. The hyperbole, however, was expected of them. So, too, all the mourning rituals that would be carried out in the next year.

Perhaps Lawrence had arranged for his own coffin and the plaque was a last thumb in the eye to his wife, mother, and sisters.

For her sitting, she'd insisted the top of the coffin be lowered. The other members of the family would probably want to view Poor Lawrence once more.

"A bad heart," Enid had called it. A bad disposition as well, although perhaps she shouldn't fault him for being angry at the circumstances he'd been dealt. A semi-invalid since birth, he'd been limited in what he could do, to the point of being imprisoned in this house.

Poor Lawrence was what she called him in her thoughts.

To his face, she'd been a proper wife. "Dearest husband," she'd said on those occasions when he allowed her to visit him.

"Dearest husband, how are you feeling?"

"Dearest husband, you're looking better."

"Dearest husband, is there anything I can bring you?"

He never answered, only slitting his eyes at her like she was an insect he'd discovered in his food.

Lawrence was, whether it was right to say such a thing about the deceased, a thoroughly unlikable person. Yet John Donne, the poet, stated that every man's death was a loss to be experienced by all mankind.

With age, Lawrence might have changed. He might have become a better person. He might have even been generous and caring.

How foolish it was to ascribe virtues to the dead they never owned in life. Lawrence wasn't a hero and he wasn't kind. Look at how he'd thrust them all into poverty.

She could easily understand his antipathy toward her. After all, didn't she feel the same for him? Why, though, would he treat his sisters and mother with contempt? Why punish them when it was obvious they hadn't done anything but treat him with kindness and care?

Every day, Eudora and Ellice called on their brother. Even if Lawrence wouldn't see them, they still returned, time after time. Eudora selected books she thought he'd like to read from their library. Ellice relayed stories to him of their days and the world outside the house.

Enid was as fond as any mother could be, worrying about Lawrence's health, querying his attendant about his cough, his color, his weakness. Despite his wishes, she insisted the doctor make regular visits, and listened when his examination was done.

What had Lawrence done to repay them? Guaranteed they would forever be dependent on others.

He could, just as easily, have given some of her father's money to his mother—or to her—to ensure their future was secure. Or he could have spent it on personal property not subject to his will.

But he hadn't done anything kind or caring.

At least, now, she would never again have to pretend to be a loving wife. These sleepless hours were little enough sacrifice for such blessed freedom.

Custom dictated the curtains be drawn, but she'd opened them at midnight, unable to bear the closed-in feeling of the room. The mirror was swathed in crepe. Candles sat burning on the mantel beside a clock stopped at the time of Poor Lawrence's death.

The room celebrated death, but she'd never been afraid of death. She was not overly fond of the dark, heights, or the ocean, however, and she detested spiders.

"The world is not going to swallow you whole, Virginia," her father had said more than once. "There's no reason to be a timid little mouse."

She circled the bier, her fingers trailing over the polished top of the coffin, closer to Poor Lawrence in death than she'd ever been in life except one time, the night their marriage had been consummated, six months after their wedding. On that occasion, he'd kissed her, so passionately it jolted her. The coupling, however, had been a painful experience, one she'd not wished to repeat. To her relief, he felt the same and they never touched again.

Enid, Dowager Countess of Barrett, pulled open the sliding doors of the parlor, then closed them just as quickly.

Her mother-in-law was stocky and short, her shoulders as wide as her hips. When Enid headed toward her, it was like facing a solid wall of determination. Enid's brown eyes could be as warm as chocolate sauce. Now they were as cold as frozen earth.

"Have you decided?"

Even though it was just before dawn, her mother-in-law was dressed in a black silk dress with jet buttons. Her hair was pulled back from her round face and contained in a black net snood. Although she wore a full hoop, she expertly navigated the room filled with furniture, moving to occupy a chair close to the bier.

"What you propose is so . . ." The words trailed away.

"Practical? Logical?" Enid asked.

Virginia walked to the window, trying to find some way to respond.

"Do not think Jeremy will support us, my dear. He will banish us from this house with a quickness that will surprise you. What he doesn't do, his harridan of a wife will. They'll care nothing for what happens to us."

"Would you?" she asked, glancing over her shoulder at her mother-in-law. "If the situation were reversed, would you care for Jeremy and his wife?"

"And their brood of children?" Enid sighed deeply. "I don't know. They're badly behaved children."

Virginia bit back a smile. Yes, they were, and she dreaded any occasion when she had to encounter Jeremy's seven children.

If Lawrence had left behind one child, they wouldn't be having this conversation.

Her mother-in-law was a planner, witness her brilliance in arranging a marriage between Lawrence, an invalid, and an American heiress. One thing Enid hadn't been able to do, however, was inspire Lawrence to bed his wife on more than one occasion.

She rarely called Enid "Mother," falling back on a habit of not addressing her at all unless it was in the company of others. Her own mother had died at her birth, a fact she'd been reminded of endlessly as a child. Not by her father, who seemed surprised when she was trotted out for his inspection at Christmas and during his one summer visit. A succession of nurses and governesses, all hired to tend her and keep her out of her father's way, ensured she knew her entrance into the world had been accompanied by the greatest tragedy.

She couldn't even imagine her mother's disembodied voice on this occasion. Would she have sided toward logic and survival? Or would her mother have been horrified at Enid's suggestion?

"Something must be done," Enid said. "You know as well as I."

The title was going to pass to Lawrence's cousin, Jeremy. He was a perfectly agreeable sort of person, pleasant to Virginia when they met. She didn't see anything wrong with him assuming the title. The problem was, everything Lawrence had purchased since receiving the bulk of her estate: the numerous houses, parcels of land, dozens of horses, farm equipment, and furnishings. Lawrence had ensured they would also go to his cousin by willing them to the "male heir of his body." Without an heir, the property traveled back up the family tree to Jeremy.

Without any cash or assets they could sell, they'd be penniless.

All she had was her quarterly allowance, and it wouldn't buy more than a few bottles of perfume. She had her mother's jewels, but they were more sentimental than valuable since her mother evidently had not been ostentatious in her dress. One good ruby brooch and a carnelian ring could be sold. How much would those bring her? Not enough to care for all the people who needed to be supported.

They were in dire straits, indeed.

Unless she produced an heir to the estate.

What Enid was proposing was shocking. Somehow, she

needed to get with child and quickly enough that he would be viewed as Lawrence's heir.

"It's a solution to our dilemma," Enid said. "Have you given any thought to it?"

She nodded. She'd thought about nothing but their situation in the last four hours. God help her, but here in this room with her husband's body in a casket, she'd thought about nothing but him.

Macrath.

The Witch of Clan Sinclair

Chapter 1

Edinburgh, Scotland
October, 1872

Nothing about the occasion hinted that it would change Mairi Sinclair's life. Not the hour, being after dinner, or the day, being a Friday. The setting didn't warn her; the Edinburgh Press Club was housed in a lovely brick building with an impressive view of the castle.

Still, possessing an inquiring mind, she should have somehow known. She should have seen the carriage pull into the street behind them. She should have felt something. The air should have been different, heavy with portent. Hinting at rain, if nothing else.

Perhaps a thunderstorm would have kept her home, thereby changing her fate. But on that evening, not a cloud was in the sky. The day had been a fair one and the night stars glittered brightly overhead, visible even with the glare of the yellowish gas lamps along the street.

A gust of wind brought the chill of winter, but her trembling was due more to eagerness than cold as she left the carriage. Straightening her skirts as she waited for her cousin to follow, Mairi wished she'd taken the time to order a new cloak—her old black one was a bit threadbare at the hem. She would like something in red, perhaps, with oversized buttons and a hidden pocket or two for her notebooks and pencils.

Her dress was new, however, a blue wool that brought out the color of her eyes and made her hair look darker than its usual drab brown. At the throat was the cameo that her brother and sister-in-law had given her on their return from Italy.

"We saw it and thought it looked like you," Virginia said.

She'd responded with the protest that it wasn't a holiday or her birthday.

Macrath had merely ignored her and pinned it on her dress. "The best presents are those that are unexpected," he said. "Learn to receive, Mairi."

So she had, and today she was grateful for the thought and the gift. The brooch enhanced her dress.

She didn't see, however, that the finely carved profile looked anything like her. She didn't have such an aristocratic nose, or a mouth that looked formed for a smile. The hairstyle was similar, drawn up on the sides to cascade in curls in the back. Perhaps that was the only point of similarity.

Fenella joined her in a cloud of perfume, something light and smelling of summer flowers.

Her cousin was a pretty girl, someone people noted even though she rarely spoke in a group. Fenella's blond hair created a halo around her fine-boned face, accentuating her hazel eyes.

Mairi had seen a swan once, and the gentle grace of the bird reminded her of Fenella.

In addition, Fenella was far nicer in temperament than she was. Whenever she said that, her cousin demurred, but they both knew it was the truth.

Fenella's cloak was also black, the severe color only accentuating her blond prettiness, while Mairi was certain that she herself looked like a very large crow. However, she wasn't going to be deterred by her appearance or any other minuscule concern on this most glorious of occasions.

She strode toward the building, clutching her worn copy of *Beneath the Mossy Bough* in her left hand, her reticule in her right. Her hated bonnet was atop her head only because Fenella had frowned at her in censure. Otherwise, she would have left it behind on the seat.

Before they could cross the street, three carriages passed, the rhythmic rumble of their wheels across the cobbles a familiar sound even at night. Edinburgh did have quiet hours, but normally only between midnight and four. Then, the castle on the hill above them seemed to crouch, warning the inhabitants to be silent and still, for these were the hours of rest.

She knew the time well, since she was often awake in the middle of the night working.

"Are you very certain this is proper, Mairi?" Fenella asked as they hurried across the street.

She turned to look at her cousin. Fenella was occasionally the voice of her conscience, but tonight nothing would stop her from attending the Edinburgh Press Club meeting.

"It's Melvin Hampstead, Fenella," she said. "Melvin Hampstead. Who knows when we will ever have the chance to hear him speak again?"

"But we haven't been invited," Fenella said.

Mairi waved her hand in the air as if to dismiss her cousin's concerns. "The whole city's been invited." She shook her head. "It's Melvin Hampstead, Fenella."

She climbed the steps to the top, opened the outer door and held it ajar for her cousin. Inside was the vestibule, a rectangular space large enough to accommodate ten people. Yellow-tinted light from the paraffin oil sconces illuminated the door at the end, guarded by an older man in a dark green kilt and black jacket.

At their entrance, he stood, folded his arms across his chest and pointed his gray-threaded beard in their direction.

"Is it lost you are, then?"

Mairi blinked at him. "I don't believe we are. This is the Edinburgh Press Club, is it not?"

"That it is, but you're a woman, I'm thinking."

"That I am," she said, clutching the book to her bodice. "We've come to hear Mr. Hampstead speak."

"You'll not be hearing him here," he said. "The meeting is closed to women."

The man didn't even look at her when he spoke, but at a spot above her, as if she were below his notice.

"That can't be true," she said. "Otherwise, it wouldn't have been publicized so well."

"This is the Edinburgh Press Club, madam. We do not admit women."

"I'm a miss," she said, stepping back. "Miss Mairi Sinclair, and I've a right to be here. I'm the editor of the *Edinburgh Gazette*."

"You're a woman by my way of thinking," he said. "And we don't admit women."

She had the urge to kick him in the shin. Instead, she batted her eyes ever so gently. She'd been told she had beautiful blue eyes—the Sinclair eyes—plus she was occasionally gifted with the same charm that Fenella effortlessly commanded.

"Are you very certain?"

Evidently, he was immune to both her eyes and her lashes, because he frowned at her.

"It's Melvin Hampstead," she said. "I adored his book," she added, holding it up for him to see. "If we promise to slip in, not speak to anyone, and simply stand in the corner, wouldn't you allow us to enter?"

"No."

No? Just no? No further explanation? No chance to convince him otherwise? Simply no?

She frowned at him, one hand holding the book, the other clenched tight around her reticule and the notebook inside. She carried her notebook everywhere, and the minute she could, she was going to record everything this man said, plus his refusal on behalf of the Edinburgh Press Club to allow her to enter.

"Is there a problem?"

She turned her head to find a man standing there, a bear of a man, tall and broad, with a square face and eyes like green glass.

"No, Provost Harrison, no problem. I was just telling this female that the Edinburgh Press Club did not allow women."

She'd listened to tales of Scotland's history from her grandmother, heard stories of brave men striding into battle with massive swords and bloodlust in their eyes.

This was one of those men.

He, too, was attired in a kilt, one of a blue and green tartan with a black jacket over a snowy white shirt. She could almost imagine him bare-chested, a broadsword in his right hand and a cudgel in his left. The sun would shine on the gleaming muscles of his arms and chest. He'd toss his head back and his black hair would fall over his brow.

There were men, and then there were men. One was male only because he wasn't female. The other was the definition of masculine, fierce and a little frightening, if her heartbeat was to be believed.

He braced his legs apart, folded his arms and regarded her with an impassive look.

She knew who he was, of course, but she'd never seen the Lord Provost of Edinburgh up so close. If she had, she'd have been prepared for the force of his personality.

If he meant to intimidate her, he was doing a fine job of it, but she would neither admit it nor let him see that she was wishing she'd thought to remove her cloak so he could see her new blue dress.

Nonsense. Was she turning into one of those women who couldn't be bothered with anything more important than her appearance?

Perhaps she should ask herself that question when she wasn't standing nearly toe-to-toe with the Lord Provost, with him looking half Highland warrior, half gentleman Scot. Or if she could have ignored his strong square jaw, full lips, and his sparkling green eyes.

"Is there a problem, miss?"

At least he'd gotten the miss part correct.

"No problem. But I don't understand why I can't attend Mr. Hampstead's lecture."

He raised one eyebrow at her.

"The Edinburgh Press Club does not allow women as members, I believe."

"Mr. Hampstead's lecture has been promoted throughout Edinburgh."

"For men to attend."

She could feel her temper rising, which was never a good sign. She had a tendency to do and say foolish things when she forgot herself.

She was very aware that there were inequities in society. For that reason, Macrath was the titular owner of the Sinclair Printing Company. For that reason, she signed her columns with either her brother's name or another male's. For that reason, she pretended Macrath was out of the office temporarily when men came to call to discuss a matter with the owner of the *Gazette*. She always took the information, made the decision, and wrote the supplicant with her answer, once more pretending to be her brother.

She had to hide behind a man to do her daily tasks, run a business, be a reporter, and publish a newspaper, but she'd never been faced with the situation she was in at the moment: being refused admittance solely because she was a woman.

It should have occurred to her, but because it hadn't, she felt the curious sensation of being blown off her feet.

"What does it matter that I'm a woman?" she asked. "Does Mr. Hampstead's lecture only appeal to men?"

Right at the moment, she didn't like the Edinburgh Press Club very much. Nor did she like the gatekeeper or the Lord Provost. Most of all, she didn't like the burning feeling in her stomach, the one that felt like humiliation and embarrassment, coupled with the knowledge that she wasn't going to win this skirmish.

Fenella evidently noted the signs, because she grabbed her elbow. "Come, Mairi, we should leave."

"I believe that would be the wisest course," the Lord Provost said.

She narrowed her eyes at him.

Did he think he was the first man to have tried to put her in her place? She was faced with criticism every day, and every day she had to deflect it, fight it, or ignore it.

"I would have thought, in your position, that you would speak for all citizens of Edinburgh, not just the men. Or is it because I don't have the ability to vote that you dismiss me so easily?"

He didn't say a word, the coward.

"Your silence indicates that you can't dispute that."

His lips curved in a faint smile. "On the contrary, my silence might be wisdom instead. I have found that it isn't wise to argue with those who are overemotional."

The breath left her in a gasp. "You consider women to be overly emotional?"

"I do not address women, miss. Only you. The club is a private organization, not one funded by or for the citizens of Edinburgh. I have nothing to do with its workings. I am simply a guest. Had I the authority, I would allow you entrance."

She smiled. "Then you do think women should be admitted."

"I think it's the only way to silence you."

She almost drew her foot back, but a soft sound from Fenella stopped her.

"Thank you, sir," Fenella said, stepping in and preventing Mairi from responding by grabbing her arm and pulling her toward the stairs. "We'll be on our way."

In her daydream, she sailed past the Lord Provost with dignity and poise while he wistfully stared after her. The truth was somewhat different. She left, but when she looked back, he was grinning at her.

Logan Harrison watched as the woman went down the steps, glancing back at him from time to time.

She had high cheekbones stained with pink and a chin that looked stubborn enough to double as a battering ram.

He smiled at her frown, which made her scowl even deeper.

He normally avoided angry women, but something about her made him want to annoy her further, just to see how fast her temper rose.

Her eyes blazed at him and her lush mouth was thinned in irritation. As he watched, she said something to her wiser companion. She evidently didn't want to leave. She'd probably be content to argue with him all night.

He rarely had the opportunity to argue with people. Gone were the fevered discussions of his earlier political life. He was at the point now that people respected his position too much to counter his pronouncements.

They practically backed out of the room.

Although he was the Lord Provost of Edinburgh, he wasn't God. Granted, his position dictated that he was also the Lord Lieutenant for the city, which meant he greeted members of the royal family—some of whom did think they were God.

"Who is she?" he asked. Robertson glanced at the woman then back at him.

"A Miss Sinclair, sir. She claims to be the editor of the *Edinburgh Gazette*."

"Does she?"

He knew the paper but he made a mental note of her name. She claimed to be its editor? Another interesting facet of the woman, one that had nothing to do with the fact that she had an arresting face and a figure that hinted at lushness beneath her cloak.

He watched as she entered the carriage, regretting that circumstances wouldn't allow him another chance to continue their discussion.

"He had no right to insult me," Mairi said as she entered the carriage.

"He didn't insult you," Fenella said. "If anyone did, it was the Edinburgh Press Club. They're the ones who refused to allow women."

"Next you're going to tell me it's the way of the world and I should simply accept it."

"Men are stronger," Fenella said.

Mairi glanced at her. "And smarter, I presume?"

Fenella didn't answer.

It was one thing for a woman to be treated with disdain by a man. Another thing entirely, Mairi thought, for another woman to feel the same. Unfortunately, Fenella wasn't alone in her thoughts. A great many women believed that men were stronger, smarter, more capable of being leaders. Let them protect women, and women—frail and helpless—would be the better for it.

She shouldn't be so critical of Fenella. Her cousin was

nothing if not loyal. Despite not being a fan of Mr. Hampstead, Fenella had donned one of her better dresses, had her blond hair curled in ringlets, and came with her tonight.

"His eyes are green," Fenella said, sighing. "I do wish my eyes were that color."

Mairi turned to look at her cousin, surprised. Fenella was not the type to long for something she didn't have. Nor was she the type to notice a man's appearance. Or at least she had never been in the past.

"Your eyes are lovely," she said, and it wasn't a lie. Fenella's hazel eyes had the ability to change color depending on what she wore. Tonight they appeared a soft brown.

Her own eyes were a deep Sinclair blue. Her brother and sister had a similar shade. If she wished to be different in any way, it would be that her hair wasn't a simple brown, but light and blond like her cousin's.

However, wishing to be different was a waste of time.

"I didn't notice his eyes," she said.

The lie embarrassed her. Of course she'd noted his eyes. And his face, looking as if it had been hewn by God's axe.

"He's entirely too large."

Fenella glanced at her.

She frowned at her cousin's smile.

"Well, he is. I prefer a man who's less imposing."

"He was certainly that," Fenella said on a sigh.

"I'm surprised he didn't throw us down the stairs."

Fenella's eyes widened.

"He seemed very polite, Mairi."

Mairi nearly threw her hands up in the air.

"I wanted to hear Mr. Hampstead. Not go all agog over a man."

Fenella's face turned a becoming shade of pink, and Mairi knew she shouldn't have said what she had. Her cousin had a delicate nature, one that required diplomatic speech. She always had to rearrange the words she was going to say before talking to Fenella, for fear of offending her or hurting her feelings.

"You have to admit he is a handsome man," her cousin said. "He's tall and has such broad shoulders. And his mouth . . ." Fenella sighed again.

"What's wrong with his mouth?"

"Oh, there's nothing wrong with it," Fenella said, sounding as love-struck as a silly girl. "He looks like he's about to say something shocking." She glanced over at Mairi. "Or kiss you."

Rather than just sit there and listen to Fenella wax eloquent over the Lord Provost, she pulled out her notebook and began to write down the conversation as she remembered it. Thankfully, she had a very good memory from years of practice recalling tidbits and snippets of information.

She didn't want to miss a minute of it.

Chapter 2

"**I** would talk to you," Robert said when she and Fenella arrived home.

"Could it wait?" she asked, striding through the kitchen still smelling of tonight's dinner of mutton and onions. She'd taken time off to hear her favorite author speak, reasoning that she could write about the lecture for the paper. Since she couldn't do that now, she had to find something else for the new edition.

Fenella moved past her, smiling apologetically as she whisked a maid from the room. At least there wouldn't be any witnesses to this dressing down. Normally, Robert didn't care where or when he criticized her.

After Macrath had purchased a home far from Edinburgh, he wanted her and Fenella to join him. She refused to leave the city, so they'd compromised. He purchased a large home for them, and instilled Robert, their second cousin, as chaperone and financial advisor, and their driver, James, as spy.

Mairi had told her brother that she and Fenella were capable of protecting themselves, however weak and defenseless he thought they were. Macrath had only smiled and done as he wished.

Robert was her daily trial.

The man's face bore evidence of each of his years, the last few making their mark with more impact. The pockets beneath his eyes sagged more each day, as if his face couldn't bear the weight of his skin.

His beard, thin and pointed, made his face appear even longer and accentuated the down-turned corners of his mouth.

His hair had thinned considerably in the last year, but he still maintained the notion that no one but he could tell, wrapping long strands around the top until they covered most of his bald pate. He was endearingly vain about his hair, but seemed not to notice when he'd splotched ink on his cuffs or shirtfront.

He was a private man, one who occupied a large room on the second floor surrounded by those items he'd brought from Inverness. For most of his life he'd lived with his sister, the woman dying shortly before he came to Edinburgh. No doubt Robert was another cause of Macrath's, another person who'd been helped from a bad situation by her brother's effortless kindness.

She only wished Robert had gone to some other distant relative.

But for all his dour appearance and personality, Robert was a man of great joys. He loved growing things. When he was not hunkered over the *Gazette*'s books, laboriously entering and grumbling over each expenditure, he was in their garden, transforming it into a place of beauty. Even in winter he was busy, readying the hardy shoots in the shed built for him, and laying out the beds in plans he worked on almost every night.

Now he frowned at her, the area above his nose folding into three vertical lines.

"No, it cannot wait," he said, blocking her way to the stairs. "You need to explain these new expenses. Why are you spending so much on paper?"

She sighed inwardly. He'd seen the invoice for the newsprint. She knew, from previous harangues, that nothing she said would stop Robert's fussing. She simply needed to wait him out.

"I should take over ordering your supplies."

She pushed back her irritation. "That's not necessary, Robert," she said.

"It is if you're determined to put the Sinclair Printing Company in debt."

She circled him and nearly raced up the stairs and to her room before he could manage another word. But his glare followed her, making her wish he knew her better. She'd never put the paper in jeopardy. But she had no choice. Their paper supplies were running low. Did he think it was possible to print a newspaper on air?

Once in her room, she pulled off her cloak, settling down to work. If she had her way, she would have replaced her secretary with a long, broad table so she could spread a layout on it. But the minute she arranged for it, Fenella would have just had it removed.

"You work too much," Fenella would have said. A comment Mairi heard often. "You need to have a place of peace to rest."

Fenella was the one who gifted their home with personal touches. She acted as their housekeeper, conferring with Cook over menus and recipes. Soft sheets and towels graced their rooms, and dishes of potpourri were everywhere, the scent dependent on the room.

Here in Mairi's bedroom it was something spicy with cloves and cinnamon, reminding her of apples and autumn. In the spring the scent would change, and she'd smell roses. Because of her cousin there were porcelain figurines on the fireplace mantel, and upholstered chairs with tassels. Mairi would have been just as comfortable with a bare room and a bed, but she appreciated Fenella's efforts to make their home both beautiful and comfortable.

Fenella also trained the four maids on their tasks, managed the laundry, and oversaw the purchases for the house, presenting the bills to Robert.

Her cousin was very careful with money, and whenever Mairi presented the monthly expenditures for the paper to Robert, he held Fenella up as a paragon of thrifty virtue.

She doubted her cousin had ever been lectured on frugality.

Pushing back the embarrassment she'd suffered at the Edinburgh Press Club, as well as her irritation over Robert's lecture, she undressed, washed, and donned her nightgown, pulled from a drawer smelling of oranges.

Sleep, however, would have to wait until after she worked. Grabbing the sheaf of submissions, she sat and began to read.

Early on, she'd realized that the *Edinburgh Gazette* would have to change from what it had been in her father's day. Once, they printed six pages of legal notices, bankrupts declared or adjudicated, debt announcements, and official proceedings at Parliament. If the paper was going to attract subscribers, she knew it had to offer more content for people, ranging from information about citizens of Edinburgh to housekeeping tips.

The only thing she didn't write about was politics, reasoning that the numerous larger papers handled that topic better than she could.

She wrote three columns herself, each signed with a male pseudonym. But she also accepted submissions from other writers. Her newest idea, to begin in the new year, was to serialize a novel, something that had been done successfully in England for decades. She could only afford a fraction of what a London paper might pay a writer, but could offer something the other papers didn't: opportunity. She was more than willing to hire a woman writer.

If she had the money, she'd employ a few full-time reporters and take on the job of being solely the editor of the *Gazette*. That was for the future. For now, she'd continue to be the chief writer for both the paper and the broadsides they printed three times a week.

She selected two columns from the ten she read and wrote acceptance letters to the writers. Tonight, it irritated her even more than usual to sign Macrath's name.

One day, perhaps, she'd be able to use her own name as the proprietor of the *Edinburgh Gazette*. People would know that she was responsible for the success of the paper, that she was a woman of influence.

When would that ever happen?

The Lord Provost had looked at her like she was a beetle, one he'd found on his shoe and quickly dispatched.

Why had he looked down his rather bearlike nose at her? Very well, perhaps his nose wasn't bearlike, but the rest of him certainly was. He was entirely too large a man. When she was standing next to him she felt almost tiny, and she was tall for a woman.

He epitomized those minor irritants she'd experienced all her life. Now they gathered in a ball and sat, like lead, in the pit of her stomach.

What was wrong with a woman running a business? And the newspaper was as much a business as a millinery shop.

She hadn't heard anyone say she couldn't buy Melvin Hampstead's book because she was a woman. Why, then, wasn't she good enough to hear his lecture?

If she was competent enough to be editor of the *Edinburgh Gazette,* why couldn't she be a member of the Edinburgh Press Club?

Why wasn't she treated with the same respect as a man, especially if she could do a man's job?

She never asked for help moving the reams of newsprint into place. She might not accomplish the task as quickly as a man, true, but she did it nonetheless.

Nor did she ever ask a man to write her columns, or gather the information for the broadsides she wrote. How many of the men who purchased their broadsides were aware that a woman had written them?

Perhaps that's why she felt the insult at the press club so acutely. She'd fought inequity all her life but never lost a battle face-to-face the way she had tonight.

She'd been treated like a beggar at a feast. Go away, don't bother us. How dare you think yourself the equal of us?

The injustice of it made her seethe.

More and more women were daring to stand up and announce their displeasure with a society run by men. Josephine Butler's campaign against the Contagious Diseases Acts was a model for women who believed their gender was being treated unfairly.

Strides were being made each day. Look at the Married Women's Property Act passed just two years earlier.

How did she change her own circumstances? It seemed to her that she could either continue to be treated as shabbily as she'd been tonight or act as an instrument of change. Standing in front of the Lord Provost and demanding that he treat her better hadn't accomplished anything. He'd only smiled at her.

There was a newly formed organization—the Scottish Ladies National Association—that was taking up women's causes, one of them suffrage. She could almost imagine herself standing at a podium, imploring a crowd of women before her to vote for anyone other than the Lord Provost.

A few minutes later she caught herself staring off into the distance, then brought her focus back to finishing the letters.

Once they were done, she pulled out a blank sheet of her stationery. She knew exactly to whom she'd write, one of the founders of the SLNA, a woman who lived in Edinburgh.

When she heard the hall clock chime midnight, she pushed back her fatigue and continued writing. A half hour later, after reviewing her letter a dozen times, she sealed it and went to bed, only to lay there staring up at the ceiling.

Normally when she couldn't sleep, it was because she was caught up in worry about their subscription numbers. Tonight, however, she was on fire with ideas.

Would it be enough to just volunteer to assist a group? What could she do to awaken the women of Edinburgh?

She rose from the bed, walked to the window, and pulled open the drapes. A flagstone path, showing gray and black in the moonlight, led to the garden. A copse of trees stood on this side of the lawn. Saplings speared upward from the ground like arrows, the mature trees guarding them like protective mothers.

No wind shivered the leaves. They were perfectly still and waiting. Death could not be as silent as this night.

She was abruptly and painfully lonely.

Pushing that emotion aside, she walked back to her secretary, lit the lamp and sat.

If she couldn't write about the Hampstead lecture, she would write about something else: the Right Honorable Lord Provost of Edinburgh himself. She wouldn't put it in a column. Instead, she'd make him the subject of one of their broadsides.

Without hesitation, she began to write a poem. She finished it only a few minutes later.

> *When shameful Vice began our streets to*
> *tread,*
> *And foul Disease reared his deathlike*
> *head,*
> *When the fate of sacred womanhood was*
> *profan'd,*
> *And fair Edinburgh's character was*
> *stain'd ;*

Then (by the Grace of God) Harrison
  came,
(Ye residents of Edinburgh tremble at the
  Name!)
He showed himself to our admiring sight,
Indeed a burning and shining light.
Yet weep my friends for more's the pity.
He did not labor to clean the city.
He doth not strive to cure the profane
Or clean the vice and scrub the stain,
No, Harrison dared show his face,
Only to keep a woman in her place.

She added a small essay to the poem, explaining the situation and adding that the time for women to stand up and come out of the shadows had arrived. Otherwise, men like Logan Harrison would forever try to keep them from achieving their rightful place in society.

Smiling, she put the poem down, consulted her watch, and decided that she could sleep for a few hours. Then she'd head for the paper and begin her campaign to win equality for women.

She couldn't wait to hear what the High and Mighty Lord Provost thought of that.

SIZZLING ROMANCE FROM
USA TODAY BESTSELLING AUTHOR
KAREN RANNEY

The Devil of Clan Sinclair

978-0-06-224244-0

Widowed and penniless unless she produces an heir, Virginia Traylor, Countess of Barrett, embarks on a fateful journey that brings her to the doorstep of the only man she's ever loved. Macrath Sinclair, known as The Devil, was once rejected by Virginia. He knows he should turn her away, but she needs him, and now he wants her more than ever.

The Witch of Clan Sinclair

978-0-06-224246-4

Logan Harrison, the Lord Provost of Edinburgh, needs a conventional and diplomatic wife to help further his political ambitions. He most certainly does not need Mairi Sinclair, the fiery, passionate, fiercely beautiful woman who tries to thwart him at every turn. But if she's so wrong for him, why can't the bewitched lord stop kissing her?

The Virgin of Clan Sinclair

978-0-06-224249-5

Beneath Ellice Traylor's innocent exterior beats a passionate heart, and she has been pouring all of her frustrated virginal fantasies into a scandalous manuscript. When a compromising position forces her to wed the Earl of Gadsden, he discovers Ellie's secret book and can't stop thinking about the fantasies the disarming virgin can dream up.